THE WOMAN IN BLUE

BOOKS BY ELLY GRIFFITHS

THE MAGIC MEN SERIES
The Zig Zag Girl
Smoke and Mirrors

THE RUTH GALLOWAY SERIES
The Crossing Places
The Janus Stone
The House at Sea's End
A Room Full of Bones
A Dying Fall
The Outcast Dead
The Ghost Fields
The Woman in Blue

THE WOMAN IN BLUE

A RUTH GALLOWAY MYSTERY

Elly Griffiths

HOUGHTON MIFFLIN HARCOURT

BOSTON • NEW YORK

2016

First U.S. edition

Copyright © 2016 by Elly Griffiths

All rights reserved

For information about permission to reproduce selections from this book, write
to trade.permissions@hmhco.com or to Permissions, Houghton Mifflin Harcourt
Publishing Company, 3 Park Avenue, 19th Floor, New York, New York 10016.

www.hmhco.com

First published in Great Britain in 2016 by Quercus

Library of Congress Cataloging-in-Publication Data is available.
ISBN 978-0-544-41785-4

Printed in the United States of America
DOC 10 9 8 7 6 5 4 3 2 1

For Giulia

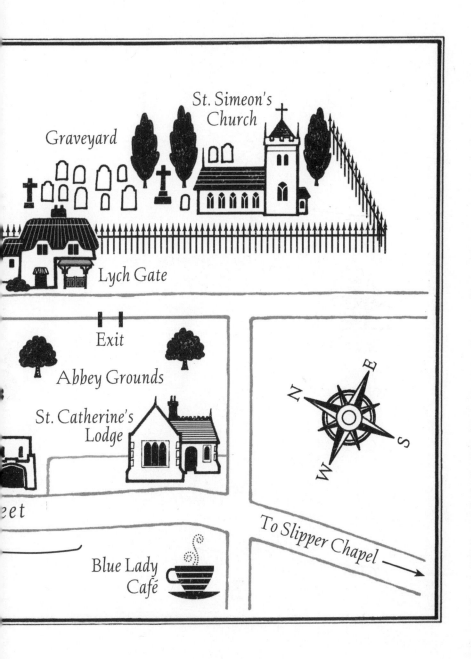

Weep, weep, O Walsingham,
Whose dayes are nights,
Blessings turned to blasphemies,
Holy deeds to despites.
Sinne is where Our Ladye sate,
Heaven turned is to helle;
Satan sitthe where Our Lord did swaye,
Walsingham, O farewell!

— Ballad of Walsingham, anonymous,
   sixteenth century

PROLOGUE

19th February 2014

Cathbad and the cat look at each other. They have been drawing up the battle-lines all day and this is their Waterloo. The cat has the advantage: this is his home and he knows the terrain. But Cathbad has his druidical powers and what he believes is a modest gift with animals, a legacy from his Irish mother who used to talk to seagulls (and receive messages back). He has a companion animal himself, a bull-terrier called Thing, and has always enjoyed a psychic rapport with Ruth's cat, Flint.

This cat, whose name is Chesterton, is a different proposition altogether. Whereas Flint is a large and lazy ginger Tom whose main ambition is to convince Ruth that he is starving at all times, Chesterton is a lithe and sinuous black creature, given to perching on top of cupboards and staring at Cathbad out of disconcertingly round, yellow eyes. This is Cathbad's third day of house- and cat- sitting, and so far Chesterton has ignored all blandishments. He has even ignored the food that

Cathbad carefully weighed out according to Justin's instructions. He might be living on mice, but Chesterton does not look like an animal who is governed by his appetites. He's an ascetic, if Cathbad ever saw one.

But Justin's sternest admonition, written in capitals and underlined in red, was: DO NOT LET CHESTERTON OUT AT NIGHT. And now, here they are, at nine o'clock on a February evening with Chesterton staring at the door and Cathbad barring the way with his fiery sword. The biblical reference comes to hand because the house is part of an ancient pilgrimage site and is decorated with etchings from the Old Testament. Justin, a custodian of the site, is on a fact-finding trip to Knock, something Cathbad finds extremely funny. He has left the fifteenth-century cottage — and the accompanying cat — under Cathbad's protection.

Chesterton meows once, commandingly.

'I'm sorry,' says Cathbad. 'I can't.'

Chesterton gives him a pitying look, jumps onto a cupboard and manages to slide out through a partially opened window. So that's why he has been on hunger strike.

'Chesterton!' Cathbad lifts the heavy latch and opens the door. Cold air rushes in. 'Chesterton! Come back!'

The cottage is attached to the church, with a passageway through it at ground-floor level forming a kind of lych-gate. Worshippers have to pass underneath the main bedroom in order to get to St Simeon's. There's even a handy recess in the wall of the passage so that pall-bearers can rest their coffins there. The back door of the cottage opens directly onto the churchyard. 'But you won't mind that,' said Justin, 'it's right up your street.' And it's true that Cathbad does like burial grounds, and all places of communal worship but, even so, there's something about St Simeon's Cottage, Walsingham, that he doesn't quite like. It's not the presence of the cat, or the creaks and groans of the old house at night; it's more a sort of sadness about the place, a feeling so oppressive that, during his first evening, Cathbad was compelled to call upon a circle of protection and to ring his partner Judy several times.

He's not scared now, just worried about the cat. He walks along the church path, the frost crunching under his feet, calling the animal's name.

And then he sees it. A tombstone near the far wall, glowing white in the moonlight, and a woman standing beside it. A woman in white robes and a flowing blue cloak. As Cathbad approaches, she looks at him, and her face, illuminated by something stronger than natural light, seems at once so beautiful and so sad that Cathbad crosses himself.

'Can I help you?' he calls. His voice echoes against stone and darkness. The woman smiles — such a sad, sweet smile — shakes her head and starts to walk away, moving very fast through the gravestones towards the far gate.

Cathbad goes to follow her, but is floored, neatly and completely, by Chesterton, who must have been lurking behind a yew tree for this very purpose.

1

DCI Harry Nelson hears the news as he is driving to work. 'Woman's body found in a ditch outside Walsingham. SCU request attend.' As he does a handbrake turn in the road, he is conscious of a range of conflicting emotions. He's sorry that someone's dead, of course he is, but he can't help feeling something else, a slight frisson of excitement, and a relief that he's been spared that morning's meeting with Superintendent Gerald Whitcliffe and their discussion of the previous month's targets. Nelson is in charge of the SCU, the Serious Crimes Unit, but the truth is that serious crime is often thin on the ground in King's Lynn and the surrounding areas. That's a good thing — Nelson acknowledges this as he puts on his siren and speeds through the morning traffic — but it does make for rather dull work. Not that Nelson hasn't had his share of serious crime in his career — only a few months ago he was shot at and might have died if his sergeant hadn't shot back — but there's also a fair amount of petty theft, minor drugs stuff and people complaining because their stolen bicycle wasn't featured on *Crimewatch*.

He calls his sergeants, Dave Clough and Tim Heathfield, and tells them to meet him at the scene. Though they both just say 'Yes, boss', he can hear the excitement in their voices too. If Sergeant Judy Johnson were there, she would remind them that they were dealing with a human tragedy, but Judy is on maternity leave and so the atmosphere in the station is rather testosterone heavy.

He sees the flashing lights as he turns the corner. The body was found on the Fakenham Road, about a mile outside Walsingham. It's a narrow road with high hedges on both sides, made narrower by the two squad cars and the coroner's van. As soon as Nelson steps out of his car he feels claustrophobic, something that often happens when he's in the countryside. The high green walls of foliage make him feel as if he's in the bottom of a well and the grey sky seems to be pushing down on top of him. Give him pavements and street lighting any day.

The local policemen stand aside for him. Chris Stephenson, the police pathologist, is in the ditch with the body. He looks up and grins at Nelson as if it's the most charming meeting place in the world.

'Well, if it isn't Admiral Nelson himself!'

'Hallo, Chris. What's the situation?'

'Woman, probably in her early to mid-twenties, looks like she's been strangled. Rigor mortis has set in, but then it was a cold night. I'd say she's been here about eight to ten hours.'

'What's she wearing?' From Nelson's vantage point it looks like fancy dress, a long white robe and some sort of blue cloak. For a moment he thinks of Cathbad, whose favourite attire is a druid's cloak. 'It's both spiritual and practical,' he'd once told Nelson.

'Nightdress and dressing gown,' says Stephenson. 'Not exactly the thing for a February night, eh?'

'Has she got slippers on?' Nelson can see a glimpse of bare leg, ending in something white.

'Yes, the kind you get free in spas and the like,' says Stephenson, who probably knows a lot about such places. 'Again, not exactly the thing for tramping over the fields.'

'If her slippers are still on, she must have been placed in the ditch and not thrown.'

'You're right, chief. I'd say the body was placed here with some care.' Stephenson holds out an object in a plastic bag. 'This was on her chest.'

'What is it? A necklace?'

Stephenson laughs. 'I thought you were a left-footer, Admiral. It's a rosary.'

A rosary. Nelson's mother has a wooden rosary from Lourdes and she prays a decade every night. Nelson's sisters, Grainne and Maeve, were given rosaries for their First Holy Communions. Nelson didn't get one because he was a boy.

'Bag it,' he says, although the rosary is already sealed in a plastic evidence bag. 'It's important evidence.'

'If you say so, chief.'

Nelson straightens up. He has heard a car approaching and guesses that it's Clough and Tim. Besides, he's had enough of Chris Stephenson and his breezy good humour.

His sergeants come towards him. Both are tall and dark and have been described (though not by Nelson) as handsome, but there the resemblance ends. Clough is white and Tim is black, but there's much more to it than that. Clough is heavily built, wearing jeans and skiing jacket. He's looking around with something like excitement and there's a half-eaten bagel in his hand. Tim is taller and slimmer, he's wearing a long dark coat and knotted scarf and could be a politician visiting a factory. His face gives nothing away.

Nelson briefs them quickly. He calls over the local officer, who explains that the body was found by an early morning dog-walker. 'Her little dog actually got into the ditch and was . . . well . . . shaking the deceased.'

'If she's in nightclothes,' says Tim, 'she could be a patient at the Sanctuary.'

The same thought has occurred to Nelson. It was the waffle-patterned slippers that first gave him the idea. The Sanctuary is a private hospital specialising in drug rehabilitation. Because a lot of the patients are famous (though not to Nelson), the place exists in an atmosphere of high walls, secrecy and rumours of drug-fuelled orgies. It is quite near here, about a mile across the fields.

'Good thinking,' he says. 'You and Cloughie can go over there in a minute and ask if any patients are missing.'

'Foxy O'Hara's meant to be there at the moment,' says Clough, swallowing the last of his bagel.

'Who?'

'You must have heard of her. She was on *I'm a Celebrity* before Christmas.'

'You're jabbering, Cloughie.' Nelson turns to Chris Stephenson, who has emerged from the ditch and is taking off his coveralls. 'Anything else for us, Chris? No handy nametapes on the dressing gown?'

'No, but it's a good one. Pricy. From John Lewis.'

'Costs a bit to stay in the Sanctuary,' says Nelson. 'I think that's our best bet.'

'Excuse me, sir.' It's one of the local policemen, nervous and respectful. 'But there's a man asking to see you. Looks a bit of a nutter, but he says he knows you.'

'Cathbad,' says Clough, without looking round.

Clough is right. Nelson sees Cathbad standing beyond the police tape, wearing his trademark cloak. How strange, and slightly unsettling, that Nelson was thinking about him only a few moments before. He strides over.

'Cathbad. What are you doing here?'

'I'm house-sitting in Walsingham.'

'What about Judy? Have you left her alone with a newborn baby?'

'Miranda's ten weeks old and she's an old soul. No, Judy's taken the children to visit her parents.'

'That doesn't explain why you're here, at a crime scene.'

'The woman you've found,' says Cathbad. 'Was she wearing a blue cloak?'

Nelson takes a step back. 'Who says we've found a woman?'

He half-expects Cathbad to say something about spiritual energies and cosmic vibrations, but instead he says, 'I heard the milkman talking about it. Useful people, milkmen. They're up and about early, they notice things.'

'And what did you mean about a cloak? I'm sure the bloody milkman didn't see that.'

Cathbad exhales. 'So it is her.'

'What are you talking about?'

'The cottage where I'm staying, it overlooks the graveyard.' That figures, thinks Nelson. 'Well, last night, I saw a woman standing there, a woman wearing a white robe and a blue cloak.'

'What time was that?'

'About nine.'

Nelson lifts the tape. 'You'd better come through.'

The scene-of-the-crime team have arrived. In their paper suits and masks they look like aliens taking over a sleepy Norfolk village. As Nelson and Cathbad watch, the dead woman's body is slowly winched out of the ditch. The corpse is covered with a sheet, but as the stretcher passes them they both see a length of muddy blue material hanging down. Cathbad crosses himself and Nelson has to stop himself following suit.

'Any idea who she was?' asks Cathbad.

'She was in nightclothes,' said Nelson. 'Your "cloak" was a dressing gown. I'm sending Clough and Heathfield to the Sanctuary.'

'Do you think she was a patient there?'

'It's a line of enquiry.'

The aliens have now erected a tent-like structure over the ditch. The atmosphere has somehow stopped being that of an emergency and has become calm and purposeful.

'Look, Cathbad,' says Nelson. 'I'm going to brief the boys and finish up here. Then I'll come and talk to you about what you saw last night. Where's this place you're staying?'

'St Simeon's Cottage. Next to the church.'

'I won't be long.'

'Time,' says Cathbad grandly, 'is of no consequence.' But he is talking to the empty air.

Ruth Galloway doesn't hear about the body in the ditch until she's at work. She did listen to the radio in the car, but what with the hassle of getting her five-year-old daughter, Kate, to school in time, it all became rather a blur. 'Have you got your book bag?' . . . Here's Gary with the sports news . . . 'Can you see a parking space?' . . . Thought for the Day with the Revd . . . 'Quick, there's Mrs Mannion waiting for you. Love you. See you later.' . . . Icy winds, particularly on the east coast . . . If the dead woman did make it on to the *Today* programme, Ruth missed it altogether. It wasn't until she was at her desk, trying to catch up on emails before her first tutorial, that her head of department, Phil Trent, wandered — uninvited — into her office and asked if she'd heard 'the latest drama'.

'No. What?'

'A woman found dead in a ditch out Walsingham way. It was on *Look East*.'

'I must have missed it.'

'I thought you had a hotline to the boys in blue.'

Phil is jealous of Ruth's role as a special advisor to the police and sometimes she likes to tease him, dropping hints of high-level meetings and top-secret memos, but this morning she doesn't have the energy.

'I doubt it will have anything to do with me. Not unless there's an Iron Age skeleton in the ditch as well.'

'I suppose not.'

Ruth turns back to her screen, and though Phil hovers in the doorway for a few minutes, eventually he drifts away, leaving her to concentrate on her emails. They are the usual collection of advertisements from academic publishers, departmental memos and requests from her students for extra time to finish their essays. Ruth deletes the first and the second and is settling down to answer the third when she sees a new category of email. The subject is 'Long time no see'. This is either intriguing or worrying, depending on your mood. Ruth is probably fifty–fifty on that. She clicks it open.

Hi, Ruth,

Do you remember me, Hilary Smithson, from Southampton? Where have the years gone? I understand that you're in Norfolk, doing very well for yourself. I'm coming to Norfolk next week, for a conference in Walsingham, and I wondered if we could meet up? I'd like to ask your advice on a rather tricky matter. And I'd love to see you of course.

Looking forward to hearing from you.

All best,

Hilary

Ruth stares at the screen. It's the second time that Walsingham has been mentioned that morning and, as Nelson always says, there's no such thing as coincidence.

2

The Sanctuary is an imposing Victorian edifice, more suited to a sooty city centre than the Norfolk countryside. Even softened by trees and gently rolling hills, it looks like a town hall or a railway station that has somehow planted itself in the middle of a field.

Clough, though, is impressed. 'Look at this place. It's like a stately home.'

'Looks more like a prison,' says Tim.

They have stopped at the electronic gates but, before Tim can speak into the intercom, they open soundlessly.

'Not very good security for a prison,' says Clough.

Tim says nothing. In fact, both have brothers who have been in prison, but they are not in the habit of discussing their families. Tim puts the car into gear and they approach the house via a sweeping gravel drive. Wide steps lead to the front door and, facing them, there's a perfect ring of grass with a stone fountain in the middle. There is not a soul to be seen.

They ignore signs to the visitors' car park and leave the car at the foot of the steps. Tim presses the bell and, this time, a voice answers. He has hardly finished saying the word 'Police' when the double doors open.

Inside it's definitely more like a hotel than a prison — a baronial hall with a monstrous stone fireplace and a round table bearing an arrangement of waxy-looking flowers. A grandfather clock ticks ponderously, and gloomy oil paintings look down from the walls. There's even a reception desk where a woman is flashing her teeth at them.

'How can I help you?'

Tim shows his warrant card. 'Can I speak to whoever's in charge?' They agreed in the car that he should take the lead in the interview. Clough hovers supportively at his shoulder.

The receptionist looks at them nervously. 'That's Doctor McAllister.'

'Can I speak to him then?' asks Tim.

'I'll see if she's free.' The receptionist picks up a phone and Clough murmurs, 'You've got to watch these sexist assumptions, Tim.'

'Bugger off,' says Tim without moving his lips.

Doctor McAllister arrives very quickly. She's an attractive middle-aged woman with short brown hair and narrow intimidating glasses. She ushers them to a leather sofa in front of the fireplace. Tim was going to suggest somewhere more private but as — apart from the receptionist who seems oblivious — the lobby is as empty as the grounds, he subsides.

'What's all this about, officer?' The doctor takes charge

immediately, smoothing her white coat and adjusting her glasses.

'We were wondering if any of your patients were missing?' asks Tim.

'What do you mean, "missing"?'

'It's a simple enough question,' says Clough. 'Are any of your inmates missing?'

'They're not inmates, officer, they're patients,' says Doctor McAllister.

'And *are* any of your patients missing?' asks Tim.

'Our patients are free to come and go. They sign themselves in for treatment.'

'Did anyone sign themselves out yesterday?'

'I don't think so,' she admits.

'So everyone is where they should be?'

'Well, we haven't done the rounds of the rooms yet, so I can't be a hundred per cent sure.'

'The thing is,' Tim says, and leans forward confidentially, 'a body has been found.'

'A body?'

'The body of a woman in her nightclothes. We wondered if she was one of your patients.'

'But that's impossible.'

'I thought people were free to come and go,' says Clough.

'Yes,' says Doctor McAllister and shoots him an unfriendly look. 'But we wouldn't sign anyone out just wearing their nightclothes. And, as I say . . .'

The pocket of her white coat starts to vibrate: they can see a red light flashing under the fabric.

'I think someone wants you,' says Tim.

Doctor McAllister pulls out her phone and has a brief monosyllabic conversation. Then she gets to her feet, saying, 'Excuse me, gentlemen.'

Clough and Tim exchange glances, then get up and follow her.

There's a grand staircase to the right of the fireplace. Doctor McAllister takes the stairs two at a time, with the policemen following her. On the landing she opens a door and immediately the country-house hotel vanishes and they enter a world that is altogether more institutional: numbered doors, hand-gel dispensers; even the carpet looks different. Two men in white coats (nurses? doctors? orderlies?) stand by one of the doors. Doctor McAllister hurries forward to speak to them and Tim hears the word 'missing'. He holds out his warrant card and asks, 'Is somebody missing?'

The doctor shoots him an irritated look, but says, 'Apparently, one of our patients isn't in her room.'

A white-coated man pushes open door number 12. It's a pleasant but functional room: single bed, table, wardrobe, armchair and a beautiful sash window that is slightly too big for the space.

'The patient's name?' asks Clough briskly.

Doctor McAllister confers. 'Jenkins. Chloe Jenkins.'

'And when was Miss Jenkins last seen?'

One of the white coats replies, 'Last night, at about eight, when I took supper round.'

A covered plate lies on the bedside table. Clough lifts the lid, revealing uneaten shepherd's pie congealing at the edges.

'And after that?'

'No. She didn't ring her bell.'

Tim has opened the wardrobe. 'What would Miss Jenkins have been wearing?'

The orderly replies nervously, 'She was in her nightclothes and a dressing gown.'

'What colour?'

'Blue.'

Tim turns to Doctor McAllister. 'I think you'd better come with us.'

What with one thing and another, it's nearly eleven o'clock when Nelson knocks on the hobbit-sized front door of St Simeon's Cottage. The door is opened immediately, but is held ajar, with only Cathbad's face showing through.

'Quickly,' he says. 'I don't want to let the cat out.'

'Trust you to be looking after a mad cat,' says Nelson, squeezing through the aperture.

'He's not mad,' says Cathbad, showing Nelson into a low-ceilinged sitting room. 'He's disconcertingly sane.'

The slim black cat is sitting by the wood-burning stove. He gets up, shoots Nelson a look of contempt and stalks out of the room.

'Friendly creature,' says Nelson.

'I think he's the reincarnation of my old Latin teacher,' says Cathbad. 'He looks at me with exactly the same expression of disappointment.'

Nelson laughs and then realises that this might not be a joke.

'Why's he not allowed out?' he asks.

'He's allowed out in the day, but not at night,' says Cathbad. 'But I've got twitchy about letting him out of the front door. I keep thinking that he'll get run over just to spite me.'

'When's the owner of the house back?'

'Tomorrow. Thank the gods.'

'It's an interesting place,' says Nelson, though privately he thinks that all those beams and uneven floorboards would get him down after a while. There doesn't seem to be a straight line in the whole place. To his surprise, though, Cathbad shudders. 'It's got bad energies,' he says. 'Oppressive. Can't you feel it? I've had a headache all the time I've been here.'

'It's probably just because you keep hitting your head on doorposts.'

Cathbad laughs. 'Probably.'

'So, tell me about this woman you saw last night.'

'I'll show you.'

Cathbad leads Nelson through a door and into a narrow stone passageway. The cat is waiting by the door at the end of it.

'I'll let you out, Chesterton,' says Cathbad, 'if you promise to come back.'

The cat ignores him.

The back door opens directly onto the graveyard. Some of the stones are almost as big as the low house; others lean towards it in a rather threatening way.

'Blimey.' Nelson follows Cathbad along the path through the graves, saying, 'Talk about dead centre of town.'

'It's a very old church,' says Cathbad. 'Anglo-Saxon. It's older than the priory.'

The word 'Anglo-Saxon' reminds Nelson of Ruth, who is fond of throwing around historical eras as if she is unaware of the fact that Nelson has never worked out whether Bronze Age comes before the Iron Age or who the hell Homo Heidelbergensis is. The Anglo-Saxons he thinks came after the Romans, but that's as far as he's prepared to go.

'Where did you see the woman?'

'Here. By this white tombstone.'

Nelson looks at the grass around the stone. It's slightly flattened, but there are no footprints or any signs of a struggle.

'What time was this?'

'About nine. I'd just rung Judy and I try to do that before nine because she goes to bed early these days.'

'What happened next?'

'She smiled at me. Honest to God, Nelson, she had such a beautiful smile, like an angel. I thought . . .'

'What did you think?'

'Walsingham is a shrine to the Virgin Mary. And she was wearing a blue cloak. Well, I thought it was a cloak at the time.'

'You thought you'd seen a vision of Our Lady?'

'Our Lady. You're still such a Catholic, Nelson.'

'Stop trying to wind me up. What happened next?'

'She turned away and started walking towards the gate. I tried to follow but Chesterton jumped out and tripped me up.'

'Chesterton, the cat?'

'Yes. He's like some malign sprite. I'm sure he did it deliberately. When I got back he was sitting by his bowl in the kitchen as if nothing had happened.'

'Forget the cat for a minute. What happened to the woman?'

'When I got up, she was gone. I went to the gate and looked down the lane but there was no sign of her.'

'Show me.'

They walk through the churchyard. There are a few impressive tombs, with weeping angels and towering crosses, but most graves are simply marked by stones, their edges blurred by time and exposure to the elements. Some gravestones have fallen over and others are lined up against the low brick wall; a few are lying flat, sunk into the grass as if laid out for a macabre game of hopscotch. Nelson tries to avoid treading on them. The gate opens easily and leads into another narrow lane with high hedges. It's a fairly straight road, though. The woman must have been walking fast, thinks Nelson, to have got out of sight so quickly.

He looks at Cathbad, who is examining the inscription on a stone angel. 'You didn't think to tell anyone about your vision?'

'No. What was there to tell? The church and graveyard are free to everyone.'

'Was the church open?'

'No. It's shut when they're not having services there. I don't approve. Churches should be open at all times.'

'I suppose they're worried about burglaries.'

'Yes, but a church should be there for the people. A place of sanctuary. Afterwards I wondered if that's what she was doing. Seeking sanctuary in the church.'

There's not much else to see. Nelson walks the perimeter of the graveyard, still taking care not to step on the dead. Then he says goodbye to Cathbad who sidles into the cottage, careful not to let the cat out. When Nelson gets back to his car, he checks his phone. There's a text from Tim saying that the dead woman has been formally identified as Chloe Jenkins, aged twenty-five, a patient at the Sanctuary.

3

'What was she being treated for?'

'Drink and drug dependency, apparently.'

'Does she have any family?'

'Parents live in Surrey. The local police are informing them now. Then they'll be on their way here.'

'Poor sods.' Nelson, Tim and Clough are back at the station. The briefing room has already been prepared for a major incident. Tanya Fuller, an extremely keen Detective Constable (Acting Sergeant, as she tells everyone), has pinned up a map of Walsingham and the surrounding area. There are pads and pencils on every desk and extra phonelines are being put in.

Nelson puts a red pin at the spot where the body was found.

'Have you got a photograph of the victim?' he asks Tim.

'The hospital gave us this.' He offers a passport-sized photograph. Nelson squints at it; he really should get his eyes tested. The unsmiling head-and-shoulders shot gives nothing away.

'But we Googled her,' says Clough. 'Look.' He pushes an open laptop towards Nelson.

'Bloody hell.'

The screen is full of images. A beautiful blonde woman stares out at him, replicated again and again, in swimwear, bridal gowns, prom dresses, gothic black and fishnet tights, covered in artistically placed leaves.

'She was quite a well-known model,' says Tim.

'Bloody hell,' says Nelson again.

'I know,' says Clough. 'Looks a lot like your missus, doesn't she?'

What had struck Nelson at first was that Chloe looked like his elder daughter, Laura. But, of course, Laura resembles her mother, and actually what is staring out at him from the myriad images is a younger Michelle. Nelson's wife, a runner-up for Miss Blackpool 1988, was offered modelling work as a younger woman, but hadn't been interested. 'It was all car shows and strip clubs anyway,' she says, 'nothing glamorous'. Besides, Michelle, though aware of her own beauty, doesn't like having her photograph taken.

'Isn't she the image of Mrs Nelson?' Clough turns to Tim.

'Maybe,' says Tim. 'I don't know.'

'The image of her,' says Clough. 'Twenty-odd years ago.'

'Don't let Michelle hear you say that,' says Nelson. 'She doesn't admit to a day over thirty.'

He keeps his voice light, but he's shaken. Resemblance is a funny thing. Michelle is always saying that the girls look like him but he can never see it. They're girls, for one thing. But this likeness is shocking. Maybe in the flesh it wouldn't be so striking — gestures and voice make up so much of what a person is — but here, pixellated on the screen, the similarity is almost frightening. Chloe Jenkins is looking at him out of a face that he has known and loved for more than twenty years.

'What do we know about this girl?' he asks.

'She's twenty-five,' says Tim, 'been modelling since she was sixteen. Two other sessions in rehab, one when she was just eighteen. Parents, Alan and Julie, live in Weybridge in Surrey. Father's an airline pilot. Chloe lived in London and was in a relationship with an actor and model called Thom Novak. She entered the Sanctuary on 27th January and was apparently making good progress. Last seen last night at about eight when an orderly brought round the evening meal. Her body was identified by Doctor Fiona McAllister, the chief medical officer at the hospital.'

Nelson pulls a pad of paper towards him. 'Well the first thing we need to know is Novak's whereabouts last night.'

'Checked,' says Clough. 'He's in rehab too. In Switzerland.'

'Jesus wept. What a set.'

'Doctor McAllister said that it was impossible to leave the hospital without signing out,' says Tim, 'but from what Cloughie and I saw it would be easy enough. There are plenty of side doors and more than one way out.'

'Any idea what she was doing in Walsingham?'

'No. We don't know if she was ever in the village. The road where she was found was on the way to the Slipper Chapel, the Catholic shrine.'

'She was seen in the village,' says Nelson. He describes Cathbad's sighting of Chloe Jenkins in the churchyard.

'Typical bloody Cathbad,' says Clough. 'Trust him to think it was some religious vision and not contact the police.'

'To be fair,' says Nelson, 'he had no reason to know that she was in danger. There are lots of odd people in Walsingham, pilgrims and the like.'

'Should we go door to door in Walsingham,' says Clough. 'Check if anyone else saw her last night?'

'Yes,' says Nelson. 'Let's track the route she might have taken across the fields too. Get some dog-handlers on the scene. Tim, will you speak to the boyfriend in Switzerland?'

'You should have a lot in common with a male model,' says Clough.

'It's not a joking matter,' says Nelson.

'That wasn't a joke.'

'The parents will be here soon. They've lost a daughter, let's not forget that. Tanya, will you look after them? I'll speak to them too.'

'Yes, boss.' Nelson thinks that Tanya looks slightly disappointed to be left with the soft, family liaison role. But someone has to do it and he needs Tim and Clough elsewhere.

'Clough, you organise the door-to-door. Appeal for witnesses on the road too. Tim, after you've spoken to the boyfriend, get on to Intel. We need to know if there's anyone in Chloe's background who might be a suspect.'

'Yes, boss.'

Nelson is getting into gear now, feeling as if the inquiry is really starting. The first hours are the most important. If they can hit the ground running, they have a good chance of finding out who killed Chloe Jenkins. Nelson thinks of the little body in the nightdress and dressing gown and his resolve hardens.

'Right, let's get going.'

Then Leah, Nelson's PA, puts her head round the door. 'Superintendent Whitcliffe wants to see you.'

Whitcliffe, perma-tanned and smooth, is Nelson's nemesis. He's a local boy, a graduate who sees King's Lynn CID as a stepping stone to greater things. He loves phrases like 'twenty-first-century policing' and 'three-hundred-and-sixty-degree appraisal'. He's passionate about community involvement as long as he doesn't actually have to meet any members of the community. Nelson is a major thorn in his side. Nelson's methods are frequently unorthodox and at heart he's an old-school copper who prefers being out in the field to directing strategic operations (another of Whitcliffe's favourite phrases). Whitcliffe would like to get rid of Nelson and bring in a smart young graduate, someone like Tim, perhaps. But Nelson's team are loyal to him and he seems to get results. Whitcliffe lives in hope that Nelson will one day want to go back to the North, a place as remote and shadowy to Whitcliffe as the north side of the moon. But he prides himself on getting on with everyone, so he greets Nelson heartily.

'Ah, Harry, sit down. Good of you to spare the time. Bad business about this young girl.'

'Chloe Jenkins,' says Nelson, remaining standing. 'I'm in the middle of an investigation. The vital first seven hours.'

'Of course. I gather that the dead girl, Chloe, was a well-known model?'

'Yes.'

'Well, you know what this will mean?'

Nelson says nothing, so Whitcliffe expands on his theme. 'It will mean increased press interest. You know how it works, Harry. A good-looking victim and all the papers will be on it. We'll have to call a press conference.'

'But there's nothing to tell them.'

'It's good PR, Harry. You know how important that is. And we can appeal for witnesses. Would you like Tim Heathfield to do it?'

'No, I'll do it,' says Nelson. 'When?'

'Tomorrow, first thing.'

'I'll be there,' says Nelson. 'And now, if you'll excuse me, I'm expecting Chloe's parents.'

They arrive just after four in an unmarked police car. Watching them approach, Nelson thinks that Alan and Julie Jenkins don't seem suited to tragedy. They're a good-looking couple, probably in their early fifties, smartly dressed even on this occasion. But they are shrunken with grief; Julie has her arms wrapped tightly around her body, Alan — a man clearly born to command — looks lost and somewhat frightened.

Nelson greets them. 'I'm so sorry for your loss.' When did they all start saying that? The police used to say, 'My condolences'. This recent phrase probably comes from American TV shows. At any rate, it doesn't register with the bereaved parents.

'Would you like to see her?'

'Yes, please,' says Julie.

'Would you like me to come with you?'

'No,' says Alan, 'we'll be all right.'

'I'll wait here,' says Nelson, relieved, but slightly ashamed of himself all the same. What can it be like, being asked to view your dead child's body? Nelson tries not to think about his own daughters, but that's impossible as he's been thinking about them all day.

A few minutes later the Jenkins emerge, both crying. Nelson takes them into the quiet room, offers tea and coffee and asks a few simple questions. It's too soon for a proper interview.

'When did you last see Chloe?'

Julie takes a long, shuddering breath. 'A week ago. You're not allowed to see patients for their first few weeks at the Sanctuary. It's meant to purge them of all outside influences, something like that. But Doctor McAllister — she's the doctor in charge — said that we could visit last week.'

'And how was Chloe when you saw her?'

'She seemed well.' Julie looks at her husband for corroboration, but he appears to have been struck dumb. 'I mean, she hadn't been there long, but I could already see a difference. When she went in she . . . she wasn't taking care of herself and she was far too thin. When we saw her last week, well, she was still thin, but her hair was clean and her skin looked better. It was lovely, wasn't it, Alan?'

'We were so happy driving home,' said Alan, his voice hoarse with misery. 'We really thought that she was going to get better. And now . . .' He buries his head in his hands.

'I'm so sorry,' says Nelson, 'but anything you tell me now

might help me find the person who did this. Did Chloe say anything last week that might explain why she was in Walsingham last night?'

'No,' says Julie. 'We didn't think they were allowed out at night. We thought she'd be safe.'

Both of them are crying properly now. Nelson can't bring himself to question them any more.

'The car's outside to take you home,' he says. 'Is it all right if I send an officer down to talk to you on Monday? Just to keep you up to date with the inquiry and to see if there's anything you can add?'

He wishes he could send Judy, but it'll have to be Tim. He's good at this sort of thing too.

'That's OK,' says Julie. 'I can't really think of the days ahead. We'll have to start planning her funeral. Her sister's still in the States. She's coming home today.'

'If there's anything I can do to help,' says Nelson, 'you've got my number.'

'She looked so beautiful,' says Julie Jenkins. 'She wouldn't have suffered, would she?'

'No,' lies Nelson. 'Death would have been almost instantaneous.'

'We had our troubles with Chloe,' says Alan, 'but she was a good girl really.' He looks at Nelson as if it is very important that he understands this.

'I know she was,' says Nelson. 'We'll catch the person who did this. I promise you.'

4

It's nearly nine o'clock by the time that Nelson leaves the
station. He races through the quiet streets, feeling tense and
strung up, as he always does when involved in a murder
investigation. The fact that, this time, the victim is a young
girl — and, what's more, a young girl who bears a striking
resemblance to his oldest daughter — brings the whole thing
closer to home. He thinks of Chloe's parents, her father saying,
'she was a good girl really'. His daughter Laura is a good
girl. Well, both his daughters are, but Laura always seemed
to lay special claim to this title. Laura is beautiful, clever
(by his lights, anyway) and sporty. As a child she reminded
Michelle of Beth in *Little Women*, sweet and domesticated,
happy to help around the house. Not having read the book,
Nelson was horrified when he saw the film of *Little Women*.
Why had no one warned him that Beth actually dies? He had
been forced to leave the room and blow his nose loudly in
the hall. Afterwards, he had asked Michelle not to compare
Laura to Beth any more. In any case, her late teenage years

saw Laura become slightly less sweet and domesticated. She acquired a boyfriend and a penchant for short skirts and late nights. She still managed to get to university, studying marine biology at Plymouth, to Nelson and Michelle's mingled bemusement and pride. Now she's working as a holiday rep in Ibiza. 'A three-year gap year' is how Nelson's younger daughter, Rebecca, describes it. It's not quite what Nelson expected when he attended Laura's degree ceremony in a wind-swept marquee on Plymouth Hoe, but it could be worse. Thinking of Chloe Jenkins, he concedes that it could be a lot worse.

Michelle's car is in the drive when Nelson reaches the house. He's pleased. Over the last few months Michelle has been working later and later at the salon. He knows that the hairdresser's is expanding and that she is assuming a lot of responsibility but, deep down, he's a northern man who likes his wife to be waiting for him at the end of the day. Sure enough, as he opens the front door he can smell cooking and hear the television (*Masterchef*, that's the only downside).

'Hi, love. I'm home.'

'Harry.' Michelle appears in the sitting-room doorway. 'You're late.'

'I did text you. Got a big murder enquiry on. Did you see the news?'

'No.' Michelle's not a great one for the news. When the news jingle comes on the radio she usually switches over to another station.

'Young girl found dead just outside Walsingham.'

'How awful.'

'Yes.' Nelson decides not to tell Michelle about the resemblance to Laura. She'll know soon enough when Chloe's picture is in the papers. In fact, in her TV-watching clothes of baggy jumper and leggings, Michelle herself looks hardly older than Chloe.

Nelson goes into the kitchen and gets a can of lager from the fridge. Michelle goes to the oven. 'I've kept your steak warm. Do you want some salad with it?'

'No thanks.'

'Have you heard from the girls?' he asks.

'Rebecca sent me a text asking for a cupcake recipe.' Rebecca is living in Brighton and working for a training company. It's not very well paid, but at least it's making use of her degree and Rebecca loves her adopted town. She's sharing a flat with three other girls and has recently developed an interest in baking.

'What about Laura?'

'She'll Skype us on Saturday.'

'But have you heard anything today?'

Michelle looks surprised. 'She put a picture on Facebook. She was in a club with Andre.'

Nelson breathes a sigh of relief. That was the way of the world now. You rely on Facebook to tell you that your daughter's alive and well, even if she's in the company of Andre, a public schoolboy who thinks he's an American gangster DJ.

'Are you OK, Harry?'

Nelson adds ketchup to his steak and chips. 'I'm fine. It's just this case.'

'I hope you catch whoever did it,' says Michelle, but she

says it vaguely, as if she's more interested in who won *Masterchef*. They've been married for twenty-five years; she's used to murder.

Ruth is trying to write. Kate is in bed (after a seemingly endless reading from *Josie Smith at School*) and Ruth is at her desk with a brain-boosting packet of chocolate biscuits to hand. Three years ago she wrote a book called *The Tomb of the Raven King* about a dig in Lancashire. Rather to her surprise, she acquired a publisher, an editor and something called a 'two-book deal'. Now she is desperately trying to write the second book, about a Bronze Age dig in Norfolk which became inextricably tangled up with the discovery of a body from the Second World War. The first book came easily, partly because no one was waiting to read it (Ruth dreads the cheery 'Hi there' emails from her editor, Javier), and partly because it was a story that ended with a satisfactorily juicy discovery. The new book, *The Shadow Fields*, is proving much more difficult, the story is fractured and complicated and the archaeologists involved are still some way off a final discovery. Ruth is trying to work on her book for an hour a night. If she writes a thousand words a day, she calculates, she will have the book finished in eighty or ninety days. So far she has written 15,000 words.

Ruth stares at the screen. Surely it wouldn't hurt to check her emails. Maybe there will be one from Frank, the American academic with whom she had . . . What? An affair sounds too steamy, a fling too casual. But, for some weeks last year, she had almost believed that she and Frank might have a future together. Frank was going to come to England. He too was writing a book. They were going to write, go on dates, have sex, spend weekends together. Maybe they would even move in together . . . Frank could be a stepfather to Kate, who adored him. Only one thing had stopped them. Ruth, for some stupid reason, couldn't get Nelson out of her head. Nelson with whom she has spent precisely two nights. Nelson, the father of her daughter. Nelson, who is married. It seemed that Ruth couldn't embark on a future with Frank whilst Nelson remained in the background. That's the trouble with Nelson, he never seems to stay in the background. He's always there, annoying her, nagging her about Kate, yet making it impossible for her to contemplate life with another man. Ruth clicks to open up her emails.

The first word she sees is 'Walsingham'. Flint jumps onto the desk and tries to sit on the keyboard. Ruth pushes him off. She is looking at another email from Hilary Smithson.

Hi, Ruth!

Wondered if you'd got my last email? I'm arriving in Walsingham on Sunday. Perhaps we could meet on Monday for a coffee at the Blue Lady? Say 11? I really would like to see you. Hilary x

What does she remember about Hilary, this woman who signs herself with a kiss? She was another graduate student at Southampton. Where had she studied before? Somewhere impressive like Oxford. Ruth's first degree and her MA are from University College London, impressive enough, but somehow real life as opposed to ivory tower. Hilary had been earnest, she remembers, but with a surprisingly good sense of humour. Their PhD advisor had been the great Erik Anderson, a charismatic Norwegian archaeologist of whom Ruth was much in awe. Hilary, she remembered, admired Erik, but sometimes used to tease him in a daringly icon-oclastic way. She remembers Erik talking about sacred landscape, how the same particular stretch of ground was important to different peoples over hundreds and thousands of years, and Hilary saying, 'Or it could just be coincidence'. She can still see the dangerous flash of Erik's light-blue eyes before he had answered, 'And it could just be coincidence, Miss Smithson, which is another word for serendipity.'

Is this a coincidence, two mentions of Walsingham in one day? And isn't Cathbad in Walsingham at the moment, house-sitting for one of his mad, religious friends? That's three things and, as Cathbad is always saying, bad news comes in threes.

Despite living near the famous shrine, Ruth has never visited it. Religion is not her thing, probably the result of being brought up by evangelical Christian parents. Mind you, her parents view shrines and pilgrimages with extreme sus-picion. Anything Catholic or Anglo-Catholic is almost worse than Satanism (although at least a Satanist will offer you a good fight, with the chance of talking in tongues and prob-ably an exorcism too). But Ruth tries to avoid anything to do with churches. Kate goes to a secular primary school and though she had both pagan and Catholic christening cere-monies (to please her godfather, Cathbad, and her actual father, Nelson), Ruth is determined that her child will have no religious indoctrination whatsoever. Christmas is about presents, Easter is about chocolate and she's hoping that birth, sex and death will wait a few years before rearing their ugly heads.

She Googles Walsingham (anything to avoid going back to the book), and finds that it was once two villages, Little Walsingham and Great Walsingham and that it is famed for its religious shrines in honour of the Virgin Mary. Confusingly, the bigger village that contains the ruined priory is actually Little Walsingham. Another site tells her that the 2001 census recorded a population of 864 in 397 households. She scrolls down, looking for references to archaeology and finds one to a dig in 1961 which excavated the site of the original holy house. The holy house, built on what is now the abbey grounds, was panelled in wood and contained a statue of the Virgin and — apparently — a phial of her breast milk. For years Walsingham was a centre of pilgrimage. Many kings, from Henry III onwards, trod the pilgrim path to Walsingham. Henry VIII paid a visit to celebrate the birth of a son to Catherine of Aragon, but the little prince died and eventually, of course, Henry destroyed the English monasteries. Walsingham Priory at first escaped the dissolution of the monasteries thanks to the abbot, Richard Vowell, doing some serious crawling to Thomas Cromwell. However, the sub-prior, Nicholas Milcham, protested against the destruction of the smaller monasteries and, in 1537, was executed for his pains. In 1538 the priory was dissolved and a private mansion built on its ruins. The abbey's treasures were sent to London and the statue of the Virgin was burnt.

Ruth skips the next few hundred years and clicks on the link 'Walsingham Now'. She learns that Walsingham is now a centre of both Anglican and Catholic worship. There's the Anglican shrine in the village itself and the Roman Catholic Slipper Chapel a mile away. There's even a Russian Orthodox chapel in an old railway-station booking office. Thousands of pilgrims come to the village every year and there's a Passion Play in the abbey grounds at Easter.

Ruth remembers taking part in a dig near Walsingham a few years ago. They'd hoped to find the site of the original Roman shrine but, in the end, the land had yielded nothing apart from some rather dull pottery shards, some glass and a coin or two. What is this conference that Hilary is attending? Is she still an archaeologist? And what is this 'tricky matter' about which she needs some advice? A very Hilary word, 'tricky', she seems to recall. Ruth's finger hovers over the mouse. Should she send a polite response, regretting that she's not available next week? Delete it? Answer that she'd be delighted to meet, can't wait to catch up, whatever happened to old so-and-so?

As she hesitates another email appears on the screen. It's from Hilary.

Ruth—did you get my last email? I really would like to see you. I'm in trouble and I think you're the only person who can help me.

Cathbad was right; third time means bad news. Ruth sighs and clicks 'Reply'.

5

Cathbad celebrates his last day in Walsingham by having lunch with his friend Janet Meadows. They are eating in The Bull, an old pub in the market square, which is actually an odd rhomboid shape with a brick pump-house in the centre. Cathbad likes The Bull because the walls are a palimpsest of prayer cards, black-and-white photographs and articles from long-forgotten magazines on subjects like the mystical Body of Christ. A sign outside the pub welcomes pilgrims from St Thomas More Church, Tring, and inside a bishop in full regalia is finishing a large ploughman's.

Janet, though, is not impressed. 'Couldn't we go somewhere else?'

'Not in Walsingham,' says Cathbad. 'Anyway, I thought you liked religion.'

He is referring to the fact that not only is Janet a local historian, but she's also a prominent member of her parish church. She often invites Cathbad to Christingle services and harvest festivals. Cathbad, who loves ritual, usually accepts.

'I don't like Walsingham,' says Janet. 'It has a nasty

atmosphere. When Tom was little he had friends here. Perfectly nice people, but whenever I went to pick him up from their house I felt as if I couldn't get him away quickly enough. The whole place seemed to be closing in on us.'

Cathbad is interested by the mention of Janet's son, Tom. He knows that Janet doesn't see Tom, who is now grown up, also that Janet (whose name was once Jan) is not Tom's mother, but his biological father. Janet is open about her gender realignment surgery, but rarely mentions her old life.

'I know what you mean,' he says. 'St Simeon's Cottage is beautiful but, when I sit there in the evenings, I feel as if the ceiling's getting lower and lower. I wake up at night struggling to breathe.'

'Some people say that Walsingham was cursed by the monks who were executed by Henry the Eighth. They swore that darkness would descend on the place and never leave.'

Cathbad shivers. He's always susceptible to a good phrase and this seems particularly chilling. Was it that same darkness that he felt pressing down on him in the cottage?

'What about that woman you told me about?' says Janet. 'The one in the churchyard.'

'Did you see today's paper? They've identified her. She was a young model, a patient at the Sanctuary. Strangled and left for dead. Peace be upon her.'

'I wonder.' Janet gets a book out of her handbag. 'I wonder if that was really what you saw.'

'What do you mean?'

Janet opens the book at a place marked by a dried leaf.

Cathbad's attention is momentarily distracted because the menu arrives at the same moment. He chooses fish pie and looks back at the yellowing pages. "'The Blue Lady of Walsingham,'" he reads out loud. 'What's this?'

'It's a legend,' says Janet, who is still perusing the menu. 'I'll tell you about it in a minute. Is the sole fresh?'

Having interrogated the barman (who disclaims any knowledge of the sole), she turns back to Cathbad. 'You know that Walsingham has been a centre of pilgrimage since the eleventh century?'

'Yes. The priory must have been built at about that time.'

'The priory was established in 1156, but before that there was the holy house. Do you know about that?'

'I've heard of it.'

'The whole thing started in 1061 with a Saxon noblewoman called Richeldis de Faverches. Richeldis had a vision of the Virgin Mary, who told her to build a replica of the Holy Family's house in Nazareth. That's why Walsingham is called England's Nazareth.'

'What happened to the holy house? Was it an actual building?'

'Some legends say that it appeared magically in the night while Richeldis was praying. But there was definitely some sort of structure. It's said to form the basis for the priory. There was an excavation in 1961, and a more recent dig too. Ruth might know something about it.'

'And the Blue Lady is the Virgin Mary?'

'That's what people say. She's appeared to various people throughout the centuries and it occurs to me that St Simeon's must be very near the site of the original structure. After all, it's very old, eleventh century.'

'The cottage isn't so old, though. Fifteenth century. Added on later.'

'I'm sure there are some old graves in the churchyard, though.'

'There are. I love looking at old graves.'

'The thing is,' says Janet, 'when the Virgin Mary appears to someone it's usually because she wants something. Think of Bernadette in Lourdes, those children in Fátima.'

'Yes,' says Cathbad thoughtfully. He remembers his first sight of Chloe, how he had crossed himself, thinking that there was something unearthly about her. He likes the idea that he might have had a holy vision, rather than just a tragic sighting of a murder victim. But then he thinks back to the woman's face, her sweet, sad smile. He felt a connection, but it was a very human connection. He remembers now that the woman reminded him of someone. Someone who is very definitely alive.

'I think I saw the dead girl,' he says. 'And I think she wanted me to help her.'

The morning press conference was, from Whitcliffe's point of view, a moderate success. Nelson, managing to sound fairly civil, informed the press that, no, he hadn't caught the killer yet. Press questions had been respectful and, though Nelson had glowered alarmingly throughout, he had answered them in a concise and professional manner. Tim had been there for back-up. 'You're Whitcliffe's pin-up boy,' Clough had told him, but Tim knows that the superintendent values him simply because he's the only black officer on the team. Still, Tim is ambitious too, so he went along with it, nodding and looking appropriately serious as Nelson told the assembled journalists that there were several ongoing lines of enquiry, please respect the family's privacy and give them time to grieve.

Now Nelson is driving to the Sanctuary. He wants to see the place for himself and to interview the doctor in charge, Fiona McAllister. He hopes that seeing the Sanctuary will help him to re-create Chloe's last journey. So far they have had no sightings after Cathbad's vision in the graveyard. What made a recovering addict — doing well, according to her parents — sneak out at night and walk a mile across several fields to visit a country churchyard? And who did she meet after she left the church? Chloe's body was found near the Catholic shrine, the Slipper Chapel, a good twenty minute walk from Walsingham. Chloe was brought up C of E, according to her parents. 'We don't really go to church,' said her mother, 'but we do believe in God.' Typical Anglicans, Nelson's mother would say. Well, Nelson hopes that, whatever faith they have, it's giving them some comfort now.

Like Clough and Tim, Nelson is impressed with the building, though the outside reminds him of a prison or magistrates' court, places where he's spent rather too much of his adult life. As he waits impatiently in the hall, he looks at the oil paintings, flower arrangements and soft furnishings and tries to work out how much this place costs per week. More than most people can afford, that's for sure. On the other hand, it stops rich drug addicts from cluttering up

NHS wards. It's not that he's not sympathetic — he's seen enough of the misery that drugs can cause — but he can't help thinking that it's almost a lifestyle choice for some people, the sort of people who go on reality TV programmes, the sort of people who come to the Sanctuary.

'Detective Chief Inspector Nelson?'

He turns. A short-haired woman in glasses is holding out her hand. 'I'm Doctor McAllister.' She has a faint Scottish accent and a disconcertingly straight gaze behind the glasses.

'Good of you to see me, doctor.'

She inclines her head, but doesn't say that it's a pleasure or her duty or anything like that. 'Shall we go to my office?'

She leads him up the stairs (more gloomy oil paintings and a stag's head or two), through several doors and finally into a modern office that was once obviously part of a bigger room, the fireplace neatly bisected by a plasterboard wall. She offers coffee, which Nelson politely declines.

'How can I help you, Detective Chief Inspector?'

'Tell me about Chloe Jenkins,' says Nelson. 'How long had she been here?'

'Just over three weeks,' says Doctor McAllister. 'She arrived here on Monday 27th January.'

'Did she check herself in?'

'Her parents brought her, as I recall, but she was self-referred, if that's what you mean.'

'And what sort of treatment would she have had?'

'We offer a mixture of medical and psychotherapeutic treatment.'

'Which means?'

'We can prescribe opioid medications such as methadone or buprenorphine, but we also offer various therapies such as cognitive behavioural therapy or motivational interviewing. Basically, prescribing drug substitutes won't work unless the patient actually wants to change.'

'And did Chloe Jenkins want to change?'

Doctor McAllister is silent for a moment. 'Yes, I think she did. She'd been in rehab before, of course. Not here. I think the first time was in a specialist centre for teenagers and the second time somewhere abroad. But I did sense a real will to get her life together at last. That's what makes it so sad . . .'

Doctor McAllister's voice doesn't break, but she does look momentarily stricken. Encouraged by this first sign of humanity, Nelson says, 'What was Chloe like as a person?'

'You should talk to her personal therapist. She knew her best. But I would say that Chloe was a bright girl. I don't think she had any formal qualifications, but she was a great reader, keen to learn more about the world around her. This sometimes led to rather strange enthusiasms, but basically she just wanted to improve her mind. And she was charming. But a lot of addicts are charming. That's how they persuade friends and family to collude with their addiction.'

'I'd like to speak to her therapist.'

'I'll give you her number. Her name's Holly Barrett.' She scribbles on a Post-it note.

'Did Chloe have any special friends here?'

Is it his imagination or is there a slight hesitation? 'She was friendly with another couple of patients, yes.'

'Could I speak to them?'

'I'll let you have the names.' But, unlike Holly Barrett's, it seems that she doesn't have the names to hand.

'Doctor McAllister.' Nelson tries to sound confiding, the way Judy does, but he has a feeling that it's coming out wrong. Fiona McAllister, at any rate, does not look reassured. 'I know this is a difficult question, but do you have any idea who could have killed Chloe Jenkins?'

The doctor looks surprised. 'But wasn't it just some random madman?'

'Random madmen are rarer than you'd think. Victims usually know their murderers.'

'What are you suggesting?'

'Was there anyone she was scared of? Did she mention someone, maybe in her past, who was threatening her or making her feel uncomfortable? She was a very attractive woman, maybe someone had become obsessed with her or was stalking her.'

'I don't know,' says Doctor McAllister. 'She never mentioned anyone like that to me. But maybe she spoke to Holly or one of the other patients.'

'And have you any idea why Chloe left her room on Wednesday night?'

'No.'

'When was the last time you saw her?'

'That morning. It was a group therapy session. Chloe seemed her usual self, quite bouncy and happy.'

'Bouncy?'

Doctor McAllister twitches impatiently. 'It was how she

was. I didn't mean she was manic or anything.'

Interesting, thinks Nelson. 'What was the group session about?'

'Families. Sometimes we do family therapy too. Often the problems with addiction go back to childhood and the family dynamic.'

'What was Chloe Jenkins' family like?'

'They seemed supportive enough. They visited last week. We try to discourage too many outside influences, but Holly and I felt that a visit from her parents wouldn't do Chloe any harm. And it seemed to go well.'

Nelson remembers Julie Jenkins saying 'She seemed well', and Alan describing the happy journey home, both parents thinking that their child was getting the help she needed.

'I've just met her parents,' he says. 'They seem nice people.'

'Oh yes,' says Doctor McAllister. 'Chloe had a privileged background, nannies, boarding school, pony club etc. No lack of money.'

Nelson thinks of the well-dressed couple in the quiet room. He can imagine them being part of a prosperous, middle-class set. But something in Doctor McAllister's voice makes him feel as if a judgement is being made. Maybe it was just because the Scottish accent became more pronounced.

'What was there a lack of?'

The doctor shrugs. 'I don't know. Time maybe. But the family were very supportive of her problems, they paid for rehab several times, bought her a flat, tried to keep her out of trouble. It's wearing, having an addict in the family.'

'What about the boyfriend, Thom Novak?'

'I never met him. I know he has problems with addiction too.'

'He's in rehab at the moment.'

'It's a real problem when addicts get together. A kind of *folie à deux* situation. They enable each other. For Chloe's rehabilitation to work, I think she would have had to break up with Thom.'

'Did you say that to her?'

'Yes.'

'And what was her answer?'

'She said that she loved him. And I'm sure she did. Sadly, sometimes love isn't enough.' Now she really does look sad. Nelson wonders about Doctor McAllister's background. He can't see a wedding ring; maybe she's married to the job.

He thanks Doctor McAllister for her time and says that he can see himself out. She doesn't seem too keen on this and calls a member of the ground staff to escort him. Even with the man's surly chaperonage Nelson is able to see that Chloe would not have found it difficult to leave the hospital unnoticed. There are several fire exits, presumably unlocked, and, although you need a passcode to open the doors from outside, from inside all you have to do is press a red button marked 'Open'. It's hardly *The Great Escape*.

When he gets back to his car, there's a message from Chris Stephenson saying that he has the preliminary autopsy results. Nelson rings him back and tries not to wince when the pathologist calls him 'chief'. 'It's much what you'd expect, chief. Death by manual strangulation. No sign of recent sexual activity. Deceased had no traces of alcohol or drugs in the bloodstream. One odd thing. We found traces of cleaning fluid on her hands and under her nails. Do they have them scrubbing floors in the Sanctuary?'

No, thinks Nelson. He's pretty sure that's not one of the therapies on offer. Then he thinks back to yesterday and Cathbad pointing out the spot where Chloe had appeared to him. 'Here. By this white tombstone.' The other stones had been grey, covered with lichen and the accumulated grime of the years, but the grave which Chloe had been standing next to was white. As if it had been newly cleaned.

6

If Chesterton is pleased to see Justin, he doesn't show it. When his owner arrives the cat stares at him coldly for a moment and then stalks out of the room with his tail in the air.

'Still the same old Chesterton,' says Justin.

'Yes,' says Cathbad. 'I think we came to some sort of understanding, though I wouldn't say we bonded exactly.'

Justin has bought Cathbad a bottle of Irish whisky and a small statue of the Virgin Mary. Cathbad is delighted with both presents and balances the glass figurine on his hand.

'She glows in the dark,' says Justin. 'Very useful if you're lost on a lonely road with only a religious icon to keep you company.'

Cathbad is never quite sure about Justin's religious convictions. He's a layman, but Cathbad knows that he once studied for the priesthood. Now he seems happy being a waspish, slightly cynical presence on many local committees and charities. He's also a guide at the priory and a volunteer at the museum. He's a respected historian too and often gives lectures in London. Cathbad first met Justin when they were both concerned with saving the remains of an anchorite's cell in the grounds of a Norwich church. Justin hadn't minded Cathbad turning up to meetings in his druid's robes and referring to the spiritual energies of the site. Cathbad, for his part, had overlooked Justin's weakness for waistcoats and foppish cravats. The campaign had been successful and, by the end of it, Justin and Cathbad were firm — if respectfully distant — friends.

'I had a religious visitation of my own when you were away,' Cathbad says now.

He tells Justin about seeing Chloe Jenkins in the graveyard and the subsequent discovery of her body.

'So that's why there were all those policemen on the Fakenham Road,' says Justin. 'I had to go the long way round.'

'My friend Janet tried to persuade me that I'd seen a vision of the Virgin Mary.'

'Like good old Richeldis de Faverches? It's possible, I suppose.'

Cathbad looks at his friend. 'Have you ever seen anything in the graveyard? Or in the house?'

Justin smiles and bends to stroke Chesterton, who has come back into the room. 'This is a holy house, did you know that?'

'What do you mean?'

'It was once owned by a holy woman called Dame Judith de Hare. She was an anchoress, like Julian of Norwich. Dame Judith used to see regular visions of the Virgin Mary. She described her as being dressed in blue with a heavenly countenance. It's documented in the parish records.'

'Have you ever seen her?'

'No.' From his tone, Cathbad thinks Justin sounds disappointed.

'I think Chesterton's seen Dame Judith, though. Sometimes he's sitting here with me in the evening and suddenly he stiffens and stands up, his hair standing on end, eyes staring.'

Cathbad wouldn't put it past Chesterton to be putting this on, but he doesn't voice this thought. Instead he says, 'So you haven't seen any ghosts here?'

'No I haven't,' says Justin. 'And I don't suppose even the ghosts will get any rest now with all these policemen flat-footing around.'

'I'm sure they won't bother you.'

At that moment there's a knock on the door. It's Nelson, asking if he can look in the graveyard.

Nelson had intended to go straight into the churchyard via the lych-gate. But then he had seen Cathbad silhouetted in the window of the cottage and thought that he'd call in and ask a bit more about the events of Wednesday night. He hadn't reckoned on the door being opened by a man in a tweed suit and a yellow waistcoat. He has a neat moustache and reminds Nelson of one of the animals in *The Wind in the Willows*, memories of a far-off school adaptation with Rebecca as Ratty.

Nelson introduces himself. The man grins delightedly and says that his name is Justin something double-barrelled.

'My friend and I were just discussing the case.'

'Hi, Nelson.' Cathbad appears at Ratty's shoulder.

'Hallo, Cathbad. Might have guessed that you'd be gossiping.'

Justin Double-Barrelled looks from one to the other. 'Do you two *know* each other?'

'We're old friends,' says Cathbad. 'We've even solved a few crimes together.'

'Starsky and Hutch,' says Nelson. 'That's us.'

Justin stands aside to let Nelson into the house. 'Can I offer you anything to drink, Detective Chief Inspector? I've just returned from a work trip so things are in a bit of a state.' He gestures at the perfectly tidy room, which has a wheelie suitcase in the centre of it.

'No, thank you very much. I'd just like to see the church-yard again.' Nelson despises wheelie suitcases.

The three of them walk through the graves. Although it's only three in the afternoon, it's already getting dark. A fine mist hovers in the air, making the tombstones and the trees merge into a hazy grey backdrop. The grave where Chloe Jenkins was seen stands out like a beacon. Nelson crosses over to examine the stone.

'Doreen Westmondham,' he reads, '1940 to 2002. Beloved wife, mother and grandmother.'

He turns to Cathbad and Justin, who are watching him intently. 'Do you know anything about this woman?' he asks.

'No,' says Justin. 'I only moved here in 2006. It's one of the newest graves. Look how white it is.'

'It's white,' says Nelson, 'because it's recently been cleaned.'

And by the wall, hidden under a holly bush, he finds what he's looking for. A cloth and a bottle of something called 'Deluxe Stone Cleaner'.

7

Ruth is late for her meeting with Hilary. She took Kate to school, then had planned to spend a couple of hours at work before heading off to Walsingham for eleven o'clock. But at the university she got caught up first with one of her PhD students anxious about his thesis, then with a colleague who wanted to complain about Phil. Normally this is one of her favourite pastimes but, when she catches sight of the clock, it's ten thirty.

'Sorry, Bob, I've got to go. I've got a meeting.'

Bob's voice follows her plaintively down the stairs: 'And he's even changed the loo paper in the staff bogs.'

She hurries to the car park, book bag bumping on her hip. Her car is parked under a lime tree that drops sticky resin onto the bonnet but this has always been Ruth's spot, and at the university you don't change things unless you really have to. The marks on the paint didn't matter when Ruth had a battered old car, but this one is new, bought last year. It's smart and comfortable, but instead of a key it comes with a whizzy card device that you click to open the doors.

Ruth always had problems finding her car keys, but the card is something else. Now she has to upturn her bag to find it, nestling at the bottom amongst the Polo crumbs and loose tampons. By the time she has inserted the card to start the ignition, the time on the dashboard clock says ten forty-five.

Ruth races through the back roads to Walsingham. This car is faster than her old one, but that doesn't help when she ends up behind a horse trailer for the first mile and then a man in a hat driving a Nissan Micra for the second. When she finally gets to Walsingham she follows signs to the car park and ends up at the top of the hill behind the farm shop. What was the name of the cafe Hilary mentioned? The blue something. Well, it can't be far away. Walsingham seems very small, just a village, really. She passes an odd-looking pump-house with a brazier on top, a pub and a couple of shops selling shrine souvenirs. 'Everything £1', says one, Ruth's first experience of a religious pound shop. She walks down the road, past flint and timbered houses, others painted in delicate pastel shades. Halfway down there's a gateway that's signposted as leading to the abbey grounds. The heavy wooden gates are shut now, apart from a grille showing a tantalising glimpse of green. The gate with its worn stone gargoyles looks odd amongst the picturesque houses, like a grey growth forcing its way through the wattle and daub. Ruth hurries on, looking in the shop windows for signs that one of them might be a cafe in disguise. As she does so she realises that these are very particular retail outlets. One sells priest's vestments, gorgeous shades of green, purple and gold. Another has life-size models of the Holy Family, Mary in blue and white with upturned eyes, Joseph solid in russet red and brown, a disturbingly adult-looking baby Jesus. Aid to the Church in Need, The Pilgrim Shop. This must be where priests and vicars go for a spending spree. But, although the car park had been fairly full, there's not a soul to be seen.

At the bottom of the street she finds the Blue Lady. It's part-cafe, part-bookshop and, at first, this too looks empty. Then she sees a woman browsing the shelves. Could that be Hilary? She's about the right height and shape, but this woman has grey hair, cut in a glossy bob. Ruth has a few white hairs, but they always disappear if she changes her parting. Hilary is about her age, forty-five. Could she have gone completely grey?

The woman turns and all thoughts of hair colour vanish. Because the woman is definitely Hilary and she is equally definitely a priest.

'Hallo, Ruth.'

'Hallo.' For one lunatic moment Ruth wonders if she should address her as 'Reverend'.

Hilary gestures at the dog collar. 'Sorry to spring this on you, but I couldn't think of a way to tell you via email.'

'That's OK,' says Ruth. She wonders if it would be socially acceptable to slip out of the cafe and run back up the high street screaming.

'Shall we sit down?' Hilary indicates a table in the window. 'They do nice cakes in here. Do you fancy a cake? I do. It's not Lent yet.'

Ruth has no idea when Lent is, but she's surprised to hear a vicar sounding so enthusiastic about cakes. Aren't

they meant to live on bread and water? She only knows one
other member of the clergy and he seems to eat and drink
fairly normally. But he's Irish and a Catholic. Her parents'
church has elders, ordinary people who are just holier (and
smugger) than the rest of them. She doesn't really have any
experience of C of E vicars, aside from *Rev* or reruns of *The
Vicar of Dibley*.

Hilary orders tea and a slice of carrot cake. Ruth goes for
coffee and a chocolate brownie.

'Have you lived in Norfolk long?' Hilary asks her.

'About seventeen years.' Christ, is it really that long?

'And you work at the university? I've looked you up. Very
impressive.'

Why? thinks Ruth. Why have you looked me up? Instead
she says, 'Are you still working in archaeology? I mean . . .
not now obviously . . .' Her voice trails away.

'I worked as an archaeologist for a while,' says Hilary. 'Did
some fantastic digs in Sussex. At Boxgrove and Whitehawk.
But then . . .' She shrugs. 'I found God.'

Why do people keep doing this? Ruth's parents discovered
God when she was ten and her life was never the same again.
Why couldn't He just stay hidden?

Feeling she should show an interest, she asks Hilary how
long it takes to become a vicar.

'Ages,' says Hilary with a brilliant, ageless smile. 'First
there's the discernment period — where you ask yourself
if this is really what God wants for you — then there's the
training. That took three years in my case. Then I was a curate
for four years. Now I'm a parish priest in south London.'

'Where?' asks Ruth. 'I'm from south London originally.'

'I know,' says Hilary, rather worryingly. 'My church is in Streatham. Quite a challenging area, very mixed.'

What does 'mixed' mean in this context, wonders Ruth. Black and white? Rich and poor? Sheep and goats?

'I'm very happy,' says Hilary. 'I love my work and I'm married with a four-year-old son.'

'I've got a five-year-old,' says Ruth. 'A daughter. Kate.'

This is something Hilary doesn't know about her. She beams. 'That's wonderful! I wish we could get them together. What does your partner do?'

'I'm single,' says Ruth. 'I'm not with Kate's father.'

Hilary gives her a compassionate smile. 'Must be hard work.'

'It is, sometimes. But I have a lovely childminder and friends help out a lot.'

'That's good.'

'Yes, it is.'

Their drinks and cakes arrive and Ruth divides her attention between the chocolate brownie and wondering how she can get round to asking why it was so important that they meet and have this fascinating chat about lifestyles. Then Hilary, cutting her cake into tiny cubes, says, 'Are you wondering why I wanted to see you?'

'Well, I . . .'

'The thing is, Ruth . . .' For the first time Hilary's sunny glow falters. She looks older, and afraid. 'The thing is, I've been getting these letters.'

'What sort of letters?'

'The thing is,' says Hilary again, cubing the cubes, 'there are some people who just don't like the idea of women priests.'

Ruth knows. She's read about it in the *Guardian*. Though, to be honest, she usually skips those articles on the way to the TV listings.

'Most women priests get abuse of some kind, people saying things, refusing to come to their services. When I first started getting the letters I didn't think anything of it. A rite of passage, that's what Brian, my husband, says.'

'What does Brian do?' Well, Hilary had asked her.

'He's a priest too.' Hilary smiles. 'Crazy, isn't it? But we met at theological college. He's a school chaplain.'

'So what do these letters say?'

'Well at first it was the usual stuff about all the disciples being men, women not being worthy, women's vocation being motherhood and domesticity. I could ignore all that. You get it all the time. Then, at the end of last year, the tone seemed to change, to become nastier, more sinister. But what worried me most were the references to archaeology.'

'To archaeology?'

'Yes. And that worried me because it was specific to me. The letter-writer must know that I used to be an archaeologist. And recently there are references to Norfolk. He must have found out that I was coming to this conference.'

Ruth notes that Hilary assumes that the writer is male. In her experience misogyny is not always confined to men.

'So I thought,' Hilary goes on. 'I thought, why don't I talk to Ruth? She's in Norfolk and she knows all about archaeology.

And, when I looked you up, I saw you were a special advisor to the police.'

Damn that LinkedIn profile. Ruth says, 'If the letters are threatening, you must go to the police. I'm not a member of the police. I'm just an archaeologist who advises them on buried bones. I can't investigate this for you. I'm not Miss Marple.'

'But if you would just look at the letters . . .'

'Look,' says Ruth. 'I know a policeman. Someone fairly senior. He's a good man. He'll take this seriously. Believe me, I know. Will you talk to him?'

Hilary looks at her squarely. 'If you'll read the letters.'

'Am I being blackmailed by a priest?'

Hilary reaches out to touch her hand. 'No, of course not. It would just be a comfort to me if you would read them. You can pass them on to this policeman if you think it's worth it.'

Ruth sighs. 'All right.'

Hilary reaches into her voluminous backpack and Ruth realises that she had the letters with her all the time. Did she always count on being able to persuade Ruth?

'Thank you, Ruth. And maybe we could meet up again? The conference lasts for a week.'

'What's it about?'

Hilary grins and Ruth sees the first trace of the old Erik-baiting Hilary. 'Preparing for Episcopacy. That should really upset the letter-writer.'

Ruth looks it up later; it's something to do with becoming a bishop.

*

Tim, too, is out of his comfort zone. He is in a room that could almost be the setting for some early evening costume drama: low sofas, a herd of spindly-legged tables, an upright piano, doors leading onto a perfect, landscaped garden. Only the giant TV screen embedded in the Regency wallpaper spoils the illusion. That and the hundreds of condolence cards displayed on the marble fireplace, the bookshelves and many of the little tables. Tim, looking for somewhere to put his coffee cup, can't escape the words: sympathy, sorrow, love, consolation, angel. But, then again, what do you say when someone has died? When he was at school one of his friends lost a brother in a shooting incident (it was that kind of school) and, whilst Tim's mother had had all the words, or at least knew where to find them in the Bible, Tim had found himself avoiding that friend because he didn't know what to say. He had hated himself for it.

Julie Jenkins sees him looking and slides a silver coaster under the cup.

'Thank you.' Tim smiles at her and is encouraged to get a wobbly smile back. 'Be charming,' Nelson had said to him, as if suggesting that he employ the dark arts. 'Some people find you charming, I hear.' Maybe that was a reference to Superintendent Whitcliffe. Even so, the remark had made Tim uneasy.

'Thank you so much for seeing me,' he says now to Julie and Alan, sitting close together on one of the sofas. 'I know how hard this must be for you, but it's very important for us to get a complete picture of Chloe.'

He wishes he hadn't used these words because, over the

fireplace, there is an actual picture of Chloe, an oil painting, presumably of her with her sister. The two faces, both impossibly beautiful, stare sadly down at him.

Julie sees him looking. 'That's Chloe and Lauren. It was painted when Chloe was seventeen and Lauren twenty.'

'It's beautiful.' Tim's no expert but he doesn't think the artist will be winning any prizes — the style is painting-by-numbers crossed with Athena poster — but there is no doubt that the girls themselves are lovely.

'Yes. They were very close.' Julie catches herself using the past tense and her mouth wobbles as the tears begin to flow again.

'Where's Lauren now?' asks Tim, as Alan silently passes his wife a tissue.

'She's a flight attendant,' says Alan. 'Working long-haul. She came home as soon as she heard, but she's with her boyfriend today. I don't think she likes being here.' He gestures at the luxurious room with the flowers and the angels and the messages of condolence.

'Are you in the aviation business too, Mr Jenkins?' Tim knows the answer already but, even if he hadn't, the room would have given him a clue. Apart from the one of the girls over the fireplace, most of the pictures are of planes: biplanes coasting over grey seas, modern jumbos on the runway, uniformed men with wings and gold braid on their caps. But he meant to give the bereaved father something else to think about, and it works. Alan straightens up immediately.

'Yes. I used to be in the RAF, but now I'm a commercial pilot.'

'The whole family are mad about planes,' says Julie. 'Both girls have amateur pilots' licences.'

'Really?' It's hard to imagine Chloe, the glamorous model, flying a plane, but, of course, that's what this interview is for. To see the whole person, not just the murder victim.

'It started when they were young,' says Julie. 'When we were still living on the base. At RAF Skulthorpe.'

This name rings a faint bell with Tim. A bell that seems to speak in the voice of his sat nav.

'Skulthorpe. Is that in Norfolk?'

'Yes.' Julie holds the tissue to her eyes. 'It's very near where she was . . . It's near the Sanctuary.'

This is interesting. As far as he knows, the investigating team have no idea that Chloe was originally from Norfolk.

'When did you leave Norfolk?' he asks.

'When Chloe was eight. She was sad to go. She loved it there. But Alan left the RAF and we needed to be near the big airports.'

'Tell me something about Chloe,' says Tim. 'What sort of a child was she?'

'Very happy,' says Julie. 'Always smiling. Everybody loved her. She was an angel, that's what her childminder said. Her problems . . . well, they didn't start until later.'

Tim waits. 'She was too pretty for her own good,' says Alan. 'She was scouted by a model agency when she was only fourteen. I didn't want her to take it up. I wanted her to have a proper career. She was a very bright girl. She just didn't try at school.'

'I made her wait until she was sixteen,' says Julie, with a

flash of spirit. 'But I couldn't stop her. She wanted to be a model. Her head was quite turned by it all, and no wonder really.'

'At the age of sixteen she was travelling all over the world on assignments,' says Alan. 'Drugs were everywhere. Chloe always found it hard to say no. By the time she was eighteen she had a real problem.'

'That must have been hard for you as parents,' says Tim.

'It was awful,' says Julie. 'At first we didn't realise. We didn't know the signs. But then I actually saw her taking the drugs. Here in her bedroom. Snorting them with a fifty-pound note! I confronted her, Alan confronted her, even Lauren begged her to get help. And, eventually, she agreed.'

'She went to this special rehabilitation place for teenagers,' says Alan. 'It was tough but it worked. She got clean. She was our little girl again. She even started studying for her A-levels.'

'What happened next?' asks Tim.

'She met him,' says Alan. 'Thom Novak.'

This time there is real anger in his voice. Julie looks at her husband apprehensively. 'She went back to modelling,' she explains to Tim. 'We didn't want her to, but they were offering such good money. She met Thom on a shoot. He's an actor and a model too, he's really handsome. Well, he is!' This to Alan, who makes a derisive noise. 'You can't say he's not handsome. And charming too. We liked him at first. You know we did, Alan.'

'He was all right,' says Alan. 'A sight too pleased with himself, I always thought. Public school type. But he got Chloe back into drugs. He was part of that "in the gossip papers every weekend" set. We were always seeing him and Chloe falling out of some nightclub.'

Tim has seen the pictures too. There are some in the crime file. Chloe, wearing nothing much more than a brilliant smile, clinging on to Thom's arm at red-carpet events. Chloe stumbling out of a taxi. Chloe in dark glasses at the airport. Chloe at a pop festival, flowers in her hair.

'So when did you suspect that she was taking drugs again?' he asks.

'It was Thom himself who told us,' says Julie. 'He rang us one weekend and just said "We need help." He was crying on the phone. We drove to their flat. They had this really nice place in Chiswick. Well, it was a tip. Bins overflowing, empty wine bottles everywhere. Chloe was lying on the bed. I thought she was dead at first. She was so thin, the marks on her arms . . .'

'I phoned the Sanctuary at once,' says Alan, in a voice that suggests he took charge of the situation. 'We drove her there that night.'

'What about Thom?'

'I called his parents. They got him into a rehab place in Switzerland. I suppose he's still there. He wasn't our responsibility.'

Tim remembers speaking to Thom on the day that Chloe's body was found. He had wept then, too.

'How did Chloe get on at the Sanctuary?' he says. 'I understand you went to see her.'

'She seemed to be doing well,' says Alan. 'It was early days, but she liked Holly, her therapist, and the main doctor. She'd made some friends there, she said. Adults, not stupid young models.'

'She looked so much better,' says Julie, 'after only a few weeks. She'd put on weight, her eyes were brighter. She was talking about taking a course. Chloe was always taking courses. It was a sign that she was feeling better.'

'What was she taking a course in?'

'I can't remember,' says Julie. 'Something spiritual. Chloe was very spiritual.'

'The coroner told us that there were no drugs in her bloodstream,' says Alan. 'Sounds strange, I know, but that was a real comfort to us.'

'I can understand that,' says Tim. He looks around the room, at the perfect furniture and the florist's arrangements in muted, funereal colours. Despite the cards and the flowers, he thinks that comfort must be hard to come by.

Ruth rings Nelson as soon as she gets back to the university. He answers on the second ring.

'Ruth. Is anything wrong with Katie?'

Ruth counts to ten. Not only does Nelson always assume she's ringing with bad news, he always insists on calling their daughter Katie when he knows full well that her name's Kate.

'Kate's fine. I'm ringing about something else.'

'Oh?' Ruth thinks that Nelson sounds nervous. Does he think that she's about to demand that he leaves Michelle and marries her? Not likely after all this time. Not least because she knows he'd say no.

Ruth explains about Hilary and the letters. 'I told her to contact you. I hope that's OK.'

Nelson is silent and Ruth wonders whether she has crossed some invisible line. Maybe he thinks it's too trivial a matter for a DCI? Maybe he's just annoyed because she has given his name to a third party.

Then Nelson says, 'Do these letters mention Walsingham?'

'I haven't read them yet. I'm going to do it tonight.'

'When you've read them, can you ring me?'

'OK. Is something up?'

'Have you read about the woman found dead just outside Walsingham?'

'Yes. She was an actress or a model or something, wasn't she?' Ruth seems to remember a lot of pictures in the papers. Easy to get coverage if you're beautiful, blonde and dead.

'It's probably nothing, but if there's some nutter threatening women . . .'

'This guy — if it is a man — seems to be fixated on women priests, though.'

'Yes. There's probably no connection. Tell your friend to give me a ring. There are laws against this sort of harassment now.'

'I will. Thanks.'

'And call me when you've read the letters.'

'I will.'

Nelson puts down the phone, feeling thoughtful. Ruth's letter-writer may have nothing to do with Chloe Jenkins' murder, but it's worrying that there might be two woman-haters focusing on Walsingham. He has learnt to ignore such vitriol at his peril. Equally he knows that it can be fatal to assume that people who write violent letters are always violent themselves. That was the mistake the police made in the Yorkshire Ripper case. And the thought that Ruth actually knows a woman priest is surely the most astonishing aspect of all. They were at university together, says Ruth. Well, you get all types at university (so he's heard; he left school at sixteen), but, even so, he can't imagine Ruth being friendly with anyone overtly religious.

The case is frustrating him. He still has no idea why Chloe was wandering around Walsingham last Wednesday. He has spoken to Chloe's therapist, Holly Barrett, on the phone and she seemed to have no particular insights into her patient's state of mind. Chloe appeared to be making good progress, she was in a 'good place', no she hadn't complained about any stalkers or sinister ex-boyfriends. Maybe Chloe's friends from rehab will be more forthcoming. Nelson is seeing them at the Sanctuary this afternoon.

Even Nelson's hunch about the gravestone is proving inconclusive. Intel have traced Doreen Westmondham. She was a local woman from Houghton St Giles, married with three children and five grandchildren, a former school dinner-lady and, according to tributes following her untimely death from cancer at sixty-two, 'loved by all who knew her'. Doreen and her husband had also fostered over a hundred children. Her funeral at St Simeon's Church was standing room only. What was Doreen's link with Chloe Jenkins, model, socialite and drug addict? It's hard to see the connection.

At one o'clock Tim returns from his trip to Surrey. Nelson accosts him before he has had time to eat his lunchtime salad. Salad! Sometimes Nelson worries about Tim.

'Did you get anything from the family?'

Tim puts down his plastic fork. 'They're still in shock. But they're nice people, very respectable. They seemed to have done their best to help Chloe. They're heartbroken.'

'Did you find anything that might help with the enquiry?'

'Well, they weren't keen on the boyfriend, Thom Novak, but he's got a pretty solid alibi. He was in Switzerland. I spoke to him myself.'

Nelson grunts, trying to work out how long it would take to get from Switzerland to Norfolk. He doesn't believe in solid alibis.

'Anything else?'

'Well, one interesting thing. Did you know they were from Norfolk?'

'No,' says Nelson, 'I didn't.'

'Yes. They lived near here when Chloe was little. Alan was stationed at RAF Skulthorpe. They moved when she was eight.'

'That's interesting.' It could explain, thinks Nelson, how Chloe was able to find her way to Walsingham at night across the fields. Isn't RAF Skulthorpe quite near Walsingham?

'I'm going back to the Sanctuary this afternoon,' he says. 'Do you want to come?'

'OK,' says Tim, turning back to his salad.

'For God's sake,' says Nelson, 'have a burger to go with that. You'll never make a detective inspector living on lettuce.'

———

8

Tim remembers Alan Jenkins saying that Chloe's new friends were 'adults, not stupid young models'. Even so, he is surprised by the two people waiting for them in the television lounge of the Sanctuary. Stanley and Jean are middle-aged and, not to put too fine a point upon it, dowdy. Jean, a food technology teacher, has dyed red hair, grey showing at the roots, and a round placid face. Stanley, who doesn't vouchsafe his occupation, is thin and stooped, fiddling nervously with a Styrofoam cup of coffee. Both are dressed in tracksuits. The boss's face gives nothing away as he makes brisk introductions, but Tim is sure that he too is surprised by the friends Chloe made while having her treatment. Surely she should have palled up with that pop star that Cloughie's always going on about, Foxy something?

'Holly Barrett says that you were particular friends of Chloe Jenkins,' says Nelson.

Tim almost expects the two impostors to deny this, but, instead, Jean says in a voice trembling with emotion, 'Dear

Chloe. I just can't believe she's gone. We loved her, didn't
we, Stanley?'

'Yes.' Stanley too looks on the verge of tears. 'We loved
her.' He tears a large portion of Styrofoam off his cup and
coffee starts dripping onto the carpet.

'Here. Give that to me.' Jean is motherly and capable, tip-
ping the coffee into a plant pot and handing Stanley a tissue
(all the rooms in the Sanctuary are equipped with large boxes
of tissues). Is this why Chloe liked these people, because
they were substitute parents? Maybe more accessible parents
than the smart, attractive couple in the room dominated by
pictures of airplanes?

'How did you get to know Chloe?' asks Tim.

'We hit it off right away,' says Jean. 'I sat next to her in
one of the group sessions and we just started chatting. She
was so open and easy to talk to. Not like some of the younger
ones here.'

'She was like an angel,' says Stanley.

What had Julie said? That Chloe's childminder had thought
she was an angel. There are getting to be too many angels
around for Tim's liking.

'I know this is very difficult,' says Nelson, 'but we're
looking for any reasons why someone might have wanted
to kill Chloe. Did she ever tell you about anyone threatening
her? Maybe someone from her past?'

Jean shakes her head. 'She talked about her boyfriend Thom.
Poor thing, he sounded like another troubled soul. But she
wasn't scared of him, if anything she felt she needed to protect
him. She was a very caring person.' She reaches for the tissues.

'Did Thom contact her while she was here?' asks Tim.

'I don't think so. Visitors aren't encouraged. You're meant to purge yourself of all influences. Chloe's parents came once. They seemed a nice couple. Chloe only had good to say about them. A lot of addicts, they blame their parents. I used to do it myself before I went into therapy.'

Jean looks too old to have parents living, let alone culpable for their daughter's lifestyle. Before Nelson can stop her Jean has launched into her life story.

'. . . blamed myself because I was never good enough. My sister was always my mother's favourite. I did everything to win Mum's approval, even becoming a teacher like her. I started drinking at teacher-training college. I coped for years, drinking and taking drugs at the weekend, teaching all week. Then my marriage broke up and it all unravelled. I was coming to work hungover, drinking in my lunch break . . .'

She stops for a sip of coffee, and Nelson takes his chance. 'Can you think of anything else Chloe said or did that might have relevance here? It could be the smallest thing, something that didn't seem significant at the time.'

He is looking at Jean, but it's Stanley who says, 'She was religious.'

'Was she?' says Nelson encouragingly.

'Yes. I don't mean that she was any particular religion, but she was very spiritual. She used to pray. A lot of people here meditate, but she actually used to pray. She'd light candles in the recreation room and pray every night. She said that she thought her guardian angel was looking after her. Turns out he wasn't,' he adds, with sudden bitterness.

'Her mother said that she wanted to take a course,' says Tim. 'Something spiritual, she said. Do you know what that was?'

Jean and Stanley look at each other and smile. 'It was a course in angel therapy,' says Jean. 'You tap into the healing vibrations of the angels.'

More angels. Tim doesn't dare look at Nelson. 'Where did she find this course?' he asks.

'Online,' says Jean. 'You get a certificate and everything.' She obviously thinks some sort of explanation is needed because she says, 'Chloe loved angels. She collected pictures of them. She gave me this beautiful angel brooch. I'll never take it off.' She points at her chest, where a little gold cherub nestles in the grey fleece. 'She was interested in all sorts of spirituality, though. As an ex-teacher I recognised a truly curious mind. She meditated, as Stanley says, she did mind, body and spirit courses and she went to conventional C of E church services.'

'She went to church?' says Nelson. 'Where?'

'St Simeon's in Walsingham,' says Stanley. 'I went with her sometimes. Doctor McAllister drove us, but she never came into the church.'

'That figures,' says Jean. 'Fiona McAllister's an atheist if I ever saw one.'

'Did Chloe ever talk to you about anyone she met at St Simeon's?' asks Nelson.

'She said she used to see her guardian angel there,' says Stanley, in a matter-of-fact voice.

'What do you think she meant by that?' asks Tim.

'She said she'd seen a vision of her guardian angel,' says Stanley, 'in the graveyard.'

'Did you believe her?'

'Oh, yes,' says Stanley. 'She was telling the truth, I'm sure of it. I've learnt to spot true mystics in my line of work.'

'What line of work is that?' asks Nelson.

Stanley gives him a sad smile. 'I'm a priest,' he says.

'Bloody hell,' says Nelson, driving back through the darkening lanes. It's still afternoon, but already the daylight is fading. 'You don't expect to find a priest in a drying-out clinic.'

'I don't know,' says Tim. 'They must come under tremendous strain. People dump all their problems on their ministers. I don't know if they have enough training or counselling to help them to cope. I should imagine it's enough to make you turn to drink.'

It's a characteristic, measured Tim response. 'Is your family religious?' asks Nelson.

'My mum is,' says Tim. 'She goes to church every Sunday. All her social life is bound up in the church too. I don't believe myself, but her faith's got Mum through some very bad times. It's been a real support to her, a real community.'

Nelson wonders what the bad times entailed. Tim never mentions a father — perhaps he died or deserted the family. It's typical of Tim to answer a question in a very open, friendly way and yet not tell you much.

'My mum's religious too,' he says. 'Roman Catholic. We were all brought up as Catholics but none of us practise now.

For my mum, though, it's the centre of her world. She's like your mother, never misses a Sunday.'

She goes on Fridays too, for some obscure reason that Nelson can never remember. Something to do with collecting brownie points for the souls in purgatory. He has a super-stitious impulse to cross himself. He remembers Cathbad saying, 'You're still such a Catholic, Nelson.'

'Stanley wasn't a Catholic priest, though,' he says aloud.

'"Anglo-Catholic", he said.'

'It's not the same,' says Nelson. 'Anglo-Catholics are still Protestants.' He can still hear his mother criticising her parish priest, Father David, who's a Church of England convert ('He only came over to us because he couldn't stand the thought of female priests'). She'd adored the previous incumbent, Father Damian. Come to think of it, Damian went back to Ireland to recover from a drink problem. Maybe Tim's right: there's more of it around than you think.

He's about to ask Tim what he thought of Stanley and Jean, when his sergeant says, so urgently that Nelson turns to look at him, 'Boss. I've got something to tell you.'

'What?' Nelson swerves to avoid a fallen branch.

'I want a transfer.'

'What?!' Nelson swerves again, causing Tim to say, reck-lessly, 'Look out!'

'Don't tell me how to drive,' growls Nelson. 'What do you mean, you want a transfer?'

'I want to move. Away from Norfolk.' After a pause Tim adds, 'I'm sorry.'

They have come to the outskirts of King's Lynn. Nelson

slows down, but only slightly. He says, 'You've had a tough few months, what with that business at Blackstock Hall.'

He's referring to the time when Tim shot a man. There has been an inquiry, and Tim was completely cleared (there were extenuating circumstances, like the fact that he saved Nelson's life), but there's no doubt that the whole business was incredibly stressful for everyone involved.

'Take some time off,' says Nelson. 'Think about it.'

'I have thought about it,' says Tim. 'I've really enjoyed working for you, but I think it's time to move on.'

'Where will you go?'

'Maybe back to Essex. To be near my family.'

Nelson understands this. He sometimes feels a real pull to go back to his home, Blackpool, away from Norfolk and its flat, alien fields. But Tim doesn't sound like a man yearning for home. He sounds disconsolate, as if he's got nothing left to look forward to. When Tim first moved to Norfolk Nelson assumed it wouldn't be long before he got himself a girlfriend and settled down. As far as Nelson knows, this hasn't happened, although Tim's a decent-looking boy who keeps himself fit.

'We'll miss you,' he says now. 'Cloughie will have no one to wind up.'

'He'll find someone,' says Tim. But he still sounds depressed.

9

Ruth doesn't open the letters until Kate has gone to bed. She feels that they need her full concentration and that's impossible with Kate organising her Sylvanians into Hogwarts houses and insisting that every one of her bath toys takes to the water. There's another reason too. She looks at the letters on her desk: brown envelopes (bad sign), addresses in capitals (ditto), and their appearance of having been read and reread several times. She's reluctant to open them and let the nastiness out. Cathbad would say that it was about bad energy. He would have recommended lighting candles and drawing up a circle of protection, but Ruth takes her own precautions by pouring herself a large glass of red wine and putting on a Bruce Springsteen CD.

Dear Doctor Smithson,
I won't call you Reverend because, as I will elaborate in this letter, you do not deserve the title. I am prepared to call you Doctor because this title you have

earned without fear or favour. But I will never accept your right to call yourself a priest. 'Man and Woman Created He Them' (Genesis 1:27). Men and women are different, Doctor Smithson. Not better or worse. Different. I am not a misogynist, as you women academics would have me. I simply believe that men and women have different tasks in the world. Women have the privilege of bearing children. Men are the appointed protectors of the family. And Jesus appointed men to be the protectors of his church. Yes, all the disciples were men and to these men was given the gift of the Holy Spirit and the task of spreading the word of God. You and your fellow harpies are bringing this holy church into disgrace. It is obscene to see a woman on the altar, her hands on the Blessed Chalice. Our Blessed Lord said, 'Anyone who has seen me has seen the Father' (John 14:9). Priests are in His image. The Father, not the Mother. The imagery of the scriptures is entirely masculine. A male priest symbolises the power, the masterfulness, of our Saviour. In the church, as in the family, the man has the authority, the guardianship, the duty of care. A women's sphere is motherhood and domesticity, not arguing from a pulpit. 'I do not permit a woman to teach or to have authority over a man' (1 Timothy 2:12). I will pray for you.

There's no signature.

Flint jumps on to the table and tries to sit on the letters. Ruth moves him gently. In the background Bruce Springsteen sings about a wreck on the highway. She thinks about the letter-writer. Is he a priest? A theologian? The painstaking biblical notations certainly seem like the work of someone with biblical knowledge, or at least someone who wants to seem learned. Maybe he's a thwarted academic? The reference to 'you women academics' sounds bitter and personal. Maybe he has been passed over for promotion by a woman. Ruth takes a sheet of paper and starts noting the biblical references. The Genesis quotation sounds as if it comes from an old translation. The writer is obviously the sort of person who likes archaic syntax. She's willing to bet that he's a Tolkien fan. Is the writer definitely a man? It's certainly someone who believes that men should have 'authority' over women, but plenty of women believe that too. Ruth has heard similar arguments in her parents' church, all about what a relief it is to have someone to make all the decisions, it's so *peaceful*. Well, so is a prison cell peaceful, after a fashion. And isn't there something of the submissive woman about the emphasis on God's 'masterfulness'? Not that Ruth knows any submissive women. She's proud to say that she hasn't even read *Fifty Shades of Grey*.

The letters aren't dated, but someone (Hilary presumably) has written the date they were received on the envelopes. The next two letters are sent a few months apart and more or less reprise the arguments of the first: the disciples were men, God is a man, men and women are different. With the fourth letter there is a distinct change of tone. According to the note on the envelope this letter was received on the first of November. Kate's birthday. All Saints' Day.

Dear Doctor Smithson,

You haven't replied to my letters. [Difficult to do, thinks Ruth, when there's no return address.] I fear you are mired in sin and in the wrongness of your ways. Do you follow the True Cross? 'I warn you, repent, for the Kingdom of Heaven is near at hand' (Matthew 4:12). 'He will put the sheep on his right hand and the goats on his left' (Matthew 25:33). You and your fellow she-devils are the goats, make no mistake about that. 'The Son of Man will send forth His angels, and they will gather out of His kingdom all stumbling blocks, and those who commit lawlessness, and will throw them into the furnace of fire; in that place there will be wailing and gnashing of teeth' (Matthew 13:42).

The last letter was received on 27th December, which probably meant that it had been sent just before Christmas. The writer had obviously decided on a new salutation.

Dear Jezebel,

They dug in Walsingham but they did not find the True Treasure. Nor will you find the Truth there. You may have borne a child (O sacrilege that anyone calling themselves a priest should do so!), but you have not suckled from the Virgin's breast. She stands before you, clad in blue, weeping for the world.

> *Weep, weep, O Walsingham,*
> *Whose dayes are nights,*

Blessings turned to blasphemies,
Holy deeds to despites.
Sinne is where our Ladye sate,
Heaven turned is to helle;
Satan sitthe where our Lord did swaye,
Walsingham, O farewell!

Beware, Doctor Smithson, for the Lord knows your ways
and His eye follows you wherever you go.
    Yours in Christ –

Ruth Googles Jezebel and learns that she was the wife
of Ahab, who encouraged him to worship false gods. Her
punishment was to be eaten alive by dogs. Ruth takes a
thoughtful sip of wine. Bruce is still singing about driving
and highways and the treacherous lure of his home town.
Flint purrs loudly, wanting to be noticed, and Ruth strokes
him with her spare hand. She can see why these last letters
so disturbed Hilary. There are the threats of hellfire and dam-
nation, but, worse still, the mention of her child and the
implication that the letter-writer, as well as the Lord, will
be watching Hilary wherever she goes. And the letter-writer
knows that Hilary will be in Walsingham. Well, maybe that's
not too difficult to find out. Presumably Hilary is listed as
attending the conference on preparing for bishopness, or
whatever it's called. The phrase 'They dug in Walsingham'
is interesting. Hilary thought it referred to an archaeological
dig, and Ruth knows that there were some excavations in
the sixties. She must look them up.

She looks at her list.

BIBLICAL

'Man and woman created He them' (Genesis 1:27)
'Anyone who has seen me has seen the Father' (John 14:9)
'I do not permit a woman to teach or to have authority over
a man' (1 Timothy 2:12)
Jezebel
'Repent, for the Kingdom of Heaven is near at hand' (Matthew 4:22)
'He will put the sheep on his right hand and the goats on
his left' (Matthew 25:33)
'The Son of Man will send forth His angels . . .' (Matthew
13:42)

HISTORICAL

The True Cross
'Weep, weep, O Walsingham' (Where is this from?)

ARCHAEOLOGY

They dug at Walsingham.

She remembers making a similar list, years ago, on the case
where she first met Nelson. The thought of that case, and
the places where it led, makes her feel suddenly uneasy. She
has been sitting by the window. Outside all is blackness, but
she knows the marshes are there, with their secret paths and

treacherous waterways, miles of grassland and sand leading to the sea. Ruth gets up and pulls the curtains. Flint jumps off the table with a thud. Ruth switches on the television, wanting the noise and distraction. It's the ten o'clock news. She had promised to ring Nelson when she'd read the letters, but is it too late now? She decides it is; besides, she never likes ringing him at home.

But, just as she settles down in front of the TV, he rings her.

'Ruth. Have you read the letters?'

'Yes.'

'I thought you were going to ring me.'

'I was, but then it seemed a bit late . . .'

'Bollocks. It's not late. Michelle's still out at her book group.' (Why tell me that? thinks Ruth. But she's interested, nonetheless. Michelle has never struck her as much of a reader.) 'Anyhow, is there anything in the letters? Have we got another madman on our hands?'

'I don't know,' says Ruth, 'but they certainly read like the work of someone disturbed. What sort of person sends anonymous letters in the first place? And there's lots of stuff about death, judgement and hell. Plus a nasty reference to Hilary and her child.'

Nelson is silent for a moment. Ruth thinks she can hear him thinking. 'Can you bring them in to the station tomorrow?' he asks. 'They sound like they're worth looking into. Anything else?'

'I've made a list.'

'Good girl.'

Ruth hates being called a girl, but she can't help smiling. A love of lists is one of the few things she and Nelson have in common.

'The letter-writer obviously has a real problem with women,' she says.

'Haven't we all?' says Nelson.

'He's even worse than you. Actually, I'm not even sure it is a man.'

'A female woman-hater?'

'They do exist, believe me.'

There's another silence and then Nelson says, 'Tim's leaving.'

'What?'

'Tim says he wants a transfer. He wants to go back to Essex.'

'Because of what happened before Christmas? The shooting and everything?'

'I asked him that. He just says it's time to move on. I've said he should take some more time to think about it. I've even offered him counselling.'

Nelson sounds aggrieved. Ruth knows that it will have cost him a lot even to say the word 'counselling'.

'You'll miss him,' she says.

But Nelson seems to regret confiding in her. 'Plenty more police officers where he came from,' he says, before ringing off with a brusque injunction not to forget the letters tomorrow.

Ruth stares unseeingly at the news for a few minutes, then she gets up and pours herself another glass of wine. She feels unsettled and not just by the letters. Last year, before Christmas, she saw Michelle and Tim together in the car park of the sports club. They were locked in a passionate embrace, an image that somehow Ruth cannot delete from her mental inbox. Were they having an affair? *Are* they having an affair? Ruth doesn't know, but, in the light of the car park kiss, Tim's request for a transfer seems to make a kind of sense. He is removing himself from temptation and taking the threat to Nelson's marriage away with him. So, although Nelson is obviously aggrieved at Tim's defection, Ruth, as his friend, should be pleased for him. But is she?

Ruth takes a long drink of wine and considers whilst, on the television, the weather forecast promises sunny spells and warns of squally showers. Ruth wants Nelson to be happy, of course she does, and, much as she sometimes hates to admit it, for him happiness probably means a solid marriage and a home to which his daughters can return whenever they feel like a dose of family life. So, if Tim disappears into the wilds of Essex, the Nelson marriage is saved for the nation. The only problem is, when she saw Michelle and Tim together, Ruth — the loyal family friend — suddenly saw an image of herself married to Nelson and, much as she tries to press that delete button again, the idea has imprinted itself on her imagination. Does she want to be married to Nelson? On the face of it, no. Ruth has never wanted to be married to anyone. Once she shared this house with her boyfriend Peter, but, after Ruth ended the relationship, she vowed never to live with anyone again (except her cats). But then Kate came along and now she is knitted into the very fabric of Ruth's life. A man would change (spoil) everything: giant shoes on the stairs, alien books on her shelves, a heavy body in her bed. This last image, she has to admit, is also slightly exciting.

But, even with Frank, though she did imagine living with him, she never thought of marriage. She considered him as a potential stepfather, not as a potential husband. Why then these shamefully retro thoughts of a white dress, a registry office (even in her fantasies she doesn't go as far as a church) and Kate dressed up as a bridesmaid. Is it because of Kate? If Ruth married Nelson, then Kate could live with her actual father. Wouldn't that be neat? No — as the seemingly endless local weather forecast continues ('Areas of low pressure spreading eastwards') — Ruth has to admit it. Somewhere, deep down, she is still in love with Nelson.

Warnings of thundery weather ahead.

10

Ruth has agreed to meet Hilary in the abbey grounds at ten.

'We can go for a walk and see the snowdrops,' she had said.

'Snowdrops?' For the moment Ruth thought she was referring to some strange religious sect.

'Flowers, Ruth.' Hilary laughed, in that slightly patronising way that was becoming familiar all over again. 'They're famous. Don't tell me you've never seen the snowdrops in February?'

'Somehow the abbey's not on my usual route.'

On her way to work Ruth drops the letters into King's Lynn police station with a note for Nelson. The desk sergeant, a grey-haired man who looks like Captain Birdseye, greets her with alarming friendliness.

'Hallo there, stranger. How are things?'

'Fine. Thank you.' She can't remember the man's name, but she knows that she has met him before. How come they are on 'Hallo there, stranger' terms? Does he just remember her as the archaeologist who helped on earlier cases, or is it something else? She never knows how much the other police officers know about her relationship with Nelson.

'How's your little girl?'

'She's fine. She's five now.'

'Five! I can't believe it. She must be at school then.'

'Yes. She's in Reception.'

'Where? At St Faith's?' He names a local private school.

'No.' She gives him a look. 'At Bridge Street Primary.'

'That's a nice little school. My niece used to be a TA there.'

'Yes, it's a lovely school. Can you see that DCI Nelson gets this package?'

'Will do. Shall I call him down? He'll be starting the briefing in a minute.'

'No. Don't worry. If you could just give him the package . . .'

Ruth doesn't think she could stand greeting Nelson in front of the sergeant's benevolent grin. She doesn't know what's worse; him suspecting that Nelson is Kate's father or him thinking that she would send her daughter to a private school.

It's still early when she gets to the university. The corridors are deserted, but, when she gets to her office, she sees that Phil's door is open. Her head of department is at his desk.

'Have you got a minute, Phil?'

'Yes, of course.' Phil looks surprised, but immediately composes his face. Maybe he's hoping that she's come to resign.

'It's about the 1961 Walsingham excavation.'

'Rather before my time, Ruth.'

'I know that,' says Ruth patiently. 'I was wondering if you knew where the finds are. Would they be at the museum?'

'I suppose so. There was a rather beautiful figure of

Mercury, I remember, and a bust of a strange three-horned god. But the rest was just the usual medieval pilgrim relics. Pilgrim badges and ampullae for carrying oil and holy water. That sort of thing.'

'Is there a write-up somewhere?'

'There'll be a list of finds at the museum, I suppose. Why this sudden interest in Walsingham, Ruth? Not getting religious in your old age, are you?'

'No, a friend of mine was looking at funding for a dig.' Ruth is pretty sure that Phil won't bother to check this story. Besides, if there was any funding going, he would have devoured it years ago.

'I doubt they'll get an English Heritage grant,' he says. 'Anything good has been excavated years ago. They think they found the site of the original holy house, but, as it was made of wood, there was nothing much left. You did a dig near Walsingham a few years ago, didn't you?'

'Yes,' says Ruth. Phil was meant to be involved too, she remembers, but he had left for a coffee break on the first morning and never reappeared. 'We were hoping to find the site of the original pagan shrine, but it was rather disappointing. The land had been really broken up by ploughing. All we found were some coins, a few pottery shards and some glass.'

Phil is busy straightening the objects on his desk: stapler, hole-punch, pens in a British Museum mug, stone paperweight. His in-tray contains just one sheet of university-headed paper. How the hell has he managed that? Ruth's in-tray regularly overflows onto the floor.

'There was one interesting find,' he says. 'A sort of cross-shaped reliquary. The chaps at UCL thought that it might have been made to hold a fragment of the True Cross.'

'The True Cross?' Wasn't there a reference to the True Cross in the letters? Ruth tries to remember.

'Yes. It's one of those crazy religious things. You know, as if Christ's cross managed to find its way to medieval Norfolk. But they believed anything in those days.'

Phil always sounds as if bygone generations were a completely different species. In Ruth's opinion, humans haven't really changed that much. We're just as credulous now, she thinks, except about different things.

'I'll let my friend know,' she says, standing up. 'Maybe she should visit the museum and see what they've got there.'

'There's no money in medieval relics these days,' says Phil, straightening the single sheet of paper. 'It's all about dead kings. I blame Richard the Third.'

Ruth hadn't really been expecting much from the snowdrops but, when she and Hilary walk through the gates, she actually catches her breath in wonder. Nothing much is left of the priory at Walsingham, just the arch and a few free-standing walls. But stretched out between them is a carpet of white, as if the church has risen again in all its finery. Trees rise up like organ pipes and, far above them, a skylark is singing.

'It's amazing,' says Ruth. 'Is there still an abbey here?'

'The Prior's lodging was converted into a private house which is now called The Abbey,' says Hilary, 'but the medieval priory was destroyed. This is all that remains of it. There was a friary too, you can see the remains of that behind St Simeon's Church. I can't believe you've lived in Norfolk seventeen years and never been here.'

'I'm not religious,' says Ruth. 'You must remember that about me.'

Hilary laughs and takes her arm. Ruth stiffens. She's not keen on people holding on to her. Apart from Kate, who doesn't count, she can't remember the last time she held another person's hand. Maybe it was Max, an archaeologist with whom she had a brief relationship a few years ago. Max liked holding hands, going out for meals, watching television together; all the coupley things. Maybe that was why Ruth had ended the relationship. She just couldn't act the part convincingly. It feels odd, having to adjust your pace to someone else's. As soon as possible, she stops and disentangles herself.

'This must be where the original holy house stood,' she says.

There's a wooden sign saying: 'Site of the 11th-century, Anglo-Saxon shrine of the holy house of Nazareth (excavated 1961)'. But, of the original structure, there's no trace at all, just smooth grass studded with white flowers. The only marker is a small cross fixed into the ground.

'Did you look up the 1961 excavation?' asks Hilary. It's the first time either of them has mentioned the letters, even obliquely.

'I talked to my head of department this morning,' says Ruth. 'He said there are some finds at the museum, a figure of Mercury, for example. You know that they think Walsingham was once a shrine to Mercury?'

Hilary ignores this information about Walsingham's pagan past. 'I went to a talk at King's Lynn Museum once,' she says. 'They have quite a lot of artefacts there, mostly medieval, but a few Roman ones too.'

'Yes. Phil mentioned some pilgrim badges and ampullae. I took part in a dig near Walsingham a few years ago and we found some Roman coins and pottery. But it was pretty disappointing on the whole. My boss did mention something interesting, though.'

'What?' Hilary takes her arm again.

'It was a cross-shaped reliquary. The experts thought it might have been made to hold a fragment of the True Cross.'

'The True Cross,' repeats Hilary, dropping Ruth's arm. '"Do you follow the True Cross?" That's what the letter-writer said.'

'Do you know what that could have meant?'

'Well, there's meant to be a relic of the True Cross at the Anglican shrine.'

'Do they really believe that it's *the* cross?' asks Ruth. 'The one Jesus died on?'

'You sound very doubting,' says Hilary.

'Well, it's not very likely, is it? What's the provenance?'

'That doesn't matter,' says Hilary. 'What matters is that people believe that it was the True Cross. Do you see?'

'Not really,' says Ruth. They carry on walking, across the grass pitted with the remains of walls and odd flat squares of ground where fragments of paving can be seen. Eventually they reach parkland and a picturesque bridge over a fast-flowing river. They stand on the bridge, watching the water rushing between the grassy banks. It's a beautiful day, bright but cold, the sky high and palest blue. Ruth says, 'The letter-writer says: "They dug in Walsingham but they did not find the True Treasure".' She had read the letters again after her discussion with Phil. 'What do you think he meant?'

'I don't know. I thought it was a reference to the Holy Spirit, the true treasure in men's hearts. That sort of thing.'

'Men's hearts,' says Ruth. 'Not women's.'

Hilary sighs, lifting up her face to the sun. Her hair gleams almost white, but otherwise she looks ageless, her skin unlined and her eyes clear.

'It's very wearing,' she says. 'How much some people hate us.'

'Why do you carry on then?' says Ruth. 'Why not do a job where people don't hate you just for being a woman?'

Hilary gives Ruth her sibylline stare, eyes wide and haunted. 'Because God's love is for everyone. We're all made in God's image, not just men. Besides there aren't enough priests to go round. Without women, the priesthood would die out.'

Ruth doesn't really see why that's a bad thing, but she doesn't voice this thought. Instead she says, 'What about the other women on your course? Have any of them received letters?'

'I don't think so,' says Hilary. 'I haven't asked, though.'

'It's just, if they have, it might prove that the link's Walsing-ham, rather than you.'

'That's true.' Hilary gives her a more considering look, the sort of look that she used to give Erik in lectures. 'But I was getting letters before I even booked to come on this course.'

Ruth thinks that Hilary sounds slightly reluctant to consider that she might not be the letter-writer's only target.

'It might be worth asking them all the same,' she says.

'You sound like a detective,' says Hilary. 'Have you spoken to your policeman friend about the letters?'

'He's not . . .' begins Ruth and then she stops. How can she possibly explain her relationship with Nelson to Hilary? 'Yes,' she says. 'I dropped the letters into the police station this morning. You said I could,' she adds, as she thinks that Hilary looks slightly annoyed.

'Yes, I know. I'm very grateful.'

'You said you'd talk to him too. About being threatened.'

'Do you think the letters are anything to worry about?' asks Hilary. 'Or is it just some nutcase with a grudge against women priests?'

'I don't know,' says Ruth. 'It's probably nothing, but there was a nasty tone to the later letters. The mention of your child, for one thing.'

'I'm not scared,' says Hilary. 'I have complete trust in God. Plus — ' she grins suddenly — 'I have a black belt in taekwondo.'

'I'm impressed,' says Ruth. 'Shall we go and get a cup of tea? I've got about half an hour before I have to get back to work.'

'Good idea,' says Hilary. They walk quickly back through the grounds, passing an almost complete section of the priory, a chamber with four walls, windows and a door, although with a roof open to the skies.

'They say this was the crypt,' says Hilary, pointing to a sign set into the grass, 'but I don't think it was. There are the remains of a vaulted ceiling and there's a fireplace too.'

'It must have been a magnificent place,' says Ruth. The grounds are filling up. A flock of nuns passes by, excited as schoolgirls, their veils flying in the wind. They pass a walled garden with gardeners at work on the flowerbeds. Ruth points out silvery shapes in the newly turned soil. 'Oyster shells. Those monks lived well.'

'Yes,' says Hilary. 'There are all sorts of tales about riotous living at the priory in the old days. There was a report in 1514 that mentions the "scandalous life of the monks". Mind you, this priory wasn't suppressed until 1538, two years after the dissolution of the monasteries. I think that's because the abbot was very quick to swear allegiance to Henry the Eighth.'

Ruth supposes that Hilary, as a good Protestant, would approve of the suppression. She has mixed feelings herself. She's no fan of monks and nuns, but she always thinks there's something grand, something illogically heroic, about the pre-Reformation Church. And didn't the monks look after the poor, too, as well as feasting on oysters?

'The verse in the last letter,' says Hilary, 'it was part of an anonymous sixteenth-century ballad lamenting the dissolution of the monasteries. I was wondering if it meant that the writer was a Catholic.'

'I thought the same thing,' says Ruth. 'There's a lot about the Virgin Mary too. That suggests Catholicism.'

Hilary laughs and waves her hand, encompassing the white lawns, the ruined priory, the blue sky above. 'Look at all this. It's a shrine to the Virgin Mary and both Catholics and Anglicans come here. England has always had a special devotion to Mary. That's why it was called "Mary's dowry".'

Ruth doesn't like Hilary's tone, which she thinks is both patronising and unpleasantly fervid. 'There's a lot of scripture quoting in the letters, though,' she says. 'That's not a particularly Catholic thing. Or am I wrong about that too?'

Hilary takes her arm again and squeezes it in apology. 'No, you're absolutely right. It's a bit different now, but Catholics used not to be encouraged to read the scriptures. And some Catholics — and some Anglo-Catholics for that matter — would still like the Bible to be in Latin, as if Martin Luther had never existed.'

If he had never existed, thinks Ruth, would this priory still be standing, its vaulted roof in place? But maybe it's more beautiful this way, the building becoming landscape, its aisle and nave filled with snowdrops. Gently, she disengages her arm from Hilary's.

'So you think the writer might be a Catholic?'

'I don't know,' says Hilary. 'He mentions the "Blessed Chalice". If it was a Catholic surely he'd say something about the chalice containing the Blood of Christ?'

It all sounds rather horrible to Ruth, but then many religions do, including the gentle paganism practised by Cathbad. She wonders how Cathbad enjoyed his stay in Walsingham.

She must ring him tonight. She notes that Hilary knows the letters by heart; also that she's convinced the writer is a man.

They are almost back at the great arch, standing on its own by the entrance. Looking at it, Ruth is reminded of a building site in Norwich, where an arch was the only thing remaining of the original house. Under the arch, which once framed a doorway, Ruth had found a child's bones. The memory makes her feel anxious and slightly dizzy. She hurries through the archway and bumps into a priest. That's the problem with Walsingham. There are priests everywhere.

'I'm so sorry,' she says.

'My mistake,' says the man courteously in an Irish accent. Then 'Ruth? Is it you?'

It's as if Ruth's thoughts have conjured up the past. Because there in front of her is Father Patrick Hennessey, the priest involved with the ruined house in Norwich. They have kept in touch sporadically over the years — it was Father Hennessey who baptised Kate — but now, to see him here, in Norfolk, under another archway, seems almost like a miracle.

'Father Hennessey! What are you doing here?'

Is it her imagination or does the priest look slightly embarrassed, almost furtive? 'Just a private pilgrimage, Ruth. Just a private pilgrimage. But how are you and your lovely baby?'

'She's not a baby any more. She's five and at school. Oh, sorry . . .' Ruth is suddenly aware of Hilary standing beside her, looking extremely curious. 'This is my friend Hilary Smithson.'

'The Reverend Smithson, I see.' Father Hennessey doffs his hat, an old-fashioned trilby. 'Delighted to meet you.'

'Delighted to meet you too.' Hilary seems rather confused to be receiving so much respect from the elderly clergyman. She puts her hand up to her clerical collar, as if surprised to find it there.

'We're just going for a cup of tea,' says Ruth. 'Would you like to come?'

'Thank you, no,' says Father Hennessey. 'I've only got a few minutes before Mass. Just time for a quick look at the snowdrops. I'm sure we'll meet again.' And he raises his hat again and disappears through the archway like the White Rabbit.

Nelson is preparing for the morning team meeting. Some-times these briefings can be fairly perfunctory affairs — Nelson reading through the logbook while Clough eats a McDonald's breakfast — but, with a major incident under way, the team meeting is crucial. Nelson will need to make sure everyone is up to speed on all developments, assign lines of enquiry and answer idiotic questions from Roy (Rocky) Taylor, the slowest policeman in the country. So, when there's a knock on his door, Nelson makes his most discouraging noise and hopes that the visitor is going to go away.

To his annoyance, the caller mistakes the sound for 'Please come in'.

'Boss, can I have a word?'

It's Tim. For one moment, Nelson thinks that he's come to tell him to forget the whole transfer conversation, that he's reconsidered and is happy to stay in Norfolk. This thought makes him sound unusually welcoming.

'Of course. What is it?'

'It's about Chloe Jenkins.'

'What about her?'

'It was something her mother said. That, when she was little, Chloe's childminder had said that she was like an angel.'

'Everyone seems to be talking about angels. Chloe was seeing angels here, there and everywhere, going on courses to feel their vibrations and what have you.'

'The same thought struck me,' says Tim seriously. 'Anyway, I thought it might be worth talking to the childminder, especially if she's local. So I rang the parents last night and asked for her number.'

'Good thinking. Are you going to go and see her?'

'That would be difficult,' said Tim. 'She died in 2002. She's buried in the graveyard at St Simeon's.'

He looks at Nelson, who slowly gets the message.

'Good God. So Chloe's childminder was . . .'

'Doreen Westmondham. Julie, Chloe's mother, says that Chloe was devoted to Doreen. She was devastated when the family left Norfolk, and they had to say goodbye. She never forgot her.'

'You can say that again,' says Nelson, 'if she was sneaking out at night to clean the woman's grave. Fiona McAllister said that Chloe had been in a family therapy session on the day before she died. Maybe that's what put Doreen into her mind.'

'I looked up the Westmondhams,' says Tim. 'Doreen had three sons, as well as lots of foster children. They all still live locally.'

'What do they do?'

'Steven's a plumber, lives in Fakenham. Married with two daughters. Kevin's divorced and lives in Holt with his new partner. But Larry, the youngest son, is the interesting one.'

'Why?'

'He's the vicar at St Simeon's.'

Nelson thinks of the church which didn't provide sanctuary to Chloe Jenkins, of the overgrown graveyard and the one white stone, so lovingly tended.

'You'd better go and see him,' he says.

Ruth and Hilary are back in the Blue Lady tea rooms. Ruth has virtuously refused a brownie, but accepts half of Hilary's scone. It's a well-known fact that shared food doesn't contain calories.

Hilary chats brightly about her course.

'Everyone's so friendly. It's a real tonic. We went to a service at St Simeon's last night. It was really beautiful. And then Larry, the vicar, invited us back to his house for lasagne.'

'Did the vicar cook for you all?'

'Well, his wife did. She was charming.'

Ruth reflects that vicars still have charming wives who do the cooking. She wonders whether Hilary's husband could rustle up a lasagne.

'What sort of people are on the course?'

'All women priests. Most of them are like me and have been in post several years. So we're ready for the next step.'

'Which is becoming a bishop?'

Hilary smiles modestly. 'I wouldn't say I was ready, personally, but we're hoping that the General Synod will give its approval to women bishops in July. It's as well to be prepared.'

'Who's running the course? A woman priest?'

Hilary looks slightly embarrassed as she says, 'No, it's a theologian called Robin Rainsford. He's very well respected, though, and a big supporter of the cause. I went on another course that he ran last year.'

Ruth rather envies Hilary all these courses. She wanted to go on a course a couple of years back — something to do with DNA-dating techniques — but Phil had flatly refused. 'We just don't have the budget, Ruth.' This before disappearing on a weekend fact-finding trip to Padua.

'The other women seem lovely,' Hilary is saying. 'So supportive and friendly. In fact . . .' She looks speculatively at Ruth.

'What?'

'Well, we're going out for a meal tomorrow night. You should come. I know they'd love to meet you.'

Why? thinks Ruth. Why should they want to meet me and why should I want to meet them? She takes refuge in her usual excuse. 'I'll have to see if I can get a babysitter.'

'Of course.' Hilary is looking supportive again. 'It must be hard when you're on your own.'

'I'm sure it's hard with both of you working,' counters

Ruth. 'Especially with you and your husband both being priests. It's not exactly a nine-to-five job, is it?'

Hilary doesn't seem to want to discuss her domestic arrangements.

'Who was that priest you introduced me to?' she says. 'Is he a friend of yours?'

Ruth hesitates — is Father Hennessey her friend? She liked him from the first, he's clever and funny and surprisingly non-judgemental. But can a priest be a friend? Then again, here she is sharing a scone with her old university friend Hilary, who is also a priest.

'He's called Father Patrick Hennessey,' she says. 'I met him when I was working on a case in Norwich.'

'A police case?' says Hilary.

'Yes. The field archaeology team found some bones buried in a house that was about to be demolished. The house used to be a children's home. Father Hennessey ran it.'

'Oh.' Hilary looks as if she has some more questions, but, to her credit, she doesn't ask them. Instead she says, 'What's going to happen to the letters now?'

'I think Nelson . . . the police . . . just want to look at them to see if there's anything . . . suspicious.'

Hilary looks at her shrewdly. 'There's something you're not telling me.'

That's the trouble with Hilary. She always was sharp, even in the old days. Ruth sighs. 'You know there was a murder here last week?'

'Yes. Some poor drug addict. I read about it in the papers.'

'Well, Nelson thinks there's a possibility — just a possibility, mind you — that there's a link.'

'Between my letters and the murder of that poor girl?'

'It's just a theory. He has to explore every lead. I probably shouldn't have told you this much.'

'Is that why you asked me if any other women priests had had letters?'

'I suppose so.'

For some reason Hilary is smiling. 'I was right. You have become a detective.'

'No I haven't.' Ruth is feeling rather stupid, an emotion she realises that Hilary often engenders in her.

'You have. You really must come out with us tomorrow night. Do some sleuthing.'

Ruth is about to reply — to recall some vital prior engagement — when she sees a dark figure hurrying past. It's Father Hennessey. She's about to tap on the window to invite him in, but there's something about the black-clad figure that makes her hesitate. Father Hennessey looks like a man on a mission. And not a particularly divine one either.

11

Even without Tim and Clough, the briefing room seems full. Tanya is sitting at the front, glasses glinting. Rocky Taylor is at the back. He has his notebook open, though Nelson notices that he has neglected to take the cap off his pen. Officers from other stations take the remaining seats, most of them trying not to look excited. This is the biggest case most of them will have seen.

Nelson runs through the investigation so far.

'Chloe Jenkins left the Sanctuary at approximately eight p.m. on Wednesday 19th February.' He points at the map. 'A woman answering her description was seen by Michael Malone, commonly known as Cathbad, in the graveyard of St Simeon's Church, Walsingham, at about nine o'clock. Chloe's body was found by a dog-walker the next morning. Her body was in a ditch, about a mile outside Walsingham on a road known as the Pilgrim Route to the Slipper Chapel, the Catholic shrine. Chloe had been strangled. No sign of sexual assault. She was still in her nightclothes: white nightdress, blue dressing gown. No underwear was found. A rosary was also found in the ditch. It had hand-carved wooden beads and a silver cross. We've followed it up and it's a design sold both at the Walsingham Shrine shop and the Slipper Chapel. The pathologist puts the time of death at between ten o'clock and midnight on the Wednesday night. So we are looking for any sightings between eight o'clock and midnight.'

'What was Chloe doing when this Malone saw her?' The question comes from a young officer from another district. Anyone from King's Lynn would know Cathbad.

'She was standing by a gravestone. I've got reason to believe that she'd been cleaning it. There were traces of cleaning fluid on her fingers and cleaning equipment was found hidden in the undergrowth nearby. The grave belonged to one Doreen Westmondham, who died in 2002. It turns out that Doreen was also Chloe's childminder when the family lived in Norfolk.'

Tanya says, 'So Chloe was visiting the grave of her old nanny? That's very sad.'

'I don't think she was a nanny as much as an occasional babysitter,' says Nelson, 'but I want to find out more about her. Heathfield and Clough are interviewing Doreen's son Larry now. He's the vicar at St Simeon's. Chloe was making good progress at the Sanctuary, according to her doctor, Fiona McAllister. I've also spoken to her personal therapist Holly Barrett, and Heathfield and I have interviewed her closest friends amongst the other guests.'

'Are they models?' asks Rocky hopefully.

'No, they're a middle-aged couple. A retired teacher and a retired vicar. Fuller . . .' He turns to Tanya, who sits up even straighter. 'Chloe was doing an online course. Something to do with angels. Can you follow it up? Find out a bit more about it?'

'Yes, boss.' Tanya sounds less than enthusiastic to be given the angel brief. Nelson decides to cheer her up. 'But first you can go to Walsingham and co-ordinate the scene-of-the-crime search. They're concentrating on the area where Chloe's body was found.'

Tanya brightens immediately. Co-ordinating is almost as good as being in charge.

'Chloe had a boyfriend called Thom Novak,' continues Nelson. 'He's also in rehab, in Switzerland. Heathfield spoke to him on Thursday and he seemed very shaken by Chloe's death. He's got an alibi for Wednesday night, but nevertheless we should keep an eye on him. I don't need to tell you that the killer is usually someone close to the victim. Miller and Cannivan — ' he turns to two DCs from Norwich — 'you look into Novak's history. See if there's anything we need to know about. If you need to speak to the family, go through DS Heathfield.'

'We need to trace Chloe's footsteps on Wednesday night,' says Nelson. 'I simply don't believe that no one saw a young girl in her nightdress wandering through the fields. We could do a reconstruction. Her sister might be willing to play Chloe's part. Taylor — ' he turns to Rocky who is chewing his pen lid — 'You make sure there are signs on all the roads leading in and out of Walsingham, asking for witnesses.' Surely Ricky can't mess this up?

'Yes, boss,' says Rocky. 'Witnesses to what?'

*

Tim and Clough arrive just as the morning service is finishing and have to endure an excruciating few minutes listening to the Reverend Larry Westmondham praying aloud to a congregation of three old ladies and a sleeping man who looks as if he might be homeless.

When the old ladies leave they look at the two policemen curiously.

'Good morning,' says Clough.

The women move closer together as if for safety.

'Good morning,' whispers one. And they scuttle out through the church porch. The homeless man sleeps on.

Larry Westmondham comes to greet them. He has taken off his vestments and is dressed in a black clergyman's suit with white dog collar. He's an affable-looking man of about forty. He's almost completely bald, but, curiously, this has the effect of making him seem young rather than old.

'DS Heathfield, DS Clough.' They shake hands and Tim thinks that Westmondham has a typical vicar's handshake, firm and controlling.

'You said you wanted to see me.' Larry Westmondham then ushers them to a pew near the front of the church. There aren't that many pews, although the church is a vast, cavernous space. To Tim it seems very bare after his mother's place of worship; no children's posters or colourful tapestries, just grey stone and a high altar that's almost invisible. There are some statues around the outside wall, but they are grey too and seem to blend into the stone. It's a cold place — physically cold too. Tim and Clough both keep their coats on.

'Thank you for seeing us,' says Tim. 'It's about the young woman who was murdered just outside Walsingham last week. Her name was Chloe Jenkins. Did you read about the case?'

'Yes.' Larry passes a hand over his smooth head. 'Such a terrible thing to happen. She was a patient at the Sanctuary, wasn't she?'

'She was,' says Tim. 'But it seems that she also had a link to your family.'

'To my family?' Larry casts a worried glance at the altar as if wondering exactly which family is being mentioned here.

'Yes. It seems that your mother, Doreen Westmondham, was Chloe's childminder. Did you know about this?'

At the mention of his mother's name, something seems to happen to Larry's face. The contours relax and he even smiles, a rather sweet, reminiscent smile.

'I didn't know, but Mum looked after so many children. She was a school dinner-lady — all the pupils loved her — and she was a foster mother. She must have fostered over a hundred children. Lots of them came to her funeral and said such lovely things about her.'

'She sounds like a wonderful woman,' says Tim, meaning it. 'So you didn't know Chloe Jenkins personally?'

Larry's brow furrows again. 'I don't think so. How old was she?'

'Twenty-five.'

'There you are. I'm forty-four. I was probably at university or working by the time Mum looked after her. The house was always full of children. My brothers and I said that, as soon as we left home, she moved some more foster children into our rooms.'

Did they resent that? wonders Tim. There's nothing in Larry's face to suggest as much, but he supposes that priests — like policemen — become adept at disguising their true emotions.

'We also believe that Chloe attended services here,' says Tim. 'Do you remember speaking to any patients from the Sanctuary?'

'I don't know,' says Larry. 'I try to speak to everyone after Sunday services, but I wouldn't know where they came from unless they told me.'

'Here's a picture,' says Clough. In deference to Larry's holy orders they have selected the least provocative of Chloe's modelling pictures. It shows her in a demure white dress, standing in a field of buttercups. She is turning, laughing, towards the camera, one hand holding back her long blonde hair.

Larry blinks and, indeed, the picture, so golden and sun-drenched, seems to glow like a beacon in the gloomy church.

'Do you recognise her?' prompts Tim.

'Yes,' says Larry. 'I think so. I remember . . . I think I remember seeing her at services.'

I bet you do, thinks Tim. From what he has seen of Larry's congregation, Chloe would definitely stand out.

'Did you ever speak to her?' asks Clough.

'I may have done,' says Larry. 'Just hallo and goodbye. As I say, I try to have a word with everyone.'

'Can you tell us where you were on the evening of the 19th February?' This is Clough, in his role as bad cop.

Larry doesn't seem unduly fazed by the question, though.

'That was a Wednesday, wasn't it? There's no Evensong on a Wednesday. My wife has a knit and natter group at the house so my job is usually keeping the kids out of her hair.'

'How many children do you have?' asks Tim, good cop.

'Four,' says Larry. 'Girls aged ten, eight and six and a baby boy, eighteen months old.'

'You must have your hands full.'

'Well, my wife does really. It's a full-time job running this place. I've got three other parishes as well.'

'Really?' Clough is surprised out of his hard-boiled persona. 'I thought vicars only had one church.'

'That was in the good old days of the Vicar of Dibley,' says Larry. 'These days vicars in rural communities have three or four parishes each. And these big old churches cost a bomb to keep up.' Larry's eyes wander to the giant thermometer propped up by the back wall labelled 'Parish Improvement Fund'. Judging by the level achieved so far, the patient is critical.

'So you were at home all evening on Wednesday?' says Tim.

'Yes. I supervised the girls' homework and bath time. When the children were in bed Daisy and I watched television.'

'What did you watch?'

'*Rev*,' says Larry with enthusiasm. 'It's our favourite programme.'

'That's a comedy, isn't it?' says Clough.

'It's both comic and tragic,' says Larry. 'Like life.'

'Chloe was seen in the graveyard of St Simeon's on the night she died,' says Clough. 'Do you know anyone who would have been near the church then?'

'No,' says Larry. 'The church is locked and the verger lives in Great Walsingham, a few miles away. Justin, who lives in the cottage, was away then. He had a friend house-sitting. A charming chap, very interested in church history.'

That sounds like Cathbad, who is interested in everything. Still, it appears that Larry doesn't have anything to add about Chloe Jenkins, and he has an alibi for the night of the 19th (though that will have to be checked).

'If anything else occurs to you,' says Tim, 'here's my card. Don't hesitate to be in touch.'

'I will,' says Larry, pocketing the card without looking at it. 'Goodbye. God bless you.'

As they leave, the homeless man is still snoring in one of the back pews.

When he gets back to his office, Nelson sees a yellow sticky note on his desk: 'Ruth Galloway called. She left a package for you.' He goes downstairs and finds Tom Henty, the doughty desk sergeant, holding several envelopes tied together with string. 'Ruth left these,' he says. 'She's looking well. Can't believe her little girl is at school.' Nelson looks at Tom suspiciously. He never knows how much the staff at the station guess about Kate's parentage. His team know, but the subject is never mentioned unless Nelson raises it first. He grunts something non-committal and heads back to his office, taking the stairs two at a time.

At first he skims through the letters, pausing only to wonder how people can get so upset about a subject like this. He has no problem with the idea of women priests — or married priests for that matter — though he's sure that his mother would have something to say on the subject. But Maureen would never buy into all this a woman is not to 'teach or to have authority over a man' nonsense. As far as Nelson can see his mother has preached to everyone all her life, and she's the most authoritative person he knows.

But when he gets to the last letter his expression changes. He reads it again, frowning. Then he picks up the phone.

'Ruth. It's Nelson.'

'I know.' She sounds irritated. He dimly realises that this might not be a convenient time to call.

'Sorry. Are you teaching? Lecturing?'

'No. I'm just getting into the car.'

'Late start?'

'No. I met my friend in Walsingham.'

'Is that the friend who received these letters?'

'Yes. Is something the matter? It's just that I've got to get back to the university. I've got a tutorial in half an hour.'

'There's something in the letters that worries me. Have you spoken to Cathbad recently?'

'No. I was going to call in on him and Judy on the way home tonight.'

'Well, on the night that Chloe Jenkins was murdered, Cathbad was house-sitting in Walsingham. He was staying at a cottage attached to the church, St Simeon's. Anyway, he went out at about nine to call the cat in and he saw a woman standing in the graveyard. A woman wearing a white dress and a blue cloak.'

'What? Oh . . . There's something in the letters about a woman wearing blue.'

'"She stands before you, clad in blue, weeping for the world",' quotes Nelson. 'It's a bit of a coincidence isn't it? When Chloe was found she was wearing a white nightdress and a blue dressing gown. Keep that bit of information to yourself, though.'

'She was a patient at the Sanctuary, wasn't she? That much was in the papers.'

'Yes. Poor kid. I don't like coincidences, as you know. I think I need to talk to your friend.'

'But the letters were all written before Christmas. How could the writer know about Cathbad's vision? I bet Cathbad thought it was a vision, didn't he?'

'Of course he did. But what I'm thinking is that there may be this madman wandering about Walsingham, incensed about women in general, obsessed with the Virgin Mary. The sight of a woman dressed in blue might have driven him over the edge.'

'But why would he kill her? Wouldn't he be more likely to fall on his knees and worship her?'

'Madmen do mad things, Ruth, as we both know.'

'Yes.'

'I'd like to speak to your friend. What's her name?'

'Hilary Smithson. She's staying at the conference centre.'

'What's the conference about?'

'Women wanting to be bishops.'

'Jesus wept.'

'Yes, very probably.'

'I can't see you being friends with a priest somehow.'

'Really? I'm going out with them tomorrow night. Just me and seven women priests.'

'I'll send Clough to give you some police protection.'

'Please don't.'

There's a short silence, and then Ruth says, 'Nelson? I saw Father Hennessey just now.'

'Really? Where?'

'Here. In Walsingham.'

'I suppose priests go there all the time. Pilgrimages and what have you.'

'Yes, but I thought he seemed a bit odd. Have you spoken to him recently?'

'Just a card at Christmas. He didn't sound odd on the card but then no one does, do they?'

'I suppose not. I don't send Christmas cards.'

'Well, Michelle does ours.'

Another silence.

'Well, I just thought I'd tell you. I'd better go now. I need to get back to work.'

'All right, Ruth. Take care of yourself now.'

'He recognised her all right,' says Clough, as they drive back to the station.

'She's hard to miss really,' says Tim.

'Weird how much she looks like Michelle, isn't it?' says Clough, then, when Tim is silent — 'You know, the boss's missus. You have met her, haven't you?'

'Yes, I've met her.'

'She's a cracker. Not a patch on Cassie, though.'

'I can't think what Cassie sees in you.'

'It's my charm,' says Clough. 'Can you look in the glove compartment? I'm sure I've got some crisps in there.'

Tim looks and comes up with a half-eaten bar of chocolate, which he passes to Clough.

'Thanks.' Clough shoves it into his mouth.

'You should be the size of a house,' says Tim. 'The amount of crap you eat.'

'I exercise,' says Clough thickly. 'I burn it off.'

Tim doesn't like to ask what form this exercise takes. Instead he says, 'What did you think about our vicar?'

'OK. He seemed fond of his mum. He looked a bit shifty when he saw the picture of Chloe, I thought.'

As ever, they are all on first-name terms with the victim. Only this time it seems especially poignant to think of that glowing girl — immortalised in so many photographs and in oils above her parents' fireplace — lying dead in the morgue. Tim supposes that he will be the one to attend the funeral.

'He did look shifty,' he agrees.

'Shall we pop into Fakenham for some chips?' asks Clough.

'I've got something to tell you,' says Tim.

He tells Clough about wanting a transfer. Clough listens in silence and takes the turning back to King's Lynn and the station. He doesn't mention chips again.

12

Ruth calls in to see Cathbad and Judy on her way home. Gone are the days when Cathbad resided in a caravan on Blakeney Beach. Now he and Judy and their two children live in a fisherman's cottage in Wells-next-the-Sea. Judy's Fiat is parked outside and there are spring flowers growing in tubs on the steps. You'd be forgiven for thinking that this was a conventional family home, that is until Cathbad answers the door in his wizard's robes, accompanied by a bull-terrier wearing a bandana.

'Ruth. Lovely to see you.'

'I said I'd pop in. Kate!' This last as Kate rushes past Cathbad shouting 'Mikey! Mikey!' She loves Judy and Cathbad's four-year-old son Michael and recently announced to Ruth that she is going to marry him whether he wants to or not. Thing, the bull-terrier, follows her.

'Where's Michael?' asks Ruth.

'Hiding,' says Cathbad, standing back to let her come in.

'I don't blame him.'

'But he wants to be found.'

Whether Cathbad is right or not, no sooner have Ruth, Cathbad and Judy sat down at the kitchen table than Kate enters triumphantly, holding him captive by the hand.

'Got him. We're going to play being teenagers.'

'Why don't you ask Michael what he wants to play?' asks Ruth. She feels quite faint at the thought of Kate being a teenager.

'He wants to play it too.'

'Do you really, Michael?' Ruth wants to hug the solemn-faced little boy — she has always had a soft spot for Michael — but she knows that he is an intensely private person who will hug you only if he feels like it.

'Oh yes,' he says now with his rare, sweet smile, and Kate drags him away.

Judy settles the baby, Miranda, in her rocker, and puts on the kettle. 'Or would you rather have a glass of wine?'

'I can't. I'm driving.'

'What about my home-made elderberry wine?' says Cathbad, pulling faces at Miranda to make her laugh. 'That's practically non-alcoholic.'

'You know that's not true,' says Ruth.

'Cathbad thinks that natural ingredients don't make you drunk. Or fat,' says Judy.

Ruth has long since ceased to marvel at the union (unofficial, so far, unless you count a druid hand-fasting ceremony) of efficient policewoman Judy and fey wizard Cathbad. It works, that's all you can say for it. They seem blissfully happy together and have two gorgeous children. If some of their arrangements are unconventional (Michael, for example, has two fathers, Cathbad and Judy's ex-husband Darren), then that's no one's business but theirs. Now, sitting in the tiny kitchen lit by fairy lights and candles, their home seems an oasis of safety and comfort.

Judy pours the tea and Cathbad pushes the rocker with his foot. Thing comes back into the room and sits by Ruth's chair, leaning on her legs.

'I could make some pancakes later,' says Cathbad. 'It's Shrove Tuesday next week.'

'What's the point of Shrove Tuesday?' says Ruth. She's beginning to feel slightly sleepy. It will be an effort to gather up Kate and embark on the dark drive over the marshes. She thinks of Hilary saying 'It's not Lent yet'. Isn't Shrove Tuesday the start of Lent?

'It's a way of using up all your flour, eggs and milk before Lent,' says Cathbad. 'In Latin American countries they have carnivals on Shrove Tuesday. The word "carnival" means "giving up meat", or something like that.'

'I'm not giving up meat,' says Judy. 'I'm always a real carnivore when I'm breastfeeding.'

'I'll take you to the carnival in Brazil one day,' says Cathbad. 'We'll dance in the streets.'

They smile at each other. Ruth is beginning to feel left out. 'I was in Walsingham earlier today,' she says. 'I've never heard so many people talking about Lent.'

'What were you doing in Walsingham?' asks Judy. 'I remember going to the Slipper Chapel shrine with my school. Slightly weird, I found it. Cathbad loves it, of course.'

'I was visiting a friend who's at a conference there,'

says Ruth. 'We went to see the snowdrops in the abbey grounds.'

'I've been house-sitting in Walsingham,' says Cathbad, 'and I'm not sure I love it any more.'

'Tell her about the woman in the churchyard,' says Judy.

'I've heard about it from Nelson,' says Ruth. 'He says he thinks it was the girl who died.'

'Yes,' says Cathbad. 'Poor soul. I can't stop thinking that she was asking for my help in some way. I keep seeing her standing there by the gravestone. So beautiful and so sad. Like a visitor from another world.'

Ruth shivers but she notices that Judy accepts this statement with equanimity. She also notes that Cathbad is always susceptible to a pretty face, and Chloe Jenkins, whose modelling shots have been plastered all over the papers, was very beautiful indeed. She also reminds Ruth of someone. She thinks of the letters. *She stands before you, clad in blue, weeping for the world.*

Aloud, she says, 'I've been looking up archaeological digs in Walsingham. There was one in 1961 to find the site of the original holy house.'

But Cathbad's sixth sense is on alert. 'Is there an archaeological link to Chloe Jenkins' murder then?'

'No . . .'

'So you're just researching archaeology in Walsingham for fun?'

'No . . .' Ruth ends up telling Cathbad and Judy about the letters, as she had always known she would. After all, Cathbad is already involved in the case, and Judy is still a police officer.

'So Nelson thinks this letter-writer could have killed Chloe?' says Cathbad.

'It's just a line of enquiry,' says Ruth.

'There'll be prints on the letters,' says Judy, 'maybe DNA too, if the envelopes are the sort that you lick. Nelson could get an enhanced search done.' Ruth knows that Judy is itching to get back to work as soon as her maternity leave is over. She sounds every inch the police professional, an impression that does not diminish even when Miranda starts crying and Judy picks her up to feed her.

'She's such a good baby,' says Ruth. 'She only cries when she's hungry.'

'Which is all the time,' says Judy. She arranges the baby with practised one-armed ease. Cathbad puts a cushion in the small of her back. 'You look like a Madonna,' he says.

'I feel like a bottle of stout,' says Judy. 'There are some in the larder. Don't bother about a glass.'

Nelson is about to leave the station when he gets the call from Tanya, who is still with the scene-of-the-crime team.

'Boss. I think we've found something.'

He can hear the excitement in her voice but tells himself to be cautious. Tanya is so keen to contribute to the case that she could be making something out of nothing.

'What is it?'

'Some blue fabric. Looks like it came from Chloe Jenkins' dressing gown.'

'Where did you find it?'

'On a hedge by the Slipper Chapel. About a mile from where the body was found.'

'Stay there. I'll be with you in fifteen minutes.'

The Slipper Chapel is a small stone-and-flint church facing directly onto the road. With its stained-glass windows and stone saints in alcoves, it looks somehow too important for its size, like a miniature cathedral. Beside it is a bigger, more modern church. Nelson parks in the car park, empty now but obviously designed for busloads of the faithful. Tanya and Mike Halloran, from the SOCO team, are standing by the visitors' entrance. It seems to have got darker in the last few minutes and Nelson can only pick them out by Mike's fluorescent jacket.

'Right,' says Nelson. 'What have you got for me?'

Mike leads the way. It's a lonely stretch of road, open to the fields on one side, with a tall hedge on the other. Mike shines a torch. A few yards along, fluttering on the dark hedge, is a tiny piece of material, hardly more than a few threads. The fabric looks white in the torchlight, but when he goes closer Nelson sees that it is unmistakably blue.

'Can't be sure before we do the tests,' says Mike, 'but it looks like material from the dressing gown. We've taken photographs, but I wanted you to see it in situ.' Carefully, reminding Nelson of Ruth in archaeologist mode, he removes the material with a pair of tweezers and seals it into an evidence bag.

'At that height,' says Nelson, 'she might have been being carried.'

'That's what I thought,' says Mike, 'more likelihood of an unconscious body brushing along the foliage.'

'Unless she was hiding in the hedge,' says Tanya.

'Then she'd be crouching down,' says Nelson. 'This is about waist height on a tall man.'

'But why would he carry her down the road to leave her in a ditch a mile away?' says Mike.

'I don't know,' says Nelson. 'And we shouldn't speculate too much until we get some tests done. Have you spoken to the people at the chapel?'

'Yes,' says Tanya. 'I spoke to the custodian before they closed for the night. I said I'd be interviewing him tomorrow.'

'I'll be interviewing him,' says Nelson. Then, relenting slightly, he says, 'You can come too, Fuller. What do we know about the chapel place?'

It's Mike who answers. 'It's the Catholic shrine. Called the Slipper Chapel because pilgrims used to leave their shoes here and walk the last mile into Walsingham in their bare feet. That was when the shrine at Walsingham was Catholic, of course. Now it's Anglican, so the Catholics come here.'

'Why do you know so much about it?'

'With a name like Halloran, you don't have to ask. Lapsed Catholic at your service.'

There are a lot of them about, reflects Nelson. The thought doesn't make him feel exactly comforted.

13

Nelson and Tanya are back at the Slipper Chapel first thing in the morning. Already the road has been cordoned off and plastic sheets cover the section of the hedge where the material was found. A defiant 'Open As Usual' notice is stuck onto the sign for the car park.

'It's coming up to our busiest time of year,' says the custodian apologetically to Nelson. 'Easter, you know.'

Nelson is a bit vague about Easter now that his daughters are no longer at home demanding Creme Eggs. When he was at school — a Catholic boys' grammar in Blackpool called St Joseph's, but inevitably known as Holy Joe's — Lent loomed large in his life. Ash Wednesday, the itchy grey dust on your forehead all day, 'Remember, man, that thou art dust', giving things up — sweets usually — and failing on the first pocket-money day, Stations of the Cross, Good Friday Mass, the statues shrouded with purple drapes, Easter Sunday and the glory of that chocolate that tastes like no other.

'It's Ash Wednesday next week,' the custodian, Father Bill, is saying. 'A lot of pilgrimages start then.'

Pilgrimage, like Lent, is now almost a foreign word to Nelson. But a thought comes to him that maybe that was what Chloe Jenkins was doing, walking over the fields towards the Slipper Chapel. Going on a pilgrimage. And she hadn't been barefoot, she had actually been wearing slippers. He thought of the body in the ditch, the little feet in the white slippers. One way or another, he would catch the bastard who had done that to her.

'You probably know,' he says, 'that we're investigating the death of a young woman, Chloe Jenkins.'

'Yes. Poor soul.' Father Bill crosses himself. He's an elderly man, stick-thin, but with a certain wiry strength to him. He looked anxious when the two police officers arrived, but has been hospitable, offering them coffee and making them comfortable in his office, a tiny space spilling over with boxes and stacked chairs and a large statue of the Virgin Mary. Most of the boxes are marked 'Votive candles'.

'We have reason to believe that Chloe came this way, perhaps into the shrine itself. Would anyone have been here between eight o'clock and midnight on Wednesday 19th February?'

Father Bill shakes his head. 'No. We close at six unless there's a vigil mass or something.'

'Do you have CCTV?'

The priest sounds apologetic. 'Yes we do. It's a sad fact but people sometimes steal from churches and we've got a lot of valuable objects, icons and relics, that sort of thing.'

'That's good from our point of view. Can you give Sergeant Fuller — ' he nods at Tanya — 'access to the tapes from the 19th?'

'It's all digital now,' says Father Bill. 'But that shouldn't be a problem.'

Tanya nods importantly and makes some swipes at her iPhone. Nelson knows that she's dying to ask some questions.

'In the weeks preceding the 19th,' he says, 'did you notice anyone suspicious hanging around the chapel? Anyone at all?'

Father Bill looks more worried than ever. The statue of the Virgin seems to be looking down on him, almost with embarrassment. She's a definite presence in the room, over six foot of painted plaster, blonde hair, blue cloak, outspread arms. One of her bare plaster feet is stepping on a snake. Nelson wonders why she's been relegated to the back office.

'We get a lot of strange people,' says Father Bill. 'This is a shrine after all. People come here because bad things have happened in their lives, because they want to forget or ask for forgiveness. And people come to the church for sanctuary. That's why I always feel a bit bad about it being locked at night.'

Had Chloe gone to St Simeon's for sanctuary? wonders Nelson. Tim said that Larry Westmondham hadn't known that his mother's former charge was a member of his congregation. But was it the Westmondham connection that made Chloe feel safe there, even in the graveyard in the night?

'Do you have a record of who visited on the 19th?' asks Tanya, determined to get a word in.

'I can tell you which parties were booked in,' says Father Bill, 'but other people are free to visit. We don't take a register.'

'Is it free?' asks Tanya.

'Of course it's free,' says Father Bill, sounding rather acerbic. 'You never have to pay to enter a Catholic church. Even St Peter's Basilica at the Vatican is free. Unlike the Church of England.'

The Counter-Reformation is alive and well, thinks Nelson. Aloud, he asks if they can look round the chapel and the grounds. 'Now we know it's free,' he can't help adding.

'Donations are always welcome,' says the priest hopefully.

The visitors are starting to arrive. A bus is pulling up in the car park: a handwritten notice on the back window proclaims 'Our Lady, Queen of Peace, Portsmouth. On Tour'. Inside the bus excited OAPs can be seen jostling to be first out.

'We get a lot of young people too,' says Father Bill, rather defensively. 'We have a youth pilgrimage every year. And we have Student Cross in Holy Week.'

'What's Student Cross?' asks Tanya.

'It's a pilgrimage,' says Father Bill. 'Students walk from London, taking turns to carry a heavy cross. It's to seek forgiveness for the sins of students everywhere.'

'That's a tall order,' says Nelson.

To his surprise, the priest laughs. 'Yes, when I think of my own student days . . . Still, the walk does them good. The Milky Way, that's what they call the pilgrimage route.'

The chapel is surprisingly small. 'It used to be a wayside chapel en route for Walsingham,' explains Father Bill. 'It fell into disrepair after the Reformation — it was even a cowshed for a time — but was restored in the nineteenth century by an amazing woman called Charlotte Boyd. She was an Anglican, but converted to Catholicism. Do you want to look inside?'

Nelson says yes, more from curiosity than because he thinks it will help the case. Even if he visited the shrine the murderer is unlikely to have left any clues behind in the chapel, although, as Ruth is always telling him, we always leave some trace of ourselves behind. Still, it might give him some insight into the sort of person who would spend the time to trek halfway across the country just to see a church that isn't even the original.

The inside is beautiful, though. All reds and golds, like an expensive cigar box. Even though it is only just after nine o'clock many candles have been lit and people are kneeling in front of the altar, which is draped in blue and white. The church is high and narrow, with arched windows that let in very little light. The air smells of candlewax, incense and flowers. Father Bill points at a box in front of the altar. 'You write your intention and put it in the box. It'll stay on the altar all day.'

'Why would anyone do that?' says Tanya, too loudly. One of the praying pilgrims gives her a distinctly un-Christian look. Next door is another chapel, filled entirely with candle-holders.

'This is the Holy Ghost Chapel,' says Father Bill. 'By the end of the day it'll be blazing with light.'

Outside, pilgrims are wandering in the garden or heading for the Shrine Shop. Nelson notes that Father Bill's principles do not extend to the banning of commercialism altogether. He thinks of the rosary found on Chloe's body. Was it bought here?

The shop is a treasure house of angels and crucifixes and

sundry glittery objects. There are endless replicas of Our Lady of Walsingham sitting rather stiffly on a throne with the infant Jesus on her knee. You can, if you wish, buy an Our Lady of Walsingham fridge magnet. Nelson briefly considers getting one for his mother. There are CDs of devotional songs and Benedictine chants. There are books and postcards and soaps made from Norfolk lavender. One wall is entirely given over to rosaries.

'These are pretty.' Tanya fingers some blue and green beads. 'What do you do with them?'

'Pray,' says Nelson. 'You say a Hail Mary for each bead with an Our Father in between.'

'But there are so many beads.'

'Exactly. It's not meant to be fun. Have you got a photograph of the rosary found on Chloe's body?'

'Yes.' Tanya was given the job of tracing the origins of the rosary and she bristles slightly now. 'I followed it up and it's sold here and at the Shrine Shop.'

'Let's ask again. They might remember Chloe.'

'I thought the idea was that the perpetrator left the rosary on her body.'

'It could have been Chloe's. We shouldn't rule anything out. We know she liked angels and that sort of thing.'

The shop assistant is a surprisingly alternative-looking young man with dreadlocks and multiple piercings. But he's extremely polite and helpful. He looks closely at the pictures of Chloe and the rosary.

'I'm pretty sure I didn't serve her,' he says. 'I would have remembered. And the rosary is one of our standard designs.

It's popular because it's got an icon of Our Lady at the end rather than the traditional cross.'

Nelson peers at the tiny figure: blue dress, yellow hair, golden crown.

'You wouldn't be able to remember who you sold this rosary to?'

The man looks apologetic. 'I'm sorry. It's just that we have so many people in here. Hundreds on a Sunday or a feast day.'

As if to prove him right, the shop is steadily filling up. Nelson thanks the man and makes for the exit. He holds the door open for a group of Filipino nuns, who thank him shyly. Tanya stares at them as they pass.

Outside preparations are obviously under way for an open-air mass. Four men walk past, carrying a statue on a kind of bier. Rows of seats face a wooden platform where a table is being draped with an altar cloth. As the men walk past Nelson notices ordinary-looking barrels with a sign above them saying 'Holy Water'.

'There was a holy well at Walsingham once.' Father Bill has appeared at their side again. 'You can see the site in the Anglican shrine.'

Nelson doesn't ask the source of the water in the barrels. He wonders if it gets sprinkled over the pilgrims or if they have to buy their own container from the shop.

'Is there anything else I can help you with?' says Father Bill. 'It's just I ought to be getting ready . . .' He gestures towards the activity behind them.

'No. We've taken up enough of your time,' says Nelson.

'Can you email the CCTV footage to Sergeant Fuller? Have
you got her card? Thank you very much.'

Tanya looks a bit sulky as they head towards the car.

'Can't someone else do the tapes, boss? I'd like to be more
involved with the interviewing.'

Who exactly do you want to interview? thinks Nelson. But
he doesn't want to discourage Tanya, so he says that she can
come with him to talk to Hilary Smithson. She brightens
immediately. In the distance, voices have started singing
'Morning has broken'.

Hilary Smithson meets them at St Catherine's Lodge, where
the conference is being held. At first sight it looks like a private house, a charming flint cottage like many others on the
high street, but as soon as Nelson steps through the door he
knows at once that he's in an institution. It's the carpet, for
one thing, green and hard-wearing, but it's also the notice-
boards, the shiny cream paint and a sense of practicality
over beauty. He thinks of the moment when the Sanctuary
morphed from country house into hospital. St Catherine's
even has the same hand-sanitisers. How dirty are your hands
going to get on a theology course?

Hilary, who is waiting in one of the meeting rooms, is a
surprise too. At first Nelson sees an old woman with grey
hair, neatly but unfashionably dressed in a blue trouser suit.
Can this person really have been at university with Ruth?
Then Hilary stands up and Nelson sees that she's probably
his age. In fact, her face is remarkably unlined and her eyes
are bright. It's just the hair that deceived him. He tries to

imagine Michelle letting herself go grey. If she's ever found a white hair, it's hidden in her streaky gold mane (she is a hairdresser, after all), and Nelson would be the last person to see it. But he supposes a priest is above such vanity.

But Hilary's handshake warns him not to underestimate her. She's friendly enough ('I've heard a lot about you from Ruth'), but she looks at him shrewdly, sizing him up. He introduces Tanya and she too gets the treatment.

'Doctor Smithson,' says Nelson. 'You know why we're here. It's about the anonymous letters that you've been receiving.'

'I don't want to make too much of them,' says Hilary, sitting on the orange sofa that, too, is functional, with square cushions that manage to be both hard and spongy at the same time. 'It's probably just some lost soul reaching out.'

In that case, why show them to Ruth? thinks Nelson. He's not fooled by the whole 'lost soul' business. He thinks Hilary was worried by the letters. And rightly too, from what he's seen.

'The letters may be nothing to be concerned about,' he says, sitting opposite her. 'But recent events in Walsingham have made us extra cautious.'

'Ruth said there might be a link between the letter-writer and the man who murdered that poor girl.'

'Did she now?' says Nelson.

'She was just speculating.'

Nelson is not mollified. Ruth had no business to be speculating, especially not to Hilary. That's the problem with civilians getting involved in police work. One minute they're an expert witness, the next they're Sherlock Holmes.

'We're interested in the letters because they mention Walsingham directly,' he says. 'Have you no idea who could have written them?'

'No,' says Hilary. 'There's no return address and I don't recognise the handwriting.'

'Postmark?'

'London, most of them. One is from somewhere in the Highlands.'

'Your parish is in London, isn't it? So it could be someone close to home.'

'London is a melting pot, Detective Chief Inspector. Half the world passes through London.'

But they don't stop to post anonymous letters, thinks Nelson. Hilary's condescending tone irritates him, even though she has a point.

'Have you ever had letters like this before?' he asks. 'It's my understanding that not everyone is delighted by the idea of women priests.'

'You're right, Detective Chief Inspector,' says Hilary. 'Not everyone is delighted. What are your own views?'

'It's not my business to have views,' says Nelson. 'Let's get back to you. So no one has ever written to you complaining about women priests?'

'I may have had the odd letter,' Hilary admits. 'A few emails, especially when I started as parish priest, but nothing too bad. I'm not on Twitter so I've escaped the trolls.' She smiles at Nelson, who doesn't smile back. He barely knows what Twitter is.

'It must be hard,' Tanya butts in, 'being a woman priest. Especially when you've got a child.'

Nelson wants to strangle her. Now is not the moment for misguided attempts at empathy. Judy would have known exactly when to say this sort of thing.

It's too late for Tanya. 'What do you mean?' snaps Hilary. 'My husband is a father and a priest. What's the difference?'

'The difference is that you've been receiving threatening letters,' says Nelson. 'Now is there anything in these letters that gives you a clue about the sender?'

'Not really,' says Hilary. 'I mean he seems to have some biblical knowledge and a very traditional view of the sacraments.'

'It might not necessarily be a man,' says Nelson. 'Never assume, that's what I tell my team.'

'It's certainly someone who dislikes and fears women,' says Hilary.

'Again, that might not mean it's a man. Can I ask you, what do you think the phrase "She stands before you, clad in blue, weeping for the world" could mean?'

'I don't know,' says Hilary, 'apart from the obvious.'

'Which is?'

'Oh, the Virgin Mary, weeping for mankind, Our Lady of Sorrows, that sort of thing.'

Nelson thinks of Cathbad's reaction to the words 'Our Lady'. 'Do you think the writer is a Catholic?' he asks.

Hilary looks curious, as if Nelson has succeeded in surprising her for the first time.

'I'm not sure. That's what I told Ruth too. There's a lot of veneration for Mary in the letters, but Anglicans venerate her too — just look around you. The ballad that he quotes is about the dissolution of the monasteries, though, so that might point to him being a Catholic.'

'The dissolution of the monasteries being when all the monks were chucked out and the gold melted down for Henry and his cronies?'

'That's a rather simplistic way of looking at it. The monasteries did help the poor, but there was a lot of abuse of privilege too. The monks hardly lived lives of poverty, chastity and obedience.'

Nor do you, thinks Nelson. He doesn't have any views about married clergy in general, but he does feel that the monks got rather a raw deal. There had been a monk who taught at his school, Brother Dominic, and he'd been a gentle soul, the focus of a lot of schoolboy teasing.

'Well,' says Nelson, getting up, 'I must ask you to be vigilant while you're here. The writer obviously knows you're in Walsingham. I'll have my officers keep a watch on the place. Probably nothing to worry about, but you'd be as well to keep on your guard. Try not to go out on your own too much.'

'There's a group of us going out for a meal tonight,' says Hilary. 'Ruth's joining us.' Is it his imagination or does she say this in a rather combative way?

'Would you like some police protection?'

'Oh no,' she laughs. 'It's just a girls' night out.'

Nelson tries and fails to imagine Ruth on a girls' night out. 'I hope you have a pleasant evening,' he says. 'Have you spoken about the letters to the other women on the course? They are all women, I take it?'

'Yes. They're all women priests.'

'And none of them have had letters?'

'I haven't asked, though Ruth suggested I should.'

Well done, Ruth. A good suggestion at last. 'I think it might be an idea,' he says. 'Again, there's no point in worrying them, but it might be significant if someone else has been receiving letters. Have you mentioned this to anyone else?'

'Only Robin Rainsford, who's running the course.'

'Can I speak to Mr Rainsford?'

'Yes, he's in the small sitting room, preparing for this afternoon's session. And it's Doctor Rainsford actually.'

Of course it is.

'I'll have a word with Doctor Rainsford now,' he says. 'Good day, Doctor Smithson, and thanks for your time.'

'Goodbye, Detective Chief Inspector. Goodbye.' This last is to Tanya.

'Goodbye,' says Tanya cheerily, unaware of any animosity.

Despite telling Nelson that she's intending to go out to dinner with the women priests, Ruth fully intends to cancel. She wakes up determined to cancel, and, when she drops Kate at school, she doesn't mention to her daughter that Clara might be coming to babysit that evening. It's always essential to warn Kate of these things beforehand because, although she loves Clara, if she's suddenly faced with an evening without Ruth she's likely to cling onto her legs and wail 'Don't leave me'. This clinginess is something new and something to add to Ruth's daily list of worries as she takes the road for the university. She won't go out, she'll get some work done, spend quality playing time with Kate (not trying to read the *Guardian* at the same time) and get an early night. This resolution survives Phil telling her — apropos of nothing much — that she should 'Get out more' and that he and Shona are quite worried about her. Shona is Phil's partner and one of Ruth's closest friends. Even so Ruth can just imagine her saying this. Shona won't be happy until Ruth is shackled to some gruesome Phil lookalike. But Ruth is definitely not going to Hilary's girls' night out. She doesn't care if she turns into a hermit and starts to knit clothes out of Flint's fur, she's not going to a restaurant with a lot of women who will talk about God as if He's sitting at the next table.

Mid-morning, Hilary rings.

'Hi, Ruth. I'm not interrupting, am I?'

'No. I'm just marking some mid-sessional papers.'

'What's the topic?'

'Field techniques in archaeology.'

'I do envy you sometimes. Still being in archaeology.'

'Really?' Then why, thinks Ruth, go to all the trouble — seven years wasn't it? — of becoming a priest? Especially if, by the end of it, people hate you for it.

'Ruth . . .' Hilary's voice changes. 'Your friend Detective Nelson came to see me just now.'

'He's not . . .'

'Seems a nice chap. He had this policewoman with him, glasses, very keen.'

That must be Tanya. She must be delighted to be doing interviews with Nelson. Judy would be spitting if she knew.

She wouldn't like the word 'policewoman' either, any more than Hilary would like 'priestess'.

'He seems to be taking the letters very seriously.'

'Well, he's very thorough.'

'He even offered us police protection for our dinner tonight.'

God, she had thought that was a joke. Please don't let Nelson send Clough. Or Tim.

'I said I'd thought we'd be safe enough at Briarfields. I booked there because I thought it was near you. Can't wait for you to meet the girls. We're getting cabs, so we can drink. Shall we swing by and pick you up?'

'It's OK,' says Ruth weakly. 'I'll drive myself.'

Nelson dispatches Tanya back to the station after the interview with Hilary. He says that he wants her to get going on the CCTV footage, but really he's had enough of her company for one day. When he's working with Clough they know each other so well that he has no need to telegraph when he wants his sergeant to cut in or keep silent. And, whilst Clough can be a bit un-PC sometimes, Nelson knows that his heart is in the right place because that's been tested many times. With Tim or Judy it's different, they are professionals and he can rely on them to be conciliatory or confrontational as the occasion demands. Judy, in particular, is excellent at empathy, letting the suspect think that she alone understands them and what led them to do this thing. Tim, with his good looks and quiet demeanour, gets results too. But Tanya, she's too keen to make her mark, to show how clever

she is. And she *is* intelligent and a good officer, it's just that
a suspect or any person of interest is not going to give you
marks for cleverness; most of the time you just need to listen.
The time for cleverness comes later.

Leaving Tanya to take a minicab back to King's Lynn,
Nelson heads for the small sitting room. It's not as cosy as
the name suggests; another institutional-looking room with
the same orange armchairs and hard-wearing carpet. But
someone has obviously been trying to make the room more
welcoming. The chairs are clustered in a circle around a
fireplace, dreamy chanting music is being played and there
is a smell of something like incense in the air. A man in a
pink jumper is sitting in one of the chairs, fiddling with what
looks like a mobile phone.

'Doctor Rainsford?'

The man looks up: he has round glasses and looks rather
like a grown-up Billy Bunter.

'I'm Detective Chief Inspector Nelson from the King's Lynn
police. I wondered if I could have a quick word?'

Robin Rainsford stands up. He's taller than he first
appeared. 'Of course,' he says. 'Is anything wrong?'

'Nothing to be concerned about,' says Nelson. He wonders
if he's saying this too much. In his opinion, there's nothing
wrong with putting the public on their guard. 'Shall we sit
down?'

They sit in the orange armchairs. Rainsford puts his mobile
down. 'I've succeeded in syncing iTunes to the sound system,'
he says. 'Isn't it incredible?'

'Congratulations,' says Nelson. He still has a phone that

doesn't take pictures. 'Any chance you could turn it off now?'

Rainsford clicks his phone and the chanting stops.

'Thank you. I've come to talk to you about one of your delegates, Doctor Hilary Smithson. I believe she's told you that she has been receiving anonymous letters?'

'She did mention something about it. But she said they were probably just from some troubled soul and not worth worrying about.'

'That might well be true,' says Nelson, 'but nevertheless the police are taking them seriously. Did Doctor Smithson show you the letters?'

'No, but she told me something about the contents. The usual diatribe about a woman's place being in the home and not on the altar.'

'The usual? Have you seen letters like this before then?'

'Not anonymous letters, but there's always plenty of this kind of abuse on chat forums and the like. A lot of people get very exercised about the idea of women priests.'

'I take it you're in favour?'

'Of course I'm in favour!' Rainsford jumps to his feet and waves his hand at the window, where there's a rather fine view of the priory and grounds. 'The Church needs renewing and that's what women priests are doing. The Church is our mother, we can't let her die.'

'Plenty of people don't agree with you.'

'We'll convert them. That's what priests like Hilary are doing. "By their fruits you will know them." You can't convert by words, only by deeds.'

'Doctor Smithson doesn't seem to be converting the letter-writer.'

'No.' Rainsford seems to deflate slightly.

'Are you a clergyman, Doctor Rainsford?'

'No. I'm a layman. I was an RE teacher first, but I found teaching in secondary schools very tough. I did a further degree in theology and started teaching undergraduates. Then I got involved in the fight for women priests. And bishops.' He gives Nelson a toothy, earnest smile.

'What sort of people come on these courses?' asks Nelson. He can't imagine what it must be like sitting in rooms like this listening to dreary music and talking about becoming a bishop. He went on a course last year, something about the community and twenty-first-century policing. He'd lasted about two hours.

'We've got a wide range of delegates,' says Rainsford. 'Some with a lifetime's experience in the Church, some who got the call later in life. We've only had a few sessions so far, but there's a real energy in the group. I think we're going to achieve great things.'

'And none of the other delegates have mentioned receiving anonymous letters?'

'No. As I say, the mood has been very positive.'

'Do you live in Walsingham, Doctor Rainsford?' asks Nelson.

'Not far away,' says Rainsford. 'I went to school in Sheringham and just drifted back, I suppose. I love Norfolk. I just love walking through the fields and along the beaches. The sense of peace, those huge skies. Well, you know how it is.'

Nelson doesn't know how it is. Unlike Ruth, he feels no particular fondness for his adopted county. What sort of place has only the sky to recommend it? Everywhere has sky. He ploughs on.

'Do you ever attend St Simeon's Church?'

'Yes, sometimes. It's a beautiful old building, but it doesn't get the congregation it should.'

Nelson produces the picture of Chloe in the buttercup field. 'Did you ever see this woman at St Simeon's?'

Robin looks closely. As well he might. Like Tim, Nelson is struck by the contrast between Chloe's golden beauty and the drab ecclesiastical surroundings.

'I don't think so . . . no, wait. I've seen her on the news, haven't I?'

'Yes,' says Nelson grimly. He disapproves of the glamorous pictures that have accompanied reports of Chloe's murder. 'She was murdered last week. Very near here, in fact.'

'I remember. Such a terrible story. Poor girl.' There's a pause, during which Nelson can almost see the thought bubbles forming over Rainsford's head.

'The letters sent to Doctor Smithson,' says Nelson at last. 'They mention Walsingham specifically.'

Rainsford's eyes grow large behind his spectacles. 'You don't suspect that the letters have anything to do with the murder, do you?'

'I'm keeping an open mind,' says Nelson. 'But there are some references in the letters which cause us to take them very seriously.'

'Hilary must be more worried than she seemed, then. Poor child.'

Nelson can't quite see Hilary Smithson as a 'poor child'. He doesn't know how old Rainsford is — he has receding hair, but probably isn't much more than thirty, which makes him at least ten years younger than Hilary Smithson.

'I'm going to tell you what I told Doctor Smithson,' says Nelson. 'There's probably nothing to worry about, but it's as well to be on your guard. If you see anyone or anything suspicious, don't hesitate to give me a call.' He hands Rainsford his card.

'I will,' says Rainsford, staring at the card.

'Goodbye then, Doctor Rainsford.'

'Goodbye.'

As Nelson walks towards the front door, he hears the chanting starting up again.

Outside, it has started to rain. Despite this, there's a steady stream of people walking down the high street, some in clerical robes and some in more touristy garb, carrying cameras and picnic baskets. The pilgrimage has begun.

'Don't leave me, Mum!'

It's pitiful, like a child being wrenched from its mother's arms at the pit head, or the prison gate or on board the sinking *Titanic*. When, in truth, all Ruth is doing is going out for a meal at a hotel a few miles away. With any luck, she'll be back by ten.

'I won't be long, sweetheart.' She crouches down. 'And Clara's going to play Sylvanians with you and watch a DVD.'

'*Frozen*?' says Kate hopefully.

'What about something else?' Ruth feels she's had enough of *Frozen*'s faux feminist message. How come, when Elsa sings about letting go and the cold not bothering her, she suddenly gets an hour-glass figure and a plunging neckline? Ruth thinks that both female characters could benefit from wearing anoraks, to be honest. 'What about *The Jungle Book*?'

'*Frozen*!'

'Oh, all right then.'

When Clara arrives, all smiles and home-made fudge, Ruth

tells her that she has promised to let Kate watch *Frozen* before bedtime.

'Oh great! I love that film.' Both Kate and Clara launch into 'Let it Go'. Ruth is glad that Kate has cheered up, but she suddenly feels a hundred years old. All she wants to do is go to bed with the latest Ian Rankin and *Book at Bedtime* on the radio. Well, with any luck the priests won't want to make a night of it.

'I won't be late back,' she tells Clara.

'Don't worry,' says Clara. 'I'll be quite happy. I've brought my books with me.' Clara is studying for an Open University degree. She already has a degree in law, but dropped out of law school, saying that she wanted to do good in the world. Since then, as far as Ruth can see, she has been living at home and accumulating qualifications. Ruth sometimes feels that she should advise Clara to travel and see the world, but she doesn't because she's such a good babysitter.

Hilary and her friends are meeting at Briarfields, a popular hotel on the edge of the marshes. Ruth likes Briarfields, it's smart without being intimidating, the food is delicious and it's only a few miles from her cottage. She'll have a nice meal, chat politely and come home. She imagines that all the priests will be fasting anyway and drinking water. She does hope they won't say grace before eating.

When she gets to the hotel the first thing she sees is a group of smartly dressed women in the bar. They are shrieking with laughter and drinking cocktails. She is about to back out, but she sees that one of the women, wearing tight jeans and a black lace top, has grey hair in a smooth bob.

'Ruth! Come and meet the girls.'

The 'girls', who are in their thirties, forties and fifties, greet Ruth warmly. They commiserate with her for not being able to drink alcohol. 'Have a Virgin Mary,' says one, without apparent irony. Ruth accepts a non-alcoholic cocktail and is soon engrossed in a discussion about archaeology with a woman called Paula.

'I wanted to be an archaeologist,' says Paula, who is extremely attractive, with long, blonde hair. 'But I couldn't do the physics.'

'There isn't much physics in archaeology,' says Ruth. 'It's a mixture of history, geology and guesswork.'

'Bit like the priesthood,' says Paula, 'minus the geology, I suppose.'

'What did you do . . . er . . . before?'

'I was an actress,' says Paula, accepting another Manhattan. 'Not a very good one although I did get to play Third Prostitute in *The Bill*.'

'Not even First or Second Prostitute,' says a woman called Sydney, taking a swig of her drink. 'That's rough.'

Ruth's mind is reeling. Who are these women, talking about prostitutes and drinking strong liquor? It's worse than going out with the field archaeology team. Her heart sinks when she hears the talk turn to relationships.

'I'd like to find a man,' says Sydney, 'but Christian dating sites are so dull.'

'Oh, I met Simon on a Christian site,' says another woman. 'He posted a video of himself playing the ukulele.'

'Surprised that didn't put you off for life,' says Sydney.

'What about you, Ruth?' asks Hilary.

'What about me?'

'Do you ever want a man in your life?'

Ruth hesitates. Should she tell Hilary to mind her own business (religious people can be very nosy) or explain the whole complicated story of her relationship with Nelson? Or should she tell her about Frank? On evenings like this she misses Frank — confident, gregarious Frank — very much.

'I don't need a man,' she says at last. 'I've got a daughter and a cat.'

This is met with universal approval. It turns out that, if there's one thing women priests love more than cocktails, it's cats.

Nelson has had a frustrating afternoon. The road blocks and door-to-door have failed to bring forth any new witnesses. The CCTV footage from the Slipper Chapel shows nothing between the hours of eight and midnight on the 19th apart from a dark and deserted car park. At one point a large animal stalks across the screen and there's some discussion in the station about whether it's a 'big cat'. There are always dozens of these big cat sightings in Norfolk; Nelson supposes that it gives the locals something to do.

At six o'clock Nelson is in his office reading Tanya's report on angel healing courses. The one she considers most likely to have appealed to Chloe is an online qualification in angel therapy, promising a certificate via PDF at the end of it. It has a comforting pseudo-academic feel, with each of the seven modules based on one of the archangels. Some of the names Nelson recognises — Gabriel and Michael, for example — others, like Uriel, Chamuel and Zadkiel, sound frankly made-up. He reads on, with increasing incredulity. The course promises to help the participant tap into 'vibrational energies' which will aid healing. Did Chloe really believe in this stuff? Tanya has added a note to say that the company running the course has no record of receiving payment from a Chloe Jenkins. So either Chloe thought better of studying angel healing or she booked under an assumed name. Nelson Googles and, under the coy heading 'Remuneration', he finds that the course costs a hundred and fifty pounds, including complementary angel oracle cards. Jesus wept. Purely for the pleasure of disapproving, he clicks on the link 'Angel gifts' and finds an array of crystals, bracelets, pendants and colour-therapy scarves. He's about to switch off when he notices the last item in the celestial shopping basket. 'Beautiful angel brooch, solid gold. Provides protection wherever you go.' Nelson thinks of Jean pointing out the ornament pinned to her grey tracksuit. Whether she had completed the course or not, Chloe had clearly thought enough of her friend to buy her this gift. In solid gold no less.

He is still browsing the angel healing sites (who knew there were so many?) when Tim knocks on his door.

'Boss? I've had a call from Larry Westmondham. You know, the vicar. Doreen's son. He said he has something to tell us. A matter of conscience, he said.'

'And he couldn't tell you on the phone?'

'He said he'd rather talk face to face.'

Nelson sighs and rings Michelle to tell her that he'll be late home. Or rather, he tells her answering service because she's still at the salon.

'She's always working late these days,' he says to Tim.

Tim doesn't answer. Nelson supposes that old married couples are of no interest to him.

Larry Westmondham says he'll see them at seven 'after Evensong'. Now they're sitting in the beautiful old church of St Simeon's waiting for the vicar to emerge from some shadowy space behind the high altar. The church seems very bare after the Slipper Chapel. Like all churches, it smells of incense and candlewax. It's also freezing cold.

Nelson picks up a hymnbook. 'Fancy a sing-song to pass the time?'

'I only know "Jesus loves you".'

'"Soul of my Saviour". That's the one I remember. Depressing as hell.'

'We should have Cloughie here. He loves karaoke.'

'Jesus. Do you remember all those Elvis songs at the Christmas party?'

A faint cough signals that the vicar is in their midst. Nelson is faintly embarrassed that he was caught saying 'Jesus'.

It's his first meeting with Larry Westmondham, and his immediate impression is that this is a man with the cares of the world on his shoulders. The vicar is fairly young, despite being almost bald, but his face has already settled into lines of worry. He's dressed in a black shirt and trousers and doesn't seem to feel the cold.

'Detective Chief Inspector Nelson. Good of you to come.'

'Sergeant Heathfield said that you had something you wanted to tell us.'

'Yes.' The vicar sits in the row in front and twists round to face them. Nelson feels oddly awkward, childhood memories of Confession fighting with his police officer's instinct to conduct interviews in properly regulated circumstances, not sitting in an icy church at seven p.m.

Westmondham, too, seems to be finding it difficult. He runs a hand over his smooth skull. 'I've wondered whether I should tell you this. I've prayed about it. It goes against my instincts, but there's a chance that it might have a bearing on the murder of Chloe Jenkins.'

Nelson and Tim exchange glances. 'Then you should definitely tell us,' says Nelson, trying not to sound impatient.

'Sergeant Heathfield told me that Chloe used to come to Sunday services here. I didn't know. I mean I didn't know that she was the same girl that Mum used to look after. But I did know that there were some patients from the Sanctuary. One of them I recognised.'

Another pause during which the priest seems to be fighting with his conscience.

'Stanley Greenway. He used to be a vicar at a neighbouring parish to mine. Before I came here. He had to leave.'

'Because of problems with drink?' asks Nelson.

Larry Westmondham looks at him squarely. 'No. Because he was a convicted sex offender.'

The surprise strikes Nelson and Tim momentarily dumb. Westmondham carries on: 'Almost every priest has a sex offender in the parish. It's logical. It's where you come when

the rest of the world rejects you. And mostly we manage it.
We have safeguarding guidelines. We can make sure they're
never left alone with children, for example. But, apart from
that, we leave them alone. After all, they need God as much —
if not more — than the rest of us.'

'Stanley Greenway's offences,' says Nelson, 'were they
against children?'

'Technically, yes,' says Westmondham. 'I think the girl was
seventeen. It's still abuse — abuse of power for one thing —
but it's obviously not the same as if she was a very young
child. Greenway claimed to be in love with her. The mother
found out and called the police. Terribly sad business.'

'What happened to the girl?' asks Nelson. He is thinking
of Stanley, sad and stooped in the visitors' room at the Sanctuary, saying 'She was like an angel'. Had he been in love
with Chloe too? Had that led him to kill her?

'She wasn't named,' said Larry. 'And I think the family
moved away. I hope she's put it behind her now.'

'Why didn't you tell us this before?' asks Tim.

'Well, at first I didn't link Stanley Greenway to the dead
girl. But then you showed me her picture, and I remembered
that he used to come to services with her.'

'But why didn't you tell me then? When you remembered?'

Now Larry Westmondham looks really uncomfortable. 'I
thought . . . well, there was nothing to link Stanley to the
murder. And being a sex offender — especially in his circumstances — doesn't necessarily make you a killer. And he was
in rehab, obviously getting help. I suppose I didn't want to
be the one to cast the first stone.'

'What made you change your mind?' asks Nelson.

'I prayed about it, as I said. And Sergeant Heathfield seemed a decent man. I didn't think he'd hound Stanley or anything. And I thought Mum would want me to do everything I could to help the police.'

Thank goodness for a guilty conscience and the power of mothers, thought Nelson. As he stands up, he says, 'Your mother sounds a remarkable woman.'

Larry's smooth, worried face seems to come to life. 'Oh, she was. She fostered over a hundred children, you know, and still always had time for the three of us. A lot of her foster children still keep in touch. They're nurses, teachers, social workers, all sorts. There's even a priest. They're her memorial, not the stone outside.'

'Talking of the gravestone,' says Nelson, 'I think Chloe had been cleaning it.' He describes the discovery of the cleaning materials hidden behind a bush.

Larry's face works like a child about to cry. 'That's very touching. Poor girl. To think she was still so attached to Mum. I wish she'd come and talked to me.'

It's pitch dark when they leave the church. Larry Westmondham locks up with a huge, archaic-looking set of keys. He lives at the top of the village, he tells them.

'Don't you live in the vicarage?' Nelson asks. He remembers seeing a rather grand house of this name, set back from the road near the church.

Larry laughs. 'The vicarage is worth a million or thereabouts. The Church sold it long ago. I live in a modern semi-detached.'

They walk through the graveyard, the frost crunching under their feet. A night bird calls from the trees, but otherwise everything is silent. At the lych-gate in the passage under Justin's house, Larry says goodbye and heads off into the night. They can hear him whistling as he walks. It sounds like a hymn.

'We need to talk to Stanley Greenway in the morning,' says Nelson.

'OK,' says Tim, 'but, like Larry said, there's nothing to link him to the murder.'

'He was obsessed with one young girl, he might have been obsessed with Chloe too. Didn't he tell us that he loved her? We need to get fingerprints and a DNA sample. If his DNA's on Chloe's nightclothes then we've got him.'

Their cars are parked on the road outside the cottage. Nelson calls goodnight to Tim then starts the engine of his Mercedes. But, instead of the satisfying throaty roar that he's used to, there's a feeble click and then silence. He tries again, but the engine is completely dead.

Tim appears as Nelson is looking under the bonnet.

'Is it the battery? I've got jump leads in my car.'

'No, it's not the battery. I think the starter motor's gone. Can't believe it. I've had this car ten years with no trouble.'

'Do you want me to drive you home?' says Tim. 'You can get the AA to pick it up.'

'Don't worry,' says Nelson. 'I'll call Michelle. She's not far away. She just texted to say she was leaving the salon.'

'I'll wait with you,' says Tim. 'Keep you company.'

Nelson would have thought that Tim had better things

to do of an evening than wait in a car with his boss. But he supposes it's a kindly thought.

'All right then,' he says, somewhat ungraciously. 'As long as we don't have to play I Spy.'

15

When their table is ready, the party repairs to the dining area. As soon as they sit down Hilary orders some wine: 'A bottle of each.' Ruth starts to get nervous. What are her chances of leaving at nine now? She puts in a plea for some water.

'You can have a glass of wine, surely?' says Hilary.

'I'd rather not drink at all,' says Ruth. 'The roads round here are so dark at night.'

'Do you live near here?' asks Sydney.

'About ten minutes' drive away.'

'But there's nothing here!' Sydney waves a rather uncoordinated arm towards the window, which is completely black, no street lights, no signs of human habitation. But Ruth knows that out there are the marshes, that treacherous zone between land and sea. There are other things too: sea spirits (according to Cathbad), archaeological treasures (to Ruth's certain knowledge) and endless layers of the past compressed into the uncertain, peaty soil. She doesn't feel able to explain this to the table full of priests.

'I live on New Road,' she says. 'There are two other houses

there.' She doesn't add that one is owned by weekenders who seldom visit their holiday home, and the other is occupied by a nomadic poet, currently on a tour of New Zealand.

'Don't you get lonely?' asks Paula. She doesn't say it in a judgemental way, rather as if she really wants to know. In return Ruth tries to give an honest answer. 'It's lonely sometimes, but I love the landscape and most of the time I like my own company. It's crowded places that make me nervous, not being on my own. Besides I've got Kate and Flint, my cat. Friends visit, my brother comes with his sons in the summer. It's beautiful in the summer.'

'I know,' says Paula, 'I spent some time here as a child. I remember swimming at Wells-next-the-Sea. The miles of sand and the little railway.'

'My daughter Kate loves that train,' says Ruth.

'It's an ungodly place to my mind,' says a woman called Freya. Ruth has already marked her out as the most ascetic of the women. She has a pinched, intense face, and is the only one, apart from Ruth, to be drinking water.

'How can you say that?' says Paula. 'Look at lovely Walsingham, the most holy place in England.'

'There's still a pagan feel to it,' says Freya. 'They say that there are a lot of those New Age thinkers in Norfolk.'

There certainly are, thinks Ruth. She could put Freya in touch with a fully-fledged druid in one easy phone call. Aloud she says, 'Well, archaeologists think Walsingham was a pagan shrine first, probably sacred to the Roman god Mercury. When they did an archaeological dig they found quite a few relics from that time, including a bronze figure of Mercury.'

'That's what I mean,' says Freya. 'It has an unwholesome feel.'

'Doesn't that just mean that people have worshipped there for thousands of years?' says Ruth. 'I'm not a Christian, but I would have thought that made it more special.'

'You sound like Erik,' says Hilary, with a smile. 'The sacred landscape.'

'Well, he was very knowledgeable,' says Ruth. And completely mad, she adds to herself.

'Who's Erik?' asks Freya, rather rudely, Ruth thinks.

'Our tutor at university,' says Hilary. 'Now who's having red?'

'So then I took the graduate fast-track course . . .'

Nelson tries to suppress a yawn. He supposes it is kind of Tim to stay while they wait for Michelle, but really he would have preferred to sit on his own in the car with the radio playing undemanding drive-time music. Instead of which, he is having to listen to what sounds like Tim's life story. Who knew the self-contained Tim could talk so much?

'So how did you get into the force?' Tim is asking.

'Joined as a cadet at sixteen,' says Nelson. He sees, with relief, that he has a call from Michelle. He clicks on the green 'accept' button.

'Hallo, love. Where are you? Oh, we're the other side, by the high street. I'm with young Tim. No, that's OK, I'll come to you. It's just through the graveyard. I know. That's Walsingham for you.'

He turns to Tim. 'That was Michelle. She's parked in

front of the church. I'm going to meet her now. Thanks for stopping.'

Tim gets out of the car, then he stands there, in the street, looking uncertain.

'Bye, now,' says Nelson firmly.

He takes the quickest route, via the passageway under Justin's house. His hand is on the lych-gate at the end when a terrible scream fills the air. A woman's scream. Michelle's scream.

'Michelle!' Nelson starts running, but he is knocked aside by someone rushing past him. Someone also shouting 'Michelle!'

Nelson used to be a fast runner, but he's older and heavier now. He runs blindly, stumbling over gravestones and cursing. By the time he reaches Doreen Westmondham's gravestone he finds his wife lying on the ground, sobbing in Tim's arms.

'Michelle! What happened?'

Michelle looks up at him. Her face looks white in the darkness, almost luminous. She starts to say something about someone attacking her from behind, but Nelson is distracted by Tim, who seems to be saying, 'Darling, are you hurt?'

'Why the fuck are you calling my wife darling?'

Tim stands up and Nelson thinks he hears him say 'Sorry'. But there's no time to give shape to the thoughts that are crowding, unwelcomed, into his head. Michelle stretches out her hand to him. 'Harry?'

Nelson helps his wife to her feet. He tries to force himself to think clearly.

'What happened?'

'I decided to come to meet you. You said through the grave-yard. It was so dark I stopped to put on my torch app. Then someone . . .' She stops, breathing hard.

'Someone?'

'Someone grabbed me by the throat. He . . . he pushed me to the ground. He was standing over me and he leant forward as if he was about to strangle me. Then I screamed and he ran away.'

Nelson turns to Tim. 'Don't just stand there. Get on to all units. Looks like this is our man and he might not be far away. Search the church and the grounds. Get one of the dog-handlers out.'

'Yes, boss.' They listen to Tim's footsteps retreating and Nelson says, 'Did you get a good look at the man?'

'No. It was dark and it all happened so quickly.'

'You're sure it was a man?'

'Yes. He seemed so strong and he smelt like a man.'

Nelson knows that Michelle is famous for her sense of smell.

'What did he smell of?'

'BO and soap and something else. Something like those sticks you burn.'

'Joss sticks?'

'Yes, something like that.'

Michelle is shaking. Nelson puts his arm round her. She is only wearing a thin jacket and she seems smaller than usual. Her hair has come loose from its complicated plait.

'I've lost my shoes. And I dropped my phone.'

'Let's get you to the car, and I'll come back with a torch.' He has a good solid one in his car, useful as a weapon too.

They walk back through the lych-gate and the dark passageway, Michelle leaning heavily on him. He thinks that she's crying. He helps her into the Mercedes and gives her his phone. 'Lock the doors. I'll be back in a minute.' He hears Tim radioing all units from his car. The silent village will soon be waking up.

He soon finds Michelle's high-heeled shoes and her iPhone. Then he swings the torch's powerful beam round the graveyard. The stones lean towards each other, as if they have just stopped moving, but there is not a living soul to be seen. He tries the church door. It's still locked. He remembers Larry Westmondham walking off into the night, whistling. Where is the vicar now?

As he heads back through the passageway he sees flashing lights. That was quick. He takes back everything he has ever said about the control room; this is impressive. They might even be in time to catch the attacker. Then the lights stop beside his Mercedes and a voice says, 'Did you call the AA?'

'Yes.' Nelson steps forward. 'It's this car here. Think it's the starter motor.'

He opens the door and gives Michelle her shoes. 'I need to stay here. I'll get a car to drive you home.'

'I can drive myself.'

'Are you sure?' He ought not to let her, but it would be awkward to have both their cars stuck in Walsingham.

'Yes. I just want to get home.'

'Call me when you get in. And take off the clothes you're

wearing and put them in a sealed plastic bag. We ought to get a doctor to look at you too.'

'I don't want a doctor.'

'It's for evidence. I'll get the on-call police doctor.'

'Not that Chris Stephenson please.'

'No. I'll make sure it's a woman. I'll walk you back to your car.'

As they walk back round to the front of the church they see more flashing lights. Back-up has arrived. Nelson has to get to work.

Michelle gets into her car. 'Remember, call me when you get home,' says Nelson.

'I will.' She turns to him. 'Harry. About Tim . . .'

'We'll talk later.' And he heads off towards the squad cars.

The table is getting raucous. They have finished the main course and every woman apart from Freya and Ruth is having pudding and a liqueur. Well, Ruth is only having pudding, but she makes up for it by choosing the most fattening thing on the menu, chocolate cake with home-made toffee ice cream. The priests are talking about the course, about someone called Robin and a 'dishy bish' called Peter.

'There'll never be a woman bishop,' says someone rather woozily.

'Yes there will,' says Hilary firmly. 'After all, they already have them in America.'

'The synod will vote yes,' says Freya. 'I'm sure of it.'

'But there'll be people who will vote against,' says Paula, 'so the Church will be divided. That makes me really sad.'

'Why do you want to be bishops?' asks Ruth. Her question came out louder than intended. 'I mean, what can a bishop do that a priest can't?'

'It's the purple,' says Sydney. 'Such a lovely colour.'

'It's a matter of principle,' says Hilary. 'Imagine if someone said to you that, however hard you worked, you could never be head of department. How would that make you feel?'

Effectively this is what Phil has already said, but Ruth takes the point.

'You're brave to keep persevering in the face of so much opposition,' she says. 'I don't know if I could.'

'Oh, you would,' says Hilary. 'I know you, Ruth. You never give up when you really want something.'

She's looking at Ruth rather hard, which is uncomfortable. What's she getting at?

'Hilary told us about the letters that were sent to her,' says Paula. 'It's awful to think that people hate us so much.'

It's the first time that anyone has mentioned the letters. Ruth, who didn't want to be the first to bring the subject up, asks, 'Have any of you had similar letters?'

A chorus of voices answers her. From what she can make out, although almost all the women have had abusive letters about women priests, none of them have been the victim of a sustained campaign like Hilary.

'I feel sorry for the letter-writer,' says Paula. 'He's a soul in torment really.'

'I feel compassion for him,' says Hilary, which is not the same as feeling sorry for him. 'I just wish he would leave me alone.'

'No one smelts a feeble metal,' says Freya. 'If God gives you trials it's because He knows you can survive them. You are being tested as fire tests and purifies gold.'

'Peter 1:7.' Hilary supplies the reference briskly. 'Well, I think I've been tested enough. Who's having another drink?'

Ruth looks at her watch. God, how is it already nearly eleven?

'I've got to get home,' she says.

In Walsingham, lights are flashing and the road has been sealed off. Some inhabitants have come out of their houses to see what's going on, but, mostly, blinds remain drawn and doors remain closed. Tim is organising door-to-door enquiries. He's keeping out of Nelson's way, and Nelson is glad of this. He's more relieved than he can say to see Clough striding towards him, crumpling a chocolate wrapper in his hand.

'What happened, boss?'

'Michelle was attacked in the graveyard. We think it's likely to be the same person that killed Chloe.'

'Same time, same place,' says Clough. 'And Michelle and Chloe look an awful lot alike.'

You can always rely on Clough to say the obvious. It's quite comforting really.

'Is Fuller with you?' Nelson asks.

'Are you joking? Couldn't keep her away from something like this.'

'I want her to go to see Michelle and get a proper statement. Also we need a doctor to see her.'

'Don't you want to get back to her?'

'No. I'm needed here.' Nelson looks at his phone. A text message from Michelle flashes up. One word: *'Home'*. 'Michelle's home,' he tells Clough. 'She's fine. Just get Fuller over there, will you?'

He thinks that Clough is looking at him oddly. 'OK, boss.'

'DCI Nelson?' Nelson is glad to see a handler and her dog coming towards him. He recognises the woman as Jan Adams, famous in Norfolk for having won several medals for bravery. Her dog, a beautiful long-haired German Shepherd, is a bit of a celebrity too. What was his name again?

'Barney,' says Jan, in answer to his question. 'What's going on?'

Nelson explains about the attack. Barney looks at him, head on one side, as if he too might be about to ask a question.

'So I need you to look in the graveyard. See if our attacker dropped anything.' He knows that police dogs are trained to search out evidence but not to touch it. They sit by it until it can be seized by someone wearing gloves. He wishes his team were as meticulous. 'It's pretty dark, I'm afraid.'

'Dogs work better at night,' says Jan. 'Fewer distractions, fewer people to contaminate the scene.'

'Can you search the lane and the surrounding area?' says Nelson. 'He can't have gone far.'

'Perpetrators normally hide somewhere quite close,' says Jan. 'They wait until they think the police have gone away. But if he's nearby, we'll find him.'

Barney nods intelligently. Nelson can see Tim coming towards him. He wishes that he could carry on talking to

Jan and her dog, but he knows that he has to get on with the investigation. He says goodbye and watches as Jan and Barney disappear through the lych-gate. Then he turns to face his sergeant.

Tim is accompanied by a man in a leather jacket and woollen cap. Nelson sees the flash of a white collar.

'You said you wanted to talk to the Reverend Westmondham,' says Tim.

'Yes,' says Nelson. 'This way, Reverend. Is there somewhere we can talk?'

'In the church,' says Larry Westmondham. 'I've got the keys. What's going on?'

'I'll tell you in a minute.'

They walk back through the graveyard. Nelson can just make out Jan and Barney moving steadily along by the outer wall. Larry opens the heavy oak door and they sit in the porch, opposite notices for Frugal Lent Lunches and Alpha courses.

'Reverend Westmondham,' says Nelson. 'A serious assault has occurred. I need to find out if anyone was in the church or churchyard this evening.'

'An assault?' says Larry. 'What happened?'

'A woman was attacked,' says Nelson. 'Now, I saw you lock the church at about eight o'clock. Did you go back after that?' Tim and Nelson were sitting by the lych-gate entrance, but Larry could easily have gone in the front way. Nelson looks down at the keyring in the vicar's hands. So many keys, so many doors.

Larry is still looking shocked, but he answers calmly

enough. 'I went straight home,' he says. 'Like I told you, it's only a short walk.'

'Does anyone else have the keys?'

'The verger, but he lives a few miles away.'

'Is there anywhere round here where a person could hide?'

'All the buildings are locked,' says Larry, 'but I suppose someone could hide in the churchyard. It's very dark at night.'

'You didn't see or hear anything suspicious as you were going home?'

'No. I didn't hear anything until Sergeant Heathfield knocked on my door.'

'OK. Thank you. Someone will be round to take a statement in the morning.'

'Can I go home now?'

'Yes.' Larry locks up again and walks quickly away through the graves. As Nelson watches, a rectangle of light appears in the darkness, like an Advent calendar door being opened. A man is standing in the back doorway of St Simeon's Cottage.

'What's going on?' It's Cathbad's friend, Justin. He's wearing some kind of velvet dressing-gown affair and he has the cat in his arms. As Nelson approaches, the animal narrows its eyes and hisses quietly.

'There's been a serious assault in the graveyard,' says Nelson. 'Did you hear or see anything?'

'I didn't hear anything,' says Justin. 'I was listening to music with my headphones on. But then I saw all the lights and people hurrying to and fro. No, Chesterton, you can't get down.'

The cat is struggling to escape. Nelson remembers that it was the cat who first led Cathbad to Chloe Jenkins. He wishes that he could ask it a few questions.

'Someone will be round to take a statement tomorrow,' he says.

'Always delighted to see a policeman,' says Justin, 'but I don't really think I'll be able to add anything. I'd better take Chesterton in now. I saw a big, rough dog going past.'

The door shuts, and the churchyard is dark once more. Nelson is about to go back through the passageway when he hears a noise behind him. Jan is standing by the gate to the lane. Doreen Westmondham's tombstone gleams white in the darkness. Nelson can't see Barney, but he knows he's nearby.

'Any luck, Jan?' he asks.

'There's a track,' says Jan. 'Someone has walked over this grass recently. They probably went out by this gate, but there's no one in the lane.'

She calls softly. A few seconds later Barney appears at her side.

'He's a good dog,' says Nelson.

'The best.'

'Go on searching, will you, Jan? I've a feeling our man is still around here somewhere.'

'Will do. Come on, Barney.'

Nelson watches as the woman and her dog disappear into the night. For the first time in years he misses his dog, Max, who looked a bit like Barney. Max died ten years ago and Nelson has sometimes thought about getting another dog.

If a dog were waiting for him at home, maybe he wouldn't be dreading going back there.

By eleven-thirty Ruth is desperate. The women seem in no hurry to leave and several of them have ordered more liqueurs. Ruth doesn't want to go before the bill comes (however much cash you leave, it always looks as if you're trying to get out of paying your share), but she really needs to be getting back to Kate. She escapes to the loo and texts Clara. 'Still at Bfields. Sorry! Leaving soon.' Clara texts back reassuringly. 'No prob all well here x.' On her way out of the cloakroom Ruth bumps into Hilary.

'Hilary. Look, I'm sorry. I've got to go. The childminder can't stay too late.' This isn't true, Clara never minds staying late, but with any luck Hilary will think it's all part of Ruth's tragic life as a single mother.

'Of course,' says Hilary. 'I'm sorry. You should have said. I'm afraid the others are well away.'

There are two doors between them but they can still hear the women's voices. All the other diners have gone home.

'Actually, Ruth — ' Hilary says and puts her hand on her arm — 'Could you give me a lift back? I've got a bit of a headache and I don't want to break up the party.'

'Of course,' says Ruth, glad to have a cast-iron excuse to leave. Come to think of it, her friend does look rather pale. She hopes she won't be sick in the car.

Ruth and Hilary leave cash with Freya (the self-appointed treasurer), and then Ruth is free, driving through the dark roads, headlights on full. It's a clear night with a full moon, but that doesn't help much around here. As she drives along the raised-up road there's no way of knowing whether the space on either side is land, sea or marshland. She hears Erik's voice, perfectly preserved in the peaty depths of her brain. 'Marshland is a liminal zone, neither land nor sea, neither life nor death, a bridge to the afterlife.' Hilary's voice: 'You sound like Erik. The sacred landscape.'

A fox or some other animal runs out in front of her and she brakes sharply. The new car has stronger brakes than her old one, and she skids slightly.

'Sorry,' says Ruth, as Hilary pitches forward.

'It's OK,' says Hilary. 'I wouldn't like to drive on these roads at night.'

'You get used to it,' says Ruth. Though you don't, really. She waits for Hilary to say that she doesn't know how Ruth manages it, living alone in the wilds of Norfolk without a man. But Hilary is silent for a while, as the liminal zone gives way to trees and hedgerows. When she speaks again her voice sounds thin, almost as if she's trying not to cry.

'I envy you, Ruth. You've got your life sorted out. A job that you love, a place that you love.'

'So have you,' says Ruth. 'You're doing what you wanted to do. You're a priest. You might even be a bishop one day.'

'But people hate us. How can we minister to people if they hate us?'

'People change,' says Ruth. 'Women used not to have the vote. Everyone got used to that.'

'Eventually,' says Hilary. 'I'm just not sure I've got the patience to wait.'

'Of course you've got patience,' says Ruth. 'You were an archaeologist, weren't you?'

Hilary laughs. 'You're right. Sorry, Ruth. I'm just feeling a bit melancholy. Too much wine probably.'

Walsingham is quiet. Just a security light by the abbey gates and a black cat strolling down the centre of the road. Ruth drops Hilary at her guesthouse and watches as she lets herself in. Somehow it seems important to see Hilary safely inside. Somewhere, quite close by, a clock is striking midnight. The moon is round-faced and baleful above the gateway to the ruined priory. Ruth does a three-point turn and heads back the way she came. The cat watches from the side of the road.

As Ruth passes the church she notices something that she hadn't seen the first time. There's a light on in the porch and it illuminates police tape across the entrance. Why is that there? She slows down and, as she does so, she sees something else, a man walking slowly along the lane by the church. He's tall, wearing a long black coat and a hat. But as he passes the porch she sees his face quite clearly. It's Father Hennessey.

16

It's past midnight when Nelson gets home. The AA have towed his car away and he gets a lift in a squad car. He's grateful that the driver is the taciturn sort who doesn't like to chat.

'You can stop here,' he says, at the entrance to the cul-de-sac. 'Save you turning round. Goodnight.'

The lights are on downstairs. His heart sinks and he realises that he'd been hoping Michelle was upstairs, asleep, and that any talking could wait until morning. Don't be a wimp, he tells himself. He was less scared when a madman pulled a gun on him last year.

Michelle is in the sitting room watching one of those programmes where celebrities talk about themselves and their films. She's wearing her white dressing gown and her hair is loose.

'Did Tanya come?' he asks.

'Yes. She brought a lady doctor with her. She was very nice.'

Nelson switches on the overhead light. In its unforgiving glare he can see the bruises around his wife's neck. She shields her eyes with her hand.

'Harry, please. You know I hate that light.'

She does too. She thinks it shows the little lines that are starting to appear around her eyes. She's still beautiful, though. Never more so than at this moment.

Nelson moves to stand in front of her.

'Are you having an affair with Tim?'

Even now he expects her to deny it, to be angry, to laugh at the absurdity of the idea. Instead she says, in a flat voice, 'It wasn't exactly an affair.'

'What the hell does that mean?'

'We didn't sleep together.'

'What did you do?'

Michelle sighs and starts plaiting the tassel on one of the cushions. 'We went out, we kissed, we talked. He listened.'

'How long has this been going on?'

She pretends to think. 'For about a year.'

'A *year*! Jesus Christ.'

'But we stopped seeing each other in December. After that Blackstock Hall affair.'

After Tim saved his life. Why the hell had he done that? Why hadn't he pushed Nelson into the path of the bullet and buggered off with his wife?

'Jesus Christ,' he says again. 'Why?'

So suddenly that it is almost terrifying, Michelle flares up. She tosses back her hair and her eyes flash.

'You can't talk! I didn't sleep with Tim. You slept with Ruth and she had your baby. How dare you pretend to be the one in the right? You betrayed me.'

'Is this what this is about?' says Nelson. 'Getting back at me?'

She looks at him with what is almost contempt. 'Not everything is about you, Harry.'

'What is it about then?'

'It's about me!' He can't remember the last time that he heard Michelle shout but now her raised voice makes the glasses in the cabinet ring. 'It's about me. You cheated on me and then you forgot all about it. You went on seeing Ruth. And Katie. Everyone knows about it. You humiliated me.'

'You agreed that I could see Katie.'

'Yes,' says Michelle bitterly, 'shows what a mug I am.'

'I suppose Tim told you that. I suppose he played on you, saying what a bastard I am. Jesus. The sneaking little swine.'

'It's not his fault. He listened to me. He loves me.'

'I suppose he told you that.'

'Yes, he did! He still loves me.'

And Nelson, remembering Tim's voice as he cradled Michelle in his arms, thinks that she is probably right. Doesn't stop him wanting to tear the little bastard limb from limb though. And, tomorrow, that's just what he'll do.

Ruth leaves Walsingham behind and drives home, Bruce Springsteen on full blast. The country roads with their high hedges seem like a maze, nightmarish and unending. Surely she's seen this crossroads before? If only she had her sat-nav plugged in, at least it could tell her if she was going the right way. She's just wondering if she should stop and consult her phone when the landscape opens up and she's driving over the Saltmarsh, the moon silver on the sea. Nearly home. It's been an unsettling evening one way or another: the discussion about Norfolk and the sacred landscape, Paula describing the letter-writer as a 'soul in torment', the panic of wanting to get back to Kate, the dark drive with a strangely sombre Hilary and, finally, that sighting of Father Hennessey in the graveyard. Why was he standing by a church in the middle of the night? And why was there police tape over the entrance to the church? What has been happening in Walsingham?

Clara is asleep when she gets in, dozing on the sofa with her textbooks around her. Ruth asks if she wants to stay the night, but Clara says that she ought to go because she's starting a new course in the morning. After Clara has left and the sound of her car engine has died away, Ruth stands by the door and listens to the silence. Sometimes nights on the Saltmarsh can be noisy affairs, with the wind howling and the sea roaring away in the distance. But tonight everything is deathly quiet, as if the dark is a muffling hand. Ruth gets herself a glass of water and climbs the stairs to bed. She checks on Kate, who is sleeping peacefully, spread-eagled on her Dora the Explorer duvet. Ruth tucks her in and goes into her own room. She switches on her bedside radio and soothing Radio 4 voices tell her about financial disaster and fiscal catastrophe. For the first time that evening, Ruth starts to relax.

She dreams of marshland, of bones and silence, of ancient relics washed up like flotsam and jetsam on an incoming tide. She dreams of a woman in a blue cloak, of the god Mercury, of the voices of lost children beneath the waves. She wakes suddenly while the sky outside is still dark. Her phone is ringing. It says 6.15 and 'Hilary'.

'Hilary? What's up?'

There's a silence and, for a moment, she thinks that Hilary may have called her number by mistake. Then there's an intake of breath and Hilary says, in a voice quite unlike her own, 'Ruth. Something awful has happened.'

'What is it?'

'It's Paula. She's dead. Someone's killed her.'

17

Nelson is already up when he gets the call. He hadn't slept well although Michelle, annoyingly, seemed to sleep peacefully all night. He had lain awake at four a.m., listening to her regular breathing, and wanting to shake her awake. Didn't she feel at all guilty about seeing another man for almost a year? Was it really all his fault? Yes, he had slept with Ruth and that was unforgivable, but Michelle had forgiven him, or so she said. And that one sexual act had occurred at a time of great emotional strain for him and Ruth. And afterwards, from the moment he knew she was pregnant, he really had tried to act in the best way possible, trying to be fair to all of them — his wife, the woman who was having his baby and the baby herself — even though he knew that it wasn't really possible. Was he really such a bad guy? At five he is drinking coffee downstairs and thinking that he is definitely ill-used. Some men would have run a mile if a woman got pregnant after a one-night stand. Some men would have tried to pressure her to have an abortion. He has done none of those things. He has tried to be a father to Katie and be true to Michelle and his other daughters. Except, except . . . Was Ruth really no more to him than the mother of his child? What about that other time, that other night he had spent with Ruth, with no excuse except that he had wanted her badly? No, he's not the good guy. He really wanted to have them both, Michelle and Ruth, and all three daughters. He has behaved like some backwoods patriarch who wants several wives waiting on him and bearing his children. No wonder Michelle has sought sanctuary in the arms of Tim, good-looking, polite Tim who has listened and told her that she was beautiful and that he loved her. When did he, Nelson, last say these things to his wife? He deserves to lose her, he really does. And if he does lose her . . . What if she left him for Tim, if the two of them disappeared into the sunset (or Essex)? Would he then be able to live with Ruth and bring up Katie with her? Don't think like that, he tells himself. But, sitting in the dark kitchen as the microwave clock ticks towards dawn, it is impossible to stop.

The phone call is a relief, even though a call from police control at six a.m. is unlikely to be good news.

'Nelson.'

'DCI Nelson. You're needed in Walsingham. A woman's body has been found in the abbey grounds. It looks like she's been strangled.'

Nelson goes upstairs. Michelle is still fast asleep, her hair spread out on the pillow. Nelson shakes her shoulder gently.

'Michelle? I've got to go out.'

'Why?' says Michelle, not opening her eyes.

'Someone's been killed. The thing is, I'll have to take your car. Is that OK?'

Michelle sits up. Nelson can see the bruises on her neck, darker than they were last night.

'It's OK,' she says. 'Debbie can give me a lift into work.'

'You're not going to work? After what happened last night?'

Michelle's eyes flash. 'Why not? My job's important, although you never think so.'

'You've had a shock. You should take it easy.'

'I'll be fine,' says Michelle. 'You get back to your case.' She turns away. Nelson knows he should say something more, but he's still angry after last night and, besides, he's itching to get to work. He heads for the shower, but when he's at the door, Michelle says, 'You won't do anything stupid, will you, Harry? You know, with Tim.'

Nelson has the satisfaction of not answering this question.

It is just getting light when he reaches Walsingham. A uniformed policeman whom he knows by sight is waiting for him at the visitors' centre.

The man introduces himself: 'PC Bradley Linwood. The body's through here, sir. In the grounds.'

'Who found her?'

'The groundsman. He's in the visitors' centre. He's very shaken.'

'Do we have an identity for the dead woman?'

'We rang St Catherine's Lodge because that's the nearest place. A couple of people came out and identified her as

Paula Moncrieff, a delegate at a conference being held at St Catherine's. They're in the centre too.'

'Have next of kin been informed?'

'Not yet, sir.'

'I'll do that myself once I've had a look at her. Are SOCO on their way?'

'Yes, and Doctor Stephenson.'

'Good. You've done well, Linwood. Now show me.'

They walk through the door into the grounds. The early morning sun is shining through the trees and illuminating a vast archway standing on its own in the middle of the park. To Nelson it looks both absurd and sinister. A few yards further on and a woman's body lies on the lawn, guarded by another police officer. From the distance, she could be asleep, but, as Nelson gets closer, he sees the marks on her neck and the awkward sprawl of her limbs. He thinks of the bruises that he saw on his wife's neck less than an hour earlier.

Nelson kneels next to the body, careful not to touch her. He is struck by two things. The dead woman is beautiful, and she looks very like Chloe Jenkins — and Michelle. Her long blonde hair is spread out on the grass and it glitters with what look like spiders' webs. She is wearing a black sparkly jacket, white silk vest and smart-looking trousers. Her feet are bare, but high-heeled black shoes lie a few feet away. Unlike with Chloe Jenkins, this time the murderer has made no attempt to hide the body. The dew-drenched grass is flattened as if someone has walked over it, but Nelson doubts if any footprints can be found. Standing up, he sees a small brass cross, like a stepping stone embedded in the ground.

A few yards away is a sign: 'Site of the 11th-century, Anglo-Saxon shrine of the holy house of Nazareth (excavated 1961).'

He turns to PC Linwood. 'I'd better talk to the groundsman. Let me know when Stephenson gets here.'

In the visitors' centre, under framed posters advertising pilgrimages in 'England's Nazareth', sit a young man in a heavy jacket and two people Nelson recognises as Hilary Smithson and Robin Rainsford. Hilary stands up as soon as he comes in.

'DCI Nelson. What's happening? We've been here hours.'

'Forty-five minutes,' says Linwood.

'I'm sorry Doctor Smithson,' says Nelson, 'but a serious crime has occurred. We're working as fast as we can. I need to speak to this young man first. Can we get you a hot drink or something?' By 'we' he means PC Linwood and is pleased to see that the young officer is quick to offer tea or coffee, saying that there's a machine in the office. Hilary, who is wearing a coat over what are obviously pyjamas, accepts gratefully. Rainsford, who is fully dressed, seems in a daze and doesn't seem to understand the question. 'What? Yes. Tea. No, coffee. Thank you. Yes.'

'I've phoned Ruth,' says Hilary.

Nelson looks accusingly at Linwood. 'Well, you shouldn't have. Please don't contact anyone else until such time as I give you permission. Now —' he turns to the grounds-man — 'if I could have a word, Mr . . .?'

'Peters. Lee Peters.'

'This way please, Mr Peters.' He pushes a door at random and finds himself in a sort of museum full of glass cases.

There's nowhere to sit, so they stand by a display of agricultural machinery.

'Mr Peters. Can you describe how you discovered the body?'

The young man looks nervous but speaks fluently with a strong Norfolk accent. 'I do a tour of the grounds at five, just to pick up any litter and check that nothing's happened overnight like. I were just crossing the main lawn when I saw her . . .' He pauses, wiping his brow with one of his gardening gloves.

'Take your time,' says Nelson. 'What did you do then?'

'Well, I thought she might be sleeping. Sometimes people break in to sleep in the grounds. You know, hippies and that. So I called out to her and, when she didn't answer, I shook her. I probably shouldn't have touched her. I've seen on TV . . .'

'Don't worry about that. Then what?'

'I called 999.'

'Police or ambulance?'

'Police. I were pretty sure she were dead.'

'Why?'

'When I touched her she were cold. Like a statue.'

That places time of death at a few hours back, even accounting for the cold night. Nelson must have left Walsingham at nearly midnight. How long afterwards did the killer strike, having been deprived of his victim in the graveyard?

'What time did you start work?' asks Nelson.

'Five.'

'And you didn't see or hear anything suspicious? No signs of a break-in?'

'No. I come in through the side gate as usual. It were locked.' He brandishes a key ring very like the one Larry Westmondham used to lock the church.

'Thank you, Mr Peters. I may need to speak to you later, but you can go home now. You acted very responsibly. Thank you.'

The young man looks surprised at this praise. He nods and then says, 'It were horrible. I mean, she were so pretty. Poor lady.'

'Yes, it's horrible,' says Nelson grimly.

When he goes back into the visitors' centre, Clough and Stephenson have both arrived. Hilary is sipping a cup of coffee, still looking argumentative. Rainsford is staring into space.

'Cloughie,' says Nelson. 'You go with Doctor Stephenson. We'll need to secure the site. I just need to talk to these witnesses, then I'll call the next of kin.'

'OK,' says Clough. 'Is Tim on the way?'

'No. I didn't call him.'

Clough looks both surprised and pleased. He knows better than to ask why, though. Stephenson greets Nelson heartily ('We have to stop meeting like this, Admiral') and he and Clough pass through the door marked 'To the Abbey Grounds'.

Nelson sits down next to Hilary and Robin Rainsford.

'I'm sorry,' he says. 'This must be a terrible shock.'

'Awful,' says Rainsford. He looks ashen and, when he takes off his glasses, his eyes are pink-rimmed. Hilary is made of stronger stuff. 'Is it the same man who killed the other girl, the model?' she says.

'We don't know yet,' says Nelson, 'and let's not presume

anything. Now, what time did PC Linwood contact you this morning?'

'At about five-thirty,' says Rainsford. 'He called at the house and the housekeeper woke me.'

'And you woke Doctor Smithson?'

'I was already awake,' says Hilary. 'I often wake up early. It's a good time to pray. I was in the kitchen making tea.'

'So the two of you went with PC Linwood?'

'Yes,' says Rainsford. 'I must say, I was glad of Hilary's company.'

'And you identified the dead woman immediately?'

'Yes,' says Hilary, with a shudder, 'it was definitely Paula.'

'Did you know her well?'

'I just met her this week on the course but she was a lovely person, lovely. Why would anyone . . .'

'When did you last see Paula?' asks Nelson.

'Last night. We went out for a meal. I had a headache, so I left early. Ruth drove me home.'

Nelson realises, with a slight shock, that this was the dinner that Ruth had been planning to attend. Maybe that was why Hilary was so quick to ring her.

'Do you know what time that was?' he asks.

'Midnight. I heard the clock striking. The others got back about an hour later. I heard them come in but I didn't go downstairs to join them.'

'Are you sure that Paula was with the others?'

'I think I heard her voice, but I can't be sure.'

'Doctor Rainsford, did you hear the other delegates come in?'

'Yes. I was in bed too. I didn't go down either. I thought it might spoil the party, seeing the course leader. And everyone sounded, well . . . jolly.'

'We'd all had quite a lot to drink, I'm afraid,' says Hilary.

Nelson is quite shocked. Women priests going out and getting drunk like a gang of rugby players. He wonders what Ruth made of the evening.

'Do you know what could have made Paula go out again?' he asks.

'She may have gone for a walk,' says Hilary. 'When we . . . when we saw her, she was still wearing what she wore to the restaurant. She may have just felt like a moonlight walk.'

'Is that the sort of thing she was likely to do?'

'I don't know.' Hilary blushes, very noticeable on her pale skin. 'As I say, we were all a bit drunk, DCI Nelson.'

'I'll need names of everyone who was at the dinner,' says Nelson. 'Can you provide that?'

'Of course.'

'And I'll need next-of-kin details for Paula.'

'I'll have the details on file back at St Catherine's,' says Robin Rainsford.

'I'll come with you,' says Nelson. 'And I'll need somewhere quiet to make the phone call.'

When Nelson gets back to the abbey grounds he sees that a small tent has been erected over the body and the SOCO team are searching the area nearby. He also sees Tim, deep in conversation with PC Linwood. He breaks off when he sees Nelson.

'I've organised door-to-door, boss. Cloughie's getting all the CCTV together.'

'Good,' says Nelson. 'We need to talk to everyone who was with the dead woman last night.' He waves a list.

'What do we know about her?'

'Paula Moncrieff, aged thirty. She was a priest. Lived in Kent, married with one child. I've just spoken to her husband and I've sent a car to pick him up.'

'I've fielded the press, but Superintendent Whitcliffe wants you to give a statement.'

'I bet he does. Tell him midday at the station. Then I'm going to see Stanley Greenway.'

'Do you really think he's involved?'

'He's got a motive for Chloe Jenkins. I'll be interested to see where he was last night.'

'Do you want me to come with you?'

'No. I'll take Cloughie. You keep going door-to-door, appeal for witnesses. Someone must have seen something.'

'OK.' Tim hesitates. Then he says, 'Boss, we've got to talk.'

'No,' says Nelson. 'We're not teenage girls. We don't have to talk. Michelle tells me that you didn't sleep together, which is the only reason you're still in one piece. As it is we've got to catch a murderer. When we've done that I'll approve your transfer and then I never want to see your fucking face again. Understood?'

'Understood,' says Tim. And he walks quickly away across the grass.

*

Ruth listens to the radio all morning, but there's nothing about Paula's death. When she got Hilary's call she'd asked if her friend wanted her to come to Walsingham. She hoped she'd say no; it would be a hassle getting Kate up and off to Sandra's so early and she didn't really know what help she could be to Hilary. Hilary had said no. 'Thanks, Ruth, but there's nothing you could do. I'm just waiting to be interviewed by DCI Nelson. Robin's with me.' 'OK,' Ruth had said, 'I'll call later.' The mention of Nelson had disturbed her, though she couldn't have said why.

But, as she is getting Kate ready for school, dropping her off and driving through the morning traffic to the university, Ruth keeps thinking about Paula. She'd liked her best out of all the women there last night. She'd seemed interesting and not frighteningly pious. Ruth remembers the Third Prostitute conversation. Paula hadn't taken herself too seriously, but there was no doubt that she had looked more like an actress than a priest. Ruth remembers her saying that they should reach out to the letter-writer, that he was a 'soul in torment'. Had that tormented soul now killed her?

When she reaches her office she can feel her phone buzzing in her bag. She swipes open her door and searches in her organiser handbag. Why can she never find anything in any of the compartments? Why doesn't this seem to happen to other women? When she finally unearths the phone it says: Missed call. Nelson.

'Nelson. Hi.'

'Were you at this Briarfields dinner last night?'

'I'm fine, thank you,' says Ruth in her head. But she for-
gives him. He's in the middle of a murder enquiry, after all.

'Yes. I can't believe that Paula's dead. What happened?'

'We don't know yet,' says Nelson. 'She got back to her
lodging house at about midnight last night. The women
stayed up having coffee. Apparently they were all a bit drunk.'

'They were,' says Ruth.

'At some point this Paula Moncrieff must have decided to
go for a walk in the grounds. The gardener found her body
this morning.'

'God. How awful.'

'I'm on my way to the station now,' says Nelson, 'but I'll be
speaking to all the women later. I'd like to talk to you too.'

'Of course. Do you want me to come to the station?'

'No. I'll come to your house tonight. It might be quite late,
though. Is that all right?'

'Of course.'

'Good. See you later.'

He rings off without saying goodbye, but Ruth stays staring
at her phone for a long time.

18

Giles Moncrieff, Paula's husband, arrives at the station at midday. Nelson has just finished giving a statement to the press ('No, we haven't found the murderer yet') and he finds Tanya sitting with Giles in his office. There's a box of tissues on the desk which reminds Nelson of the Sanctuary. It's times like this when Nelson misses Judy the most. She's very good with the bereaved, empathetic and caring, but also professional enough to stop the situation collapsing into tears and breakdown. Tanya is saying all the right things, but she is staring at Giles as if he's an exhibit in the zoo. Giles, a tall man in his thirties who looks like he'd be more at home in cycling shorts, has the shell-shocked look of someone who is hoping that the last few hours have been a particularly nasty dream.

Nelson greets him. 'I'm so sorry for your loss. Can I get you anything?'

Giles shakes his head. 'No. Sergeant . . . er . . . the sergeant has been very kind.'

'Sergeant Fuller,' says Tanya unnecessarily.

'You'll want to see your wife's body,' says Nelson. 'Sergeant

Fuller will take you there in a minute. You can take as long as you want.'

Giles stares at him blankly. 'I just can't believe it. Paula. I mean, she was just here for a conference. I encouraged her to go. "It'll be a break for you," I said. It's hard work with the parish and a young child. Christ, I wish she hadn't come.'

Nelson pulls round his chair so that the desk isn't between them. 'This must be very difficult for you,' he says, 'but you'll appreciate that we have to find the person that did this to Paula. I promise you that we won't rest until we do. So, anything that you can tell us about Paula now will be invaluable. Anything that might be relevant.'

'What do you mean?'

'Well, for example, had anyone been threatening her? Sending her abusive letters, for example.'

Giles looks more nonplussed than ever. 'No. Everyone loved Paula. Her parishioners adored her. When Jack was born they threw a surprise party for her. On her birthday we had so many cakes we had to give them to a shelter for the homeless. Oh God . . .' He looks helplessly at Nelson and Tanya. 'How am I going to tell Jack?'

'How old is Jack?' asks Nelson.

'He's four. He'll be starting school in September. He was so happy. Paula had already bought his uniform.' He rubs his eyes but can't stop the tears. Tanya hands him the box of tissues. 'Who's looking after Jack now?' she asks.

'My parents. They're devastated too. They loved Paula.'

'What about Paula's parents?' asks Nelson.

'They're dead,' says Giles. 'They died when she was a child.

Paula had a terrible childhood really, she was in children's homes, with various foster parents, in and out of care. But it never made her bitter. She was extraordinary.'

'How long had she been a priest?' asks Nelson.

'Only two years. She was still a curate when Jack was born. That's why it was such a big thing for her, being invited on this course. Paula was an actress when I met her. She used to joke that she wasn't very good, but she was, she could have gone a long way. I mean, she was beautiful too. Beautiful and talented. But she wanted to do good in the world, she said. Look where that got her.'

'I'm sure she did do good in the world,' says Nelson.

Giles looks at him. 'Do you believe in God, Inspector?'

'I'm not sure,' says Nelson honestly. 'Sometimes I think I do.'

'Well, I don't,' says Giles. 'How could a just God let this happen?'

Nelson has no answer to this and, after a few more desultory questions, Tanya leads Giles Moncrieff off to the morgue.

All in all, Nelson is glad of the distraction of the drive to the Sanctuary. The only problem is that he's a passenger, which he hates. He usually insists on driving (in defiance of the protocol that it should be the junior officer who takes the wheel), but he doesn't think that Michelle's little Matiz is quite suitable for the job. Besides they need room in the back for Stanley Greenway. Nelson is determined to bring him back to the station to get DNA and fingerprint samples.

Clough is obviously relishing being at the wheel. When he turned the engine on, Bastille had blasted from the CD player. Nelson recognises the group because they are one of his daughter's favourites and rightly suspects the influence of Clough's girlfriend, Cassandra. Left to himself Clough is strictly a rock ballads man.

'So,' says Clough, pulling out to overtake a tractor, 'do you think Greenway is our man?'

'Never assume,' says Nelson mechanically. He is thinking about Michelle. He had rung her from the station, but the phone had gone through to answerphone. At least she can't be with Tim because he's still going door-to-door in Walsingham. Nelson fully plans to keep him employed there for several days. Weeks, if necessary.

'But a convicted sex offender . . .' says Clough.

'Being obsessed with a young girl doesn't make you a killer,' says Nelson.

'Doesn't hurt, though,' says Clough.

'I admit I'll be interested to see where he was last night,' says Nelson. 'Whoever attacked Michelle obviously hung around and got lucky when Paula went walking in the grounds.'

'How is Michelle?' says Clough. 'Must have been bloody frightening for her.'

'She's OK,' says Nelson. 'Insisted on going in to work today.'

'Probably the best thing. Take her mind off it.'

'Yes,' says Nelson. They are stuck behind another farm vehicle. Nelson drums his fingers on the glove compartment. 'You can overtake here.'

'Better not,' says Clough, 'it's a tricky bend.'

A BMW powers past them, proving Clough right, which

doesn't improve Nelson's mood. On the next straight stretch, Clough pulls out smoothly to pass.

'That Paula didn't look like a woman vicar, did she?' says Clough.

'How many women vicars have you met?' asks Nelson. But he knows what Clough means. Seeing Paula's picture stuck up on the board beside Chloe's had been startling. Although the two women hadn't been identical — Paula was older, for one thing — the resemblance was striking. Both had long blonde hair and classically beautiful features. When Nelson had added a snapshot of Michelle — taken from home that morning — there had been gasps in the room. Not just because she was the boss's wife, but because the three women could have been sisters.

'The scene wasn't the same, though,' he says now. 'Chloe's body was hidden in the ditch. It was positioned there with care, the rosary on her chest. Paula's body seemed to have been left where she fell. No rosary, no arrangement of the body.'

'Could just be that the killer didn't have time. Maybe he was interrupted.'

'Who would have interrupted him in the abbey grounds in the middle of the night?'

'I don't know, but the murders look pretty similar to me. Same method, for one thing.'

Chris Stephenson has confirmed that Paula died from manual strangulation. 'Would have had to be someone fairly big and strong. She was a tall woman.' She was a tall, beautiful woman — like Chloe, like Michelle — but she hadn't been expecting an attack. She had been wandering in the grounds, slightly drunk, probably thinking lovely thoughts about heaven and angels and fluffy clouds. It wouldn't have taken a very strong person to have overpowered her. Only someone determined.

They drive on in rather uncomfortable silence.

Doctor McAllister is definitely less friendly than before.

'Have you got a good reason for wanting to see Stanley? He's in a rather vulnerable state just now.'

'He's a person of interest in our inquiry,' says Nelson. 'So it's very important that we speak to him. You can sit in on the interview if you like.'

The doctor looks at him squarely through her intimidating glasses. 'Is this because of his previous conviction?'

'That's part of it,' says Nelson, 'as is his relationship with Chloe Jenkins.'

'But you can't suspect him for last night's attack? He was here.'

'Are you sure of that?' says Nelson. 'Because Chloe Jenkins got out without you or your staff being any the wiser.'

Fiona McAllister shoots him an unfriendly look, but she seems to take the point. She picks up the phone. 'I'll get someone to bring Stanley here,' she says. 'It's probably better if we talk in my office.'

Stanley is wearing his usual tracksuit, and he looks thin and stooped and nervous. There's no sign, though, that he looks any more nervous than usual. He blinks at Nelson in surprise, but takes the seat offered by Doctor McAllister and awaits questions calmly, as if this is just another group session.

'Mr Greenway,' Nelson begins. 'When we came to see you last, you told us that you sometimes went to church with Chloe Jenkins. To St Simeon's. Is that right?'

'Yes,' says Stanley. 'I went a few times.'

'Did you know the vicar, Larry Westmondham?'

Stanley swallows but answers quietly. 'I think I met him before. In my former life.'

'Talking of your former life,' says Nelson, 'you didn't tell us the reason that you left the priesthood.'

'I'm still a priest,' says Stanley. 'Technically.'

'But you didn't tell us that you served a jail sentence for having sex with a minor.'

Fiona McAllister cuts in. 'Is this relevant, Inspector?'

But Stanley raises his hand, curiously dignified. 'It's all right, Doctor McAllister. No, I didn't tell you that, Inspector, because I knew you wouldn't understand. I loved Shelley and she loved me.'

'And did you love Chloe Jenkins?'

'What are you getting at?'

'Where were you on the night of 19th February?'

'Here, of course.'

'And last night?'

Stanley looks around the room. 'Why are you asking me that?'

'Just answer the question please.'

Nelson expects Stanley to say, again, that he was at the Sanctuary, blamelessly in his room. But, instead, he looks apologetically at Fiona and says, 'I went for a walk.'

It's hard to say which of the three people listening is more surprised by this. But it's the doctor who exclaims, 'What do you mean, you went out for a walk?'

'It was a lovely night,' says Stanley, 'so I went for a walk over the fields.'

'But you're not allowed out of the house at night. You have to sign out.'

'I know. I'm sorry.'

Nelson has had enough. 'Mr Greenway, I'm going to have to ask you to come to the police station with us.'

'Am I under arrest?' Stanley's voice is gently curious.

'No. This is purely voluntary. However, I would like your permission to take fingerprints and DNA swabs.'

'Do I need a lawyer?'

The question is addressed to Doctor McAllister, but Nelson answers, 'You are entitled to call a solicitor but I must stress that you're not under arrest.' Yet, he adds to himself.

'I'll need my coat.'

'I'll come to your room with you,' says Fiona McAllister.

Nelson and Clough wait in the hall with the looming fireplace and the waxy flowers. The grandfather clock ticks importantly, but Nelson notices with irritation that it's half an hour slow. He paces to and fro while the receptionist eyes him anxiously.

'Think he's made a run for it?' says Clough.

'You can catch him, if so. You're always telling me how fit you are.'

'I could beat Tim in a race.'

'I don't doubt it.' Nelson turns as he hears someone descending the stairs. But it's not Stanley. It's a tall man in clerical black. A man with white hair and broad shoulders.

'Father Hennessey?'

'Harry. My dear boy.'

'What are you doing here?'

'Visiting the sick. There are a lot of troubled souls in these places.'

'Ruth said she saw you in Walsingham the other day.'

'Yes. I'm here on a private visit. Ruth looked well. I can't believe the little one is at school.'

Nelson is never sure what Father Hennessey knows about Katie. Once, at a very low point in his life, Nelson confessed to the priest that he had slept with a woman, who then got pregnant. A year later Father Hennessey had baptised Katie, and Nelson knows that he is capable of putting two and two together. He remembers the priest saying, 'A child is always a blessing.' Well, he was right there. But, today, Father Hennessey doesn't seem inclined to talk.

'I'd better be on my way. Lovely to see you, Harry. And you too, David. God bless you both.'

And he hurries out of the door, leaving Clough staring after him.

'How did he know my name?'

'He's met you before. Remember, six years ago, when we found that body in the old children's home? He was the priest that used to run the home.'

'I remember,' says Clough. 'I never trusted him. He looked pretty shifty just now.'

And Nelson, although he both likes and trusts the priest, has to admit that Clough has a point.

*

There is a small group of reporters at the front of the station so Clough drives round to the back entrance. Stanley Greenway still seems in a dream, hardly noticing his surroundings, but Nelson dreads to think what will happen when the press pack find out about his previous conviction. He can see the headlines now.

Tanya meets them at the door, eyes wide with excitement.

'Sergeant Fuller,' says Nelson, 'can you take Mr Greenway and organise fingerprints and a DNA swab? He's not under arrest and is free to leave at any time.'

'Yes, boss.' Despite Nelson's words, Tanya grasps Stanley's arm firmly. 'This way, Mr Greenway.'

Nelson and Clough shut themselves in Nelson's office.

'What do you think?' asks Nelson.

'I don't like him,' says Clough, somewhat predictably. 'He's a convicted sex offender and he hasn't got an alibi for last night.'

'He hasn't got a motive either.'

'She looked like Chloe. Didn't he say that he loved Chloe? When you interviewed him before?'

'Yes. They both said it. Stanley and Jean, the older woman who had befriended her. At the time I thought she was a substitute child for them.'

'Stanley didn't sound very paternal towards the other girl. What was her name? Shelley. He said he loved her and she loved him.'

'No,' said Nelson, remembering the shambling figure in the tracksuit. 'There's no fool like an old fool.' And he's a fool too, he thinks. He's a fool for trusting his wife. How many times over the last year had Michelle told him that she was working late or at the gym? And he'd believed it every time, wrapped up in his work and his own life. But, curiously, it's Tim's betrayal that hurts most. He had brought Tim down from Blackpool, made him one of the team, one of the family. He had thought that Tim liked him and looked up to him. Well, you live and learn.

'Boss?'

He had been so deep in thought that he hadn't heard Tanya coming into the room.

'Where's Greenway?' he asks. 'You can't have finished taking prints yet.'

'He's with the duty sergeant. I want to show you something.'

Nelson looks at Clough, who shrugs. 'OK. What is it?'

Tanya leads them to her computer, which has a video window open. 'This is the CCTV footage from the Slipper Chapel on Wednesday 19th.'

'Thought it didn't show anything.'

'Apart from the big cat,' says Clough.

'No, but I looked earlier on in the day,' said Tanya, her glasses glinting. 'Then, when I saw that man, Greenway, I recognised him.'

Nelson leans in, interested now.

'There was a service at six o'clock in the evening,' says Tanya. 'Here are the people coming out. Look there. Next to the man in the waistcoat.'

Nelson looks. Grainy and indistinct, the man in the shabby raincoat is nonetheless definitely Stanley Greenway.

19

Ruth had almost given up hope. She managed to get Kate to bed fairly early, came downstairs, poured herself a glass of wine and tidied up by putting the books in piles and shoving everything else under the sofa. By nine o'clock she has drunk half the bottle and is convinced that Nelson won't come. He has probably had a long day at the station and has gone home to Michelle and a cooked supper. Then, just when she's considering getting into her pyjamas, car headlights illuminate the sitting room. Flint sits up, eyes popping as if he's expecting an axe murderer, and then a hand that can only be Nelson's hammers on the door.

'I thought you weren't coming,' says Ruth, ushering him towards the sofa. Flint jumps off, orange tail fluffed up in outrage.

'I said I would, didn't I?' Nelson looks exhausted, thinks Ruth. His eyes are shadowed and she can see the clenched muscles in his jaw. He hasn't shaved either and this gives him a rather desperate and piratical appearance.

'Do you want a cup of tea?' she says. Then, seeing his eyes

flicker towards the bottle on the coffee table, 'Or a glass of wine?'

'A glass of wine would be grand.'

This is a surprise. Nelson rarely drinks when he's on duty or driving. Also he prefers beer to wine. She pours them both a generous glassful.

'It's so awful about Paula,' she says. 'I've been thinking about it all day.'

'How well did you know her?' asks Nelson.

'I only met her that evening. But she seemed nice. Not at all like a priest.'

'That's what everyone says,' says Nelson. 'But her husband says that she was dedicated to her job. Her parishioners loved her, he says.'

'So she hadn't had any threatening letters?'

'No. I asked him and he seemed shocked at the idea. Mind you, the poor bloke was in shock anyway. His wife went away for a week's conference, and now she's dead. Suddenly he's a widower with a four-year-old child. Fuller said he was in pieces when he saw her body.'

Ruth shivers, imagining the scene. 'When I asked, most of the women priests said that they had had some abuse,' she says, 'but no one had received letters like Hilary's.'

Nelson smiles faintly. 'Nice to see you're doing some detective work, Ruth.'

Ruth can feel herself blushing. 'I only asked a question,' she says.

'The questions are more important than the answers. That's what you told me once.'

Ruth looks at Nelson. He seems to be behaving rather oddly this evening. Arriving late, drinking wine, remembering past conversations. For some reason, she feels it's important that they get back to the topic in hand.

'What happened after Paula got back to Walsingham last night?' she asks.

'Apparently they all had coffee and chatted in the sitting room. They all admitted to drinking too much. You wouldn't expect it of a group of priests, would you? Or maybe you would. I don't know. Anyway, one of the women — Sydney something — said that Paula decided to walk in the abbey grounds. She wanted to see them by moonlight, she said. This Sydney almost went with her, but she was tired and went to bed. She felt pretty bad about that.'

'Hilary said that she felt bad too. But they couldn't have known, could they?'

'They could have been more careful,' says Nelson, 'knowing that there was a killer on the loose. But there's no point saying that now.'

'Do you think it was the same person? The same person who killed the other girl. What was her name?'

'Chloe,' says Nelson. 'Chloe Jenkins. It certainly looks like the same modus operandi. Both women were strangled. And there are other similarities. The women looked alike, for one thing.'

'Did they?' says Ruth in surprise. 'But Chloe was so glamorous. I saw the pictures in the paper.'

'Paula was glamorous too,' says Nelson. 'And the same

type. Long blonde hair and all that.' He hesitates, then says, 'Michelle was attacked last night too.'

'Michelle?' Ruth can hardly believe she's heard right. 'Michelle was attacked?'

'Yes.' Nelson is speaking quickly now. 'She came to meet me. My car had broken down outside St Simeon's. She walked through the graveyard and someone jumped on her from behind.'

'Oh, my God. Was she hurt?'

'Just shocked. Tim and I got to her in a few minutes. The attacker got away. We had police everywhere — sniffer dog, the lot — but he must have hidden, bided his time, and attacked Paula later.'

'Lucky you and Tim were there.'

'Yes.' Nelson looks at her, his eyes very dark. 'Did you know that Michelle and Tim were having an affair?'

'*What?*' For the second time in a few minutes Ruth doubts her own hearing. Please don't let him say what I think he's said, she prays.

'So you didn't know? I thought everyone must know.'

'I don't believe you.'

'They both admitted it,' says Nelson, draining his glass. He picks up the bottle, 'Want some more?'

'No thanks.'

There's not much left in the bottle, but Nelson pours it all in his glass.

'They admitted it?'

'Well, they said that they hadn't slept together, but that's irrelevant.'

Is it? thinks Ruth. It doesn't sound very irrelevant to her. But she says nothing.

'They've been seeing each other for over a year. Christ, what a mug I've been. When you think how guilty I've felt about you and me.'

Nelson is a great one for guilt, Ruth knows, but she doesn't quite like how he puts this.

'I've felt guilty too,' she says defensively.

'Well, we needn't have worried. We could have been having an affair all this time.'

'Could we?' says Ruth.

They stare at each other. Ruth feels as if the very air is charged, as if she can see the little pluses and minuses hovering around them.

'Haven't you sometimes wanted to?' says Nelson.

'Yes,' says Ruth. 'Yes, I have.'

Nelson reaches out and touches her cheek. She can see his eyelashes, the black stubble on his chin.

'Don't, Nelson.'

'Why not?'

'Because you're just doing it because you're angry with Michelle. You need to talk to her. She hasn't had an affair if they didn't sleep together. A few meetings at the gym doesn't constitute an affair.'

'What did you say?'

The change in his tone is almost frightening. For a second he looks like a stranger.

'I said . . . I said they weren't really having an affair if they . . .'

'You said "a few meetings at the gym". How did you know they met at the gym?'

'I didn't . . .'

'Yes, you did. You knew.'

Nelson stands up. He looks very big and very threatening. Flint jumps back on the sofa as if to protect Ruth.

'I didn't know,' she says.

'You're lying, Ruth.'

Ruth stands up too, angry now. 'OK. I saw them together at the gym once. I didn't know that they were seeing each other, though. Michelle was hardly likely to confide in me, was she?'

'Why didn't you tell me?'

'Tell you what? That your wife was seen at the gym with another man? You would have thought I was mad.'

Nelson looks as if he is about to say something. Then he looks as if he's going to come towards her. Then, with a gesture as if he's pushing something away, he makes for the door.

'Where are you going?'

'I'm going to the bloody gym,' says Nelson. 'What do you think?'

And he's gone, slamming the door behind him.

20

Nelson fully intends to drive round all night. When he gets back into the car there are three messages on his phone from Michelle, but he ignores them. He heads for the sea, parking by the sand dunes at Hunstanton. He gets out of the car and takes the path to the beach. The sand is silver in the moonlight and the sea is breaking in smooth black waves. He thinks of the wooden henge with the body buried in its circle, the case where he first met Ruth. He thinks of their night together, the night Katie was conceived. It's true that Michelle has had much to forgive, because, since that night, Ruth has barely been out of his thoughts. The salt wind stings his face. He has always hated the Norfolk landscape, but tonight the sea and the sky are strangely suited to his mood, the long unforgiving miles of sand, the endless tide of water.

He walks back to Michelle's car. There's a message from Ruth too, but he doesn't read it. He heads for home because, really, where else is he going to go?

Michelle is waiting up for him. She is in her dressing gown again, her hair tied back. She should look less glamorous than normal, but, to Nelson, she looks as beautiful as ever. More so, perhaps, because he is the only person who sees her like this, her eyelashes pale, her lips slightly chapped.

'Where have you been, Harry? I've been really worried.'

'I was working late. A woman was killed yesterday, remember?'

'I'm not likely to forget, am I, considering it was nearly me?'

Nelson looks at the marks around her neck. They are greenish-yellow now. The people at the salon must think he's a wife beater.

'How are you feeling?' he asks.

'All right. Harry, we have to talk.'

'That's what Tim said to me. Stupid bastard.'

Nelson goes to the drinks cabinet and pours himself a whisky. 'Do you want one?' he asks grudgingly.

'No thank you.' From the cup beside her Nelson can see that his wife has been drinking one of her disgusting herbal teas. She's never been a big drinker.

'Harry, have you been with Ruth?'

The acuteness of her guess takes him by surprise. 'Why would I go there?' he blusters.

'I thought you'd go to her. That you'd think it would be OK to be with her now.'

Nelson looks at her curiously. 'Is that what you think I want?'

'Sometimes.'

'Is that why you had an affair with Tim?' He raises a hand. 'OK. I know you didn't sleep with him. But you were seeing him behind my back.'

Michelle fiddles with the end of her ponytail. 'Partly. Partly just to prove that someone still found me attractive. It's hard, you preferring someone like Ruth to me.'

'I don't prefer her.'

'Really?' Michelle looks at him squarely. 'Really?'

'Really. Do you prefer Tim to me?'

'No!' Her response is so immediate, so genuine, that he is touched. 'You're the only man I've ever loved.'

He makes a move towards her and she flings herself, weeping, into his arms. After a few moments he bends his head to kiss her. There are tears in his eyes too.

In the morning, he wakes before the alarm. He lies there for a few moments, letting the events of yesterday run through his mind. He can't help feeling that he's messed things up in some subtle but catastrophic way. Yesterday he had felt betrayed by Michelle, and, at the same time, drawn to Ruth. He hadn't gone round to Ruth's house determined to carry on their affair, but, all the same, he can't deny that the thought hadn't been far from his mind. But also, Ruth's little house had suddenly seemed a place of refuge, a sanctuary if you like. Ruth had turned him away, that's what it feels like anyway. And now he feels betrayed by Ruth, but — by some strange marital alchemy — reunited with Michelle. Last night they had made love and he knows that Michelle thinks that this has set the seal on their reconciliation. Soon Tim will be gone and he and Michelle can continue to mend their marriage, adjusting to life without the girls, enjoying their mid-life years. So why isn't he feeling happier?

Enough soul-searching, he tells himself. He doesn't like talking about emotions, not even to himself. There's a murderer to catch. Tanya's CCTV footage has upgraded Stanley Greenway from a 'person of interest' to a suspect with a number in the case files. But, all the same, he didn't think there was enough to arrest the man. The footage didn't place Greenway at the Slipper Chapel at the time of the murder, though it did leave him with some questions to answer about his movements that night. He'd let Stanley Greenway go back to the Sanctuary. 'After all,' he told Clough, 'he's as safe there as anywhere.' But, if Greenway's DNA is found anywhere on Chloe or Paula's clothing, then Nelson will be round at the Sanctuary gates with an arrest warrant faster than you can say 'Innocent until proven guilty'.

So, his first job today is to hassle the lab about the DNA results. It's possible to get them back in twenty-four hours, though this is expensive and, therefore, frowned upon by Whitcliffe. He also wants to go back to the Slipper Chapel with a photograph of Stanley Greenway. They need to go through all the witness reports from Walsingham too. He looks at the clock. Six o'clock. Time to get going. He'll have to take Michelle's car again, but hassling the garage will also be on his list. He gets out of bed, careful not to wake Michelle, and heads for the shower.

He's at work by seven. King's Lynn is deserted, mist rising up from the quay, everything grey and dreamlike. On the steps outside the police station there's a rough sleeper who greets him with an ironical, 'Morning, Inspector Morse.'

'Didn't I give you money to go to a shelter last time?'

'Yes, you did, God bless you.'

'Well, go and get yourself some breakfast.' Nelson slips the man a fiver and watches him hurry off down the road throwing 'God bless yous' over his shoulder. He's pretty sure that the breakfast will be entirely liquid.

Inside, there's only the night sergeant yawning over a cup-a-soup.

'Morning, Shane.'

'Morning, sir. You're early today.'

'Lots to do.' Nelson is conscious of his mood lightening the further he gets into the building. He climbs the stairs two at a time, makes himself a cup of instant coffee and sits at a computer in the incident room to go through the previous day's reports.

Tim comes in at eight, carrying his sports bag. He says good morning to Nelson, who nods at him.

'Is this all the CCTV we have? The abbey grounds and the gift shop?'

'Yes. There's a camera outside the farm shop, but it doesn't work.'

'Anything from the door-to-door?'

'I'm going to type up the reports now. One possible sighting. A woman walking her dog saw a man walking along beside the church at midnight. Said he looked furtive.'

'Description?'

'Not a very good one. But we could show her pictures of Stanley Greenway. Or have an identity parade. The CPS loves identity parades.'

Nelson knows that this is true. He doesn't want to grant Tim the satisfaction of agreeing, though.

'What are you going to do now?'

'It's Chloe Jenkins' funeral. You said that I should go. To represent the force.' Tim holds up his bag. 'I'm going to change as soon as I've done the reports.'

'All right,' says Nelson grudgingly. 'Pick up anything you can from the family. This case isn't over yet.'

'It'll be tough for them, hearing about Paula being killed.'

'Yes, it's tough,' says Nelson. 'And we haven't got time to chat about it. There's a team meeting at nine.' He can't help feeling aggrieved that Tim is in before Clough.

Clough arrives at eight-thirty, still chewing his McDonald's breakfast. Tanya is already making a health-food smoothie in the tiny kitchen. She has brought in her own blender and everything.

'Much better for you than all those carbs,' she says. 'Kale's a super-food.'

'Count me out,' says Clough, chucking the greasy wrappers in the bin.

'If you've finished chatting about food,' says Nelson, who is having his fifth cup of coffee, 'I'd like to have a meeting.'

'Do you want a smoothie?' asks Tanya, waving a container of sludge-green liquid.

'No, you're all right,' says Nelson. 'What is it?' This last to Tom Henty, the desk sergeant, who has appeared in the doorway.

'Someone to see you, boss. He says it's important.'

'Who is it?'

'He's a priest. I think I remember him from the children's home case.'

Nelson's first thought is that Father Hennessey looks as bad as he does. The priest is still an intimidating presence, with his rugby player's shoulders and boxer's nose, but his eyes are shadowed and he looks as if he hasn't slept. He puts his hat on the floor and accepts a cup of coffee.

'I'm giving up coffee for Lent,' he says. 'Better make the most of it.'

'This stuff's enough to make you give up coffee for life,' says Nelson. 'I should know. I've drunk about a gallon of it.'

Father Hennessey smiles and drinks his coffee in silence for a few minutes. Just as Nelson is wondering if the priest is ever going to speak, if he's waiting for Nelson to make the first move ('Bless me, Father, for I have sinned'), Hennessey says, 'Fiona . . . Doctor McAllister . . . tells me that you called Stanley Greenway in for questioning.'

'I can't discuss ongoing investigations,' says Nelson.

'But that much is common knowledge.'

'All right,' says Nelson, 'he did come into the station yesterday.'

'The thing is,' says Hennessey and, uncharacteristically, he looks away as he speaks, 'I can give him an alibi for Wednesday night.'

'Go on.'

'I left the Sanctuary at about eleven o'clock on Wednesday,' says Hennessey, speaking rather fast. 'It was a lovely clear night so I thought I'd walk back across the fields to

Walsingham. When I was still in the Sanctuary grounds, though, I saw a man lying on the ground. My first thought was that he might be hurt but, when I went over, I saw that it was Stanley. He was just lying there, staring up at the stars. I asked if he was all right and he said that he just liked lying there, thinking. It helped him "make sense of things", he said. He wasn't in distress of any kind, so I left him.'

'You didn't think to tell Doctor McAllister?'

'No. I knew that, strictly speaking, patients weren't allowed out at night, but Stanley seemed so peaceful. Sometimes we all need a bit of silence, a bit of time with God.'

'What did you do after you saw Stanley?'

'I walked back to Walsingham. I wanted to go and pray in the church, but it was locked, so I went back to my pilgrim house.'

The alibi isn't perfect. Paula was probably killed some time in the early hours of Thursday morning and it wouldn't have been impossible for Stanley to have stopped star-gazing, walked to Walsingham, and killed her. Not impossible but, Nelson has to admit, not that probable either. He looks curiously at the priest.

'I have to ask you, Father, what you were doing at the Sanctuary so late at night?'

He expects Hennessey to come up with some line about visiting the sick, but, to his surprise, the priest runs a hand through his white hair and utters something very like a groan. When he speaks, his words are the very last thing that Nelson expects. 'Celibacy,' says Father Hennessey, 'is very hard. A real sacrifice. Especially for a young man.'

'It must be,' says Nelson.

'When I was a young priest I was sent to a parish in Glasgow. I loved the place. It's a great city.'

Father Hennessey loves cities, Nelson remembers. It's the countryside he can't stand. He waits for the priest to continue.

'I loved Glasgow,' says Hennessey, 'but the work was hard, working in the tenements amongst the very poorest of the poor. This was the sixties. Exciting times, but lots of gang violence, lots of suffering.'

Nelson says nothing. He assumes that Father Hennessey has not come here to give him a lecture on Scotland in the swinging sixties.

After a few minutes, Hennessey says, speaking very fast now, 'None of that is any excuse, of course. I fell prey to temptation. I had an affair. It sounds terrible, put like that. I fell in love. But I loved God too. What matters is I broke my vows. I slept with a young woman and she became pregnant. I offered to leave the priesthood and marry her, but she said no. She was very strong, far stronger than me. She knew that I had a vocation and that I'd be miserable if I didn't fulfil it. So we parted. She had the child and eventually married someone else. I moved down to Norfolk and started the children's home, trying to give those children a good life even if I couldn't acknowledge my own.'

'That's a sad story,' says Nelson, 'but how is it relevant here?'

'My child, my daughter, eventually found out that I was her father. Her mother told her on her deathbed. And she got in contact.'

Nelson thinks he can guess the rest, but he asks, 'And your daughter is?'

'Fiona. Doctor Fiona McAllister. She's a wonderful woman, very like her mother. I've been getting to know her, spending time at the Sanctuary.'

Nelson remembers Jean saying that Fiona was an atheist. He supposes that it's enough to make you an atheist, having a Catholic priest as a father. But, then again, he thinks that Fiona is probably more like Father Hennessey than she realises. She has inherited his crusading zeal, for one thing.

'I understand that this might come out in the course of your investigation,' says Father Hennessey, 'but I'll leave that to your discretion.'

'I'll try to keep your relationship with Doctor McAllister out of it,' says Nelson. He doesn't really see why the priest should suffer for his former mistake. Hennessey is still a principled man who has done a lot of good in the world. And, if he were a C of E priest, he could have had any amount of children. Larry Westmondham has four, he seems to remember.

'Thank you, Harry,' says Father Hennessey. 'You're a good man.'

'I'm not a good man,' says Nelson. 'I do try to be a good policeman, though.'

'You're a better man than you think,' says Father Hennessey, 'and you're a better father than I am. At least you're involved in your daughter's life.'

So he does know about Katie.

21

Ruth wakes up knowing that she's worried about something. Is it Kate? Always her first thought. She runs through her list of Kate worries: illness, developmental delay, friendship problems at school. But no. Kate had seemed in rude health yesterday, her teacher says she's the best reader in the class, and she seems extremely popular, her book bag always full of invitations to parties and play dates. Ruth had friends at school, but she was never one of those children who is effortlessly top dog, the arbiter of playground fashions, the one everyone fights to sit next to at lunchtime. It seems amazing to her that she has given birth to one of those alpha pupils. So it isn't Kate. Is it work, her parents, the state of the world? No — as she rises from sleep it all becomes clear. It's Nelson.

What actually happened last night? Ruth ponders this, and other Nelson-related matters, as she showers and dresses, wakes Kate and supervises her washing and dressing. 'I need white socks with frills today,' says Kate informatively. 'It's too cold,' says Ruth, 'you should wear your woolly tights.' 'It's white socks with frills day,' counters Kate. 'Who says so?

Mrs Mannion?' asks Ruth. Kate narrows her eyes, wondering how far she can go with this — 'I expect Mrs Mannion thinks it's a good idea.' Ruth lays out the tights.

Making breakfast, Ruth wonders whether she should ring Nelson, just to clear the air. She dismisses this at once. What is there to say anyway? Nelson came over to tell her that his wife was having an affair, Ruth had suggested that he talk to Michelle about it and Nelson had stormed out in a temper. But that's without the subtext, without the moment when Nelson had touched her cheek, had leant towards her, the moment when she knew that he was going to kiss her. Why had she pulled away? Why had she wanted to make sure that this — this thing that she had wanted for so long — wasn't just a reaction to Michelle and Tim, but something that Nelson actually wanted too? She had spoken up, like an idiot, and in doing so had given herself away.

She makes breakfast for herself, Kate and Flint. Flint is the only one who eats heartily. Kate is a picky eater in the morning, and Ruth doesn't feel hungry. Hooray. At this rate she'll be thin, albeit with a broken heart. Is her heart broken? She thinks about it as she cuts Kate's lunchtime sandwiches into triangles (squares are unacceptable). Her heart isn't broken but only because she has immunised herself against this eventuality, building herself up with little doses of heartbreak every now and again. Every time that Nelson goes home to his wife, every time he says 'we' and means him and Michelle, every time he talks about their shared past, every Mother's Day, every birthday, every Christmas. So she isn't in pieces. She just feels numb and rather scared, terrified that the fragile relationship she and Nelson have built since Kate's birth might be shattered. That can't happen. She owes it to Kate to keep on civil terms with her father. She adds an apple to Kate's lunchbox, hoping that she won't notice that it's green instead of the more socially acceptable red.

As she drives over the marshes (silver-grey with frost this morning) Ruth makes a decision of sorts. She has a morning without lectures; she'll go to King's Lynn Museum and look up the Walsingham digs from 1961 and 2011. There might be something there that links to Hilary's letters. And, if she finds anything, then she'll have to steel herself to ring Nelson and tell him about her discovery. After all, the letter-writer might be the person who killed Chloe and Paula. She thinks of Paula's family. Hilary said that she had a husband and son. What must they be feeling this morning? How Paula would love the chance to be arguing about woolly tights (or the male school uniform equivalent). Ruth really must count her blessings.

Hilary is going home today. She has asked Ruth to meet her at the Anglican shrine at five to say goodbye. Ruth wanted to find an excuse (she never wants to go to Walsingham again), but knows that's only cowardice. She owes it to Hilary to meet. After all, they might never see each other again. All the same, the thought of the encounter makes a morning in the museum seem even more appealing.

At the school she zips into a parking space made available by some monster people carrier. As she walks Kate to the gate she sees several little girls wearing white frilly socks, their legs blue with cold.

*

Tim gets caught in a hold-up on the M25 and so only just makes it to the crematorium on time. It's a plain room, aggressively tasteful, with bleached wood and lavender-painted walls. Tim finds himself feeling nostalgic for St Simeon's with its stained glass and high altar, even for the clashing primary colours of his mother's church. But, unlike St Simeon's, this place is full to bursting. Tim has to stand at the back, next to a group of mourners who could have stepped from the *Vogue* fashion pages ('Funeral Chic Special'). Tim has attended a few funerals, both as a policeman and his mother's son, and remembers the congregations consisting mainly of old people, some clearly just looking forward to the food afterwards. But today the crowd is overwhelmingly young and beautiful. He can't see Chloe's family, but assumes that they are at the front of the room. A burst of recorded music, and people start to stand up. The girl next to Tim is crying so hard that she looks about to collapse. 'Are you all right?' he whispers. A singularly stupid question.

The coffin is carried in, a wreath of white roses on top. And following behind are Chloe's family. Julie, in a smart black dress, leaning heavily on Alan. And, behind them, a beautiful blonde woman who can only be Lauren, Chloe's sister. She is accompanied by a handsome young man with a designer goatee. Is this Thom Novak or another male relative, a cousin perhaps? An elderly couple complete the family party. Chloe's grandparents, Tim assumes. What a terrible thing it must be to outlive your granddaughter.

The service is brief, ecumenical and — to Tim — heartbreaking in its lack of certainty. Chloe was a beautiful young woman, taken too soon, who is now in some hazy location 'with the angels'. Lauren takes the pulpit to say that Chloe was the best little sister anyone could have had. A schoolfriend (Kelly or Kylie, Tim doesn't quite catch the name) remembers the fun they used to have. 'Chloe was the best friend ever. She'd do anything for anyone.' Isn't that what Alan had said, with rather more sinister overtones? *Chloe always found it hard to say no.* But Chloe wasn't killed by drink or drugs, she was murdered. The manner of her death is never mentioned, and Tim doesn't blame the family for that. This is a time for remembering Chloe in life. By the end, when Robbie Williams' 'Angels' fills the room, there's not a dry eye in the place.

As the music swells and the sobs abound, the curtains open and Chloe's coffin is borne smoothly away. What a horrific moment this is, thinks Tim, and nothing Robbie Williams can say about loving angels instead is going to change that. Chloe was alive and now she's dead. Soon, all her parents will have of their daughter is an urn full of ashes.

Robbie has finished and something classical is playing as the congregation files out, by a back door this time. Tim is one of the last to leave and he finds Alan, Julie and Lauren standing in a sea of flowers still shaking hands and managing to smile.

They don't recognise him at first.

'Detective Sergeant Tim Heathfield from King's Lynn CID,' says Tim. 'The whole team send their condolences. We're all thinking of you today.' This isn't perhaps strictly true but the team will be doing the next best thing; trying to find Chloe's killer.

'It's so good of you to come, Sergeant Heathfield,' says Julie.

'Tim, please. I wanted to pay my respects.'

'That other girl who was killed yesterday,' says Alan. 'Do you think it's the same person?'

'We're not jumping to any conclusions,' says Tim, 'but there are similarities, yes.'

'She even looked a bit like Chloe, we thought,' says Julie. 'Poor woman. We feel for her family, we really do.'

'I know you do,' says Tim, thinking that the Jenkins family are really the only people who know what today will be like for the Moncrieffs. Today, tomorrow and all the days afterwards.

'There are some refreshments at the golf club,' says Julie. 'We hope you'll join us.'

'I ought to get back to work.'

'Just for a cup of tea. Before you have to drive back. It's a long way.'

'That would be very kind.'

But Tim isn't the only person making the drive back to Norfolk. In the car park he sees Fiona McAllister getting into a smart Range Rover. Stanley and Jean are in the back seat.

King's Lynn Museum is a modern state-of-the-art establishment, brimming with the best of old and new. The timbers from the henge are there, and Ruth often visits them for old time's sake, wondering what Cathbad and the other druids who complained about their removal would think about this new chapter in the life of these ancient oaks. But today Ruth is far from the glass cabinets and interactive displays. She is in the basement, going through the archaeological finds from Walsingham. It always gives her a strange feeling to be in these subterranean rooms, surrounded by hundreds of labelled boxes. How many treasures are here, identified and catalogued, but hidden from sight? She knows that there's not room to display everything but, even so, she sometimes wonders if it wouldn't be better to leave these objects in the ground — part of the natural world, as Cathbad would say — instead of bagging them up in acid-free paper, putting them in a box and forgetting all about them.

The Walsingham finds are conveniently marked WS. As Phil said, the bronze Mercury and some of the more interesting pieces are on display in the museum, but there's plenty here: some flint tools and axe-heads, a Bronze Age knife, pieces of quern-stones, fragments of pottery, a few Late Saxon coins and a rather interesting Viking buckle. But it's the more recent finds that she's interested in, the ones relating to the medieval shrine. She finds the ampullae and the copper alloy reliquary thought to be meant for a fragment of the True Cross, plus a medieval leather boot (preserved because it was apparently found in a sewer). Most of these finds come from the 1961 dig which excavated the remains of the original holy house. But there are some objects from the dig Ruth attended a few years ago which concentrated on land just outside Walsingham, on the way to the Slipper Chapel, in fact. At the time, she remembers that the team had been disappointed, a week's digging, and all they had found were a few pieces of pottery, impossibly broken up by ploughing. There had been some flints too and a few coins, nothing that justified further excavation. She looks down the list now:

WS1025 Fragment of Roman pot
WS1026 Fragment of Roman pot
WS1027 Flint implement
WS1028 Coin, Roman: 43–409 AD
WS1029 Coin, Roman: 43–409 AD
WS1030 Lead ampulla with scallop shell design
WS1031 Medieval gilt, possibly from horse harness
WS1032 Fragment from neck of hand-blown glass phial

The scallop shell design is quite interesting. The scallop shell is the symbol of pilgrimage; Ruth seems to remember that it comes from Santiago or Saint James. She went to Santiago de Compostela with Shona once, and there had been scallop shells everywhere, including (Ruth had been pleased to see) on their dinner plates. Coquilles St Jacques, one of the great pleasures of earthly life. She and Shona had travelled by bus, but Ruth remembers seeing pilgrims, dusty and sunburnt, staggering along by the side of the road with their backpacks and staffs. At each stage you had to have the scallop shell stamped in your passport, and then you got a free meal at the end of the pilgrimage. Ruth wonders whether the same system applied in medieval times.

She looks at the last item on the list. *WS1031 Fragment from neck of hand-blown glass phial.* There's no picture, but the notes describe it as 'Early Medieval, possibly mid-to-late

12th century'. With some difficulty, she locates the correct box. She finds the pieces of Roman pottery and the lead ampulla and the horse harness, but, although she looks several times, there's no sign of the piece of hand-blown glass. It's not unknown for objects to go missing — perhaps taken for display elsewhere — but why would anyone want to show a broken piece of old glass? Ruth stares at the sheet of grid-references, troubled by a memory that's buried in some forgotten storeroom of her brain.

The golf club has put on quite a spread. Tim accepts a cup of tea and a biscuit. He looks around at the room, which is now making the kind of upper-class roar more suited to a cocktail party. Still, people have to unwind somehow after the stress of the funeral. The whole thing has made him want to write a will specifying that he wants to be buried at sea with no mourners present. Planning her own funeral is one of Tim's mother's favourite pastimes. Recurring themes include a horse-drawn hearse (with plumes), a gospel choir and internment in a proper grave with a proper headstone. 'A cross or an angel. Or one of those books like the Bible. White marble.' 'Where are we going to get the money for all this?' Rick, Tim's eldest brother, had asked after the last such conversation. 'Save it,' their mother had said darkly. 'Go without.'

Who would attend *his* funeral? thinks Tim, standing on the outskirts of the room, drinking his tea. He hopes for her sake that he will outlive his mother. His brothers, presuming they are both out of prison at the time? His sisters? His nephews and nieces? Michelle won't be there because, when this case is over, he will have to go away and never see her again. To his horror, he feels tears pricking behind his eyes.

'Detective Heathfield?' Tim puts the cup down and blinks rapidly. It's Lauren and the goatee man. He knows from their faces that they saw the tears and were touched by them. He feels oddly guilty about this.

'I'm Lauren, Chloe's sister. This is my boyfriend, Jake.'

So it's not Thom Novak. Where is Chloe's mysterious boyfriend today?

'You spoke really well,' says Tim. 'That must have been difficult to do.'

'I thought someone from the family should say something,' says Lauren. 'Mum and Dad couldn't have managed it.'

'How are they doing?' asks Tim.

'All right. Mum threw herself into arranging the funeral. I think it will hit her afterwards. Dad's been in pieces, though. I've never seen him cry before, but now he can't stop.'

It's terrible when a man like Alan Jenkins finally gives in to grief. Tim has seen it before. He asks if the family are getting counselling.

'Mum and Dad have seen someone. Mum said she was really good.'

'Maybe you should see her too,' suggests Tim gently.

'That's what I said,' says Jake.

'Maybe.' Lauren twists a strand of hair in a way that reminds him agonisingly of Michelle. 'Can I ask you something, Sergeant Heathfield?'

'Do call me Tim. Yes, of course.'

'Those people that were here from the Sanctuary. The old man. Someone told me that he was a suspect.'

There's no sign of Fiona, Stanley and Jean at the wake. They must have driven straight back to Norfolk. A good move, thinks Tim. He wonders who could have told Lauren that Stanley is a suspect.

'We've interviewed Mr Greenway,' he says carefully. 'But no charges have been brought.'

'If you've interviewed him,' says Lauren, 'then he must be a suspect.'

'I can't really say,' says Tim. 'I'm sorry.'

'I suspect him,' says Jake. 'He looks the type.'

That's the trouble, thinks Tim. Stanley Greenway *does* look the type. The trouble is that there isn't really a type. Tim has met charming, respectable murderers, people who wouldn't look out of place at a Surrey golf club. It would help a lot if they were all seedy-looking loners.

As soon as he can, he asks about Thom Novak.

'Oh, Thom,' says Lauren, sounding half-affectionate, half exasperated. 'Goodness knows where he is.'

'What do you mean?'

'Oh, he checked out of the clinic in Switzerland two days ago. No one has any idea where he is now.'

Ruth knows that something is up as soon as she gets to the Archaeology department corridor. As she stands by her door, trying to dig her keycard out of her organiser handbag, Zita, the department secretary, pokes her head out from Phil's office.

'Here she is.'

Phil himself emerges. 'Ah Ruth, there you are.' As usual, he makes Ruth feel as if she's late, although, as she has no lectures or tutorials that morning, her time is her own.

'Hi, Phil.'

'Ruth, there was a man asking for you.'

His words take Ruth back to another day. The day, almost seven years ago, when she arrived at work to find a strange man waiting for her. Nelson, wanting her help in dating bones found on the Saltmarsh. She realises that Phil is still talking to her.

'A man?' she repeats.

'No, not a man,' says Zita, appearing at Phil's side. 'A priest.'

'He's waiting in the canteen,' says Phil.

As Ruth only knows one priest (one male priest, that is) she's not that surprised to find Father Hennessey waiting for her at one of the long tables, a cappuccino in front of him.

'Hallo, Ruth. Sorry to call in on you like this.'

'That's OK.'

'Are you going to get yourself a drink? This coffee's really very good. It's truly terrible, the stuff they serve at the police station.'

'I know.' Ruth has had her own experience of Nelson's coffee. She often wonders if it's a way of torturing suspects until they confess. In contrast, the coffee at the university is excellent. Ruth gets herself an espresso. She thinks that she might need the energy. She has a feeling that, like the visit from Nelson all those years ago, this conversation is going to complicate her life.

They sit opposite each other. It's nearly lunchtime and the canteen is filling up, but the undergraduates give them a wide berth. Perhaps it's the clerical collar.

'Ruth, I've just been to see Nelson.'

'Oh?' That's the best she can do.

'I had a story to tell him and I'd like, if I may, to tell the same story to you.'

He tells her about Glasgow, the tenements, the deathbed confession, Fiona McAllister. Ruth listens in silence.

'Last night, after I left the Sanctuary, I walked back to Walsingham. I think you saw me outside St Simeon's. I recognised your car going past.'

'Yes. I was dropping off my friend Hilary.'

'I heard what happened to that poor girl. I'm so sorry.'

'She wasn't a girl,' says Ruth, suddenly irritated. 'She was a woman. And a priest.'

'I know. I'm sorry.'

'Why did you come here and tell me all this?'

'I thought that seeing me might have raised some questions in your mind. I wanted to tell you the truth.'

'What if I tell other people?'

'You won't, I'm sure. Besides I'm going to make a clean breast of it to my bishop. That's one of the things I have decided on this trip.'

'I won't tell anyone.'

'Thank you, Ruth.'

Ruth looks at the priest, one of the few people she had believed to be genuinely good and incorruptible. He looks the same: grey hair, broken nose, bright blue eyes. Who knows what secrets people are hiding? The thought makes her feel afraid, as if the brightly lit canteen has been suddenly plunged into darkness.

'It's been a strange time,' says Father Hennessey, stirring the remains of his coffee. 'It's been wonderful to get to know Fiona, but such terrible things have happened. Fiona was so upset about that young girl . . . woman . . . Chloe. And now this other death. Places like Walsingham can be dangerous.'

'What do you mean by that?'

'Pilgrimages can be very fulfilling, spiritually fulfilling, I mean. This trip has been a pilgrimage for me too. But, by their very nature, pilgrimages make people think about the past. And that can be dangerous.'

'Don't people go on pilgrimage to ask for forgiveness?'

'That's true. But forgiveness is a powerful thing.'

After Father Hennessey has gone, sweeping through the undergraduates like Gandalf on a visit to Hobbiton, Ruth wonders whether that was what the priest was doing today. Asking forgiveness, or at least understanding, from her and Nelson. Why he should want her forgiveness she doesn't know, but she gives it anyway. Fathering a child doesn't seem like such a terrible sin. She wonders what Nelson thought and whether he made his own confession in return. He was raised a Catholic, after all.

'Hallo, Ruth.'

She's not really surprised to see Phil and Shona bearing down on her. Phil always wants to know everything that happens in the department and it's not every day that one of his colleagues gets a visit from a priest complete with dog collar.

'So,' he says as soon as he sits down, 'who was the mysterious visitor?'

Ruth considers telling Phil that Father Hennessey is a long-lost uncle/serial killer/emissary from the Pope. Instead she says, 'I got to know him when we excavated that house in Norwich a few years ago. You remember, the one with the skeleton under the door. The foundation sacrifice.'

'I remember,' says Phil, losing interest slightly.

'Gosh, Ruth,' says Shona, 'you do live, don't you?'

Ruth agrees that she does. Shona starts to eat her salad and Ruth feels her mouth watering (though not for salad). She usually tries to avoid eating in front of Phil because he always has to make some comment about her menu choice. 'You do love your carbs, don't you, Ruth?'

There is something she wants to ask him, though.

'I was at the museum today,' she says, 'going through the Walsingham finds.'

'Oh, is this for your friend's dig?'

Ruth has almost forgotten the lie she told Phil at the start of Hilary's visit.

'Er, yes,' she says. 'Sort of. I wanted to ask you something. You know about old glass, don't you?'

'It's one of my areas of expertise,' says Phil modestly.

In fact Phil has a few of these rather dull specialisms. Ruth often suspects it's a way of getting maximum media attention. Looking for an expert in eighteenth-century lustreware? Phil Trent is your man. Even now he has his TV face on, head on one side, eyes crinkling encouragingly. Ruth shows him a copy of the print-out from the museum.

'This piece of glass. Could it be important, do you think? It's quite early for glassware in Britain, isn't it?'

'Not really. You sometimes get glass beads in Anglo-Saxon funerary contexts and glass was fairly common in the Roman era. Glass goblets have been found in Viking graves too. Post Roman occupation, glass-making went into decline, but it was still manufactured in monasteries using wood furnaces. They were banned eventually, because the process used too much timber. Then you get a post-medieval boom when they started using coal furnaces.'

'So this could be a rare piece?'

Phil shrugs. 'It could be Venetian. You got a lot of Venetian glassmakers coming over in the Middle Ages. Hard to tell without looking at it. But this sort of find is fairly common. The monks would have had glassware, or it could be from an apothecary or used to carry holy oil and what have you. Why are you asking?'

'I was looking through the Walsingham finds at the museum today. This one is missing.'

Phil shrugs again and takes a piece of cucumber from Shona's salad bowl. 'Things go missing all the time.'

'Not at the museum. They're very organised.'

'Why are you so interested? Is this to do with the police?'

'Oh no,' says Ruth. 'I was just curious, that's all.'

'Curiosity killed the cat,' says Phil. A singularly tactless thing to say to Ruth.

Apart from police tape over the entrance to the abbey, there's little sign that Walsingham has been the scene of a violent crime only forty-odd hours ago. The shops are still selling vestments and holy pictures; groups of pilgrims are still wandering up and down the high street taking pictures of the pump-house and the pub. Ruth sees a woman priest dressed in purple like a bishop, and a man with a long beard who looks like a Greek Patriarch. She also sees Clough sitting in his car outside St Simeon's Church eating a Crunchie bar. The car is unmarked, and Clough isn't in uniform so maybe he's undercover. Ruth is just wondering whether to approach when Clough leans out of the window and shouts, 'Hi, Ruth!' So much for the Secret Service.

'Hi, Dave.' Ruth crosses the road to talk to him. She's known Clough for years, one way and another, and is rather surprised how fond she is of him.

'Bad business, isn't it?' says Clough, nodding towards the church with the abbey behind it.

'Awful.'

'The boss said you knew her, the woman who died.'

'I didn't really know her, but I went out to dinner with her once. She was very nice.'

'That's what everyone says. Good-looking too.'

Ruth reflects that the death of someone attractive (Chloe Jenkins, Paula Moncrieff) is always considered borderline more tragic than the death of someone aesthetically displeasing. But there's no point saying this to Clough.

'Did you hear that Michelle was attacked too?' Clough is saying. 'Must have been the same bloke. She had a lucky escape.'

'I did hear, yes.'

'Lucky Tim and the boss were close by. Did you know that Tim has applied for a transfer?'

Ruth thinks it's best to pretend that she doesn't know this. She expresses surprise.

'Everyone's deserting me.' Clough sounds really aggrieved. 'First Judy, now Tim.'

'Judy'll be back.'

'So she says.' Clough's voice is gloomy. 'She'll probably bring the baby with her and insist on breastfeeding all over the office.'

That's the thing about Clough, thinks Ruth, as she says goodbye and follows the signs to the Anglican shrine. Just when he's being human, he says something that reminds you what a Neanderthal he can be. Except that the Neanderthals probably had a more enlightened attitude towards breastfeeding.

The Anglican shrine is round the corner from The Bull. Ruth almost walks straight past it because the front is modern and glass, with automatic doors. When she passes through the doors (which make a sinister swooshing sound) she finds herself in a rather charming garden. Brick paths take slow serpentine routes through the spring flowers and, apart from the occasional visitor sitting quietly on benches, the place is deserted. Along the path there are brick pillars inlaid with brightly coloured frescoes. Ruth peers at one, 'Jesus falls for the second time.' What are these called? Stations of the Cross, something like that. Underneath is a small sign saying 'Mother Mary, Pray For Us'. Ruth hurries on.

Hilary had said that she would meet her in the cafe, but instead Ruth finds her sitting on a bench near an outdoor altar covered with a sort of sail. They embrace awkwardly.

'I thought I'd wait for you here,' says Hilary. 'I couldn't cope with the cafe somehow.'

'It's nice here,' says Ruth, sitting beside Hilary on the bench. 'Peaceful.'

'Yes,' says Hilary. 'I really felt that I needed some time here before I left.'

'I'm so sorry about Paula,' says Ruth.

'It's horrible.' Hilary looks like she hasn't slept. Her hair is lank and her eyes deeply shadowed. Ruth remembers Hilary at the dinner on Wednesday night, sleek and attractive in her black top. She thinks of Paula too and feels again the shock at the finality of death. Two days ago Paula was sitting in the Briarfields bar, funny and animated, talking about her acting career, and now she isn't anywhere. She has gone. Completely, irrevocably. Except that Hilary, presumably, thinks that she's in heaven. Sometimes Ruth thinks that she'd do anything to share this belief.

'Her husband came to identify her body,' says Hilary. 'I thought he might come to St Catherine's, but he didn't.'

Ruth thinks that Paula's husband probably doesn't want to come within a million miles of Walsingham. What was it that Father Hennessey said? Places like Walsingham can be dangerous.

'The last two days have been terrible,' says Hilary. 'The police interviewing us, everyone crying. You'd think a group of priests would be able to cope better, that we'd be able to pray, to comfort each other, but everyone just seems stunned.'

'Surely that's natural,' says Ruth. 'You're only human after all.'

By mutual consent they start walking along one of the brick paths. The birds are singing and the air suddenly seems soft and springlike. They walk past a raised piece of ground with three crosses on it and more brick pillars with brightly coloured scenes of death and suffering.

'Are you going home tonight?' asks Ruth.

'Yes,' says Hilary. 'Inspector Nelson said we could go. He took all our names and addresses, though. He can be quite abrupt, can't he?'

'Sometimes,' says Ruth. 'He's got a lot on his mind at the moment.'

'The police don't seem to have any idea who did it,' says Hilary, idly crushing a piece of lemon-balm between her fingers. Ruth wonders if that's why her friend has requested this meeting, to pump her about the police investigation. She's come to the wrong place, if so.

'It's early days,' Ruth says, thinking what a meaningless phrase this is.

'Nelson asked me about the letters again. He can't really think that my letter-writer killed two women.'

'I don't know,' says Ruth. 'I really don't know what he thinks.'

'He says he's assigned me police protection. I told him that the police in Streatham have better things to do.'

'Well, be careful all the same,' says Ruth.

They stop by steps that lead to a courtyard with a fountain. A sign says sternly, 'Silence in the courtyard. People are praying.' Ruth feels that this is a message telling her not to go any further.

'Come and have a look at the church,' says Hilary. 'It's very ornate, very beautiful. They've got a replica of the holy house.'

'I'd better be going,' says Ruth. 'I need to collect Kate.'

Hilary seems to know not to push it. 'It's been good to see you again, Ruth,' she says. 'Despite everything. Do keep in touch, won't you?'

'I will,' says Ruth. It's an easy promise to make, after all.

'I'll be praying for you,' says Hilary. 'This Lent is going to be a very difficult time for all of us.'

'Thank you,' says Ruth, who feels that some response is called for.

Hilary smiles. 'You think it's all nonsense, I know. But I'll pray for you all the same.'

Somehow it sounds like a threat.

Later that evening, after Kate is in bed, Ruth makes a determined effort to dredge up the memory that's bothering her. She once saw a programme about memory that said you ought to see it as a house; everything's there, it's just that it's all folded into drawers, or shut up in cupboards, or (in Ruth's case) shoved under the sofa. Sitting at the table by the window she looks out over the blackness of the Saltmarsh and takes a trip through her memory house, which appears to be a cross between this cottage and her parents' semi in Eltham. The Walsingham dig, pottery, glass, Cathbad, St Simeon's, Clough, Nelson (Don't go there), Kate, Michael, Judy . . . She has a feeling that she's very near. Maybe some wine would help. She pours herself a glass and goes back to the window.

'She'll probably bring the baby with her and insist on breastfeeding all over the office.'

'You look like a Madonna.'

'The holy house was panelled in wood and contained a statue of the Virgin and a phial of her breast milk.'

And the letter-writer: *'You may have borne a child (O sacrilege that anyone calling themselves a priest should do so!), but you have not suckled from the Virgin's breast.'*

She thinks of the medieval glass. Is this what it was? A phial containing the Virgin Mary's breast milk? And, if so, why has it gone missing?

22

Ruth always knew that it would be a difficult conversation.

'So you think a bottle of breast milk has gone missing. And that's somehow relevant to the case?'

'A phial that may have contained something claiming to be the Virgin Mary's breast milk.'

'Oh, that makes all the difference.'

Ruth counts to ten; her usual practice with Nelson.

'The letter-writer refers to the "true treasure" of Walsingham. What if this is it? If you find out who took the glass you may find out who wrote the letters.'

'That easy, is it? How am I supposed to track down a bit of broken old glass?'

'I don't know. Check who was on the original dig, who had access to the museum. You're the detective.'

'Yes, Ruth.' Nelson is trying out his patient voice. 'I am.'

'Are you going to follow this up?'

'I'll put my special medieval-glass team on to it right away.'

Sod you, thinks Ruth. She hadn't wanted to ring Nelson. She'd wanted to let a few days go by after that awful evening at her house. But she had genuinely thought that she had uncovered something that might be relevant to the case. Now Nelson is making her feel stupid, as if she's an unworldly academic or — worse — an amateur detective. She wants to yell at him but she can't; she isn't his wife.

'See you around,' she says.

'It was good of you to call.' Nelson now sounds almost conciliatory. 'How are you doing? How's Katie?'

'We're both fine.'

'I'm taking Katie out at the weekend, remember?'

'I remember.'

'We thought we might take her to Redwings. She loves horses, doesn't she?'

Ruth notes the 'we'. 'Yes,' she says, 'she'd like that. See you on Saturday. Good luck with the case.'

'I'm going to need it,' says Nelson.

Nelson puts the phone down feeling rather ashamed of himself. Ruth was only trying to help, he shouldn't have been sarcastic to her. But, the truth is, deep down, he is still angry with Ruth. Why didn't she tell him that she had seen Michelle and Tim together at the gym? He brushes aside the thought that he would hardly have welcomed this information, or been very well disposed towards the informant. As it is, it feels as if Ruth and Michelle have both been deceiving him and, whereas Michelle is being particularly loving at the moment, Ruth remains cool and aloof, only ringing him with some ridiculous theory about the Virgin Mary's breast milk. He doesn't want to remember the moment when Ruth had looked at him in a way that wasn't cool and aloof. He doesn't like to think about what might have happened.

Nelson walks out into the incident room. Tanya is going through CCTV footage from Wednesday night. The screen is split into four. He can see the priory wall, a ruined archway and two sections of complete blackness.

'Fuller?'

'Yes, boss.' She turns round eagerly.

'Have we heard from the lab about Stanley Greenway's DNA?'

'Not yet.'

'Well, hassle them. I want it checked against DNA from Chloe's clothes and from Paula's. Where's Clough?'

'At the Sanctuary. You sent him.'

Clough is interviewing security staff. Apart from Father Hennessey's sighting in the field, Greenway has no alibi for the early hours of Thursday morning. Clough is talking to the night watchman and anyone else who may have been on duty at the time. Nelson knows it's unreasonable to be irritated that this is taking so long. It doesn't stop him, though.

'And Heathfield?'

'Talking to Interpol.'

The news of Thom Novak going AWOL has added an unwanted complication to the investigation. He checked out of the Swiss clinic two days ago, and no one has seen him since. 'We tried to stop him,' the staff had said. 'We could see that he was in a bad state. But he was free to leave when he pleased. There was nothing we could do.' 'Bloody Swiss,' Nelson had said when he heard that. 'Always so bloody neutral.' Tim (who, until a few days ago, Nelson would also have had down as one of life's neutrals) is liaising with Interpol in the search for the missing male model. It's not that he's a suspect exactly. Novak has an alibi for Chloe's murder and it's unlikely that he came to Norfolk and killed Paula on the spur of the moment just because she resembled his dead girlfriend. 'Unlikely,' Nelson reminded the team, 'but not impossible.' In any case, they need to find him.

'Have you got the witness statements from the conference delegates?' Nelson asks now.

'Yes.' Tanya brandishes a file.

'Give it here then.'

He sits opposite Tanya, under the map of Walsingham and the photographs of the two dead women, and reads through the printed witness statements. There were eight women present at the meal, including Ruth. By all accounts the meal was convivial and lasted a long time. Staff at Briar-fields confirm that five bottles of wine were consumed, as well as several liqueurs. The mood, they said, was 'lively, but good-humoured'. They were nice women, the waiting staff said, and left a generous tip. Ruth and Hilary left first, at about eleven-forty, and arrived at St Catherine's Lodge at mid-night. The other women called a taxi and got back around one. They had made coffee and chatted until about one-thirty. Then most of the women had gone to bed. Paula Moncrieff, Sydney Bowen and Freya Drew-Hayes had remained down-stairs. At about two o'clock Paula Moncrieff expressed her intention of going for a moonlight walk. 'I almost went with her,' said Sydney Bowen, 'but I was tired and went to bed.' The written statement does not convey the guilt and pain in Sydney's voice when she said these words. Nelson also has a statement from Robin Rainsford, who was woken by the housekeeper at approximately five-thirty a.m. He had dressed, gone downstairs and spoken to PC Linwood. Hilary Smithson was also there, making tea in the kitchen. Rainsford and Smithson had then accompanied PC Linwood into the abbey grounds, where they had found Paula's body. 'She was such a lovely woman,' said Rainsford, 'she had a difficult start in life, but that hadn't made her hard or bitter. She saw the best in everyone.' Her husband had said something similar. Nelson leafs through the file until he finds his notes on the interview with Giles Moncrieff.

'Paula had a terrible childhood really, she was in children's homes, with various foster parents, in and out of care. But it never made her bitter.'

'I'm going out,' Nelson tells Tanya.

'Where?' she asks, though it isn't strictly speaking her place to do so.

'Walsingham. I'm going to talk to Larry Westmondham.'

Nelson enjoys the drive to Walsingham. He has his Mercedes back and it's a joy to feel it purring through the narrow lanes rather than bouncing around like Michelle's car. He drives through the village. A couple of uniforms are standing by the entrance to the abbey, which is still sealed off. They'll have to open it soon. Nelson is getting hassle from the local bishop as well as the Norfolk Tourist Board. They'll want the abbey grounds open by Ash Wednesday, which is next week. Never let it be said that death got in the way of tourism.

He remembers Larry Westmondham's amusement at the idea that he might live in the grand Victorian vicarage by the church. As Nelson drives past the timbered cottages towards the modern estate on the edge of the village, he realises that he's entering a very different world. The garden of the Westmondhams' house is full of bicycles, punctured footballs and the remains of a rusting swing set. There are even a few chickens pecking dispiritedly behind a wire fence. The sign on the door says, helpfully, 'Ring here for the vicar', but the bell seems to be out of order. Nelson knocks loudly and, after a few minutes, the door is opened by a woman wearing the kind of apron Nelson has only seen in fifties' films. She has the face to go with it, round and cheerful, completely free from make-up. Her dark-blonde hair is pulled back into a ponytail.

'Is Larry — the Reverend Westmondham — in?'

'He's picking the girls up from school,' says the woman. 'He won't be long. Do you want to come in and wait?'

'Thank you,' says Nelson. The woman seems to expect that people will come to her door demanding to see her husband. She doesn't even ask for his name. Nelson gives it anyway and shows her his warrant card for good measure.

'Oh, is this about those poor women who were killed? Larry was so upset. We both were. To think of it happening here, in Walsingham.' She wipes her hands on her apron and holds out her hand. 'I'm Daisy. Larry's wife.'

'Pleased to meet you,' says Nelson.

'Come through to the kitchen. I'm just putting some scones in the oven.'

Scones? Oven? Has he really gone back fifty years in time? Michelle is a good cook, but he can't imagine her making scones in the middle of the afternoon. Don't all women work these days? Or, if they're not at work, they're out meeting their lovers at the gym.

In the kitchen is one reason why Daisy Westmondham is not out cracking the glass ceiling in the City or breaking the pain barrier at the gym. A large baby sits in a highchair. He's either worryingly pale or covered in flour.

'This is Samuel. He's always filthy, I'm afraid.'

'Hi, Samuel.' Nelson waves from a safe distance. The baby beams at him.

Daisy puts a baking tray in the oven. 'Can I get you a drink? Tea? Coffee?'

'Only if it's no trouble.'

'Oh no. I always make a pot when Larry comes home.' Of course she does. Other women would use teabags, but not Mrs Domestic Harmony 1952. Nelson is not at all surprised when Daisy gets out a large brown teapot complete with knitted tea cosy.

Nelson sits at the table opposite Samuel. After the emotional traumas of the last few days Daisy Westmondham's kitchen is a rather restful place to be. The radio is playing, not Radio 1 (Michelle's choice) or dull people talking on Radio 4 (Ruth), but something tuneful and undemanding. Daisy hums along as she puts out cups and saucers (cups and saucers, not mugs), and Samuel beats time with a spoon.

'It was so awful about Paula Moncrieff,' says Daisy, meas-
uring out tea leaves. 'Awful about the other girl too, but I'd
actually met Paula, which made it worse somehow.'

'Had you?' This is news to Nelson.

'Yes. I had all the delegates round for supper on their
first night in Walsingham. I always try to do that for all the
people who go on courses at St Catherine's. Nothing special,
just a big lasagne or shepherd's pie. Paula was lovely, really
chatty and friendly.'

'Everyone says what a nice person she was,' says Nelson.
His mind is still boggling at the sort of woman who thinks
that having eight people for supper (plus her family, presumably) is 'nothing special'.

'Did all the women priests come that evening?'

'Yes, and Robin too. They were a really nice bunch. Sometimes the delegates can be very serious. Women priests
especially. Somehow they seem to feel that they have to be
more . . . well, pious than the men. But this group were really
good fun. Paula had been an actress, you know. Freya had
been a teacher and Sydney used to work in a circus.'

'A circus?'

'Yes, she was an acrobat or something like that. Anyway,
they were all so interesting. We stayed talking until past midnight. Usually I'm in bed at ten, what with this one — ' she
nods at Samuel, who is now dreamily eating flour — 'keeping
me going all day.'

'How old are your other children?' asks Nelson.

'Becky's ten, Lizzie's eight and Victoria is six. They're all
at the local primary. It's walking distance, which is great. I

don't drive. I know it's ridiculous in a grown woman, but I've just never got round to it and I couldn't afford the lessons. Larry's always offering to teach me, but he's so busy.'

'Have you lived here long?' asks Nelson.

'Five years,' says Daisy. 'We lived in Croydon before this. It was a great parish, but we had a tiny flat with no garden. Not much fun with three kids. I was delighted when this came up. I've always wanted to live in the country. And this is where Larry's from. He was brought up in Houghton St Giles.'

'He must have been pleased to move back here.'

Daisy wrinkles her nose. 'Ish. The thing is, I think Larry felt that he was doing more good in an inner-city parish. Here it's all retired colonels and people who think that the church is their personal fiefdom. I mean St Simeon's is a beautiful old church, but people get furious if Larry tries to change anything. Even when he put in a hearing loop for the deaf. Half of them can't hear, but they're against anything that means drilling holes into the precious walls. And Walsingham's a funny place. I've got a friend, Janet — she's a historian — and she says that it has a dark atmosphere, something to do with a curse and the dissolution of the monasteries.'

'Do you believe that?'

'No. I mean, anywhere that's a centre for pilgrimage arouses really strong emotions. It's a beautiful place and I've met some lovely people. It's a wonderful place to grow up. Larry had a really happy childhood here.'

'Did you know Larry's mother, Doreen?'

'No.' Daisy looks genuinely regretful. 'She died just before I met Larry. He was still mourning her really. I wish I'd known her. She sounds like a wonderful woman. Larry and his brothers have all sorts of stories about her. That's her, on the noticeboard.'

She points to a cork board which is so covered with pictures, invitations, shopping lists and certificates saying 'Star Pupil: ten ace points for sitting quietly at story time' that it resembles one of those pieces of modern art collected by Juan, the co-owner of Michelle's salon. It takes Nelson a few moments to pick out a photograph of a smiling woman standing by a caravan with a surly-looking youth at her side.

'That's Doreen with Larry. They all used to go on holiday in that caravan. They had it specially adapted because Eddie, one of the long-term foster children, was in a wheelchair. You know she fostered over a hundred children?'

'I've heard.'

'I wish I could do something like that, but I find it hard to cope with four.'

'I'm not surprised. My wife and I found it hard to cope with two.'

She gestures at Samuel. 'This one was my present to myself. A boy after three girls. Now, I keep thinking, what about another baby to keep him company?'

Michelle had wanted another baby after Rebecca, Nelson remembered, but he had thought two children were enough. Well, now he has three. No wonder Michelle resented him for it. He's about to say something when there's a noise outside and Daisy's face lights up.

'In here, darlings.'

There is a lot of crashing in the hall and then three children and a dog burst into the room, followed by the Revd Larry Westmondham.

There is such a din of children shouting, the baby beating a tattoo on the tray of his highchair and the dog barking that it's a few moments before Larry registers Nelson's presence.

'Detective Chief Inspector. I'm sorry. I didn't see you there.'

'Don't worry. You've got your hands full.'

Daisy puts a cup of tea in front of her husband. 'Detective Inspector Nelson came to see you, Larry.'

'Do you want to see my picture?' asks one of the girls, the youngest, he thinks.

'Yes, please,' says Nelson.

'It's a friendly shark,' says the girl.

The picture shows a blue sea with what looks like a floating smile in it. The paper smells strongly of primary-school paint and brings back memories of Laura and Rebecca waving similar masterpieces at him.

'I like his teeth.'

'It's a lady shark.'

'Leave Inspector Nelson alone, Victoria,' says Daisy. 'He's here to talk to Daddy.'

'Are you to do with the church?' asks Victoria.

'No.'

'I didn't think you were,' she says, peeling away to play with the dog, a large excitable spaniel. One of the older girls has taken Samuel out of his highchair and there's a move towards the garden. Daisy puts a plate of scones in front of Nelson and Larry.

'I'll go out into the garden too,' she says, 'then you can talk in peace. Be careful, they're a bit hot.'

It's a few minutes before Nelson realises that she's talking about the scones.

Larry Westmondham drinks his tea with the abstracted air of one whose mind is far away from domestic minutiae, in inner-city Croydon, perhaps.

'Sorry to bother you at home,' says Nelson. 'I bet you don't get much time to yourself.'

'No,' says Larry, crumbling a scone into his saucer. 'That's the only thing about being a priest with a family. Your wife and children miss out really. There are hundreds of people out there who call you "Father" and your real kids come second a lot of the time. Sometimes I think there's something to be said for a celibate clergy.'

Nelson is glad that Daisy is not here to hear this endorsement of family life. He thinks of Giles Moncrieff going home to break the news to his son of his mother's death.

'Must be difficult for husbands of female clergy too.'

'Yes. I often think that. It's hard to share your spouse with a whole parish.'

Giles had said that Paula's parishioners had adored her. Had he found it hard to share her with them? It's a new line of thought.

'I actually wanted to talk to you about your mother,' says Nelson.

'Really?' Larry's eyebrows seem to rise into his bald head. 'Why?'

'Paula Moncrieff, the woman who died, she had been fostered. I just wondered — I know it's a long shot — if your mother had had a foster child called Paula?'

Larry's forehead wrinkles. 'I'm not sure. There were so many, and some only stayed a few weeks. They would know at the council, wouldn't they?'

'Yes. I'm going to look at the local authority records. I just thought it might be quicker to come to you. When I spoke to you in the church you said that one of your mother's foster children had become a vicar. I thought that might be Paula.'

'I heard that one of them was a vicar,' says Larry. 'I don't know who told me, but I assumed it would be a man.'

'Not a safe assumption these days.'

'No.' Larry looks at Nelson. 'Paula and the other women priests came here for a meal at the start of their course. You'd think that Paula would have mentioned it if she'd been fostered by Mum.'

'You would,' admits Nelson. 'But sometimes people don't like to talk about their childhood. Especially if it hasn't been very happy.'

'The other girl that died was looked after by Mum. Do you think that's the link then?'

'I don't know,' says Nelson. 'It's just a line of enquiry.'

Larry still looks troubled. He's about to speak when the back door opens and Victoria bursts in to demand that he plays football with them.

'We need someone who can actually kick the ball. Mum and Samuel are in goal.'

'I'm busy, sweetheart.'

'You've got a few minutes to play football, surely,' says Nelson. 'I'll join you. I once had a trial for Blackpool Juniors.'

'Oh,' says Larry vaguely. 'Have Blackpool got a football team?'

When Nelson gets back in his car, still out of breath (partly from the shock of Larry's remark) he puts in a request to Intel, asking for the names of all the children fostered by Doreen Westmondham. Could this really be the link between Chloe and Paula? That they had both been cared for by the kind-faced woman in Daisy's photograph? But, if that was the case, why was Michelle attacked? Was it simply because the killer had mistaken her for Paula? He's just about to ring the station when his phone buzzes. Clough.

'What is it?'

'We've got the DNA results. Stanley Greenway's DNA matches semen found on Chloe Jenkins' dressing gown.'

'Meet me at the Sanctuary,' says Nelson. 'We're going to bring him in.'

23

Fiona McAllister insists on accompanying Stanley Greenway to the police station.

'It's all right, Dr McAllister,' says Stanley, 'I'm sure this is all just routine.'

'I'll come anyway,' says Fiona grimly.

Nelson, looking at Fiona McAllister in the driving mirror, tries to see if he can see any resemblance between the doctor and Father Hennessey. On the surface they couldn't be less alike. Hennessey is heavily built, with strong, irregular features; Fiona McAllister is slim and attractive, radiating coolness and poise. But there is something there all the same: maybe it's just the crusading expression or the sense of certainty. Nelson knows that he must play this interview by the book.

'I want to make a statement,' says Fiona, 'stating that Stanley Greenway is on drugs which can cause paranoid delusions and blackouts.'

'You can make a statement at the station,' says Nelson.

'I've called my solicitor,' Fiona is saying now. 'She's meeting us there.'

'What's her name?'

'Khan. Nirupa Khan.' That figures. Nirupa Khan is one of the smartest lawyers around. What's more, she's no fan of the police.

Nelson drives round to the back entrance. Nirupa Khan is waiting at the front desk.

'Have you charged him with anything?' she says.

'No,' says Nelson. 'Mr Greenway is just here on a voluntary basis to answer some questions.'

'I'll sit in on the interview,' she says.

'Is that what you want?' Nelson asks Stanley.

Stanley looks confused. 'I strongly advise you to have Ms Khan with you,' cuts in Fiona.

'All right then. If you say so, Doctor McAllister.'

'It's going to be quite a party,' murmurs Clough as Stanley, Nelson, Nirupa and Fiona file into Interview Room One. Clough takes his seat beside Nelson as Nelson explains that this is an interview under caution and Greenway doesn't have to answer the questions but that anything he says may be taken as evidence. Greenway stares at him vacantly.

Nelson introduces himself and DS Clough for the tape. Then he says, 'Mr Greenway, what was the nature of your relationship with Chloe Jenkins?'

Nirupa stirs, but allows the question.

'We were friends,' says Stanley.

'Is that all?'

'We were fond of her, Jean and I. She was almost like a daughter to us.' Stanley is gaining in confidence now, sounding almost angry. 'She was such a sweet, gentle soul, very spiritual. She believed in angels. To think that someone could . . .' He dabs his eyes.

'Mr Greenway,' says Nelson, 'we have had forensic tests done on Chloe Jenkins' nightclothes, the clothes she was wearing when she was killed, and we found traces of your semen on them. How do you explain that?'

Nirupa Khan says, 'You don't have to answer, Stanley. Remember you can leave at any time.'

Nelson ignores her. 'Can you explain that, Stanley?'

Stanley stares at the ceiling. Eventually he says, in a gentle voice, as if he is explaining something to a child, 'I used to go into her room when she wasn't there and try on her clothes. I liked her dressing gown because it was big. It fitted me. I used to walk round in it. And sometimes I got excited.'

Nelson stares at him. 'You masturbated in her clothes?'

'If you want to put it like that, yes.'

'A perfectly reasonable answer,' says Nirupa. 'Now if I could have a few minutes with my client.'

'Jesus wept.' Nelson and Clough are having a hasty meeting in Nelson's office. Rather reluctantly, Nelson has asked Tim to join them. 'Can you believe it?'

'I can believe anything of him,' says Clough. 'He gives me the creeps.'

'The trouble is,' says Nelson, 'it is an explanation for his DNA being on Chloe's clothes. Being a creep doesn't make you a murderer.'

Clough looks unconvinced.

'Does he have an alibi for the night of Chloe's murder?' asks Tim.

'Says he was in bed at the Sanctuary but no alibi to confirm this. And, given his fondness for sneaking out at night, I think we could have a good go at breaking that down. We've got to be careful though. Nirupa Khan will be down on us like a ton of bricks if we ask anything approaching a leading question. Stanley's obviously quite vulnerable mentally too. That's why it's good that his doctor's here.'

'I think we'll get a confession,' says Tim. 'He's that type.'

Would you have confessed, thought Nelson, if you hadn't given yourself away with Michelle in the graveyard? Aloud he says, 'Greenway isn't a Catholic. It's Catholics who like confessing.'

'Anglo-Catholics do too,' says Tim. 'I've been reading up about it.'

At any other time Nelson might have been impressed by this, but now he just says, sourly, 'Nirupa Khan will try to stop him coming over all confessional in the interview.'

'We'll just have to press the right buttons,' says Clough. 'What an angel Chloe was, how no one understood their relationship. That sort of thing.'

'Blimey,' says Nelson, 'have you been going to empathy classes in night school, Cloughie?'

Clough looks modest. 'I've learnt a thing or two in the past few years.'

'We all have,' says Nelson. 'Come on, let's get back in there.'

*

Ruth is in a very different environment, the Humanities library at the university. Yet she too is primarily concerned with bodily fluids. She is immersed in a heavy hardback book with hand-cut pages. It is called *Relics of the Medieval Saints*. It's all here: vials of blood, St Anthony's tongue, St John the Baptist's head, the finger of Doubting Thomas, even something called the Holy Foreskin (a prized relic in medieval times apparently). There are also enough pieces of the True Cross to build an ark. Ruth reads on, turning the pages with care. Occasionally she writes in her notebook. It's quite soothing, reminding her of her student days and the slower pre-Internet world.

It's far quieter here than in the Natural Sciences library, where there's a constant whirr of photocopying and low-level chatting. The windows look out onto the ornamental lake, currently as still and smooth as glass. Faint shouts can be heard from the tennis courts behind the octagonal lecture theatre, but, in the library, there is a heavy scholarly silence. Ruth is not even sure that the woman opposite her is breathing.

'Ruth! What are you doing here?'

It's Shona, scattering the dust motes with her carrying voice and her glowing face and hair. The woman opposite wakes up with a start and glares at them.

'I thought you never came to the Humanities block,' Shona is saying.

'I managed to get past the checkpoint.'

'What are you reading?' Shona reaches out to look at the cover of Ruth's book. The title is embossed in gold. Shona peers at it. '*Relics of the Medieval Saints* . . . Are you getting religious in your old age, Ruthie?'

'Come for a coffee,' says Ruth, 'and I'll tell you. I'll just put this book back. You're not allowed to take it out of the library.'

'I bet there's a waiting list a mile long,' says Shona.

Just to give himself some thinking time, Nelson checks his emails before he goes back into the interview room. There's one from Intel listing Doreen Westmondham's foster children. Nelson scans down impatiently. There's a Pauline Berry on the list, also a Paula White. He calls, 'Fuller!'

Tanya appears at the door. 'Yes, boss?'

'Can you do something for me? Check Paula Moncrieff's maiden name. Be sensitive, mind, if you speak to the husband.'

'Of course. How's it going with Stanley Greenway?'

'If he confesses,' says Nelson, 'you'll be the first to know.'

Tanya clearly doesn't get the irony and leaves the office looking complacent.

Shona is actually a very good audience. Ruth doesn't tell her about the possible link to the letters, only that she is on the trail of the missing piece of glass. Even so, Shona listens wide-eyed, letting her cappuccino get cold.

'Those old relics are really interesting. Have you seen St Etheldreda's hand in Ely?'

'No. I love Ely, though. Is it in the cathedral?'

'No, in St Etheldreda's Church. It's apparently the oldest

Catholic church in England, but it's tucked away in a back street. You'd miss it if you didn't know where to look. The hand's in a glass case and it lights up if you put a coin in. There's a pretty good provenance to it, though.'

'That's more than can be said for these breast-milk relics.'

'Are there a lot of them around?'

'Yes. Apparently there's quite a tradition of the nursing Madonna, especially in the Greek Orthodox Church. There's a church called the Church of the White Grotto, built on white stone in Bethlehem where a drop of Mary's milk is meant to have fallen. There's also St Bernard of Clairvaux who had a vision of the Virgin Mary where he got squirted in the eye with her breast milk.'

'That's quite a vision. Did he go blind?'

'No. It cured his eye infection apparently.'

'Is there a breast-milk tradition connected to Walsingham?' asks Shona.

'Well the original holy house apparently contained a phial of the Virgin's breast milk. It's shown on some of the pilgrim badges. And the pilgrim route used to be called the Milky Way.'

'It's a funny thing,' says Shona. 'The Catholic Church is meant to be against the sins of the flesh, but it's obsessed with these corporal objects. I always remember reading that Robert Browning poem, "The Bishop Orders His Tomb", and there's a line about something being "as blue as the vein o'er the Madonna's breast". I found that quite shocking — I was a good little Catholic schoolgirl at the time — but then there are all these churches with bits of wrinkled flesh kept as holy objects. It's all very odd.'

Ruth thinks about the letter-writer and his preoccupation with the masculinity of the scriptures. Maybe the cult of the nursing Madonna is a way to combat this. She wonders what Hilary would think of it all. She also realises how much she has missed Shona and her literary take on events. She has seen far less of Shona since she moved in with Phil, and her life feels poorer for it.

Maybe Shona has been thinking the same thing.

'We could go to Ely and see the hand, if you want. Take the kids. Make a day of it. Louis would love to see Kate.'

Since Shona's little boy Louis spends most of his time beating Kate up, Ruth rather doubts that this feeling will be mutual, but the thought of a day with Shona is very enticing.

'I'd love that,' she says. She catches sight of the clock over Shona's head. 'Oh God, it's five o'clock. I've got to pick Kate up from the childminder.'

'I've got to get Louis from the nursery. They make you feel so terrible if you're late.'

That's one problem the Virgin Mary didn't have, thinks Ruth, as the two mothers hurry out of the canteen.

Time is moving on for Nelson too. Nirupa Khan is looking at her watch, and Stanley Greenway has been answering questions for over an hour. Despite Nelson's constant references to the angelic qualities of Chloe, Stanley sticks to his story pretty well. He was in bed at the Sanctuary, he didn't hear about Chloe's death until Doctor McAllister told him the next day. Yes, he'd been at the Slipper Chapel earlier in the evening. He likes to attend different churches and there's a statue he likes at the Catholic shrine. He was devastated when he heard about Chloe, had to take a tranquilliser. Dr McAllister drove him and Jean to the funeral. It was so sad, there were white roses on the coffin, and they'd played a song about angels. On the night of Paula's death he had gone for a walk, just strolling around aimlessly looking at the stars and trying to pray. He'd been back at the Sanctuary by two because he remembered the grandfather clock striking in the hall.

That clock was slow, remembers Nelson. Even so, if this is true, Stanley was back at the Sanctuary by two-thirty. Paula was killed between one-thirty and three-thirty. It's still possible.

At six o'clock Nelson takes a break. He knows that he hasn't got much time left and he doesn't think that the DNA on its own is enough for an arrest. If he doesn't get a confession soon he will have to let Greenway go and the momentum will be lost. Going back up to his office, he meets Tanya on the stairs.

'You still here, Fuller?'

'Of course. And I found out about Paula Moncrieff. Her maiden name was White and her husband said that she was fostered by a lovely woman who lived in Houghton St Giles. He remembered the name because it was like his.'

'Well done.' Nelson stands still on the stairs, thinking. If the link is Doreen Westmondham, then surely that lets Stanley Greenway off the hook. Maybe the ex-priest really is just a slightly creepy man who likes dressing up in young girls' clothes and not a murderer after all. As Nelson debates with himself, Tom Henty calls from downstairs.

'DCI Nelson? Ms Khan wants a word.'

Nirupa Khan is looking thoroughly irritated. Nelson assumes this is because he has been questioning her client for so long, so he is stunned when she says, 'My client wants to make a statement. I must tell you that this is against my advice and that of his doctor.' She shrugs. Nelson feels almost sorry for her.

Stanley Greenway's statement is brief. 'I killed Chloe. I'm very sorry. It was just that I loved her so much.'

24

17th April 2014, Maundy Thursday

The arrest of Stanley Greenway for the murder of Chloe Jenkins takes some off the pressure off Nelson and his team.
The press jump eagerly onto the idea of a defrocked vicar
as a killer, helped, Nelson thinks cynically, by the fact that
Stanley Greenway looks like everyone's idea of a sinister
predator. 'Police Arrest Paedo Priest,' screams the *Sun*. The
only problem is that there is still nothing to link Stanley to
Paula Moncrieff's murder. There were no traces of his DNA
on her clothes and, though his clothes (retrieved from the
Sanctuary laundry) were stained with mud and grass, that
could easily have come from lying in the field looking up
at the stars. Nelson is also slightly worried by Stanley's confession. Apart from saying constantly that he loved Chloe,
Stanley can't come up with any other motive. His statement,
transcribed verbatim by the police stenographer reads:

'And I was just lying there in the grass the birds blackbird
thrush robin looking at her so pretty then she was dead I

loved her but she was dead I prayed at the chapel mea culpa mea culpa mea maxima culpa . . .'

Nirupa Khan is talking about entering a plea of insanity.

Nelson hasn't forgotten the Doreen Westmondham link, but that too has proved to be a dead end. He has looked into the background of everyone involved in the case and none of them were in care. Larry Westmondham seems infuriatingly vague about his mother's foster children. 'Daisy probably knows more than me. She's been going through all the old pictures.' Nelson went to see Daisy, cunningly timing his visit for tea-time. Over Victoria sponge ('Named after me,' said the youngest girl), Daisy laid out the pictures on the kitchen table. Doreen smiled into the camera, accompanied by a variety of children, of all ages and ethnic groups, one in a wheelchair. That must be Eddie, for whom the camper van had been adapted. In some of the photographs, she was in the company of a mild-faced man who looked some years older than her. 'Larry's father,' said Daisy, 'he only died a few years ago. He was a sweet man, but somehow he doesn't come into the family stories much.' There was only one picture of Doreen and her three sons: Steven, Kevin and Larry. The three boys had stared sullenly into the camera, much less beguiling than the foster children. But, then again, maybe they had less to smile about.

There was no way of knowing if any of the pictures featured Chloe or Paula. Was Chloe the little blonde girl holding on to Doreen's skirt on Cromer beach? Was Paula the awkward-looking teenager pictured building a tent in the garden? So many children, so many lives. Nelson showed

Daisy a picture of Stanley Greenway and she examined it closely. 'I think I might have seen him at Sunday services. At St Simeon's.' 'Do you think you've seen a younger version in any of the old photographs?' asked Nelson. 'I don't think so,' said Daisy. 'But people change so much, don't they?'

Nelson had interviewed Steven and Kevin Westmondham, but they too were less than enlightening. Steven, an older version of Larry, said that he didn't really remember any of his mother's foster children. 'There were so many, they all merged into one really.' 'Do you recognise this man?' Nelson showed him the photograph. 'No,' said Steven. 'Oh, wait. I've seen him on the news. Isn't he the vicar who killed those two girls?' 'Looks like a pervert to me,' said Kevin, the other brother. 'No, I've never seen him before.'

So, more than a month after Stanley's arrest, Nelson is still trying to firm up the case. He's in Walsingham to meet the woman who claimed to see a lurking figure near the church on the night of Paula's murder. The witness, Bella Hendred, has not been terribly helpful so far. She failed to pick out Greenway in an identity parade and the description in her witness statement is vague in the extreme. But maybe he'll be able to get something better out of her.

Nelson has rather lost count of the days, so he's surprised when he arrives in Walsingham to see the village so full of people. When he cuts through the abbey grounds to have another look at the murder site, he sees that two men are erecting a huge wooden structure in front of the ruined arch. There are other such structures spaced at intervals around the park. One looks like the dock in a magistrate's court, another like a cave. The largest edifice, in front of the arch, looks disconcertingly like a gibbet with an upright and a crossbar being hammered into place.

'What's going on?' Nelson asks a passing workman.

'It's for the play tomorrow,' says the man. Then, seeing Nelson's blank look he adds, 'The Good Friday Passion Play. They act out Jesus being killed and all that.'

Nelson looks back up at the gibbet. He sees now that it's a massive cross, silhouetted against the pale-blue sky. He shivers, thinking, not for the first time, that it's a weird thing to be celebrating torture and death. Religious people might as well wear little electric chairs around their necks. Only a few yards away is the spot where Paula Moncrieff had the life choked out of her. Nelson hurries on, head down against the wind which is rattling the instruments of torture. Today must be Maundy Thursday then. A more convivial feast, the meal in the upper room, the sharing of bread and wine. But then, the agony in the garden, betrayal and death. It's a wonder they tell children these stories, though Nelson remembers taking part in a Passion Play at his primary school. He had played Judas because, as Sister Anthony kindly explained, he was good at looking angry. Blond-haired, blue-eyed Joseph O'Malley had played Jesus.

Bella Hendred lives in a cottage off the high street. The walls are pale pink and the front door is green, the knocker in the shape of a hand. Nelson fears the worst.

And he's proved right. The room contains wind chimes, statues of Buddha and the Virgin Mary and, on every surface, crystals, scented candles and tiny carved objects. The air smells of incense and over the fireplace is a sampler informing Nelson that 'The best and most beautiful things in the world cannot be seen or even touched — they must be felt with the heart'. Want a bet? thinks Nelson. He takes his seat on the blue-draped armchair and says no thank you to a glass of cranberry juice. A small fluffy dog stares at him stonily from the adjacent chair.

He has only seen Bella once before, at the identity parade, and he supposes that she had made an effort to look conventional on that occasion. Today she is wearing an orange kaftan emblazoned with silver suns and moons. Enough, in Nelson's mind, to make her lose credibility with any jury in the land.

'I'd like to ask you again about the man you saw on the night of the 19th February,' he says. 'I know it's a long time after the event, but sometimes things do occur to us when some time has passed.'

'That's so true,' says Bella. 'I think it's because those events have been in the universal subconscious for longer and so we gain greater understanding.'

'That's an interesting viewpoint,' says Nelson. 'Could I just take you through your witness statement from that night?'

'Of course.' Bella sits opposite him, and the dog gets out of its chair to sit on her lap. Two pairs of eyes stare at Nelson expectantly.

'You were walking your dog by the church at approximately ten past midnight on the 19th February . . .'

'Yes.' Bella pats the animal in question. 'I always take Francis out then. There's less chance of meeting other dogs.'

'Doesn't he like other dogs?'

'He doesn't seem to,' says Bella sadly. 'I think he must have had a trauma in a former life.'

Nelson decides to skate over this. 'So you were walking beside the church, past St Simeon's Cottage, and you saw a man. What was he doing?'

'That was it,' says Bella, 'he wasn't doing anything. He was standing in the graveyard looking up at the church. I'm the last one to stop people communing with the spirits, but it seemed an odd thing to be doing in the middle of the night. Francis barked. He could tell something wasn't right.'

Nelson suspects that Francis barks quite a lot. Though he's a fraction of the size of Jan's dog, Barney, he seems far more aggressive.

'You described the man as being "quite tall, wearing dark clothes". Is there anything else you can add now, thinking back?'

Bella shuts her eyes, Francis, though, continues to stare at him. Eventually Bella says, 'He was wearing a hat. A black hat. Like the one that Pat O'Brien wore in *Angels with Dirty Faces*. People don't seem to wear hats so much these days. My dear father . . .'

Nelson interrupts. 'Did he look at you? Respond to your presence?'

'No. He didn't even look round when Francis barked. He seemed lost in his own thoughts.'

Larry Westmondham was wearing a hat on the night that Michelle was attacked, Nelson remembers. He has a clear picture of the vicar wearing a heavy coat and black woolly hat.

Then another picture comes into his head. Catholic youth club, a black-and-white film, Jimmy Cagney on the way to the electric chair.

'Pat O'Brien in that film you mentioned. He played a priest, didn't he?'

'Yes,' sighs Bella Hendred. 'It was so affecting that last scene, where he convinces James Cagney to pretend to be afraid so as not to be a role model for those tearaways.'

And Nelson thinks of Father Hennessey sitting in his office, drinking coffee and talking about his illegitimate daughter, his black trilby hat on the floor beside him. Father Hennessey had been in Walsingham that evening. He had gone to the church to pray and found it locked. Nelson had watched Larry lock it only a few hours earlier.

'And you'd never seen this man before?' he says. 'Around the village, for example?'

'I don't think so. He was an unfamiliar presence.'

So the mysterious lurking man may have been Father Patrick Hennessey. Nelson thanks Bella and stands up to leave. On the way out she tells him that she's not a churchgoer, but she likes the spiritual energies of Walsingham. She gets strength from the Buddha as well as her guardian angel and various Christian saints.

Nelson thinks to ask who Francis is named after.

'St Francis of Assisi, of course. Patron saint of animals.'

Francis barks shrilly.

On his way back to the car Nelson makes a detour to look at St Simeon's Church and the place where Bella saw her mysterious man. On that occasion the lane had been deserted, but today it is rather more crowded than Nelson would like. Standing by the door of Justin's cottage are the house owner himself (resplendent in embroidered waistcoat), Cathbad (in cloak), Ruth, Hilary Smithson, Robin Rainsford and another of the woman priests. What's her name? Something outlandish. Freya something.

Nelson stops and considers backing away, but Cathbad has seen him.

'Talk of the devil,' he says brightly.

There's been far too much talk of angels and devils already for Nelson's liking. Also, he doesn't relish the idea that the group have been discussing him. He has seen Ruth a few times since their argument at the cottage, mostly when he has dropped off or collected Katie. On those occasions Ruth has been polite and coolly friendly. Nelson wants to apologise for losing his temper, but he doesn't know how to. Perhaps because he's still angry.

Now Ruth shoots him a distinctly hostile glance. Cathbad says, 'We were just saying that we're sure that poor vicar is innocent.'

'Really?' says Nelson. 'Well it's always nice to hear an informed viewpoint, but the CPS are happy that we've got sufficient evidence against him.' He doesn't add that this evidence is mostly in the form of a rambling, often incoherent, confession.

'There's nothing to tie him to the murder of the other woman, though, is there?' says Justin. 'What was her name?'

'Paula,' says Freya tightly. 'Her name was Paula.'

'Does this Greenway man have any links to Paula?' asks Hilary.

'That's not something that I can share with the general public,' says Nelson. 'I'm surprised to see you here, Reverend Smithson. I wouldn't have thought you'd want to come back to Walsingham.'

Hilary Smithson's face doesn't change, but she can't stop herself turning a particularly bright shade of pink, like vestments on a feast day.

'Freya and I came for the Good Friday Passion Play,' she says. 'I won't let Paula's death stop me practising my faith.'

But there's nothing to stop you practising it at home, thinks Nelson. The woman's manner strikes him as furtive.

'I'll be at the Passion Play too,' says Cathbad. 'I love a good Passion. What about you, Justin?'

'Oh, I'll be there,' says Justin. 'I'm playing Pontius Pilate.'

Ruth had been very surprised to get an email from Hilary at the beginning of April. Despite their promises to keep in touch, the two women hadn't been in contact since Paula's murder. Ruth had sent flowers to Paula's funeral, but honestly thought that would be the last she would hear from any of the women priests. But two weeks ago there had been this email:

Hi, Ruth,
Hope you're well. I've been having a peaceful and fulfilling Lent, despite everything. Paula's funeral was beautiful. Sydney led the service and all the women from the course came. Robin read the

lesson and little Jack read out a prayer he had written. He was so
brave. Giles was too upset to speak. Anyway, Ruth, I'm coming to
Walsingham for the Good Friday Passion Play. Could we possibly
meet at the Blue Lady at 11 o'clock on Maundy Thursday? There's
something I want to show you.
Love and prayers,
Hilary

Ruth had turned up at the Blue Lady to find the place
deserted and a sign on the door saying 'Spring Cleaning for
Easter'. She had walked back through the village, following
the Abbey wall, and found Hilary, Freya and a large man
in glasses chatting with Cathbad outside a cottage attached
to the church. A man in a waistcoat was standing in the
doorway, also deep in conversation with them.

'Here's Ruth now,' said Cathbad as she approached.

'Hi, Ruth.' Hilary came forward to fold her into a warm
embrace. 'The cafe was closed so I was just looking for somewhere else to go, and I ran into Cathbad. He says he's a good
friend of yours.'

'I've never seen him before in my life,' said Ruth.

Cathbad laughed, but Hilary looked troubled. 'Sorry, I . . .'

'It's a joke,' said Ruth. 'Cathbad and I go back a long way.'

'Have you met Justin Fitzroy-Jones?' said Cathbad. 'It was
his cottage I was looking after when I saw Chloe Jenkins in
the graveyard.'

'If it was Chloe,' said Justin with a slightly foxy smile, 'and
not the Blue Lady herself.'

'You know Freya, of course — ' Hilary carried on with the

introductions as if she was at a cocktail party — 'Freya and I are taking part in the Good Friday Passion Play tomorrow. We've just come from a rehearsal.'

Ruth felt out of her depth. She had only the vaguest idea what a Passion Play entailed. 'What are you doing in the play?' she asked.

'We're apostles,' said Hilary. 'And Robin is an apostle too. Have you met Robin Rainsford? He was running the . . . well, the course that I was on.'

Ruth thought that Robin looked rather embarrassed at the mention of the fateful course. He blushed pink, matching his jumper.

'We were talking about the case,' said Cathbad. 'I'm really worried about the police arresting this Stanley Greenway fellow. He looked very vulnerable to me. Do you know anything about it, Ruth?'

Ruth was quick to deny any inside knowledge, but they had got into an enjoyable discussion about wrongful arrests and general police brutality when Nelson spoilt it all by strolling up looking like a thundercloud. He hadn't addressed a word to Ruth, but sparred briefly with Cathbad and expressed surprise at seeing Hilary in Walsingham. Hilary replied that she was there for the Passion Play, but she coloured when she said it, confirming Ruth's suspicions.

Now Hilary, Cathbad and Ruth are in The Bull, which is filled to the brim with Easter pilgrims. Hilary seemed anxious to shake off Freya and Robin ('I know you'll want to rest') and now Ruth sees why. As soon as they sit down,

Hilary rummages in her voluminous handbag and pulls out a handwritten letter.

'I wanted to show you this.'

Ruth's first thought is that, if Hilary has had a new letter, this proves that Stanley Greenway can't be the killer. Then she remembers that the letter-writer and the killer aren't necessarily the same person. She and Nelson have been fooled that way once before.

Cathbad takes the letter. Ruth isn't quite sure how Cathbad has inveigled his way into Hilary's confidence, but it seems that he has; maybe because he appeared to be so sure of himself with Nelson earlier. Or maybe it's just the cloak.

Ruth reads over Cathbad's shoulder.

Dear Jezebel [nice to see that the letter-writer's salutation has not changed, she thinks],

You would not heed my warnings. If you want to know why those two fallen women had to die, meet me at the holy house on Good Friday at 3 p.m., the hour Our Saviour died for our sins. Do not tell the police, especially Harry Nelson, for he is a sinful man, guilty of the sin of adultery. Come on your own, and I promise that all will be made plain to you. For now we see through a glass darkly, but then face to face.
Yours in God —

Ruth stares at the letter. The phrase 'for he is a sinful man, guilty of the sin of adultery' seems to be growing bigger

and bigger, almost pulsating on the page. How can the letter-writer know about her and Nelson? Only a few people
know, and they are the people closest to them: Michelle,
Judy, Cathbad, Clough, Shona. Even her parents don't know
who Kate's father is. How can this person know? Or maybe
it's just a shot in the dark. She mustn't give herself away.
She is grateful to hear Cathbad's voice, sounding uncharacteristically serious. 'Hilary, you aren't planning to meet this
character, are you?'

Hilary takes a sip of her tomato juice. 'I certainly am.'

'But it's madness. If you really suspect that this man is
the murderer, you must tell the police at once. Let me ring
Nelson.'

'No,' says Hilary, pointing at the letter, 'he says not Nelson.'

'When did you get this letter?' asks Ruth.

'A few weeks ago.'

'A few weeks . . . And you didn't tell anyone?'

'No.' Hilary has her martyr's face on again. 'He wrote to
me. It's up to me to see this thing through.'

'You can still meet this person,' says Cathbad, 'but the
police can be nearby, watching, ready to pounce if he attacks
you.'

'Where would they hide? The site of the holy house is out
in the open. By three o'clock tomorrow the grounds will be
full of people watching the Passion Play.'

'They can mingle with the crowds,' says Cathbad, 'or you
can wear a mike. Seriously, they have ways of doing these
things.'

It's quite amusing to hear Cathbad, the man who once

hated the police, sounding like an expert on their procedure. Ruth weighs in too.

'You have to tell the police, Hilary. If this man is the killer, you'll be in terrible danger.'

'I'm not afraid,' says Hilary, sounding stubborn. 'I'm a black belt in taekwondo.'

Nelson is back at the station when he gets the call from Cathbad. He listens impatiently, then with mounting incredulity.

'Do you mean to say that Hilary Smithson was planning to meet this person and not inform the police?'

'That's right. But Ruth and I talked afterwards and thought that you should know. Even if Hilary asked us not to tell you.'

'Very kind of you both. Why on earth didn't Hilary want to tell the police?'

'The letter says not to. In fact it mentions you by name.'

'Does it? What does it say?'

There's a slight pause then Cathbad says, 'Something about you being a sinful man.'

'Go on.' Something tells Nelson that there's more.

'Oh, more Old Testament stuff. Something about you being an adulterer.'

'I see.' Nelson is beginning to understand why Ruth didn't make this call.

'It's very over the top,' says Cathbad. 'About looking through a glass darkly — though that's a beautiful phrase — and all being revealed. But it's worth taking seriously, don't you think?'

'Yes, I do,' says Nelson. 'I'll make sure I have people at the site of the holy house tomorrow. Three o'clock, was it?'

'Yes. The hour that Jesus was crucified.'

How the hell do they know that? thinks Nelson. He has trouble getting his team to fill in their timesheets correctly, let alone keep count from two thousand years ago.

'We'll be there,' he says. 'Thank you for telling me.'

'That's OK,' says Cathbad. 'Perhaps now you'll let that poor priest go.'

'Goodbye, Cathbad.'

Nevertheless, thinks Nelson as he puts down his phone, Cathbad might have a point. Greenway is in custody, but someone claiming knowledge of the killings is still out there. And there's nothing to link Stanley Greenway to the letters, although the biblical knowledge could point to someone with theological training. A handwriting expert has concluded (as far as these people ever conclude anything) that the writing in the letters does not match Stanley's. Is it possible that there are two killers out there, that a different person murdered Paula Moncrieff? Never assume, that's what Nelson tells his team, but is he guilty of assuming that the two murders were committed by the same person? There were some differences, as he pointed out at the time. Chloe's body had been laid out carefully, the rosary on her chest; Paula's left where it had fallen. These details have never been released to the press. Could Paula's even be a copycat crime, based on what had actually made it to the papers? Are there two murderers in Walsingham?

He thinks of Justin saying that there is nothing to link

Stanley Greenway to the murder of Paula Moncrieff. Not that he wants to take policing lessons from some waistcoat-wearing . . . Nelson stops. Something is chiming in his brain, a tiny alarm bell somewhere. What is it? Stanley Greenway, Chloe Jenkins, Paula Moncrieff, Cathbad, Justin . . .

Nelson goes into the incident room. Tim and Tanya are both there, glued to screens.

'Fuller,' says Nelson. 'Can you find the CCTV footage of Stanley Greenway at the Slipper Chapel?'

'Sure,' says Tanya. She clearly wants to ask why, but doesn't dare to. Tim looks up from his work.

Tanya clicks on various icons and a grainy window appears on the screen.

'There he is,' says Tanya, 'on the left.'

But it isn't Stanley Greenway that Nelson is looking at. He has remembered Tanya's words when she first spotted Greenway in the footage. 'Look there,' she'd said. *'Next to the man in the waistcoat.'* And the man next to Greenway is none other than waistcoat-wearing Justin Fitzroy-Jones.

25

Maundy Thursday, afternoon

Ruth drives home, feeling that her hard-won serenity is, once again, under threat. Over the last few weeks she has concentrated on work and looking after Kate and has almost succeeded in not thinking about Nelson. Well, not much anyway. When he arrives to pick up Kate she manages to chat to him pleasantly enough, not rising when he reminds her about new child car-seat regulations or reminding him how to pronounce his daughter's name. She hopes that he quakes before the new ice-queen Ruth and feels shrivelled inside but she has a nasty feeling that he hasn't noticed any difference.

Still this last month hasn't been without its pleasures. She and Kate went to Ely with Shona and Louis. They visited St Etheldreda's Church and were shown the relic by the charming parish priest, Father Tony. The hand itself, enclosed in a small curtained niche, was surprisingly ungrisly. It was just a grey object, made innocuous by its surroundings.

Shona, of course, had crossed herself and genuflected madly, partly for Father Tony's benefit (he was a man, after all, and all men are susceptible to Shona). But it had been a lovely day. Louis didn't attack Kate once. They visited the soaring cathedral and had tea by the river. Perhaps there is life after Nelson.

But now Hilary's visit has brought everything back: the murder, the sinister letters, the row with Nelson. Ruth and Cathbad agreed to tell Nelson about the latest missive, despite Hilary asking them not to. 'You ring him,' Ruth said to Cathbad. 'It'll sound better coming from you.' Cathbad had looked quizzical, but hadn't asked any questions. They have arranged to meet at the Passion Play tomorrow. 'That way we can keep an eye on things,' said Cathbad, clearly desperate not to miss any of the action. Ruth had agreed, but now she has a feeling of dread in the pit of her stomach. She doesn't feel that an afternoon spent watching the re-enactment of a violent death will help matters very much. Besides, she's dreading seeing Nelson again.

She collects Kate from Sandra, the childminder, at two. At least it's the holidays, which means she can spend some quality time with her daughter. Unfortunately Kate has had a great morning doing potato prints with Sandra and doesn't want to come home. It's at times like this, when Kate actively prefers the company of her childminder to that of her mother, that Ruth feels her whole life — all the juggling of work and childcare and school parents' evenings — is a complete failure.

'Come on, Kate,' she says, trying to keep a happy 'fun

mother' smile on her face. 'We can go to the beach and dig in the sand.'

'I hate sand,' says Kate. 'And digging,' she adds, perhaps knowing that this is what would hurt Ruth most.

'Well let's go and see Flint then,' says Ruth, keeping the smile plastered on.

Kate eventually allows herself to be shepherded to the car and Ruth drives off, waving cheerfully.

Ruth keeps up a merry flow of chat as far as the turn-off for New Road. Then she lapses into silence. The tide is out and the sand stretches forever, interspersed with cool blue lakes and patches of wind-blown grass. Even Kate cheers up a bit at the sight. 'We *could* go and dig in the sand,' she says, as if making a huge concession.

'Not if you don't want to,' says Ruth. Honestly, she thinks, what kind of person scores points off a five-year-old?

But, as they get nearer the house, they see a car parked outside.

'Is it a visitor?' asks Kate. Such apparitions are rare in her life, but usually mean that fun is cancelled in favour of Mum sitting on the sofa chatting and drinking glasses of wine. Her lower lip starts to protrude.

Ruth is no less apprehensive. She doesn't recognise the car, so it can't be Cathbad or Nelson, her only two regular callers. Maybe it's just someone going for a walk over the Saltmarsh. But there's a perfectly good car park about half a mile away and bird-watchers are never scared of walking. As Ruth comes to a halt behind the car she sees that the driver is still in their seat. Again, she doesn't recognise the person's back view. She takes her phone out of her bag and clicks on Nelson's number. One false move from her caller and she'll summon the cavalry.

But, as Ruth gets out, so does the other driver and Ruth recognises her. It's Freya. Why is she here when Ruth only saw her a few hours ago? Besides, they hardly know each other. At the Briarfields dinner Freya had seemed rather humourless and intense. She was the one who said Norfolk had an 'unwholesome feel'. Ruth had felt insulted on behalf of her adopted county. And, if Freya hates the place so much, what's she doing here now? Ruth seems to remember that she lives in Wiltshire.

Still, the woman doesn't seem to be actually dangerous, so Ruth gets Kate out of the car.

'Hallo,' she calls. 'Have you come to see me?'

'Yes,' says Freya, walking towards her. 'I hope it's not an intrusion.'

'Not at all,' says Ruth. 'Come in and I'll make a cup of tea.'

Kate sighs heavily.

When Ruth last saw Freya she was very smart and controlled. Whippet-thin, with short dark hair and a penchant for neutral clothing, she had seemed like the sort of woman who made Ruth feel more than usually untidy and inadequate. But, today, something is different. Freya is still neatly dressed in jeans and a black windcheater, but there's something about her face that looks slightly hysterical. She sits bolt upright on Ruth's sofa and places her hands carefully on her lap, as if this is the only thing that will stop her wringing them together. Flint wanders over nosily, but something in Freya's rigid stance seems to repel him and he meanders off again. Kate gets out her Sylvanians and starts a rather bad-tempered game with them.

'I'm sorry if I'm intruding,' says Freya again.

'You're not,' says Ruth. 'It's fine. Tea or coffee?'

'Just water, please.' Ruth remembers Freya drinking water at the Briarfields evening. Well, she had been too, but only because she was driving. Freya's choice, then and now, seems more of a moral standpoint. Only bread and water for me, please. The rest of you carry on with your gluttonous eating and drinking. Just don't expect me to bring you a glass of water while you're burning in the everlasting fires of hell. Ruth goes to the kitchen and makes herself a cup of tea, whilst running the water so it's cold enough for Freya. She's certainly not going to offer biscuits.

When she gets back, Freya is watching Kate lining up her Sylvanian babies in front of the schoolhouse.

'I used to have some toys like that when I was young,' says Freya. 'Whimsies, I think they were called.'

'Do you have children?' asks Ruth.

'No,' says Freya. 'I don't have a husband either. I suppose I'm married to the job.' She gestures at her neck as if she's wearing her dog collar. And, even though she isn't, her plain black sweatshirt still looks like some sort of uniform.

'I haven't got a husband either,' says Ruth. 'They're rather hard to come by, aren't they?' She remembers the conversation about Christian dating sites. Hadn't one of the priests met her husband that way? Ruth dreads the day that her mother learns how to work a computer; she'll be sending Ruth the hyperlinks in a nanosecond.

'I suppose you're wondering why I came,' says Freya.

'I know you're here for the Passion Play,' says Ruth. Although this doesn't explain why Freya is here, in her house, drinking water and watching Kate play with her miniature woodland animals.

'Yes,' says Freya. 'Hilary suggested it. She thought it might be a way to come to terms with Paula's death. Visiting the place where it happened and praying for her.'

It occurs to Ruth that her old friend is very fond of managing people. Meet me here, do this, read that. Hilary might say that it's all for altruistic reasons, but it's rather bossy all the same.

'I've never been to the Passion Play,' she says, 'but Cathbad and I are going to watch it tomorrow. We'll look out for you.'

'The thing is,' says Freya as if Ruth hadn't spoken, 'do you remember Hilary talking about those anonymous letters?'

'Yes,' says Ruth.

'Well, I've had one,' says Freya, twisting her hands together.

'Have you?' Ruth's heart sinks.

'Can I show you?'

Please don't, screams Ruth silently. But Freya is already getting a piece of paper out of her backpack.

Dear Jezebel [the old ones are the best],

Good Friday is the day of Our Lord's Passion and Death. We kneel before the True Cross and know that we are not worthy. Beware, for the Lord sees into your soul. He will strike you down in your wickedness. You strut

and fret your hour upon the stage, but then you will
be heard no more.

There's no signature. Even so, Ruth is pretty sure that this
is the same person who wrote to Hilary. There are too many
similarities: Jezebel, the True Cross, the threatening suggestion that the Lord (and, by association, the letter-writer)
is watching at all times. Only the last line sounds different somehow. That's not the Bible, is it? It sounds like
Shakespeare.

'*Macbeth*,' confirms Freya, 'I read English at university. It's
the "Tomorrow and tomorrow" speech: "Life's but a walking
shadow, a poor player, That struts and frets his hour upon
the stage, And then is heard no more. It is a tale, Told by an
idiot. Full of sound and fury, Signifying nothing."'

As Freya quotes the lines, she suddenly reminds Ruth of
Shona, who has an encyclopaedic knowledge of Shakespeare.
It's not a comparison that would have occurred to her before,
what with Shona being a Titian-haired beauty and Freya
being a priest who wears windcheaters and sweatshirts. It's
more the rapt look that came over Freya's face when she said
the words. She might not love Shakespeare more than God,
thinks Ruth, but it's a close thing.

'When did you get this?'

'After I saw you in Walsingham I went back to my B&B.
This was waiting for me. Hand-delivered.'

So the letter-writer is someone who lives in or around
Walsingham, thinks Ruth. Aloud, she says, 'Have you shown
this to Hilary?'

'No,' says Freya. 'I thought I'd come to you first.'

Of course, thinks Ruth, that makes perfect sense. Accost a woman you've hardly met, but don't consult your friend and colleague who has actually received similar letters herself. But she doesn't think this is the most important issue here.

'You need to show this to the police,' she says.

'They won't be interested.'

'I think they will. Please tell DCI Nelson about it.'

'DCI Nelson interviewed us after Paula died,' says Freya. 'I can't say I took to him much. He was rather brusque.'

'He can be like that,' says Ruth, thinking, *Tell me about it*. 'But he's a good policeman. He'll take it seriously.'

'The reason I'm showing it to you,' says Freya, 'is because of the True Cross reference. Hilary said that a relic of the True Cross had been found near Walsingham. I thought you might know something about it, being an archaeologist.'

'A holder, supposedly meant to contain a relic of the True Cross, was found at Walsingham,' says Ruth. 'I've been doing some research, though, and apparently there were loads of such relics about at the time.'

Freya doesn't ask why she was doing the research. Instead she says, 'I've got no patience with that sort of thing. Icons and relics and angels and incense. It saddens me that some of my fellow women priests seem to have a weakness for ritual.'

'I'm not a believer,' says Ruth, 'but there's evidence that even the earliest human societies practised some forms of ritual. There are Stone Age bodies buried with animal bones and special stones, for example.'

'What do you mean, special stones?'

'There are fossils called shepherd's crowns,' says Ruth, 'you can find them on the beach here. Well, they've also been found in Palaeolithic graves.'

Freya looks less than interested in Palaeolithic burial practices. Ruth remembers that Freya has no time for so-called 'New Age' thinking.

'You're an old friend of Hilary's, aren't you?' she says.

'Yes,' says Ruth, wondering if this is really true. 'We were at university together.'

'Both studying archaeology?'

'Yes.'

'You must have been surprised when she decided to become a priest.'

'Yes, I was,' says Ruth. 'But we hadn't been in contact for quite a few years. People do change. I know I have.'

'I haven't changed,' says Freya. 'I've wanted to be a priest for as long as I can remember. Of course, at first it seemed impossible, as if the Church of England would never change its position. But I prayed. I prayed fervently. And it came to pass.'

Freya says this with a certain smugness, as though her prayers alone have changed the mind of the General Synod. Ruth thinks it's time to get the conversation back on track.

'Are you going to take this letter to the police?' she asks. 'I really think you should. It's quite threatening. All that stuff about striking people down in their wickedness.'

'It's not worth it,' says Freya, gathering up her backpack. 'It's like the *Macbeth* quotation. "Full of sound and fury, Signifying nothing."'

But *Macbeth*, thinks Ruth after Freya has left, is not the best omen. Not only is the play notoriously unlucky, but she seems to remember that quite a few people get murdered in it. Why did Freya want to show her the letter? After all, they had only spoken a few words at that fatal dinner. Was it really because of the vague archaeological reference or was it something altogether more sinister? Should she, Ruth, tell Nelson, even if Freya refuses to? The fact that the letter was hand-delivered must be significant, after all.

She sits on the sofa and Kate, miraculously sunny again, comes and sits on her lap. 'I do like you, Mum,' she says. 'I love you,' says Ruth, giving her a fierce hug. She is certain of one thing. Kate will not be coming to the Passion Play with her tomorrow. Kate will stay safely with Sandra making potato prints or playing in the sandpit. Places like Walsingham can be dangerous.

Justin Fitzroy-Jones greets Nelson politely, with just a hint of a raised eyebrow.

'How can I help you, Inspector?'

'Could I have a few minutes of your time?' says Nelson. 'There's something I'd like to clear up.'

'Of course.' Justin stands back to let Nelson in. He has to duck under the low beam. 'I warn you, I haven't got long. I've got a meeting at three. We're protesting about the plan to build new houses on Badger's Copse.'

'This won't take long,' says Nelson.

He takes a seat in the low-ceilinged sitting room. The room exudes order and comfort. Like Bella Hendred, Justin obviously enjoys collecting *objets d'art*, but his are minimalist and tasteful: a china vase on a low table, a collection of watercolours, a single orchid on the mantelpiece. Chesterton, the black cat lying on the white brocade sofa, seems to be placed there purely for aesthetic impact. A bowl of white hyacinths on the coffee table fills the room with a subtle yet heady fragrance. An ornate clock ticks above the fireplace.

Justin offers tea or coffee, both of which Nelson declines. Justin sits beside Chesterton on the sofa. Without looking at his owner, the cat gets up and moves away.

'Mr Fitzroy-Jones,' says Nelson, 'Can I ask your where-abouts on the 19th February?'

Justin raises both eyebrows now. 'I was in Ireland. I'm surprised you ask. Cathbad was house-sitting for me and I know you two are friends.'

The word 'friends' is said slightly maliciously.

'The thing is,' says Nelson, 'I have CCTV footage that places you at the Slipper Chapel that evening.'

He keeps his eyes on Justin and is rewarded by a tiny flicker of fear on the neatly whiskered face. Eventually Justin says, 'What do you mean, CCTV footage?'

'As part of our investigations we looked at the CCTV from the chapel. We've got a picture of you leaving a service with Stanley Greenway, the man charged with the murder of Chloe Jenkins.'

Justin looks from left to right, a cornered woodland animal now.

'I don't know the man.'

'Oh, come on,' says Nelson, 'you can do better than that.'

'You wouldn't understand.' More nervous eye movement.
'Try me.'

Justin adjusts a coaster on the spindly table beside him. 'It's
a brotherhood,' he says. 'The Brotherhood of the Madonna
Lactans. We meet at the Slipper Chapel because there used to
be a statue there which belongs to the brotherhood. Father
Bill has hidden it in his office now. He's suspicious of us,
thinks we're a dangerous cult. He doesn't understand our
deep love for the Madonna. When you lose your mother as a
child, like I did, you turn to the Holy Mother. She nourishes
us, she cares for us.'

'What is the Madonna Lactans?'

'The nursing Madonna,' says Justin. 'The brotherhood
started in the twelfth century. There's a fresco showing the
breastfeeding Virgin in Santa Maria Trastevere in Rome and
on several Greek and Russian icons. It was revived by the Cis-
tercians in this country. There was a phial containing Mary's
milk above the high altar at Walsingham. Women would pray
to the relic for help with conception or childbirth.'

This account seems to have given Justin confidence. He
even over-pronounces the Italian in a way that strikes Nelson
as deeply pretentious. Nelson himself is still trying to get
over the fact that Ruth's ridiculous idea about the phial of
breast milk seems to have some basis in reality.

'Who else is a member of this . . . brotherhood?' he asks.

'I can't tell you. I swore a vow.'

'You'd better, unless you want to be arrested for obstructing
a police enquiry.'

Justin rolls his eyes heavenward. 'Stanley Greenway is a

member and Larry Westmondham, the vicar here. Also Robin Rainsford, a theologian.'

'Why did you pretend to be in Ireland that week?'

'I wanted to go on retreat. There's a retreat house near the Slipper Chapel. I couldn't tell Cathbad, though I think he'd understand. We're sworn to secrecy, you see. I gave Cathbad a glow-in-the-dark statue and told him it came from Ireland. In fact I bought it at the Shrine Shop.'

'There's a piece of glass missing from the museum,' says Nelson. 'Is that anything to do with you?'

Now Justin looks really amazed. 'How did you know about that?'

'I have my methods,' says Nelson.

'I volunteer at the museum,' says Justin, 'and I found the glass in the basement, just stored in a box with bits of old stone and pottery. I thought it was possible that it was from a phial that had contained the Virgin's milk. Perhaps it was even the very phial that had sat on the high altar at the priory. And to see it kept in such a way, with no reverence, no respect! I took custody of it. We worship it as a holy relic.'

Nelson thinks 'I took custody of it' sounds a lot better than 'I stole it'. It never ceases to amaze him, the way people find comfortable language for uncomfortable actions. Justin has relaxed slightly, but he and the cat are both still looking at Nelson warily. As far as Nelson is concerned, Justin still has some explaining to do.

'What did you do after you left the service at the chapel?' he says.

'I went back to the retreat house,' says Justin. 'I had a simple meal and went to bed early.'

'And did you see Stanley Greenway during that time?'

'I said goodbye to him at the Slipper Chapel. I think he was going to walk through the fields back to the Sanctuary.'

Stanley Greenway certainly likes walking through fields, thinks Nelson. Was he walking home when he saw Chloe and attacked her? The material found on the hedge suggests that, at some point, Chloe was brought back to the chapel. Did Stanley bring her there to commune with the Madonna Lactans? He remembers Stanley saying that there was a statue that he liked at the Slipper Chapel. Justin had mentioned a statue too. He asks Justin.

'Yes,' says Justin. 'It's a beautiful work of art. It shows the Virgin Mary with blonde hair. I don't hold with all those modern depictions of her looking swarthy and dark. She was golden-haired, like an angel.'

And like Chloe Jenkins too, thinks Nelson. And Paula Moncrieff. He thinks of Stanley saying that Chloe used to meet her guardian angel at St Simeon's. But, of course, on that night, she had met someone else entirely.

It's just that he's still not sure who it was.

Nelson drives straight from St Simeon's Cottage to the Slipper Chapel. In contrast to his last visit, the place is absolutely heaving. The car park is jammed with tour buses, and there's an open-air mass going on. Nelson stands at the back, remembering bits of it: the sitting and the standing, the responses, the incense, the readings, the odd little ritual before the gospel reading when you are meant to trace a cross on your forehead, lips and chest. Nelson has to stop himself doing it with the rest of the congregation. He spots Father Bill at the altar. He's not the main priest, but seems to be assisting. In fact the altar is as crowded as the car park. Nelson counts five priests and ten altar servers (a job he once did, earning himself a bronze Guild of St Stephen medal). He wants to talk to Father Bill, so decides to stay for the rest of the service. It's quite soothing, standing there amongst the swaying crowd, feeling the soft early evening breeze as it ripples the altar clothes and the white robes of the priests.

After the homily, there is a movement amongst the congregation and several men rise and make their way to the altar. A vague memory starts to take shape in Nelson's mind and, as the men sit on a bench in front of the altar table and start to take off their shoes and socks, the memory crystallises and hardens. The Washing of the Feet. Before the Last Supper, Jesus is meant to have washed the disciples' feet. Peter, who gets everything wrong, protests, and Jesus promises him: 'One day you will understand . . . I have given you an example so that you may copy what I have done to you.' It's in the words of the reading that they have just heard. And, on Maundy Thursday masses, the priest washes the feet of twelve members of the congregation, in remembrance of this act of humility. Nelson remembers the ritual as embarrassing; the men with their callused, often dirty, feet, Father O'Brien fastidiously patting at them with a snowy white towel. The altar servers had to carry the bowl of water, not that any real washing was done. Pope Francis apparently went into a prison and washed the inmates' feet. He washed women prisoners' feet too. No women on the altar today, just as there are no women in the Brotherhood of the Madonna Lactans.

Finally the mass is over and the participants surge towards the car park. Nelson manages to catch Father Bill as he processes out.

'Can I have a word, Father?'

The priest looks round at the crowds, at the new pilgrims now taking their places at the benches in front of the altar.

'It won't take a minute,' says Nelson, 'but it could be important.'

'All right, but we've got another mass in twenty minutes. I'm concelebrating.'

'I'll be quick,' promises Nelson.

In Father Bill's office, under the gaze of the plaster Madonna, Nelson explains about the brotherhood that meets at the Slipper Chapel. Father Bill doesn't look surprised, and Nelson remembers that Justin implied that the priest knew about the group and didn't approve.

'I did know about it,' Father Bill confirms. 'You do often get things like this. Odd little devotions and so on. But this seemed a bit . . .' He pauses, looking up at the dusty ceiling.

'A bit what?'

'A bit extreme, I suppose. It's dangerous to make Our Lady into a living and breathing woman. It's dangerous to see her as our actual mother.'

'Dangerous?' says Nelson. 'That's an odd word to choose.'

'A woman is dead.' Father Bill looks at him steadily. 'Two women. I'd say it was dangerous.'

'Justin Fitzroy-Jones and Stanley Greenway were both here on the 19th February,' says Nelson. 'Did you see them?'

'I can't be sure, but it's fairly likely. They often come to early evening mass.'

'We've got footage of them leaving the service at five past six. Did you see them leave?'

'No. Sometimes, after mass, they go into one of the smaller chapels to pray.'

'And you don't go with them?'

'No.'

'You know that Stanley Greenway is under arrest for the murder of Chloe Jenkins?'

'Yes, I'm praying for him.'

'Did he ever say or do anything that made you feel that he could be a danger to women?'

'No. I knew that he was troubled, but I thought that he was a dreamer, a fantasist. I never would have thought that he could be violent.'

Fantasists can kill, thinks Nelson. In fact, they often kill when real life disappoints them by not living up to their fantasies. Was this the case with Stanley and Chloe?

'What about Justin Fitzroy-Jones?'

'He's an odd man, but I believe that he has a sincere faith.'

'He says he was at a retreat on the 19th.' Nelson will have to get this checked.

'It's possible. There is a retreat house near here.'

'What about the other men in the so-called brotherhood? Larry Westmondham and Robin Rainsford?'

'Larry I know slightly. He's a traditionalist, but his heart's in the right place. His wife is a very pleasant woman. She invited me to Sunday lunch once. Roast lamb and all the trimmings.'

Father Bill's voice is wistful as he says this. Is he regretting the absence of Sunday roasts in his life or something fundamentally more substantial, the right to a wife of his own?

'And Robin Rainsford?'

'He's a layman, a moderniser. Very committed to the cause of women priests.'

'Seems an unlikely person to be obsessed with the Madonna.'

'When you've been a priest for as long as I have, you cease to be surprised by people's obsessions.'

'You said that too much devotion to Our Lady was dangerous. Do you think that one of these men killed Chloe Jenkins?' Nelson notices himself using the title 'Our Lady'. Half an hour in the Slipper Chapel and he's turning back into a Catholic.

Father Bill looks up at the statue. 'I can't say,' he says slowly. 'But I do think that the Madonna is at the heart of it somehow.'

Nelson is looking at the statue too. 'Justin and Stanley both mentioned a statue that was important to them. Was it this one?'

'Yes,' says Father Bill. 'It's a fairly undistinguished Victorian work, but they fixated on it for some reason. Maybe because Mary has golden hair. Of course, most depictions of Mary nowadays show her with dark hair, which is ethnically more convincing. There was a real outcry when they put up a modern statue of a fair-haired Mary in Ely Cathedral recently.'

But the brotherhood liked the blonde Mary. Was this covert racism or something even more sinister? Nelson doesn't think that Father Bill can answer this question. The bells are ringing and mass is starting again. Nelson leaves Father Bill to prepare. But, instead of going straight back to the car park, he takes a detour to the Slipper Chapel. It's empty, perhaps because everyone is at the open-air mass. But Father Bill was right; the tiny room is blazing with light from hundreds of candles, some of them newly lit, some burnt almost to their wicks. Nelson takes a piece of paper from the pile by the door. After a second's thought, he writes the names of his daughters. Laura. Rebecca. Katie. Then he puts the paper in the box in front of the altar, offering up his intentions.

When he gets back to his car, his phone is still plugged in and he has a missed call from Ruth.

'Ruth. It's Nelson. You called me.'

'What's that noise in the background?'

'Just some hymns.'

'Some *hymns*?'

'I'm at the Slipper Chapel in Walsingham.'

'Oh.' He hears Ruth digest this. 'I hope this isn't a bad time. It's just that something's come up.'

'Is it about that letter sent to Hilary Smithson? Cathbad already told me about it.'

'No. It's about another letter actually.'

'Hilary's had another letter?'

'No. This one was sent to Freya Drew-Hayes. Another one of the women priests who was on the course at St Catherine's.'

'Freya . . . The miserable-looking one I met yesterday?'

'I don't know what you mean.' Nelson suspects Ruth knows exactly what he means, but she's not going to admit it in her present mood. 'Anyway Freya's in Walsingham for the Passion Play. A letter was hand-delivered to her today. It looks to me like it was sent by the same person who wrote to Hilary.'

'Does he want to meet her at three o'clock tomorrow too?'

'No, but he says God will strike her down in her wickedness.'

'And she didn't think to call the police? What's wrong with these people?'

'What do you mean, "these people"? Women or women priests?'

Nelson thinks it's best to ignore this. 'What else did the letter say?'

'Something about Good Friday and not being worthy. And there's a quote from *Macbeth*.'

'But you think it's from the same person.'

'Yes, I do. It was addressed to "Dear Jezebel".'

Nelson is silent for a few minutes and Ruth says, 'So this must mean that Stanley Greenway can't have written the letters.'

'Leave the policing to me, Ruth.'

'I'm only too happy to.'

Another silence. Nelson tries for a conciliatory tone. 'Do me a favour, Ruth, stay away from Walsingham tomorrow.

It's probably nothing, but there's obviously someone rather disturbed wandering around.'

Ruth laughs and, for a moment, Nelson thinks that it's all right again. Ruth has forgiven him and they can go back to their previous spiky but affectionate relationship. Then Ruth says, in a hard, tight voice, 'Why would I want to do you a favour?'

26

18th April 2014, Good Friday

Walsingham is already buzzing with activity by the time
that Ruth arrives at one o'clock. The streets are full of robed
people, not just priests, monks and nuns, but also sundry
apostles and residents of first-century Jerusalem. Ruth has to
park her car some way out of the village and, as she walks,
she sees more men with tea-towels on their heads than she
would have thought humanly possible. Women too, and
children, some with wings and halos, and even a patient-
looking donkey or two. But even the thought of how much
Kate would enjoy seeing a real-life donkey does not make her
wish she had brought her daughter with her. She thinks of
the line in the last letter that was sent to Hilary: 'You would
not heed my warnings', and of the threat wrapped up in the
quotation from *Macbeth*: 'then you will be heard no more'.
No, Kate is much safer with Sandra.

She is meeting Cathbad at The Bull Inn, where they are
having lunch. Cathbad has booked a table, knowing that

the place will be heaving. 'We don't want to end up with no room at the inn,' he said, 'although that has a biblical precedent, of course.'

Ruth has to fight her way through a regular army of apostles to get into the pub. Inside she can see more tea-towels, as well as a man apparently dressed as Herod. Does he even come into this bit of the story?

Cathbad is sitting at a corner table under a noticeboard crammed with Technicolor saints and sepia photographs of priests. The whole place is beginning to make Ruth feel rather anxious. She was never, for one moment, going to stay away because Nelson told her to, but, all the same, it is a rather frightening feeling that somewhere amongst the robed hoards there is the person who wrote to Freya 'Beware, for the Lord sees into your soul. He will strike you down in your wickedness'. Don't be stupid, she tells herself. The letter-writer is probably not the same person as the murderer and Nelson knows all about it: the place will be swarming with police. But, looking around, she can see disciples, angels, Mary and Joseph — but nobody in police uniform.

Still, Cathbad has already got her a glass of red wine, which does help. He fights his way through the disciples to order them two roast beef sandwiches.

'I thought there were only twelve apostles,' says Ruth, when he gets back.

'There are twelve apostles in the Passion Play,' says Cathbad. 'This lot are just the audience. They like to come dressed up.'

'Are the rest professional actors?'

'Some of them. I think Jesus and some of the main people are professionals. The rest are just keen amateurs. You heard Justin saying that he was Pontius Pilate.'

'That's a good part.'

'The best. Some great lines. "Truth? What is that?" Fabulous stuff.'

That's not quite how Ruth would describe it, but she knows that the crucifixion makes terrific drama. Even in the Nissen hut where her parents get to grips with being 'born again', they can't deny the power of the story. She remembers, as a child, watching Zefferelli's *Jesus of Nazareth*. It probably delayed her coming out as an atheist for a few years. Who played Pontius Pilate in that?

'Rod Steiger,' says Cathbad. 'He was incredible. I remember watching it in Ireland. Of course, Robert Powell was far too western-looking to be Jesus. There's no way He would have had blue eyes.'

'Rather lovely blue eyes, as I remember,' says Ruth. 'That intense stare. I was still nominally a Christian at the time and it had a great effect on me. Mind you, I was probably going through puberty, which didn't help.'

'It's all connected,' says Cathbad. 'Religion and sex. Birth and copulation and death. Speaking of which, I've been reading the letters.'

Ruth had been rather surprised when Hilary had given Cathbad the letters yesterday, saying that she would value his opinion. She wasn't surprised that the two had got on so well — religious people always liked Cathbad — but it seemed odd that Hilary, who refused to involve the police, was so willing to involve a part-time druid whom she had only just met. Ruth wonders what Hilary would say if she knew that Cathbad had told Nelson about her plan to meet the letter-writer today.

'What did you think?' she asks.

'I found them very disturbing,' says Cathbad. 'All that hatred, both towards Hilary and towards women in general. All that religious feeling, which should be a force for good, turned inwards.'

'Is religion ever a force for good?' asks Ruth.

'Well God is love,' says Cathbad, 'and love is always good.'

Is it? wonders Ruth, thinking of the times when she has witnessed crimes committed in the name of love. Thinking, too, of the times when love has led her to places that she would rather not revisit. She doesn't say this to Cathbad, though, and they are both momentarily distracted by the arrival of their sandwiches. It might not be as powerful as love, but food is pretty important too.

'Look who's here, scoffing away in a dark corner.'

Ruth looks up, embarrassed, as ever, to be caught in the act of eating. (*Scoffing?*) They are being addressed by a tall man in a dark-blue robe and a red headdress. The costume is professional in the extreme — not a tea-towel in sight — and it is a few minutes before Ruth recognises DS Dave Clough.

'Dave! What are you doing here?'

'I'm undercover, aren't I?' says Clough, pulling a chair over to their table. 'I'm an apostle.'

'Which one?' asks Cathbad.

'The most important one,' says Clough. 'Who's the most important apostle?'

'Peter,' says Cathbad. 'On this rock I will build my church.'

'I can't be Peter,' says Clough, 'they've got a proper actor for him. John too. I'll be one of the others.'

'Andrew?' suggests Cathbad. 'Matthias? Philip? Bartholomew?'

'Bartholomew,' says Clough. 'I like that.'

'So what are you doing, Bartholomew?' asks Ruth. In the background a woman in purple robes is looking vainly for her chair.

'Keeping an eye on your friend Hilary,' says Clough. 'Apparently she's meeting some nutter at three o'clock. The boss told me to stick to her like glue. She's an apostle as well, so it's easy. Cassie got me the gear, her theatre company's involved in this malarkey. Cassie's Mary Magdalene.'

That figures, thinks Ruth. She's only met Cassandra a few times, but she looks the type who would grab the only glamorous part in the gospels.

'Is Nelson coming?' she asks.

'He said he'd be here,' says Clough. 'Of course, we've got the killer, but we still want to catch the letter-writer bloke.'

'What if you've got the wrong man?' asks Cathbad.

'Oh, you would think he's innocent,' says Clough. 'You always think everyone's innocent. Greenway's the killer, mark my words.'

Cathbad is about to answer, but a diversion is caused by

Mary Magdalene appearing and enfolding Bartholomew in a passionate embrace.

Nelson is planning to set out for Walsingham when he gets a message that Stanley Greenway wants to speak to him. Clough and Tim are already mingling with the crowds at the Passion Play. Clough had assured Nelson that Cassandra would provide costumes for the two policemen.

'You can be the only black apostle,' Clough told Tim.

'Simon of Cyrene was black,' said Tim.

'Who was he when he was at home?'

'The man who helped Jesus carry His cross.'

Nelson remembers what Tim had said about his mother, that her life revolved around the church. Clearly some biblical knowledge has rubbed off.

Despite it being a bank holiday, the team are working full strength. They still haven't made an official arrest for Paula's murder and all non-essential leave has been cancelled. Nelson finds Tanya in the incident room.

'Come on. We're going to prison.'

Stanley is being held in a remand prison just outside Norwich. It's a Victorian building, not unlike the Sanctuary in appearance, and not unpleasant on this bright spring day. As they pass through the two checkpoints the guards nod at Nelson, but give Tanya covertly appraising glances. He sees her noticing and wants to apologise for this sexist behaviour, but doesn't know how to start the conversation. Better leave it. Tanya's a professional, after all.

Stanley is sitting with Nirupa Khan in the visitors' room.

He's still wearing his tracksuit — remand prisoners are allowed to wear their own clothes — and actually looks calmer and better fed than he did in the Sanctuary.

'I've remembered something,' he says in greeting.

'I'll be looking for some recognition of my client's co-operation,' says Nirupa.

Nelson ignores her. 'What have you remembered?' he asks Stanley.

'I went to the service at the Slipper Chapel,' he says. 'There's a group of us and we have a special relationship with the Madonna.'

'The Madonna Lactans,' says Nelson.

Nirupa looks at him in surprise, but Stanley just smiles and nods. 'Exactly so. Well after the service I went to walk back to the Sanctuary across the fields. I love walking in the open air. Then, I don't know, it all went black and Chloe was lying there at my feet.'

Nelson shifts impatiently. He's heard all this before. *Then it all went black.* Does Stanley take him for an idiot?

'What's this new information you have for us, Stanley?' he asks. 'I haven't come here for the good of my health.'

Stanley smiles his vague, irritating smile. 'There was a smell.'

'A smell?'

'Yes, like incense. I always use incense in my services. The smoke rising up, like our prayers rise up to God. Some of my parishioners complained. They thought it was too High Church . . .'

His voice drifts away, perhaps thinking of other things that his parishioners complained about. Nelson's mind is racing. Michelle said that the man who attacked her smelt of body odour, soap and joss sticks. Joss sticks are a kind of incense. But these aromas could have come from Stanley himself. After all, he had just come from a Catholic service where, presumably, incense was being wafted all over the place. What's the incense thing called? Memories of his altar-serving days come back to him. The thurible. He'd enjoyed swinging the thurible.

'Anything else?' he asks. 'Anything about Paula Moncrieff, for example?'

Stanley blinks at him. 'Paula who?'

Nelson gives up.

Cathbad and Ruth follow the crowds towards the abbey gate. Clough and Cassandra have gone for a last-minute cast briefing in the church.

'I don't envy the person who explains the Stations of the Cross to Dave Clough,' says Cathbad.

'Or tells him that he can't be Bartholomew.'

There are so many people at the gate that it takes a few minutes to pass through. Once inside, Ruth thinks how different the grounds look from that day in February when she walked amongst the snowdrops with Hilary. The snowdrops have gone, and the grass is already being churned into mud by the footsteps of the faithful. The vast archway still dominates the scene, but now, in front of it, there's a platform with a huge wooden cross. The cross casts a shadow over the crowd as they gather by the platform where the first station is due to be enacted.

'So dramatic,' breathes Cathbad. But the whole thing seems rather nightmarish to Ruth: the cross, the crowds, the gloomy music that is blaring out from loudspeakers high in the trees. She can't shake the thought that something awful is about to happen — apart from the crucifixion, that is.

'The first station is right by the site of the holy house,' she says. 'How is the letter-writer going to meet Hilary with all these people about?'

'They'll have moved off by then,' says Cathbad. 'The stations are dotted all over the grounds.'

'But they come back here at three,' says Ruth. 'For that.' She gestures at the cross.

'Maybe everyone will be so caught up in the drama that they won't notice one of the disciples slipping away,' says Cathbad. 'Of course, in the scriptures the whole lot of them up and run.'

'You know a lot about scripture for a druid.'

'I was brought up a Catholic, as you know. And I love the stories. It's an essential human act, telling stories.'

As long as you don't make the mistake of believing them, thinks Ruth, as she follows Cathbad to the first station.

Nelson and Tanya drive straight to Walsingham. Well, straight isn't quite the word, as the journey across Norfolk is convoluted and frustrating. Every time Nelson takes a side road, it is blocked by a tractor or slow-moving holiday traffic. His temper isn't helped by Tanya yacking on about the case. 'Does he think Stanley Greenway is insane? Could Greenway have had an accomplice? What about Justin Fitzroy-Jones? Or that woman, Jean Something, in the Sanctuary?' Eventually, to shut her up, Nelson switches on the radio. It's R.E.M, a band he likes, but Tanya starts singing along so he turns it off.

'Was that the first time you've been to the prison?' he asks.

'No,' says Tanya. 'I've been there to conduct post-arrest interviews.'

'The atmosphere can be a bit intimidating,' says Nelson, thinking of the guards and the way they'd looked at Tanya.

'I don't care about men staring at me,' says Tanya. 'If they keep on, I just tell them that I'm gay.'

'Why would you say that?' asks Nelson.

'Because I am.'

Nelson knows he should say something, to show that he's not embarrassed (he is embarrassed), to show that this is all in a day's work for the modern, twenty-first-century policeman.

'Have you got a . . . a partner?' That's the best he can do.

Tanya beams. 'Yes. Her name's Petra. She's a PE teacher. We're thinking of getting married next year. Perhaps Hilary Smithson could conduct the service. It would be nice to have a woman priest.'

That's not a view shared by everyone, thinks Nelson. Someone out there thinks women priests are a very bad idea indeed. And it's not necessarily Stanley Greenway.

'If you don't want this known at work,' he says, 'you can count on my discretion.'

'Oh, I think they've all guessed,' says Tanya. 'Apart from you and Clough.'

The rest of the journey passes in silence.

It's nearly two o'clock when they arrive in Walsingham. The Passion Play is due to start at two and people are pouring through the main gates into the abbey grounds. Nelson parks on a double yellow line and hurries to join them. Like Ruth, he is slightly thrown by the number of people in costume. He'd assumed that only the participants would be dressed up, and that it would be easy to spot Hilary as one of the disciples. But almost everyone seems to be in robes and some sort of headdress. They are all moving in the same direction, so Nelson follows, feeling uneasy. He hates crowds. So much potential for crime in a crowd — even a holy one like this.

Tanya veers off and comes back with a printed sheet. 'Apparently we walk around the grounds for the different scenes,' she says. 'It's called the Stations of the Cross. Does that make sense to you?'

'I think so,' says Nelson. He remembers walking in a procession around the sooty church where they had worshipped in Blackpool. A prayer at each station, wood-carvings so crude that it was hard to tell which was Jesus and which was the cross. A swing of the thurible, a bit of chanting. He thinks of Stanley Greenway saying, 'I always use incense in my services. The smoke rising up, like our prayers rise up to God.' There's something here that he's not quite getting. What is it?

'I think the first one's over here,' says Tanya. 'Where the platform is. It's called "Jesus is Sentenced to Death".'

'How many stations are there?' It's quite a few, he remembers that much.

'Fourteen.'

A large crowd has already gathered around the raised platform. It's very near the site of the holy house, notes Nelson, and close to the giant cross where — presumably — the procession will end. Tanya and Nelson stand at the back, Tanya on tiptoe, anxious not to miss anything, Nelson looking around for potential murderers.

'After this,' he tells Tanya, 'you move on with the rest of the crowd. I'll stay here.'

'OK, boss.'

He has told Clough not to let Hilary out of his sight, so, if she tries to slope off for her assignation, Clough should be close behind. Tim won't be far away either. It's hard to see how anyone can manage to have an assignation in the middle of such a crowd, but Nelson doesn't want to take any chances. He texts Clough: '*R u in place?*' In a few seconds he gets a text back: '*Yes. Feeling holly.*' He hopes this is a predictive-text misspelling of 'holy'.

He scans the crowd, searching for familiar faces. He thinks he sees Father Bill, the custodian of the Slipper Chapel, as well as people he vaguely recognises from his daughters' schools and Michelle's work. Then, standing on the very edge of the crowd, he sees a tall grey-haired figure. Father Hennessey. Is Fiona McAllister with him? It doesn't seem so. The priest appears to be on his own; his face is sombre, deep in thought.

'Nelson!' Nelson swings round to see two very familiar, but definitely not welcome, faces. Cathbad and Ruth. Cathbad is wearing a purple robe, but, of course, in this setting he blends in nicely. Ruth is wearing jeans and an embarrassed expression.

'I thought I told you two to keep away.'

'We're not living in a police state yet,' says Cathbad serenely. 'We're here to see the Passion Play.'

'Bollocks. You're interfering in my investigation.'

'We felt compelled to be here,' says Cathbad.

'Bollocks,' says Nelson again. A mother with two young children gives him a reproving look. 'Stay away from Hilary Smithson or you could ruin everything. I've got it covered.'

'Yes, we know,' says Cathbad. 'We've seen Clough in costume.'

Nelson turns to Ruth. 'I wouldn't have thought that this was your idea of a fun day out, Ruth.'

Ruth raises her eyebrows, but her retort is silenced by a sudden blast of trumpet music. 'Shh,' says the mother with the children, 'it's starting.'

The music stops and the crowd parts to allow a group to pass through. 'The disciples,' says someone. The disciples pause near Nelson and Peter and John start speaking. You can tell who the professional actors are. John, dressed in pinkish robes, is almost ridiculously handsome, and Peter is emoting away as he denies Christ three times. The extras are less convincing. They include Hilary Smithson and Robin Rainsford, as well as Clough and Tim. Nelson also spots Freya Drew-Hayes, the woman who received a poison-pen letter yesterday. Obviously, this is a progressive group of disciples that admits women. Freya looks grim, but Nelson suspects that this is her usual expression. Does the fact that she received a letter – hand-delivered, no less – mean that the writer is very close, amongst this crowd in fact? After all, he or she is planning to meet Hilary Smithson in less than an hour's time.

Nelson does a quick disciple count. Why are there only eleven of them? Oh yes, Judas must already have betrayed Christ and deserted the cause. He commits suicide, Nelson seems to remember. Sister Anthony used to say that Judas's worst crime was not believing in the possibility of forgiveness. But then she said a lot of things. The loudspeakers blare out with the sound of a cock crowing. Peter falls to his knees. John turns away, covering his face. The other disciples attempt to look concerned/frightened/sad. All except Clough, who is grinning and has his mobile out. Still, at least he is still close to Hilary. Tim, in dark robes, looks the most serious of the lot. Pity he's not playing Judas. Now that would be good casting.

Peter, his big scene done, disappears into the crowd. The other apostles process to the platform and arrange themselves on the steps. Only John, his face anguished, is still acting. Hilary is smiling at someone in the crowd, and Clough is taking pictures with his phone. A trumpet blast, and a man in purple appears on the stage and takes his seat. It's a few seconds before Nelson recognises Justin playing Pontius Pilate. There's a moment's silence, and then a man in white robes steps onto the stage. This must be the actor playing Jesus. Nelson is too far away to hear the words, but he's surprised at how effective it is: the man in white standing in front of the seated Roman prelate, the crowds, the birds singing.

Then Pilate points, and Jesus is led away. He walks back through the crowds between two Roman soldiers. The apostles follow, and then, at a discreet distance, the audience. On to the next station, where it says: 'Jesus Is Given His Cross to Carry'.

Tanya, Cathbad and Ruth all move away, but Nelson stays where he is. He doesn't want to leave the holy house site. It feels oddly peaceful now that the crowds have gone.

'Hallo, DCI Nelson.' Nelson turns and sees a woman with a pushchair. She has a dog on a lead and is accompanied by another robed man. Daisy and Larry Westmondham.

'Hallo,' says Nelson, bending to pat the dog. He turns to Larry, who seems uncomfortable in brown robes that look like they were meant for someone bigger. 'Aren't you part of this affair?'

'I'm Joseph of Arimethea,' says Larry. 'I don't come in until the end.'

'I love the Passion Play,' says Daisy. 'Becky, our oldest, is in the children's choir, but I thought I'd better keep my distance. Samuel can be a bit noisy and Lulu gets overexcited in crowds.'

Lulu's the dog, Nelson remembers. She always seemed slightly mad to him and is now panting enthusiastically, straining at her leash.

'Why are you here, Inspector?' asks Larry. 'I wouldn't have thought this was your sort of thing.'

This is effectively what Nelson has just said to Ruth, but that doesn't stop him feeling obscurely offended. 'I thought it would be worth seeing,' he says. 'I was brought up a Catholic.'

'I didn't know that.'

'I'm going to catch them up,' says Daisy, 'I don't want to

miss the singing. You won't forget to bring Becky home, will you, darling? I have to leave early to collect Lizzie and Victoria.'

'I won't forget,' says Larry. Nelson thinks that he wouldn't bet on it.

Daisy says goodbye and sets off, bumping the pushchair over the grass, the panting spaniel at her side.

'Your wife,' says Nelson, 'is a very nice lady.'

'Yes,' says Larry, 'she is. Funny thing, she reminds me of my mother sometimes.'

Larry hurries off after his wife, his brown robes billowing, leaving Nelson wondering why he finds this last remark quite so unsettling.

As he watches the vicar rounding the corner by the trees, Nelson's phone rings. It's Michelle.

'Harry! Please come home. I think he's back. The man who attacked me.'

27

Good Friday, afternoon

It's half an hour's drive from Walsingham to Nelson's house on the outskirts of King's Lynn, but he does it in twenty minutes, siren on, lights flashing. He screeches to a halt outside his house to find Michelle waiting in the doorway.

'What is it? Have you seen someone hanging around the house?'

As he speaks he scans the cul-de-sac. It's a sunny afternoon, so several of his neighbours are outside, mowing their lawns and getting barbecues out of garages. It's hard to see how any sinister stranger could infiltrate this cosy, suburban scene.

'Look at this.' Michelle is holding out her phone. There's a message on the screen. *'I'm coming back for you.'*

'Who's it from?'

'Caller unknown.' Michelle, who was so brave about an actual physical attack, is white and shaking.

'I can trace the number,' says Nelson. 'Mobile phones have a unique number that they send out when they make a call.

I'll be able to trace it to its local base.' He's already dialling the station.

'He's coming back for me.' Michelle grabs his arm. 'I'm sure it's the man in the graveyard.'

'It's OK, love.' Nelson steers her to the sofa. 'I'll look after you. I'll get someone to stay with you.'

Michelle grabs hold of him again; her eyes look almost wild. 'No! I want *you* to stay.'

Nelson is talking to Tom Henty. 'I need a trace on a phone. Here's the number . . . and I need someone to come here and guard my wife. Really? Are you sure? There's no one else? OK. Send him at once.'

Nelson crouches down in front of his wife. 'I'm getting a policeman to come and stay in the house.'

'Why can't you stay?'

'I'm in the middle of an undercover operation. But I won't leave until he gets here.'

Michelle seems to accept this. She leans back against the cushions, her eyes closed.

'I'll make you some tea,' says Nelson. 'A proper cup, not that crap you like.'

Michelle smiles faintly. 'Just some water would be nice.'

In the kitchen Nelson checks that the back door is locked. Then he goes upstairs and does a quick sweep of all the rooms, shutting all the windows. Going back into the kitchen, he pours water from the purifier into one of Michelle's favourite glasses. When he comes back into the sitting room, Michelle is replaiting her hair. He takes this to be a good sign. Her face has lost some of its pallor too.

'Who's coming from the station?' she asks. 'Anyone I know?'

'Roy Taylor.'

'Is he the one you call Rocky?'

'That's right.'

'Isn't he meant to be stupid?'

'No,' lies Nelson. 'That's someone else.'

Thank God Michelle never pays attention when Nelson talks about work, otherwise she would have heard him describe Rocky as 'proof that evolution works both ways'. Nelson just prays that he's smart enough to watch a house.

After her initial doubts, Ruth is surprised to find herself enjoying the Passion Play. It is pleasant to walk through the abbey grounds with Cathbad at her side. It's nice to be with such a good-natured, friendly group of people, moving back to let children get to the front, listening to the actors in respectful silence. And, though this is harder to admit to herself, she is finding the play itself rather moving. It's one thing to hear — in her parents' Nissen hut, for example — that Jesus carried His own cross, quite another to see the actor lifting the heavy piece of wood and carrying it, with obvious difficulty, through the watching crowds. When Simon of Cyrene steps forward to help him bear the weight, an audible sigh runs through the audience. And when the actor takes his place in front of the cross, arms uplifted, and the children's choir sings 'There is a green hill far away', their voices sweet and fragmented in the open air, she has to turn her head away so that Cathbad won't see the stupid tears in her eyes.

They are nearly at the end now. She looks at her watch. Ten to three. Saint John, the Virgin Mary and Mary Magdalene (Cassandra, wearing a dress that owes much to the character's origins as a prostitute) stand at the foot of the cross. The actor playing Jesus still has his arms outstretched, and the choir sings something about Jesus remembering us. Ruth looks across at the apostles standing a little way away. Although the gospels tell a different story, in this version Jesus's followers are all present at His death. Clough is easy to recognise in his red headdress. He's also the only disciple looking at his iPhone. Tim is there too, in dark-green homespun, his eyes downcast. What is he thinking? wonders Ruth. Is he regretting everything that has happened with Michelle or is he just concentrating on the job in hand? Tim is hard to read at the best of times. She suppresses the ignoble thought that it's hard to see what two complex, intelligent men can see in Michelle. She must have hidden depths, that's all. Ruth sometimes suspects that she, herself, has hidden shallows.

Hilary is standing near Clough. As Ruth watches, she too glances down at her wrist. Then, with a quick look around her, she starts to walk away.

'Jesus remember me,' sings the choir, 'when you come into your kingdom.'

Ruth looks at Cathbad, and they start to make their way out of the crowd. It's hard to do this surreptitiously. The play is nearing its climax and people are standing, or kneeling in prayer. Ruth apologises as she trips over one pair of legs after another. She hears someone say 'Jesus!' in a distinctly unreligious way. When they are finally free they hurry to the place where the holy house once stood. It's only a few hundred yards from the main stage, but the neat square of grass is completely deserted.

Clough runs towards them, holding up his skirts. 'Did you see where she went?'

'No.' Ruth looks around helplessly, but they are in the open, there's nowhere to hide.

Suddenly a bell rings and people in the crowd start to fall to their knees. Three o'clock. The bell continues to toll, and, appropriately enough, a cloud passes over the sun. Tim appears from a southerly direction. 'She was seen going out of the gate,' he says.

'Which way did she go?' says Clough.

'She turned left, they thought.'

'Come on!' Clough pulls off his headdress and starts towards the exit.

'Hang on,' says Cathbad. The bell stops suddenly, and his voice carries further than he intended. Several of the crowd look round disapprovingly.

'The holy house,' says Cathbad, in a lower voice, 'it could be somewhere else.'

'Where?' says Clough. 'Almost everywhere in this bloody place is holy.'

'I remember Justin saying something to me about his cottage. You know, the place next to St Simeon's. "This is a holy house," he said.'

'Justin?' says Tim. 'The man who owns the cottage? Isn't he in the play?'

'He was here at the beginning,' says Cathbad. 'He's not here now.'

Ruth looks back towards the stage. The characters are still frozen in tableaux. Pontius Pilate is nowhere to be seen.

'Do you really think it could be Justin?' says Ruth.

Cathbad nods. 'That was the thing that really disturbed me about the letters. They sounded like they were written by someone I knew.'

Nelson reaches Walsingham just as the bell starts ringing. The high street is deserted, but, as he parks, he sees a woman with a pushchair hurrying up the road, tugging a reluctant spaniel behind her. Daisy Westmondham, obviously late for her two younger daughters. As he watches, she takes the track by the farm shop. Nelson has a ridiculous urge to call after her, to tell her to be careful. Why? It's broad daylight in a Norfolk village. Anyway, she has the dog to protect her. Not that Lulu seems much of a guard dog. As he thinks this, another dog approaches, a small furry creature barking angrily. Francis, patron saint of animals, taking Bella Hendred for a walk. Anxious to avoid talking to her, Nelson hurries towards the abbey entrance. With any luck, Clough will have intercepted the letter-writer by now.

But, as Nelson passes the gift shop, he sees his two sergeants, still in their robes, running through the archway. They are followed by Cathbad and Ruth.

'What the hell . . .?'

'St Simeon's Cottage,' says Clough, not breaking stride.

'Where's Hilary Smithson?' says Nelson. But the three men

have run past him, and he is forced to address the question to Ruth.

'She got away,' pants Ruth. 'Cathbad thinks she might be at the cottage. With Justin.'

Nelson opens his mouth to speak, but, thinking better of it, turns and follows his officers. Ruth trots after him.

In the background the crowd are chanting the Lord's Prayer.

Daisy doesn't know why she is so worried. Lizzie and Victoria are spending the afternoon with their friends Grace and Ella and won't mind at all if she's a bit late. Grace and Ella's parents are the laid-back type too. They are probably all out in the garden, enjoying the bank holiday sunshine. There's a treehouse and a swing; Lizzie and Victoria won't be in any hurry to leave. In fact, last time Victoria had said, embarrassingly, 'I wish our house was like yours.' Grace's mother had been understanding: 'All children say things like that. I'm sure you like your home best.' Daisy wouldn't bet on it. Victoria's views on lifestyle are already diametrically opposed to her mother's. Victoria announced the other day that, when she was grown up she was going to have a 'flat with glass all round and no children in it'.

So why is Daisy hurrying along the lane behind the farm, bumping poor Samuel over the ruts and potholes? Partly because she doesn't want to hear, as she hears so often, 'Daisy's late again', or see the look that goes with this statement, half-affectionate, half-irritated. She's going to be the kind of calm, composed mother who's always first at the school gates and always has plasters and wet wipes in her bag. She stops because she's lost a shoe. Lulu whines and pulls at the lead. Daisy would like to let her off the lead, but, last time, Lulu ran four miles across country and had to be brought back by a farmer in his trailer.

'Stop it, Lulu. We're nearly home.'

She gets her shoe on and looks at her watch. Ten past three. Damn, she told Victoria that she would be there at three, and, even if Victoria is enjoying herself in the tree-house, she'll still have one eye on the clock.

'Come on, Lulu.' At least Samuel has, miraculously, fallen asleep. Daisy opens the gate to the field and shoves the push-chair through. Then she follows with Lulu and turns to shut the gate. As she does so, she sees a figure hurrying along the path by the farm. Nothing strange in that — it's a public foot-path, after all — but for some reason the approaching figure makes Daisy feel uneasy. She watches as the person (it's too far away to tell if it's a man or woman) skirts the farm build-ings and continues on the track she has just taken, moving quickly. Daisy grips the wooden bars of the gate, the clouds are scudding over the grass, giving her the odd feeling that the world is moving and she is standing still.

She takes hold of the pushchair. This field is full of rape-seed, stinging yellow against the blue sky. But, there's a path running through it and, at the far side, she can see the back of her house and, further up the hill, the palatial garden belonging to Grace and Ella. She can even hear children's voices, very clear on the still air. It reminds her of the choir, earlier. 'There is a green hill far away, without a city wall.'

How beautifully they had sung. She sets off again, almost running now, Lulu silent at her side.

Ruth knew she should have carried on going to the gym. There's a slight hill towards St Simeon's, but even that's enough to make her slow to a walk. By the time she gets to the cottage the door is swinging open and all four men are inside. She has no idea whether Clough and Tim kicked the door down, but, as she stands for a second on the doorstep, she can hear raised voices and a rather sickening thump. She dreads what she will find inside.

What she finds are Clough, Tim, Cathbad and Nelson standing almost helplessly as Hilary kneels in front of them, pinning Justin's head to the floor. On the sofa a black cat is washing itself, oblivious.

'You see,' Hilary says, when she sees Ruth, 'I told you I was a black belt in taekwondo.'

'I think you might be killing him,' says Ruth.

'No. He can still breathe.'

Ruth is not so sure about this. Justin's face is turning blue. Nelson obviously thinks the same thing because he says, 'Let him go now, Doctor Smithson. We've got this.'

With obviously reluctance, Hilary loosens her grip and stands up. Justin remains on the floor, gasping and choking. Tim kneels beside him and helps him onto the sofa. Cathbad disappears and comes back with a glass of water.

'Now, Doctor Smithson,' says Nelson. 'Perhaps you could tell us what's happening here.'

Hilary sits on an armchair, looking perfectly composed.

She holds out her hand for the water, although Ruth is pretty sure that Cathbad meant it for Justin.

'I had a letter asking me to meet the writer at the holy house at three,' she says. 'I was pretty sure that meant here. It's often called the holy house in medieval records. But I let Ruth and Cathbad think that it meant the site of the holy house in the abbey grounds. Sorry,' she says to Ruth.

'You could have been killed,' says Ruth.

'Oh, I was almost certain that he wouldn't kill me,' says Hilary. 'When I got here, Justin was sitting in this chair. I asked him if he wrote the letters, he said yes, and I got him in a headlock.' She smiles sweetly, smoothing out her robes.

Nelson turns to Justin. 'Did you write the letters?'

Justin massages his throat for a minute, and then he says, 'It's sacrilege for a woman to call herself a priest. Women are called to motherhood, not the priesthood.'

'The Church is our mother,' says Hilary. 'A loving, gentle mother.'

'With a black belt in taekwondo,' suggests Ruth. Nelson gives her a look.

'You should be at home with your child,' Justin tells Hilary, still rubbing his neck.

'I'm called to serve God,' says Hilary, 'why can't you understand that?'

'Let's get this straight,' says Nelson. 'Mr Fitzroy-Jones, you wrote a series of malicious letters to Doctor Smithson.'

'I met her when she came to a talk at the museum,' says Justin. 'She seemed to represent everything that I deplore about women priests.'

Ruth thinks that Hilary looks rather proud to hear this. She takes a thoughtful sip of water.

'So you sent her threatening letters?' says Nelson.

'They weren't threatening,' says Justin, 'they were meant to point out the error of her ways.'

'I've read them,' says Nelson. 'They sounded pretty threatening to me. You also sent her a letter asking her to meet you today. In that letter you said you'd explain why Chloe and Paula had to die.'

Hilary looks reproachfully at Ruth. 'You told him about the letter.'

'I told him,' said Cathbad. He is sitting on the window seat. As Ruth watches, the cat comes up to him and rubs against his legs.

'What did you mean by saying you'd explain about the murders of Chloe and Paula?' says Nelson.

'I know why they died,' says Justin, 'but I didn't kill them.'

'You don't have an alibi for either murder,' says Nelson. 'I'd start talking if I were you.'

'He has an alibi for Chloe's murder,' says Cathbad. 'He was in Ireland.'

'No, Cathbad,' says Nelson. 'Justin lied to you. He was in Walsingham that night. We've got CCTV footage of him at the Slipper Chapel. He belongs to a secret society called the Brotherhood of the Madonna Lactans. They meet at the chapel.'

Lactans, thinks Ruth, that's breastfeeding isn't it? Is it possible that her hunch about the glass phial was correct?

Justin is looking apologetically at Cathbad. 'I'm sorry for lying to you,' he says.

Cathbad says nothing. He looks very shocked. The cat is still purring against his legs, and he strokes it mechanically.

'What did you mean by saying that you knew why the women had been murdered?' says Nelson again.

'I can't tell you.'

'You'd better,' says Nelson, 'if you don't want me to arrest you for the murder of two women.'

There's a silence, and then Justin says, looking out of the window, 'They were murdered because they were sinful. The first woman was a drug addict, the second was an actress.'

He says 'actress' like it is the most wicked profession imaginable. Ruth sees Clough stir angrily. She thinks about Freya, ascetic, severe Freya, with her dark clothing and hatred of ritual.

'Why did you write to Freya too?' she asks.

'She was like Doctor Smithson,' says Justin. 'She thought herself worthy to be a priest. The two of them came to the rehearsal yesterday, wanting to play apostles. Sacrilege. There were no female apostles.'

'What about Mary Magdalene?' cuts in Hilary. 'Most theologians concede that she was an apostle. She stood with the Virgin Mary at the foot of the cross. She was the first to see the risen Christ. And she was a prostitute. Jesus loves the outcasts of society. The drug addicts, the prostitutes.'

Ruth glances at Nelson, expecting him to break into this theological debate. Instead she is surprised to see that he is looking out of the window, towards the graveyard. His face has a look of frowning concentration that Ruth knows well.

'Boss?' says Clough at last.

Nelson turns. 'Tim, do you know where Doreen West-mondham was a dinner-lady?'

'I can't remember,' says Tim. 'But I think I made a note.' He gets out his phone. 'Yes, it was a boarding school in Sheringham.'

'Come on,' says Nelson to Clough. 'You come with me. Heathfield, you stay here. Ruth and Cathbad, go home.'

Ruth is still trying to find the words to protest at being spoken to in such a way when the door slams behind Nelson.

28

Daisy hears the field gate open and shut. Lulu turns and barks loudly. 'Come on,' says Daisy pulling at her lead. Now is not the time for Lulu to develop bravery. Daisy keeps moving. Samuel's head lolls as the pushchair rattles along. Could she take a short cut across the field? But the rapeseed grows high on either side, almost shoulder-height in places. She'd never get the pushchair through. She must just keep on the track. Keep right on till the end of the road. She contemplates singing, but, when she opens her mouth, only a croak comes out. She met Larry when she was singing in the choir at the church in Croydon where he was a deacon. On his days off they used to get a bus to the South Downs or the Pilgrims Way. They'd take a picnic and they'd walk for miles. Sometimes they'd sing as they walked, harmonising naturally, pop songs and favourite hymns. 'O lord my God, when I in awesome wonder consider all the works Thy hand has made.' In those days the countryside had seemed like heaven.

Daisy starts to jog. She always claims that walking everywhere has made her fit, but now she's out of breath in seconds, a stitch like a knife wound in her side. One of the soldiers plunged his spear into Jesus's side and at once blood and water poured out. The Passion Play seems years away. She stops. Silence, just a bird singing somewhere very high up. Blue sky, yellow flowers, like one of Victoria's paintings. Has her pursuer taken another path? Is she safe? Or have they stopped too? This last is somehow the most terrifying thought of all. She wants to look round, but finds she can't turn her head. She starts to run, faster than before, oblivious to the pain in her ribs. And, behind her, the footsteps start to run too.

For a few minutes Hilary, Cathbad, Ruth and Justin all stare at each other. In some ways, thinks Ruth, there is so much to say; in other ways, nothing at all. It is Tim who says, slightly apologetically, 'I expect you'll all be wanting to get on your way.'

Ruth looks at her watch. It's twenty past three. She has to collect Kate at four.

'I'd better be going,' she says. 'Cathbad?'

Cathbad is looking at his friend. 'How could you lie to me?' he says.

'I'm sorry,' says Justin. 'I didn't think you'd understand about the Madonna Lactans.'

'Don't I usually understand things like that? I'm a druid, remember. I understand the mystical.'

'You say you do,' says Justin, 'but underneath I think you're pretty hard-nosed, Cathbad. You're more like your friend Nelson than you think.'

Cathbad looks deeply hurt and doesn't reply.

'Goodbye, Justin,' says Hilary serenely, standing up. 'I hope we meet again.'

Justin stands too. As the two of them are still in biblical dress, it gives the moment a strange solemnity.

'I'm sorry if the letters frightened you,' says Justin.

'I wasn't frightened,' says Hilary. '"The Lord is my strength."'

And, with that, the three of them file out of the door.

Outside, they stand, uncertain, in the lane. People are streaming out of the abbey grounds, returning to cars and lodgings. The mood seems oddly cheerful, considering the drama that has just been re-enacted. Hilary too seems almost elated, humming under her breath. Ruth can't be absolutely sure that it isn't 'Onward, Christian Soldiers'. Cathbad, on the other hand, seems extremely depressed. For the first time since Ruth has known him, he looks too slight for his druid's robes, as if he's merely dressing up.

'I should have known,' he says. 'The cat's called Chesterton, after all.'

'You couldn't have known,' says Ruth. 'We can never know what people are really like.' She's thinking of Michelle and Tim, of Father Hennessey and Hilary. Of everyone, really.

'I'd better get home,' says Cathbad. 'Can I have a lift, Ruth?'

'Of course,' says Ruth. She notices that he brightens up at the thought of home. 'Let's fight our way through the pilgrims.'

Nelson and Clough are caught up in the crush at the main gates. 'Police,' shouts Nelson. 'Let us through.' This causes consternation as people try to get out of their way and end up creating more of a bottleneck.

'Call Fuller,' Nelson tells Clough. 'Find out where she is.'

Nelson pushes his way through and finds that the grounds are almost empty. The grass has been trampled into mud, and men in overalls are picking up litter. Clough is still trapped at the gate. Where the hell is Tanya? As he stabs impatiently at his phone he sees a familiar figure in brown coming towards him. It's Larry Westmondham, bald head gleaming, holding a girl of about ten — presumably his daughter — by the hand.

'There, you see,' he says to Nelson. 'I didn't forget her.'

'Yes, you did, Dad,' says the girl. 'Miss Lewis had to remind you.'

'Larry,' says Nelson. 'Have you seen Robin Rainsford?'

'Robin who? Oh, the teacher. Wasn't he one of the apostles?'

Thank God. Tanya is on the phone.

'Fuller. Where's Rainsford? Remember, I told you to keep an eye on him.'

Tanya sounds flustered. 'He left just before the end.'

'Didn't you follow him?'

'You told me not to leave the grounds.'

'Jesus.' Nelson turns back to the rather shocked Larry. 'Have you heard from your wife?'

'Daisy?' Larry's forehead crinkles. 'No. But she'll be collecting Lizzie and Victoria.'

'They're at the Hendersons',' says his daughter. 'Lucky things. They have ice pops in their freezer.'

'Do you know which way she will have gone?'

'She had the pushchair so she probably went by the road.'

'No,' says the daughter. 'She had Lulu, so she would have gone over the fields behind the farm. It's quicker that way too.'

'Can you show me?'

'Of course.' She skips forward happily, followed by her father, Nelson and, seconds later, a red-faced Tanya.

Tim is left alone with Justin. Of the two of them, Tim feels that he is the most embarrassed. Justin just sits there on the sofa. The cat jumps up and sits next to him. Tim finds the animal rather creepy, with its jet-black fur and green eyes. He is sure that his mother would say that a pure black cat was bad luck.

Tim looks out of the window, at the strange view of the graveyard with its tilting stones. St Simeon's is in the background, a solid grey shape surrounded by blossoming trees. It all seems a million miles away from the abbey grounds, where a killer might still be at large. Why did the boss go charging off like that? And why did he tell Tim to wait at the cottage? Was it just to keep Tim out of the action or to make sure that Ruth and Hilary got away safely? Tim looks at Justin, still sitting serenely on the sofa, stroking the demonic cat. It's hard to see this man as dangerous. Weird, certainly, with some pretty nasty views about women. But not dangerous.

'I'm going now,' says Tim. Justin doesn't look up, and Tim feels an urge to jolt him.

'You'll be hearing from us,' he says. 'About the letters.' He doesn't know if this is true. Hilary may well not want to press charges now that she has succeeded in half-strangling the perpetrator. In fact, Justin might want to bring charges of actual bodily harm against Hilary. But he suspects that neither of these things will happen. The letters will be forgotten, especially as it seems they weren't written by the murderer.

Justin turns his head towards Tim. 'I meant what I said in the letters, you know.'

'Which bit in particular?' asks Tim.

'About DCI Nelson being an adulterer. He's had an affair outside wedlock.'

'Who told you that?'

'Cathbad. In confidence.'

'Well, you don't seem to have respected the confidence,' says Tim. One way or another he's not really in the mood to talk about Nelson's marriage.

'Those girls were killed because they were sinful too,' says Justin. 'That's what I think.'

'They were killed because there's a murderer out there,' says Tim, moving towards the door. 'You'll be hearing from us again.'

Justin stays sitting on the sofa, the cat at his side.

Outside Tim takes off his robe, folds it neatly and leaves it by Justin's front door. Then he walks quickly towards the abbey grounds, hoping to catch up with Nelson and Clough. If there's a race to find the killer, he wants to be involved. He wonders where Ruth and Hilary have got to. With any luck, they will have gone home.

But, when he reaches the grounds, he finds that almost

everyone has gone home. It seems amazing that a place that was so full only ten minutes ago is now almost deserted. Discarded prayer sheets litter the grounds and two men with black sacks are picking them up. Someone else is loading music stands onto a trolley. The Stations of the Cross remain in place: the stage where Pilate (a.k.a. Justin Fitzroy-Jones) sentenced Jesus to death, the tomb where His body was laid and, towering above the rest, the cross on its raised platform. As Tim looks towards the platform, he sees something hanging from one of the arms of the cross. Is it a discarded costume? No, it looks too bulky for that. Tim starts to run across the grass. One of the litter-collectors shouts at him, but he keeps on running.

When he gets closer he sees what is hanging from the cross. A man's body, dressed in pink robes. Something in the way it twists and turns tells Tim that it's too late, but he calls the ambulance anyway, shouting into his phone as he gets closer. The litter-collectors look in his direction and soon they are running too. Tim climbs onto the stage and fumbles with the rope around the man's neck.

'Here, use this.' One of the litter-collectors is proffering a dangerous-looking knife. Tim must remember to question him about it afterwards.

The knife does the trick, though. The rope gives way and the body sags into Tim's arms. He lays it on the platform. The man is clearly dead. Despite the distorted features, Tim recognises him immediately as the handsome actor who had played John, the disciple Jesus loved.

'Who is it?' says one of the litter-men. 'He's dead all right. Poor bastard.'

'One of the actors,' says the other. 'Do you know his name?' he asks Tim.

Tim shakes his head but, in his heart, he is certain of the dead man's identity. He thinks that he has found Thom Novak.

The hymn is still echoing in Daisy's head as she runs. 'When through the woods and forest glades I wander, And hear the birds sing sweetly in the trees . . .' She can see the houses now, the white gate leading to the Hendersons' garden, that paradise of treehouse and swings. She's nearly there — in a few seconds she'll be with her darling daughters. She'll tell the Hendersons about her fears and they'll laugh together, they'll give her tea and biscuits and offer her a lift home.

The next minute she is on the ground. There's a heavy weight pressing her into the mud and hot breath on the back of her neck. She has let go of the pushchair and she hears Samuel give a startled shout as it topples over. Lulu is barking. Protect Samuel, she sends a thought message to the dog. Protect Samuel, don't worry about me. She struggles, but her assailant is too strong for her. Now his hands are round her neck. Lulu's barking seems to be coming from a long way away. She tries to pray, to say an act of contrition, but all she can think is how unfair this is, she's only thirty-five, she has four children, how will Larry ever be able to cope on his own?

Darkness. Is this it, the promised land?

Led by Becky, Nelson, Clough and Tanya take the path behind the farm buildings. Becky sets a good pace, obviously a child used to walking. It's Larry who stumbles, hampered by his long robe, and almost falls several times. Nelson thinks of the Stations of the Cross, 'Jesus Falls for the Third Time'. He has already telephoned the station asking for back-up and circulating a description of Robin Rainsford.

'Why do you think he's our man?' asks Clough, as they approach the gate to the rapeseed field. At least Clough has discarded his costume. Nelson doesn't think he could cope with two people in fancy dress.

'Something Stanley Greenway said,' says Nelson. 'It all fell into place back in the cottage. I think that Robin was befriended by Doreen when she was a dinner-lady at his school. It made him pathologically jealous of her foster children — and her actual children. That was the link between Chloe and Paula. Not that they looked alike, it was because they were Doreen's children.'

'But, even if that's true,' pants Larry. 'Why would he go after my wife?'

'It's a hunch,' says Nelson. 'And I hope I'm wrong. It was when you said how like your mum Daisy was. I think Rainsford's jealousy might be at work again. He met Daisy when she made supper for the delegates. Daisy seems like such a perfect wife and mother. She's Doreen's daughter-in-law. And killing her, of course, would be the perfect way to get at you.'

'Dear God,' says Larry. 'I hope you're wrong.'

They see the pushchair first. It's lying on its side, wheels spinning. Samuel is still strapped inside and he's crying in an exhausted way, as if he's been doing so for a long time.

'Daisy!' Suddenly Larry gets a burst of energy and he runs

along the path, Clough close behind. But it's Tanya, who never misses a day at the gym, who sprints past them both. Nelson suddenly grabs Becky's hand, unwilling to let her see what might be ahead.

'She's here,' shouts Tanya.

Nelson lets go of Becky and runs forward. Daisy is lying in the yellow flowers just off the track. Tanya and Clough are leaning over her. Larry has fallen to his knees and is crying.

'Look after your daughter,' Nelson shouts at him.

Plant stalks are flattened all around as if a struggle has taken place; the scent of the flowers is acrid and unpleasant. Nelson fully expects to see a dead body but, instead, Clough is phoning an ambulance and Tanya is briskly turning Daisy into the recovery position.

'She's alive, boss.'

Nelson goes back to the pushchair and frees Samuel, lifting him up into his arms. Larry is sitting on the ground with tall Becky in his lap and Nelson doesn't think he could cope with the baby as well.

'Daisy's alive,' he says. 'The ambulance is on its way.'

Larry looks at him blankly. 'Where's Lulu?' he says.

Who the hell's Lulu? Oh, the dog. Still holding the baby, Nelson sets off through the flowers. A few yards away he finds Robin Rainsford lying on the ground, with Lulu growling on his chest.

29

Tim's hunch proves correct. A search through the dead man's pockets (he is wearing jeans under the pink robes) produces a driving licence and a passport in the name of Thomas Novak. Tim calls the station and sits with the body until the coroner's van arrives, trundling self-importantly over the grass. It strikes him as immeasurably sad that this young man, with all his life ahead of him, preferred to die rather than to live it without the woman he loved. Love, he thinks, is a very frightening thing.

Back at the now deserted station he rings the next-of-kin number given in the passport. Thom's mother answers, and he gives her the news as gently as he can. What strikes him most is that she isn't in the least surprised. 'When he left the rehab place we were worried that he might . . . that he might do something stupid.' Was it stupid to kill yourself? Tim supposes so, but Novak's action has a tragic logic nonetheless. Mrs Novak seems comforted to hear that Thom had attended a religious ceremony before he died, so Tim makes a lot of this without expanding on the horror of the giant

cross and the body hanging from it. 'Thom was brought up
a Catholic. I hope he got some help from that . . . at the end.'

'I'm sure he did,' says Tim.

Next he rings Chloe's parents. Julie Jenkins listens in
silence and then she says, 'Poor Thom. He did love her really.'
'I think he did,' says Tim. He can't bring himself to say (as his
mother would) that they are together again now. 'I'll speak to
his parents,' says Julie. 'Maybe we can have his ashes buried
with Chloe's.'

'That's a nice idea,' says Tim.

He feels rather depressed after the phone calls and could
do with someone to talk to but the incident room is empty.
Surely the boss and the others should be back by now?
Tanya's computer is on, its low insistent hum filling the
silent room. Tim clicks on the screen and sees a journey
planner app showing a route from the remand prison to
Walsingham. Clough's emergency Mars bar is still on his
desk. Where is everyone?

Rainsford's trousers are torn and there seems to be blood on
the grass. But he's alive and, when he sees Nelson, he shouts
'Help' in a feeble voice. Nelson gives the baby to Larry, grasps
the spaniel's collar and pulls her off. Becky comes forward
to take Lulu from him, bending down to bury her face in
the dog's hair.

Rainsford struggles to sit up. 'That dog,' he pants, 'it's mad.
It attacked me. Bit both of my ankles.'

'Robin Rainsford,' says Nelson, pulling the man to his feet.
'You're under arrest for the murders of Chloe Jenkins and

Paula Moncrieff and the attempted murder of Daisy West-mondham. Do you understand the nature of the charge?'

'It drew blood.' Rainsford seems to be asking for sympathy.

'You do not have to say anything,' says Nelson. 'However it may harm your defence if you do not mention when questioned something which you later rely on in court. Anything you do say will be taken in evidence.'

Clough is at his side. 'She's OK, boss. More shocked than anything. Tanya's with her now.'

'And the ambulance is on its way?'

'Yes, but we ought to get to the road. They'll never find us in the middle of a field.'

'Where's Daisy?' says Larry. He too seems in shock. He gazes at Rainsford as if he's never seen him before.

'I'm here,' says a voice. It's Daisy, leaning on Tanya's arm, shoeless, her skirt ripped but her smile miraculously intact.

Larry wraps his arms round his wife, sobbing. Samuel, in danger of being crushed between his parents, starts crying too. Becky stands silently, holding the dog in her arms. Nelson puts his arm round her. 'It's all right, love. Let's get out of here. Where's the nearest road?'

'Our friends live there.' Becky puts down the dog and points to a white gate, about a hundred yards away.

'OK. Clough, have you got cuffs?'

But Clough has already handcuffed Rainsford, who is still trying to look down at his injured ankles.

'Let's go then.'

Tanya has recovered the pushchair and Larry puts the baby into it. Daisy reaches out to her daughter and gives her a hug. Together they walk towards the gate, with Larry following, pushing the buggy. Tanya hovers protectively at Daisy's shoulder. Nelson and Clough bring up the rear with the handcuffed Rainsford between them. Lulu circles them excitedly.

'That dog should be put down,' says Rainsford. 'It's quite out of control.'

'You should be put down,' growls Clough.

Back at the cottage, Ruth finds it hard to settle. Kate, over-excited after a day of arts and crafts with Sandra, is whiny and irritable. Ruth cooks supper, plays several games where the Sylvanians go to prison and/or boarding school, gives Kate her bath, reads two Josie Smith stories and still Nelson hasn't rung. What is going on? Why did Nelson and Clough rush off so suddenly? Nelson asked Tim something about a school. What did that mean?

When Kate is finally asleep, Ruth opens her computer and Googles Madonna Lactans. 'A depiction of the Virgin Mary,' she reads, 'where the Virgin is shown breastfeeding the infant Jesus.' So she was right about the breast milk. She hopes that Nelson remembers how scathing he had been about the missing glass phial. Why doesn't he ring so she can say 'I told you so'?

Ruth paces around her tiny sitting room, watched impassively by Flint. She thinks of Hilary forcing Justin to the ground. Hilary was certainly telling the truth when she said that she wasn't afraid of her stalker. In fact she had seemed positively to enjoy the encounter. Cathbad, on the other hand, had seemed to feel that he had been personally betrayed by his friend, the man whose cat he had looked after. Thinking of the cat, Ruth goes back to her laptop.

'G. K. Chesterton, English writer and Christian apologist. Best known as the creator of the Father Brown stories, Chesterton converted to Roman Catholicism in 1922.'

So that was why Cathbad had said that the cat's name should have given him a clue. Scrolling through a selection of G. K. Chesterton quotations, she reads, 'Reason is always a kind of brute force, those who appeal to the head rather than the heart . . . are always men of violence.' She thinks of Justin's letters, of the attempts to justify his views by twisted reasoning and quotations from scripture. She thinks of Hilary's own arguments, so measured and confident. Perhaps it's better just to believe things, as Cathbad does, without attempting to explain them.

Maybe Nelson won't ring her at all. After all, she's not involved in the case. She's neither a colleague nor a wife. Nelson is under no obligation to tell her what happened today. She supposes she'll hear it on the news, just like everyone else.

At nearly ten o'clock her phone rings.

'Ruth. It's Nelson.'

'Nelson. I was hoping you'd ring. What happened after you left Justin's cottage?'

'A whole lot happened,' says Nelson. 'For one thing, we've arrested Robin Rainsford for the murders.'

'Robin Rainsford? Oh . . . the man who led Hilary's course. Why did you arrest him?'

'Well, we caught him trying to murder Daisy West-mondham, for one thing.'

'Who?'

'She's the vicar's wife. Rainsford was obsessed with his mother.'

'Whose mother? The vicar's?'

'Yes, a woman called Doreen Westmondham. She was a dinner-lady at Rainsford's school. Apparently she befriended him, and he became jealous of her children and the children she looked after — she fostered hundreds of children, including Paula Moncrieff.'

'What about Chloe Jenkins?'

'Doreen was her childminder. When Rainsford met Chloe at the church, the whole thing started up again. He kept tabs on all of them. It seems that he asked Paula to come on the course specially. I remember her husband saying that she was surprised to be invited. She hadn't been a priest very long.'

'God. Poor woman.'

'Yes. It just clicked when we were at Justin's house. I remembered that Rainsford had been at boarding school near Walsingham. Then I thought about Daisy and realised that she might be in danger.'

'Why didn't he go after the vicar? After all, he was this Doreen's actual child.'

'He only attacked women, and I think it helped if they were blonde. It's all very nasty. Uniform went round to his house, and it's full of pictures of blonde women. He was also obsessed with a golden-haired statue of the Virgin Mary.'

'When Justin confessed to writing the letters I really thought it might be him.'

'Yes. The letters were a distraction really. All that stuff about the Madonna dressed in blue, weeping for the world. It turns out that it wasn't the Virgin Mary that Rainsford was obsessed with but his own substitute mother, Doreen.'

'I was right about the breast-milk link, though, wasn't I?'

Nelson laughs. 'Yes, you were right, Ruth. Is that what you wanted me to say?'

There's a small silence while Ruth thinks about what she really wants Nelson to say. 'I'd better go,' says Nelson at last. 'It's been a long day.'

'Yes. It was very kind of you to ring me. I was going mad wondering what was going on.'

Another silence, then Nelson says, 'Ruth, I'm sorry about the other evening . . . the things I said.'

'That's OK,' says Ruth. 'Have you spoken to Michelle?'

'Yes,' says Nelson. 'We've . . . well, we've straightened things out.'

'I'm glad,' says Ruth. 'I really am.'

As she clicks off the phone she thinks that, if Hilary's God can make those words come true, she might even start believing in Him.

30

20ᵗʰ April 2014, Easter Sunday

'Will he be all right on his own?'

'He'll be fine. He's got his blanket.'

'I'm not sure. He's so little.'

Nelson and Michelle both look fondly at the puppy. He looks back up at them, head on one side, stumpy tail wagging. He has no idea that they're planning to abandon him for the morning. Nelson feels his heart contract.

It was Lulu's bravery on Good Friday that had finally convinced Nelson to get a dog, but the thought had been forming in his mind ever since his last meeting with Jan Adams and Barney. He'd rung Jan late on Good Friday evening and she'd said that she knew of a rescue place that had some German Shepherd puppies. 'They're all vaccinated and chipped, ready to go to new homes.' Nelson and Michelle had driven over to the rescue centre on Saturday and had fallen in love at first sight.

Nelson had wanted to call the puppy Jimmy, after Jimmy

Armfield, a legendary Blackpool player. If he'd had a son he would have insisted that the name Jimmy featured somewhere on the baptismal certificate. But Michelle had said that the puppy just didn't look like a Jimmy, though Nelson is sure that she would have had the same reservations in the case of a son. Nelson's previous and much-loved dog was called Max, but now he dislikes the name. Michelle suggested Rocky, but, although Nelson likes the idea of naming the dog after a boxer, it still reminds him too much of PC Roy 'Rocky' Taylor. 'Roy was really sweet,' Michelle had told him after the policeman had steadfastly guarded her on Friday afternoon. 'I don't know why you're always so nasty about him.'

It was Laura who christened the new pet via her weekly Skype call from Ibiza. 'He's so fluffy and gorgeous. He looks like a bear. Let's call him Bruno. Bruno the bear.' Nelson had acquiesced. It could have been worse, knowing his daughters. Rebecca once had a hamster called Fluffykins. At least there was a boxer called Frank Bruno.

Robin Rainsford has confessed to the murders of Chloe and Paula and to the attempted murder of Daisy. He confessed while still in hospital having his dog bites treated. Perhaps he knew that DNA evidence would link him to the crimes; perhaps it was being caught attacking Daisy or perhaps he was just too tired of lying. 'How did you guess it was Rainsford?' asked Tim, when Nelson finally arrived back at the station. 'I remembered he'd been at school in the area,' said Nelson, as he had to Ruth, 'and it just clicked suddenly.' But, in fact, it was something else, words that had been running in Nelson's head ever since Stanley Greenway's taped confession: 'And I was just lying there in the grass the birds blackbird thrush robin looking at her so pretty then she was dead I loved her but she was dead . . . ' The unintelligible babble had, in fact, contained a witness statement. Some time on Good Friday Nelson's brain had unscrambled this and added punctuation:

'And I was just lying there in the grass, the birds: blackbird, thrush. Robin looking at her, so pretty, then she was dead.'

Stanley had actually seen Robin Rainsford looking down on Chloe's dead body, but, in his drug-addled state, hadn't been able to connect this with her murder. Stanley's first conscious memory was of finding himself beside Chloe's corpse and this convinced him that he must be the killer. He had carried Chloe back to the Slipper Chapel, intending to pray to his beloved Madonna. But the chapel had been closed and, in terror, Stanley had laid Chloe's body in a ditch, placing his rosary on her chest. He had then staggered back to the Sanctuary and managed to block out the whole thing.

'It's fairly typical of the drugs he was on,' said Fiona McAllister. 'They can cause blackouts and paranoid delusions. I told you that at the time.'

Yes, she had told them, but they hadn't listened. Stanley had confessed to the crime and Nelson can't acquit himself or his team of the assumption that Stanley must have been the killer because he simply looked the type. He knew that he had doubts — there was never anything linking Stanley to Paula, for example — but he had suppressed those feelings. And he hadn't trusted Robin Rainsford from that first meeting in the room smelling of incense. Robin must have been at the Slipper Chapel that evening, along with Justin and Larry. And, walking back through the fields, he had encountered Chloe Jenkins, wandering back from a visit to her beloved childminder's grave. Robin, recognising Chloe from church and knowing her to be linked to Doreen, had killed her, leaving her body where it lay. Paula, too, was a marked woman from the moment she was invited on the course. Robin had attacked Michelle in the graveyard, thinking she was Paula. But Paula was out with the other priests and all Robin had to do was to wait for her to come back to St Catherine's. He had heard her return, had heard her announce her attention of walking in the grounds and he had gone to meet her. Then he had returned to his room and, by his own account, slept peacefully until the police came to rouse him in the early hours of the morning.

Father Bill was right, in a way, Nelson thinks. The clue was the Madonna. Not Our Lady or the Virgin Mary or the Madonna Lactans. It was the mother, the foster mother, the extraordinary, ordinary Doreen Westmondham, who had enough love in her heart for her own children and for a hundred foster children, yet still had time to befriend a little boy at boarding school. As an adult, Robin Rainsford championed the cause of women in the Church, perhaps because he remembered the kindness of his surrogate mother. But, unlike the millions of pilgrims who flock to Walsingham every year, he was not willing to share the love of his mother. He was jealous of anyone she had cared for. Even Daisy Westmondham, who had never met Doreen, wasn't immune. She was her daughter-in-law, and had had the temerity to have a photograph of Robin's ideal mother stuck to her kitchen noticeboard. Robin must have seen it when he came to dinner at the start of the course.

And now Larry Westmondham has invited them to this Easter service. 'Please come, Detective Chief Inspector. All of you. It'll be a way of putting the past behind us and making a new start. That's what Easter morning is all about. Resurrection, new life, a new start.'

Nelson passed the message on to the team. Clough and Cassandra will both be there. Tim, who is leaving after Easter, was vague about his plans. Tanya, on the other hand, was keen. She's keen about everything these days, especially since Nelson has recommended her for a permanent promotion to detective sergeant. It was well deserved, too. It was Tanya who had spotted Stanley Greenway and Justin Fitzroy-Jones on the CCTV. And it was Tanya who, running like the wind through the rapeseed fields, found Daisy first. Nelson wonders if Tanya will bring her partner to the church. If so, Nelson prays that Clough won't say anything too embarrassing.

But Michelle is clearly having second thoughts. 'I don't think we should both go, Harry. Look at Bruno's little face. He'll be so sad.'

Nelson looks at Bruno's little face. He knows that he is going to the service on his own.

Ruth, too, is on her way to church. In her case, it was Hilary who did the emotional blackmail. 'Please come, Ruth. It would mean so much to me.'

'I don't believe in God,' said Ruth. 'You know that.'

'I understand,' said Hilary, though she still sounded as

if she didn't. 'But come for me, for all of us. It was such a shock about Robin. It feels important to leave Walsingham on a positive note.'

'What about Kate?'

'Bring her too,' said Hilary. 'I'd love to meet her. They're giving out Creme Eggs after the service.'

Ruth had sighed and given in. Maybe Hilary's right and they do need some sort of ceremony to mark the occasion. And you might see Nelson, says that unwelcome, but insistent voice in Ruth's head.

It's a blustery morning, and, as Ruth drives over the marshes the wind makes the long grass undulate like the sea. Kate is eating a chocolate egg (Ruth hopes she's remembered wet wipes) and clutching a woolly lamb, an Easter present from Nelson and Michelle.

'Why are we going to this place?' she asks, rather indistinctly.

'Because it'll be fun,' says Ruth. 'There'll be singing and . . . er . . . candles and . . .'

'Candles? Is it a birthday party?'

'Not exactly.'

'Christmas is Jesus's birthday, isn't it?'

In a way, thinks Ruth. She remembers Cathbad saying the Christians picked the date of the 25th December for Christmas because it coincided with a pagan feast. 'And it's traditional, of course, to have a feast in mid-winter. Light in the dark, warmth in the cold.' At least Cathbad will be at the church today and then Ruth and Kate are going back to his and Judy's house for lunch.

'Easter is celebrating life,' she says, 'and spring and lambs and all that.'

'And chocolate,' says Kate.

'And chocolate,' agrees Ruth. She hopes that there will be enough Creme Eggs for the adults.

Michelle listens to Nelson's car driving away; he's accelerating too much as usual and has to brake noisily at the entrance to the cul-de-sac. But Nelson will always drive like he's involved in a pursuit, even when he's doing something as innocuous as going to church.

Michelle looks down at Bruno, who crinkles his nose engagingly. 'You're going to like me best,' Michelle tells him, 'be a real mummy's boy.' 'We mustn't start referring to ourselves as the dog's mummy and daddy,' Nelson had said last night, 'that really would be the beginning of the end.' Too late, thinks Michelle, the process has already started in her head. 'Mummy loves you,' she says defiantly to the puppy, who looks back at her with absolute adoration.

Michelle takes out her phone. '*He's gone,*' she texts. No need for more words. A guilty text if there ever was one. Except she's not guilty, she tells herself, as she goes into the kitchen to prepare the lamb joint for lunch. She is going to do everything she can to save this marriage, it's just that she thinks she owes herself this meeting first.

Tim arrives ten minutes later. She watches him walking to the house, having left his car at the top of the road as instructed. Her next-door-neighbour is mowing his lawn, but he doesn't look up as Tim, sober and unremarkable in jeans and a grey jumper, goes past. A people-carrier parks across the road bearing her opposite neighbours' grandchildren and, under the cover of their joyful exclamations of welcome, Michelle lets Tim into the house.

He hasn't been inside the house since the time, three years ago, when Michelle cooked him lunch to welcome him to the team. She wonders if he'll think of that now, smelling the garlic and rosemary from the lamb. She always lays the table for Sunday lunch, even if it's just for two of them, but she hasn't done it today. She thinks that seeing the two places, the wine glasses, the mats showing Norfolk scenes, would be too much for both of them.

'Do you want a drink?' she asks. 'Tea? Coffee? Something stronger?'

'No, thanks,' says Tim. 'Is this the puppy?' He bends down to talk to Bruno, who flattens himself onto the carpet, in a posture that's half-welcome, half-abasement. 'Clough was telling me about him.'

'He's called Bruno,' says Michelle. 'We only got him yesterday but he's been so good. He didn't cry at all last night.' She doesn't add that this was because they took him into their bedroom at the first sign of a whimper.

Tim straightens up. He looks out of place in her sunny sitting room; too tall, too serious, too intense. He's not as big as Nelson, but he's still a rather intimidating presence. He also looks, Michelle realises with a shock, too young for a room that has matching sofas and a dining alcove. Tim is ten years younger than her, but it has never seemed to matter before. Now he almost looks like he could be one of her daughters' friends.

'Nice house,' he says.

Michelle shrugs, though, in truth, the house is her pride and joy.

'Be careful the dog doesn't chew the furniture,' says Tim. 'My brother had a German Shepherd that did that. Mind you, I think that was because it was bored. Rick didn't take him out much.'

'I'm going to take Bruno for a long walk every day,' says Michelle. 'It'll be better than going to the gym.'

They stare at each other. Eventually Tim says, 'I'm sorry my text scared you.'

'That's OK. It was just that it was an unfamiliar number.'

'I always used to call you from my other phone. In case the boss saw the texts.'

The message, '*I'm coming back for you*', had turned out to be from Tim. When Michelle found out she was almost more frightened than when she believed it was from a madman threatening to kill her. What did Tim mean, he was coming back for her? What if she didn't want him to? What if she did and the knowledge meant that she could never again live happily with Harry? Michelle hadn't slept at all last night, lying awake, listening to Harry and Bruno snoring in unison.

Now she says, 'What did it mean? The text.'

Tim spreads out his hands. 'I still love you, Michelle. I'm sorry, but I do. I know you want to stay with Nelson and I respect that. It's just . . . well, if you ever need me, you know where I am.'

It occurs to Michelle that she actually has no idea where Tim will be. She says so.

'My transfer has come through,' says Tim. 'I'm starting with Essex CID after Easter. The boss has been very fair, given me a good reference.'

'I'll miss you,' says Michelle. At that moment she wants, more than anything else, to fling herself into Tim's arms, to drag him upstairs so he can make love to her on the king-sized marital bed with French Colonial-style duvet. Why not? she thinks wildly, I might never see him again. Why shouldn't I have this to remember? But she doesn't move.

'Goodbye, Michelle,' says Tim.

'Goodbye, Tim.'

She doesn't go with him to the door. She stands still in the middle of the room, listening to the metallic hum of next-door's lawnmower. After a few minutes Bruno comes to her side and she buries her face in his fur.

The first person Nelson sees is Clough. He looks unusually smart in a blue suit and is standing with Cassandra by the church porch. Nelson is early as usual, but he's surprised to see a stream of people walking through the graveyard and into the church. Out of the corner of his eye he can see Doreen Westmondham's tombstone, very white in the spring sunshine.

'All these people,' he says to Clough. 'It'll be standing room only.'

'It's Easter,' says Cassandra. 'If you only go to church once a year, you go at Easter.' She's looking beautiful in a flowery dress and pink cardigan. Clough, as always in her presence, seems about to burst with pride.

'Is Michelle coming?' asks Cassandra. Rather to Nelson's surprise, the two women get on well.

'She stayed at home,' says Nelson. 'She didn't want to leave the puppy.'

'That dog will rule your life,' says Clough. 'You mark my words.' Clough had a dog when he was with a previous partner, Nelson remembers. He once told Nelson that he missed the dog more than the girl.

'I'll go and save us a seat, shall I?' says Cassandra. She disappears into the gloom of the church. Nelson goes to follow her but Clough puts a hand on his arm.

'Just a minute, boss. Something I want to tell you.'

Nelson looks at him in surprise. For one awful moment he thinks that Clough, too, is about to ask for a transfer. But Clough is looking too happy for it to be bad news.

'Just wanted you to know before it's all round the station. Cassie's pregnant. I'm going to be a father.'

'Congratulations,' says Nelson, shaking Clough's hand. 'Are you getting married? No, forget I said that. It's the sort of thing my mum would say.'

Clough laughs. 'That's OK. My mum said it too. Bit rich, coming from her, seeing as she didn't marry my dad or Mark's. But, yes, we want to get married. We're going to have the baby first, though. Cassie says she doesn't want to look fat on her wedding day.'

'Congratulations,' says Nelson again. 'It's wonderful news. You'll be a great dad.'

'I'm going to try.' Clough suddenly looks serious. 'I really am.'

Fatherhood changes you, thinks Nelson, as he follows Clough into the church. It makes you the sort of person who gets emotional about news like this, for a start. Nelson rubs his eyes. He hadn't cried, but it had been a dangerously close thing.

Ruth had intended to sit a long way away from Nelson but, before Ruth can stop her, Kate runs across the church to sit next to him. Ruth follows, aflame with embarrassment. The congregation smile benignly and move up to make room. After all, Ruth can see them thinking, it would be a shame to break up this happy family. Kate sits on Nelson's knee and Ruth is squashed uncomfortably between Nelson and Clough.

'This is cosy,' says Clough. His girlfriend, an irritatingly glamorous actress, gives her a superior smile. Ruth, unable to take off her jacket, can feel herself getting red in the face all over again.

The first hymn starts almost as soon as they have sat down. They scrabble to their feet again, looking for their places in the hymnbooks. Clough sings loudly in a fine tenor. Nelson mumbles the words, keeping his arm around Kate.

'Christ the Lord is risen today . . .'

It is the first time that Ruth has seen the Reverend Larry Westmondham, and she finds him rather an uninspiring speaker. He obviously feels it all very deeply, his round face gets quite anguished when he talks about purgatory, but he seems rather embarrassed about imparting any insights that he might have. Ruth is left with a general mumble of thoughts about life, death and rebirth, together with a vague idea that it might be good if we were all nicer to each other. The church is lovely, though, possibly twelfth century, with a rood screen and some beautiful stonework. There are flowers everywhere and incense swirls from a silver orb on a chain which is being swung enthusiastically by one of the altar servers. Kate flaps her hand, but doesn't say anything. Cassandra coughs and Clough pats her on the back, whispering solicitously.

Ruth doesn't see Hilary until they are all filing out at the end after another rousing hymn ('Thine be the glory'). Hilary is with Freya, and they are both wearing dog collars. Some of the congregation are looking at them suspiciously, but Larry, passing them on his way out, makes a point of shaking their hands. Bearing in mind his membership of the Brotherhood of the Madonna Lactans and the incense, Ruth assumes that Larry is fairly High Church and may be opposed to women priests. If so, he's making a pretty good job of appearing welcoming. Behind the priests, Ruth sees Janet Meadows, resplendent in a patchwork velvet coat, and Tanya, who is accompanied by a blonde woman whom Ruth doesn't recognise.

There are so many people leaving the church that Ruth, Clough and Cassandra get trapped in their pew. Nelson has managed to escape, but Ruth holds Kate firmly by the hand. Opposite them, a similarly trapped woman smiles and waves.

'That's his wife,' hisses Clough. 'The one who was attacked.'

When the crowd shuffles forward Ruth finds herself next to a pretty, fresh-faced woman in jeans and a blue jacket. She's holding a baby and has a girl of about six by the hand. Two slightly older girls hover behind her, one of them wearing a choirgirl's surplice.

'Hi, Daisy,' says Clough, behind Ruth. 'You're looking good for someone who was strangled the day before yesterday.'

Daisy laughs. She doesn't seem fazed by this typical Clough humour.

'I'm fine,' she says. 'The hospital discharged me that night. I just had a few cuts and bruises. Thanks to you and DS Fuller and DCI Nelson getting to me so quickly.'

'Thanks to your little dog,' says Clough. 'Where is she?'

'Daddy says she can't come to church,' says one of the older girls resentfully.

'What does Daddy know?' says Clough. 'Daisy, let me introduce my fiancée, Cassandra, and my friend Ruth.'

Daisy shakes hands with them both, while Ruth thinks *fiancée*?

'I've heard lots about you,' says Daisy to Ruth. 'I'm a friend of Janet Meadows. You must come to tea one day. Bring your daughter.'

'I'd like to,' says Ruth. Kate and the youngest girl smile warily at each other.

'Happy families,' says Clough, who seems in a weirdly ebullient mood. He kisses Cassandra on the cheek, and they laugh together quietly.

Outside Ruth finds another happy family: Cathbad, Judy and Michael, with Miranda in the buggy. Kate runs up to Michael.

'Did you get me an Easter egg?'

'Kate!' Ruth wonders if it's possible to die of shame.

'We're going to have an Easter egg hunt in the garden,' says Cathbad.

'Easter egg hunt!' Mad with surplus energy Kate runs off through the gravestones with Michael following. The wind has stripped the cherry trees of their blossom and the grass is full of white petals. Like confetti, thinks Ruth, although most churches seem to forbid confetti these days.

'Watch she doesn't run in the road.' Ruth doesn't have to look round to know that this is Nelson.

'I am watching.'

Kate and Michael are now playing hide-and-seek around Doreen Westmondham's gravestone. Ruth tells Kate to stop.

'Don't worry,' says a voice behind them. It's Larry Westmondham, still in his vestments, holding a basket full of Creme Eggs. 'Mum loved to have children round her.'

'Creme Eggs,' says a voice, 'my favourites.' Hilary is sailing towards them. Larry proffers the basket rather nervously.

'Thank you,' says Hilary. 'I'm going to do the same in my parish next year.'

'Where is your parish?' asks Larry.

'Streatham,' says Hilary, unwrapping silver paper.

'I know it well,' says Larry, with what Ruth, a south London girl, thinks of as misplaced enthusiasm. 'I used to live in Croydon. I hope to go back there one day.'

'Funny thing to hope for,' says Ruth, and she and Hilary walk through the graveyard together. Kate and Michael are playing a complicated game of jumping over the flat stones instigated by Larry Westmondham's youngest daughter. The curtains are drawn in Justin's cottage. According to Cathbad, he has gone away on retreat. The police, at Hilary's request, aren't pressing charges. Chesterton has been booked into a cattery; Cathbad doesn't think he'll be asked to cat-sit again.

'I feel bad,' Hilary says now. 'I felt so angry with Justin. When I got him in that headlock I really wanted to hurt him. That's a terrible thing for a priest to say, isn't it?'

'It just shows you're human,' says Ruth. 'Priests are allowed to be human. Male priests and female priests.'

As she says this, she thinks of Father Hennessey. She hasn't spoken to the priest since that day in the canteen, but she did see him in the distance at the Passion Play. She hopes that, even if he does confess, the bishop will let him carry on being a priest. It's not a job that would appeal to Ruth, but some people, Hilary included, really do seem cut out for it.

She stops to call Kate, but Nelson has already got to her and is leading her back to Ruth.

'Thanks,' says Ruth, when they reach her. Hilary has wandered away to talk to Cathbad.

'What are you doing for the rest of the day?' says Nelson.

'We're going to Cathbad and Judy's for lunch. There's an Easter egg hunt apparently.'

'Katie will enjoy that.'

'Yes, she will. Well, goodbye, Nelson. Happy Easter.'

'Happy Easter.'

She moves away, but somehow she knows that he is watching her. She has the oddest feeling that they are alone in the world, and everyone else, even Kate, is just part of a dream. Is it a dream, then, when Nelson catches up with her and, just briefly, takes her hand? She thinks he says something, but she doesn't catch the words and, before she can ask him to repeat it, Nelson is striding away through the tombstones.

ACKNOWLEDGEMENTS

As always in my books, I have made the real Walsingham into my own fictional version of the place, including real and imaginary elements. The priory, the abbey grounds, the Anglican shrine and the Slipper Chapel are all real. There is a beautiful Russian Orthodox Chapel in the old railway booking office. The snowdrops in February are justly famous and well worth a visit. However, St Simeon's Church and Cottage are imaginary, the cottage owing much to my father-in-law's house in Smarden, Kent. St Catherine's Lodge is also imaginary, although similar religious institutions established to host conferences and retreats do exist. Most importantly, with one exception, the people are all completely made up. The Slipper Chapel does have a custodian, but Father Bill is a fictional character.

Last year, a woman called Jan Adams took part in a fund-raising auction for the young people and children's cancer charity CLIC Sargent. The prize was the chance to appear as a character in these pages. When I found out that Jan had been a police dog-handler I was determined that she should feature in that role. I also wanted to include her dog, Barney. Thanks to Jan, both for bidding and for all the fascinating information about the work of police dogs.

Several people have been very generous with their time and advice. These include Francesca Lewington, Andrew Maxted and Julie Williams. However, I have only followed the experts' advice as far as it suits the plot, and any resulting mistakes are mine alone. I'm also grateful to Emma Bryant for the information about Renault key cards. Thanks to Tracy Stickland for inviting me on a pilgrimage to Walsingham, and to Father Kevin O'Donnell for sharing his knowledge of the place and explaining some of its mysteries. Thanks also to Father Kevin for recommending a wonderful book, *Walsingham: Pilgrims and Pilgrimage* by Michael Rear (St Paul's Publishing, 2011).

Special thanks, as always, to my editor, Jane Wood, and my agent, Rebecca Carter. Thanks to everyone at Quercus and Janklow and Nesbit for working so hard on my behalf. Love and thanks always to my husband, Andrew, and our children, Alex and Juliet.

This book is for my sister, Giulia, with love.